PENGUIN 🐧 CL

TALES OF HOFFMANN

HOFFMANN was born in Königsberg on 24 January 1776 and baptized
Ernst Theodor Wilhelm; he later substituted Amadeus for Wilhelm out
of admiration for Mozart. Having studied law, he entered the Prussian
civil service and held a number of legal posts in the eastern Prussian
provinces. However, his earliest ambition was to be a graphic artist and
painter. For a while he attempted to exist as a composer and critic of
music, and it was not until he was in his thirties that he turned to fiction,
becoming one of the best-known and most influential authors of his
time. The first volume of *Nachtstücke*, the earliest collection of genuinely
'Hoffmannesque' tales, appeared in 1816. Three years later he published
the first of the four volumes of his second and greater collection of
stories, the *Serapions-Brüder*. As a man of letters Hoffmann is famed
above all for his tales, in which he exploited the element of the grotesque
and the bizarre in a manner unmatched by any other Romantic writer.
He died on 25 June 1822.

R. J. HOLLINGDALE has translated eleven of Nietzsche's books and published two books about him. He has also translated works by, among
others, Schopenhauer, Goethe, Lichtenberg and Theodor Fontane, many
of these for the Penguin Classics. He is Honorary President of the British
Nietzsche Society, and was for the Australian academic year 1991 Visiting Fellow at Trinity College, Melbourne.

STELLA HUMPHRIES is an Oxford graduate in Philosophy, Politics and
Economics who has published some forty translations from German,
French and Italian, three of which were awarded prizes. Her husband
Vernon has collaborated with her since his retirement from industry in
1976.

SALLY HAYWARD was educated in Leeds and at the Institut Français,
London. She worked initially as a translator and interpreter for several
leading companies and after marriage set up a translation agency with
her graphic artist husband, dividing her time between translating and
administration (and bringing up two children). Eleven years were also
spent as Secretary of her local Chamber of Commerce in Surrey. Her
staple working diet consists of manuals, minutes, reports, specifications
and brochures from six European languages. She has also translated
popular medical texts for publication.

TALES OF HOFFMANN

—◦❦◦—

SELECTED AND TRANSLATED WITH AN INTRODUCTION
BY R. J. HOLLINGDALE

o

With the assistance of
Stella and Vernon Humphries,
and Sally Hayward

PENGUIN BOOKS

PENGUIN BOOKS

Published by the Penguin Group
Penguin Books Ltd, 27 Wrights Lane, London W8 5TZ, England
Penguin Books USA Inc., 375 Hudson Street, New York, New York 10014, USA
Penguin Books Australia Ltd, Ringwood, Victoria, Australia
Penguin Books Canada Ltd, 10 Alcorn Avenue, Toronto, Ontario, Canada M4V 3B2
Penguin Books (NZ) Ltd, 182–190 Wairau Road, Auckland 10, New Zealand

Penguin Books Ltd, Registered Offices: Harmondsworth, Middlesex, England

This translation first published 1982
10

Printed in England by Clays Ltd, St Ives plc
Set in Linotron Bembo

CONTENTS

INTRODUCTION

Hoffmann was a two-sided, schizophrenic kind of man; by day a decent citizen and a lawyer, by night a fantasist with a strong penchant for the freakish and weird. Temperamentally he was an anarchic humorist, and this affected his daytime side: his final experience with the Prussian state and legal system in which he earned his living was an official inquiry into allegations that he had abused his membership of a judicial commission to satirize the commission's proceedings. He took care of the split between bourgeois and artist by indulgence in what were in his day called 'habits of intemperance'; when he was forty-six these in turn took care of him. He was laden with talent: his earliest ambition was to be a graphic artist and painter; he then attempted to exist as a composer and critic of music; and it was only in his thirties that he turned himself into a writer of fiction and became – with four novels and about fifty stories, most of them of novella length – among the best-known and most admired and influential authors of his time. Long before his death he was the kind of author anyone who reads at all reads. His two-sided, schizophrenic type of personality informs all his fictions. A high proportion of the central characters of his tales are demented, either permanently (as is, for example, Nathaniel in *The Sandman*) or temporarily, under the impact of events their minds cannot handle. Like the other German Romantic writers, he habitually allows his heroes to lose control of themselves and run raving; but, unlike most of his contemporaries, he has a sense of humour always at hand to puncture the pretensions of these hysterics. The Enlightenment too is the subject of gentle mockery: into naturalistic scenes, often set in Berlin and described with the aid of real street names, names of restaurants, etc., there obtrude supernatural and fantastic events which are left unexplained (often it is suggested that, since the Enlightenment does not allow them, they cannot have happened). The Establishment is the subject of mockery not at all gentle: lawyers, civil servants, businessmen and their wives are represented as idiots. However, Hoffman's literary technique was not always equal to the demands he made of it, nor was his vocabulary always adequate to the depiction of the so-called abnormal psychological states (normal enough to Hoffmann, it seems) he wanted to portray.

Hoffmann was born in Königsberg on 24 January 1776 and baptized Ernst Theodor Wilhelm; he later substituted Amadeus for Wilhelm out of admiration for Mozart. His father was an advocate and his whole background that of the Prussian state service. When he was three his parents separated and he was brought up – or, as he himself says, not brought up – by an uncle. From 1792 to 1795 he studied law at Königsberg; he also gave music lessons – he had already studied music, drawing and painting – and fell in love with one of his pupils, Cora Hatt, who returned his love but was, inconveniently for both of them, married. This might not be a serious obstacle now, but in Hoffmann's day it was a Berlin Wall and, after practising law in Königsberg for not much more than six months, he fled to Glogau in an effort to break with Frau Hatt. From Glogau he went in 1798 to Berlin, and in 1800 he was sent as a member of the Prussian governmental apparatus to Posen. Here Hoffmann's Hyde persona made its first serious mistake: he drew a number of unflattering caricatures of the leading personalities of Posen, including the commandant of the military garrison, General von Zastrow. The general failed to see the humour of it and protested to Berlin about Hoffmann's continuing presence; as a consequence, Hoffmann was re-posted to the village of Płozk on the Vistula – a demotion he regarded as a virtual banishment. Before leaving Posen, however, he married a Polish girl, Michaelina Trzynska.

He spent four years at Plozk; while he was there his first published work – *A Letter from a Cloistered Monk to his Friend in the Capital* – appeared anonymously in Kotzebue's magazine, the *Freimütige* (Berlin, 9 September 1803). He was also working hard at painting and composition, and his application in these fields bore fruit when, having been transferred to Warsaw in 1804, he was able to complete, among other things, an opera to a text by Brentano, *Die lustigen Musikanten* (1804), and a symphony (1806), and to design and redecorate rooms in the restored Mniszeksche Palace (also 1806). On the title page of the *Lustigen Musikanten* he signed himself E. T. A. for the first time. On 28 November 1806 Warsaw was occupied by the French and Hoffmann became jobless and, when his house was requisitioned a little later by the occupying forces, homeless. His case was common among the members of the former Prussian bureaucracy, who had lost their livelihood through the victories of Napoleon; what was uncommon was that he could look for work in the artistic sphere, and especially in the theatre and opera house. In 1807 he completed a second full-length opera, *Love and Honour*, based on Calderon's *La Banda y la flor*. Then, back in Berlin, he began a (fortunately brief) period of near-starvation: he wrote to his friend, Gottlieb von Hippel, on 7 May that for five days he had eaten nothing but bread; but he had already made contact with the theatre at Bamberg with the object of obtaining the post of musical director and in-house composer, and the director of the theatre, Count Julius von Soden, was favourably inclined towards him, though he had to compose an opera to a text by Soden, *The Draught of Immortality*, as a proof of his abilities. In September he went to Bamberg and was appointed musical director, but after the failure of the first production he conducted there – that of Berton's *Aline, Queen of Golconda* – he relinquished the post and stayed on only as composer of stage-music and ballets.

He was again reduced to giving music lessons and again fell in love with one of his pupils, Julia Merc. This time it was Hoffmann who was married. His attachment to Julia Merc was pathologically serious, and he was led to thoughts of suicide by the insuperability of the difficulties in the way of making her his. But by this time he was definitely directing his mind towards authorship: *Ritter Gluck* appeared in the *Allgemeine musikalische Zeitung* for 15 February 1809, and on 17 May the *A.M.Z.* published his first critical review (of Friedrich Witt's Fifth and Sixth Symphonies); other stories, mostly with a musical setting, appeared during succeeding years, and on 18 March 1813 Hoffmann signed a contract for his first book, *Fantasie-stücke in Callots Manier*, a collection of tales and musical reviews and fantasies.

Things were now at last beginning to look up for E. T. A. Hoffmann. During the historic year 1812 he began his opera *Undine*, which was to prove his only real success in the theatre and which still survives in Germany as a minor classic of the early Romantic period. In February 1813 the impresario Joseph Seconda offered him the post of musical director at Leipzig, a position he took up in May, at just the time Richard Wagner was being born there. Hoffmann indeed came to know the theatre-loving Karl Friedrich Wagner, the legal (though not, it seems, actual) father of Richard, and later established a firm and long-lasting friendship with Karl Friedrich's brother Adolf Wagner, who, as Uncle Adolf, plays a significant role in the early biography of his nephew. Richard Wagner was, as a

youth, an avid reader and boundless admirer of Hoffmann, whose stories, he said, gave him bad dreams, but he
seems not to have known that Hoffmann and Uncle Adolf
were close friends. In 1814 Hoffmann began his first novel,
Die Elexiere des Teufels; and, when the government service
revived in the wake of Napoleon's retreat, he returned to
Berlin and his Jekyll side resumed its career, though Hyde
continued to write musical criticism under the pseudonym
'Johannes Kreisler, Kapellmeister'.

The year 1816 was a decisive year: *Undine* was performed in Berlin to great applause, and through it Hoffmann acquired the friendship of Weber, who wrote a
laudatory review; the first volume of *Nachtstücke*, the
earliest collection of genuinely 'Hoffmannesque' tales,
appeared; and Hoffmann was appointed a councillor of the
Kammergericht (court of appeal). Fiction now followed in
an unbroken stream of productivity, and by February 1819
he could bring out the first of the four volumes of his
second and greater collection of stories, the *Serapions-
Brüder*. His second novel, *Klein Zaches*, had already
appeared, and at the end of the year he published the first
volume of his third novel, *Kater Murr*.

In September 1819 the government instituted a Commission for the Investigation of Treasonable Organiza-
tions and Other Dangerous Activities, and Hoffmann was
appointed to it. All went well until at the turn of the year
1821–2 Hyde again committed exactly the same kind of
indiscretion that had got him thrown out of Posen: he told
several of his friends that he had inserted into the novel he
was then working on, *Meister Floh*, a satire on the proceedings of the Commission of which he was himself a member. This interesting intelligence came to the ears of the
president of the Ministry of Police, Herr Karl Albert von
Kamptz, who acted at once: at the request of Prussia, the
manuscript of the book, the parts already printed and
Hoffmann's correspondence with his publisher, Wilmans

of Frankfurt, were seized by the Frankfurt Senate and transported to Berlin, where, when he studied them, von Kamptz was unamused to recognize in 'Geheimer Hofrat Knarrpanti' the lineaments of his own important person. Hoffmann was now subjected to a judicial examination by the president of the *Kammergericht*, after which he dictated a detailed defence of what, to the official eye, looked very much like an attempt to undermine the work of the Commission by making it seem ridiculous. Prussia in 1822 was in many respects a liberal and free society, but Hoffmann's offence was no laughing matter: if proceedings had gone forward, Hoffmann-Jekyll would almost certainly have discovered that Hoffmann-Hyde had ruined him. That they did not go forward was due entirely to the fact that Hoffmann was ill: his habits of intemperance, grown to the point at which they had become self-destructive, had brought on the inability to control the limbs known as *locomotor ataxia*, which was the formal cause of his death on 25 June. To have escaped prosecution by dying was a very Hoffmannesque thing for him to have done.

The first collected edition of Hoffmann's writings was published between 1827 and 1839, and most of his fiction has never been out of print since. The eight stories in this collection are among his best-known. *Mademoiselle de Scudery* is often considered his masterpiece and has thus been placed first; the others are in order of publication.

Das Fräulein von Scuderi was written during 1818, published in September 1819 in the *Taschenbuch der Liebe und Freundschaft gewidmet* for 1820 and reprinted in 1820 in the third volume of the *Serapions-Brüder*. It is a detective story, embodying most of the tricks of the genre supposedly invented by Poe in *The Murders in the Rue Morgue* twenty-two years later. Hoffmann came to learn of Cardillac from Wagenseil's *Nuremberg Chronicle* and was probably drawn to him through recognizing in his double-sidedness a bloodstained reflection of his own.

Der Sandmann was written probably during 1815 and published in 1816 as the first story of the first volume of *Nachtstücke*. It forms the basis of the first act of Offenbach's opera *Les Contes d'Hoffmann*.

Der Artushof was written between 14 February and the beginning of March 1815, published in November 1816 in Brockhaus's yearbook *Urania* and reprinted in 1819 in the first volume of the *Serapions-Brüder*. Traugott, the businessman turned painter, is again a self-portrait, though this time a happy and modestly self-deprecating one.

Rat Krespel was written in 1816 and sent on 22 September for publication in Fouqué's *Frauentaschenbuch*, where it appeared in the edition for 1818 (Hoffmann was too late for the 1817 edition). In its original form the story was enclosed within a supposed letter and was published under the title *A Letter from Hoffmann to Baron de la Motte Fouqué*. It was reprinted in 1819, this time embedded in the conversation at the Serapion Club, as the first story of the first volume of the *Serapions-Brüder*. Hoffmann himself is again the central figure, now in grotesque caricature; Antonia is an idealized Julia Merc. The story forms the basis of the third act of Offenbach's *Contes d'Hoffmann*.

Das Majorat was written in 1817 and published in the same year in the second volume of *Nachtstücke*. The sinister Castle R. . . is a real place: Runsitten, on the Kurisches Haff on the Baltic coast.

Doge und Dogaressa, written in 1817, was published in October 1818 in the *Taschenbuch der Liebe und Freundschaft gewidmet* for 1819 and reprinted in 1819 in the second volume of the *Serapions-Brüder*. The story of the conspiracy of the Doge Marino Falieri is, of course, historical – 'one of the most remarkable events in the annals of the most singular government, city, and people of modern history' (Byron).

Die Bergwerke zu Falun was written during 1818 and 1819 and published in 1819 in the second volume of the *Serapions-Brüder*. The story is a fantasy founded on a real event: the discovery in 1719 at Falun in Sweden of the body of a miner buried in a mine-collapse nearly fifty years previously; it had been perfectly preserved beneath the earth and is supposed to have been recognized by an aged woman who claimed to have been the miner's lover half a century before. Wagner had the idea of basing an opera on Hoffmann's story and drafted a three-act scenario (March 1842) before being diverted, no doubt fortunately, to the subject of Tannhäuser.

Die Brautwahl, written in 1819, appeared in November that year in the *Berlinische Taschen-Kalender*; it was revised in mid-1820 and the revised version included in the third volume of the *Serapions-Brüder* published in the same year.

The English version of these eight tales of Hoffmann is a work of collaboration. Stella and Vernon Humphries translated *Doge and Dogaressa*. Sally Hayward translated *Mademoiselle de Scudery*, *The Entail* and *The Mines at Falun*, and I revised her translations. I translated *The Sandman*, *The Artushof*, *Councillor Krespel* and *The Choosing of the Bride*.

In helping to produce these new English versions of some of Hoffmann's best stories, I have sometimes felt the need to 'editorialize'. Hoffmann well knew how to evoke and maintain tension, but he did so, of course, in the idiom, and above all at the tempo, of his own age; this tempo was somewhat slower than ours, and it seemed to me that, for a story to produce, in modern English, the effect intended by the author, some speeding up and tightening up was sometimes called for. How far one should go in this interference can, I think, be only a matter of subjective judgement and 'feel' as one proceeds through the story; and its justification can lie only in whether or not it succeeds in its objective – whether, that is, the story affects the reader of today in the way in which, so far as one can tell, it affected Hoffmann's many thousands of readers in his own day. His aim, as a writer of fiction, was to give pleasure; and ours is nothing else.

June 1980   R.J.H.

MADEMOISELLE DE SCUDERY

A tale from the age of Louis XIV

——◦❦◦——

It was in the Rue St Honoré that the little house was situated which Madeleine de Scudery, famous for her charming poems, occupied by the grace and favour of Louis XIV and Madame de Maintenon.

Towards midnight – it would have been in the autumn of the year 1680 – there was a sudden violent hammering on the door, which echoed through the whole hall. Baptiste, who acted as cook, footman and doorman in Madeleine's small household, had gone to the country for his sister's wedding, and so it happened that only Madeleine's maid, Martinière, was in the house and still awake.

She listened to the persistent knocking . . . she remembered that Baptiste was away and that she and Mademoiselle were alone and unprotected; all the crimes ever committed in Paris – burglary, theft, murder – rushed through her mind. She was certain that a mob of cut-throats, having heard the house was unguarded, was rampaging outside, and so she remained in her room, quailing and quaking – and cursing Baptiste and his sister's wedding.

Down below, the knocking still thundered on and it seemed to her as if a voice were calling at intervals: 'For Christ's sake, open the door! Open up!'

Finally, with growing anxiety, Martinière seized the candlestick with its lighted candle and ran out into the hall; there she could make out quite clearly the voice of whoever was knocking: 'For Christ's sake, open up!'

'Indeed,' thought Martinière, 'no robber would talk like that. Who knows, it may be someone being pursued who is seeking refuge with my mistress: she is known for her good deeds. But one can't be too careful!'

She opened a window and called down, asking who was banging on the door at that hour of the night and waking everybody up . . . and trying as hard as possible to make her deep voice sound as masculine as it could. In the glimmer of moonlight which had just broken through the dark clouds she became aware of a tall figure enveloped in a light grey cloak and a broad-brimmed hat pulled well down over his eyes. She now called out more loudly, so that the figure down below could hear: 'Baptiste, Claude, Pierre! Get up and go and see immediately what ne'er-do-well is trying to knock the house down!'

Then the voice came up from below with a softer, almost pleading tone: 'Ah! Martinière, now I know it's you, dear lady, hard as you have tried to disguise your voice. I also know that Baptiste has gone into the country and you are alone with your mistress in the house. Just open the door for me without delay, don't be afraid! I absolutely must have a talk with your mistress, right this minute.'

'What are you thinking of?' replied Martinière. 'Do you think my mistress would want to talk to you in the middle of the night? Don't you realize she has been asleep for ages and I wouldn't wake her up at any price!'

'I know,' said the figure below, 'that your mistress has just this minute laid aside the manuscript of her novel *Clelia*, which she is working on so tirelessly, and is just now writing some verses which she is thinking of reading to the Marquise de Maintenon in the morning. I beseech you, Madame Martinière, have compassion and open the door for me. An unfortunate fellow's salvation from ruin depends upon it; the honour, freedom, indeed the life of someone depends on this moment; I *must* speak to your mistress. Just think how your mistress's wrath would fall on you for ever if she were to learn that it was you who stony-heartedly turned away from her door an unfortunate fellow who came to beg for her help.'

'But why do you want to beg my mistress's sympathy at this unearthly hour? Come back in the morning at a more suitable time!' rejoined Martinière. From below there came: 'Does fate come back at a certain time on a certain day when it strikes like the fatal flash of lightning? Is help to be delayed when rescue depends on a moment? Open the door for me! You have nothing to fear from a poor unprotected wretch, abandoned by the world, pursued and harassed by a terrible destiny, who wants only to implore your mistress to save him from his impending doom!'

Martinière heard the figure below sob and groan with pain at these words; the tone of his voice was, moreover, that of a young man, and it reached her very heart. Moved to her soul, she went and fetched the key.

Hardly had she opened the door when the figure pushed his way violently in, strode past Martinière into the hall, and cried wildly: 'Take me to your mistress!'

Martinière lifted the candlestick on high and the flickering light fell on a deathly pale, fearfully distorted youthful countenance; and she would have liked to sink to the ground in terror when, as the man now threw back his cloak, the shining handle of a stiletto glinted at his belt. The man looked at her with angrily flashing eyes and cried, more fiercely than ever: 'Take me to your mistress, I tell you!'

Now Martinière believed Mademoiselle to be in the most dire peril; all the affection she felt for her dear mistress welled up passionately within her and engendered a courage of which she would not have thought herself capable. Quickly she slammed the door of her chamber, which she had left open, stood before it, and said firmly:

'In faith, your wild conduct here inside the house does not suit with the plaintive words you used outside. I was wrong to feel sorry for you. My mistress should not and shall not speak to you now. If you had no wickedness in mind you would not shun the daylight. Come back in the morning.'

The man breathed a deep sigh, fixed Martinière with a terrible look, and reached for his stiletto. Martinière silently committed her soul to the Lord; yet she stood unflinching and looked the man bravely in the eye, pressing herself more firmly against the door through which the man would have to go to gain access to her mistress.

'Let me see your mistress, I say!' cried the man again.

'Do what you will,' replied Martinière, 'I am not moving from here – just finish the evil deed you have begun. You will meet a degrading death in the Place de Grève – you and your wicked friends!'

'Ha!' cried the man. 'You are right, Martinière! I do look like a murderer!' And with that he drew the stiletto.

'Jesus!' cried the poor woman, expecting the death blow; but at that moment she heard the clink of weapons and the tread of horses' hooves out in the street. 'Constables! Constables! Help! Help!' shrieked Martinière.

'You dreadful woman, do you want to ruin me? Now all is up with me! Here, take this! Take it! Give it to Mademoiselle now, today . . . in the morning – whenever you like!' So saying, the man snatched the candlestick from Martinière, extinguished the candle, and pressed a small box into her hands. 'For your salvation's sake, give the box to Mademoiselle!' he cried, and rushed from the house.

Martinière had slipped to the floor; now she stood up again and felt her way in the darkness back to her room, where, quite exhausted and incapable of another sound, she sank into the armchair. Then she heard the rattle of a key: she must have left it in the house door. Soft, uncertain footsteps approached the apartment . . . Spellbound, without strength to move, she waited for the worst . . . As the door opened, she recognized in the light of the lantern the face of honest Baptiste. He looked bewildered and deathly pale.

'For heaven's sake!' he began. 'For heaven's sake, Madame Martinière, tell me what has happened! – I don't know what it was, but something dragged me away from the wedding yesterday evening! I was back on the road when I met a patrol, horsemen and infantry, armed to the teeth. They stopped me and didn't intend to let me go; but as luck would have it, Desgrais was with them, the Lieutenant Constable – he knows me well enough. "Eh! Baptiste, what are you doing out here at night?" he says. "You must stay at home and keep guard. It's dangerous out here. We think we may still make a good catch tonight!" . . . You will hardly believe, Madame Martinière, how those words terrified me. Then, when I reached our doorstep, a cloaked figure darted out of the house with a drawn stiletto and sent me flying! The house was open, the key was in the lock. Tell me, what does all this mean?'

Martinière, no longer in fear for her life, related all that had happened. Then she and Baptiste went together into the hall. They found the candlestick on the floor where the stranger had dropped it as he fled.

'It is only too obvious,' said Baptiste, 'that our Mademoiselle was to have been robbed and probably murdered. You told me the man knew you were alone with Mademoiselle . . . indeed, that she was still awake and at her writing. For certain he was one of those accursed scoundrels who get into houses and spy out everything that may be useful to them in their devilish designs. And that little box, Madame Martinière – that I think we shall throw into the Seine at its deepest spot – who knows, it may be some mad attempt on our mistress's life, so that when she opens it she drops dead, like old Marquis de Tournay when he opened that letter he received from someone he didn't know!'

After a lengthy consultation, the faithful couple finally resolved to tell their mistress everything in the morning and, after due warning, to hand over to her the mysterious box.

Baptiste's fears were well founded. Paris was at that time the scene of horrific atrocities; the agent of them, one of the most devilish inventions of Hell. Herr Glaser, a German apothecary and the finest chemist of his time, occupied himself – a frequent temptation for people of learning – with alchemical experiments. His aim was to discover the philosopher's stone. An Italian named Exili had apprenticed himself to him; to learn the art of alchemy, however, was only a pretext; the mixing, boiling and sublimation of poisons was his real objective, and he at last succeeded in preparing a fine potion, odourless and taste-less, quickly fatal or killing slowly, and leaving behind no trace in the human body. Exili went to work very discreet-ly, yet still he fell under suspicion and was taken to the Bastille, where he was shortly afterwards joined in his cell by Captain Godin de Sainte Croix. Sainte Croix had long been living with the Marquise de Brinvillier in a rela-tionship which had brought shame on her whole family; finally, as the Marquis himself remained indifferent to his wife's crimes, her father, Dreux d'Aubray, a Civil Lieu-tenant of Paris, had compelled the miscreants to separate by means of a warrant of arrest served on the Captain. Characterless, inclined to depravity from his youth up, jealous and revengeful without limit, Sainte Croix could have encountered nothing more to his liking then Exili's devilish secret: he thought to possess in it the power to exterminate all his enemies. He became Exili's eager pupil, and he soon equalled his master, so that when he was released from the Bastille he was quite capable of working on his own.

Marquise de Brinvillier was a degenerate; under the influence of Sainte Croix she became a monster. With his aid she poisoned her own father, then her two brothers, and finally her sister; her father she killed for reasons of revenge, the others so as to obtain their inheritance. As the histories of other poisoners show, this kind of crime can become an irresistible passion: such poisoners have then killed people whose life or death must have been a matter of perfect indifference to them. So it was that the sudden death of several paupers in the Hôtel Dieu subsequently gave rise to the suspicion that the bread which the Marquise distributed there weekly as evidence of her piety had been poisoned. It is certain, however, that she poisoned the pigeon pies which she set before her guests on one occasion: the Chevalier de Guet and several others fell victim to that hellish repast.

Sainte Croix, his assistant La Chaussée, and the Marquise for a long time concealed their gruesome crimes behind an impenetrable veil: yet, fiendish though their craftiness was, the eternal power of Heaven had resolved to punish these evildoers while they were still on earth!

The poisons Sainte Croix prepared were so fine that if the powder – *poudre de succession* the Parisians called it – lay open while being prepared, a single breath sufficed for instant death; for this reason Sainte Croix always wore a mask of fine glass when carrying out this operation, and when one day it fell off as he was about to pour a prepared powder into a phial and he breathed in the poisonous dust, he fell dead on the instant. As he had died without heirs, the court hastened to take charge of his estate; there, locked in a case, they found his whole fiendish arsenal of poisons; and they also discovered letters from the Marquise which left no doubt as to her complicity in his crimes. She fled to a convent in Liège. A law officer, Desgrais, was sent after her: disguised as a priest, he presented himself at the convent where she was in hiding and soon succeeded in entering into an amorous intrigue with her. Enticed to a secret meeting place in a lonely garden outside the town, she was surrounded by Desgrais's men-at-arms, her priestly lover was transformed into an officer of the Constabulary, and she was forced to climb into a carriage standing ready outside the garden and straightway driven off to Paris. La Chaussée had already been beheaded, and the Marquise suffered a similar fate; after the execution her body was burnt and the ashes were thrown to the winds.

The Parisians for a time breathed freely again, but it soon became evident that the evil Sainte Croix had passed on his dreadful art. Like a malicious and invisible spectre, death stole into even the closest circles of family, love, friendship, and seized upon its unhappy victims. He who today was in blossoming health on the morrow staggered ill and infirm, and no physician's skill could save him. Riches, a lucrative office, a beautiful, perhaps too youthful wife: these sufficed for a man to be pursued to his death. Mistrust infected the most sacred relationships: husband feared his wife, father his son, sister her brother; meals remained untouched, wine undrunk; and where pleasure had once ruled, fearful eyes kept watch for a murderer. And still the most careful precaution was often in vain.

In an attempt to control the mounting disorder, the King appointed a tribunal to investigate and punish these crimes – the so-called *Chambre ardente*, which conducted its hearings not far from the Bastille and was presided over by La Regnie. Zealously though he went to work, La Regnie's efforts remained fruitless, for a long time, and it fell to the cunning Desgrais to penetrate the source of the outrage. In the district of Saint Germain there lived an old woman named La Voisin, skilled in soothsaying and necromancy; and with the help of her accomplices, Le Sage and Le Vigoureux, she knew how to inspire fear and amazement even in those who thought themselves un-gullible. Like Sainte Croix a pupil of Exili's, she knew how to prepare Exili's untraceable poison and so help sons to early inheritances and wives to younger husbands. Desgrais unearthed her secret and she confessed all: the *Chambre ardente* sentenced her to death by burning on the Place de Grève. Among her goods there was found a list of all those who had availed themselves of her assistance, and after that execution followed upon execution. Persons in high places did not elude suspicion: it was believed that Cardinal Bonzy had acquired from La Voisin the means of disposing of all those to whom, as Archbishop of Narbonne, he would have had to pay pensions; the Duchess de Bouillon and the Countess de Soissons, whose names were found on the list, were accused of connections with the diabolical old woman. Even the Duke of Luxembourg, Marshal of the Realm, was not spared; the *Chambre ardente* prosecuted even him and he surrendered to imprisonment in the Bastille, where La Regnie had him locked in a six-foot cell; months passed before it became clear that the Duke had committed no crime: he had once had his horoscope cast by Le Sage.

The blindness of his enthusiasm led La Regnie into illegalities and brutalities, and his tribunal assumed the character of an Inquisition: the slightest suspicion sufficed for strict incarceration, and often it was left to chance to prove the innocence of the condemned. La Regnie soon inspired the hatred of those whose avenger or protector he was supposed to be: the Duchess de Bouillon, questioned by him as to whether she had seen the devil, replied: 'I fancy I see him at this moment!'

The blood of the guilty and the innocent flowed at the Place de Grève, and as a result death by poison at length grew more and more rare; but trouble of another sort now appeared, to spread fresh consternation. A gang of thieves appeared to have set themselves the task of acquiring all the jewellery in Paris, and they were not hesitating to commit murder in pursuit of this aim. Those fortunate enough to escape with their life deposed that a blow from a fist had knocked them down and that when they came round they found they had been robbed and were in a place quite different from where they had received the blow. The bodies discovered almost every morning in the streets or within houses all bore the same death wound: a dagger thrust to the heart which, according to the doctors, must have killed so quickly and surely that the victim, incapable of making a sound, must have dropped to the ground at once. In the voluptuous court of Louis XIV there were many who, entangled in some amorous intrigue, crept to their mistress in the night, often bearing a rich gift; but often, too, the lover failed to reach the house where he anticipated enjoyment; sometimes he fell on the threshold, sometimes even before his mistress's door, who, horror-stricken, found his body in the morning.

In vain did Argenson, the Minister for Public Order, arrest anyone who seemed in the least suspicious; in vain did La Regnie rage and seek to extort confessions; watches and patrols were strengthened in vain – the villains were never detected. Only the precaution of arming yourself to the teeth, and having a lantern carried before you, was of any avail at all; even so, there were cases of servants being distracted and masters being murdered and robbed at the same instant.

What was very peculiar was that, despite investigation and inquiries in every place where jewels could in any way be disposed of, not the slightest trace of the stolen gems ever came to light.

Desgrais was enraged that the villains knew how to elude even his cunning: the quarter of the city in which he happened to be remained quiet, while the murderous thief was stalking his victim in another.

He resorted to theatricals, creating several versions of

himself all so similar in walk, stance, speech, figure and facial expression that even the constables did not know who the real Desgrais was. Meanwhile, at the risk of his life, he eavesdropped alone in secret hide-aways, and at a distance followed this person or that who on his instructions was carrying jewellery; but such a person was never attacked; the thieves knew of this trick, too. Desgrais fell into despair.

One morning he went to La Regnie, pale, with face distorted, and quite beside himself.

'What have you got? What's the news?' the president asked him.

'Ah, Sir,' Desgrais began, stammering with rage. 'Last night, not far from the Louvre, the Marquis de la Fare was attacked in my presence.'

'Heaven and earth!' cried La Regnie jubilantly. 'We have them!'

'Just listen!' Desgrais interrupted with a bitter laugh. 'Listen first of all to how things turned out. I was standing outside the Louvre, all Hell pent up inside me, waiting for the devils who are making me a laughing stock. Then there came along, walking uncertainly, constantly looking behind him, a figure who went past me, close by but without seeing me. In the moonlight I recognized the Marquis de la Fare. I was not surprised to see him there, for I knew where he was going. Hardly had he gone a dozen steps past me when a figure sprang up as if out of the ground, threw him down and pounced upon him. Momentarily amazed that the murderer should thus have been delivered into my hands, I cried out and made to leap from my hiding place. But I got entangled in my cloak and fell over. I saw the man make off as if on the wings of the wind. I pulled myself together, ran after him, gave a blast on my horn; from the distance the constables' whistles answered – everything came alive: the clatter of weapons, hoof-beats from all directions. "To me, to me – Desgrais, Desgrais!" I shouted, so that it echoed down the street. I can still see the man in front of me running in the bright moonlight; he tried to evade me, he turned off, and we came to the Rue Nicaise. As his efforts seemed to be weakening I endeavoured to redouble mine – at the most he was only fifteen paces ahead.'

'You overtook him, you seized him, the constables came up!' cried La Regnie with flashing eyes. He gripped Desgrais by the arm as if he were the fleeing murderer.

'Fifteen paces,' Desgrais continued in a dull voice, 'fifteen paces in front of me the man leaped sideways into the shadows and disappeared through the wall.'

'Disappeared? Through the wall! Are you raving?' cried La Regnie, taking a step back and throwing up his hands.

'Call me mad,' Desgrais continued, rubbing his forehead. 'Call me raving mad for ever more, a foolish ghostseer, but it is exactly as I am telling you. I was standing before the wall as several constables came running up. The Marquis de la Fare was with them, a drawn sword in his hand. We lit the torches. We groped about the wall: there was no sign of a door, or window, or any other opening. It was a solid, stone-built courtyard wall attached to a house. The people who live there are beyond suspicion. I have had everything inspected again today. It is the Devil himself we are dealing with.'

Desgrais's adventure was soon common knowledge throughout Paris. Heads were full of stories of sorcery, the evocation of spirits, of the Devil's alliance with Voisin, Vigoureux and the notorious Le Sage; and, as it lies in our nature to prefer the supernatural and miraculous to sober reason, very soon no one believed anything less than that, as Desgrais had said merely in a moment of ill-humour, the Devil himself was protecting the villains who had sold him their souls. Desgrais's story became wildly embellished and, illustrated with a woodcut depicting the Devil sinking into the ground in front of the startled Desgrais, was printed and sold at every street corner; it was sufficient to drain the constables of courage, and they now roamed the streets quaking and quailing, festooned with amulets and drenched in holy water.

Argenson saw the efforts of the *Chambre ardente* foundering, and approached the King, asking him to create a new court with still wider powers; but the King, convinced he had already given the *Chambre ardente* too much power and shocked by the innumerable executions demanded by La Regnie, rejected the proposal altogether. A further effort was made to persuade him: in Madame de Maintenon's chambers, where the King was accustomed to spend his afternoons and, indeed, even work with his ministers until late into the night, a poem was submitted to him on behalf of all the imperilled lovers, who complained that, as gallantry required them to bear an expensive gift to their beloved, they stood in peril of their life on each occasion; honourable and desirable though it might be to spill one's blood for one's beloved in chivalrous combat, it was quite otherwise with the treacherous attacks of a murderer, against whom no one could arm himself; and Louis, the star of all love and gallantry, who could rend the dark night with his bright rays and unveil the black secret which lurked therein, the godly knight who smote down his enemy, would even now flash his victorious, blazing sword and, like Hercules with the Lernaean Hydra, like Theseus with the Minotaur, do battle with the menacing evil which destroyed all pleasure in love and darkened all joy in sorrow, in wretched grief. The poem conveyed how the lover, creeping on his secret way to his beloved, was filled with such fear and distress that his anxiety killed all joy in love, every beautiful adventure in gallantry. And as it ended in grandiloquent praise for Louis XIV, the King could not fail to read it with satisfaction. He turned briskly to Madame Maintenon without taking his eyes from the paper, read the poem again aloud and then asked, smiling, what she thought of the desires of the imperilled lovers. Madame Maintenon, true to her serious nature and, as always, with a certain show of piety, replied that secret, forbidden paths did not merit special protection, but that the dreadful criminals did merit special measures for their extermination. The King, unhappy with such an indecisive answer, folded the paper and was about to rejoin his Secretary of State, who was at work in another room, when his eyes happened to light on Mademoiselle Scudery, who was present and had just taken her seat in a small armchair close to Madame Maintenon. He stepped over to her; his smile, which had vanished, now reappeared and, standing before the lady and again unfolding the poem, he said mildly: 'The Marquise wishes to know nothing of the gallantries of our enamoured gentlemen and is avoiding my question. But you, Mademoiselle, what do you think of this poetic petition?'

Mademoiselle de Scudery rose respectfully from her chair, a fleeting blush like the glow of evening passed over the pale cheeks of the worthy old lady, and, curtseying low, she said with downcast eyes:

> *'Un amant qui craint les voleurs*
> *n'est point digne d'amour.'*

The King, amazed at the chivalrous spirit of these words, which annihilated the whole poem and its tedious tirade, cried with flashing eyes: 'By Saint Denis, you are right, Mademoiselle! No measure which strikes the innocent with the guilty shall shelter cowardice: let Argenson and La Regnie do their duty!'

All the horror of the times was depicted by Martinière in the vividest of colours when, the next morning, she related to her mistress what had happened the previous night and, with much quaking, handed over to her the mysterious casket. Both she and Baptiste – who, standing in a corner as white as a sheet and twisting his nightcap in his hands with anxiety, could scarcely utter a word – begged Mademoiselle in the most pathetic way for heaven's sake to open the box only with the utmost caution.

Mademoiselle Scudery, weighing the locked secret in her hand and examining it, said with a smile: 'You look like a couple of ghosts! That I am not rich, that I have no treasures worth murdering for, is as well known to those evil assassins – who, as you yourself said, spy into the innermost corners – as it is to you and me. Can they be after my life? Who can be interested in the death of a person of seventy-three who has pursued scoundrels and disturbers of the peace only in novels she herself has written, who writes mediocre verses incapable of arousing envy, who will leave nothing behind but the wardrobe of an old maid who occasionally went to Court and a couple of dozen books with gilded edges! And you, Martinière, you can make the stranger sound as terrifying as you like, yet I cannot believe he had any evil intent in mind.'

Martinière started back three paces, Baptiste sank almost to his knees with a dull 'Ah!', as their mistress pressed a protruding knob and the lid of the box sprang noisily open.

How astonished Mademoiselle was as in the box there sparkled up at her a pair of golden bracelets, richly set with jewels, and an identical necklace. She took out the jewellery, and as she praised the beautiful workmanship of the necklace, Martinière stared at the expensive bracelets and cried over and over again that even the conceited Montespan did not possess such finery.

'But what is it supposed to be, what does it mean?' said Mademoiselle Scudery. At that moment she saw a folded note in the bottom of the box; but hardly had she read what it contained than the note fell from her trembling hand, she threw a glance up to heaven, and sank back into the armchair. Terrified, Martinière and Baptiste ran to her side.

'Oh!' she cried, in a voice half-choked with tears. 'Oh, the insult! Oh! the deep humiliation! Must this happen to me at my age? Have I behaved in a silly frivolous way, like a young, witless thing? Oh God, must words uttered half in jest bear such dreadful significance? I, who have been true to virtue and piety, irreproachable since childhood, must I then face such an accusation?'

Mademoiselle held her handkerchief to her eyes and sobbed violently, so that Martinière and Baptiste, utterly bewildered, did not know how to help their dear mistress in her distress.

Martinière picked up the note from the floor, and read what was written:

> *Un amant qui craint les voleurs,*
> *n'est point digne d'amour.*

Your penetrating wit, most esteemed lady, has saved us from great persecution – *us*, who exercise the right of the strong on the weak and cowardly, and appropriate to ourselves riches which would otherwise have been shamefully squandered. As proof of our gratitude, kindly accept these jewels. They are the most expensive we have procured for some time, although you, dear lady, should be adorned with much finer jewellery than this. We beg you not to withdraw from us your friendship and your gracious remembrance. We Who Are Invisible.

'Is it possible,' cried Mademoiselle Scudery, when she had recovered to some extent, 'is it possible that impudence and wicked mockery can be carried so far?'

The sun was shining brightly through the window-blinds of bright red silk, and made the diamonds which lay on the table by the open box sparkle with a reddish gleam.

Looking at them, Mademoiselle Scudery hid her face in horror, and ordered Martinière to take away the frightful jewels, to which the blood of the murdered victim seemed still to cling. Martinière, shutting the necklace and bracelets back in the box, thought that the best thing to do would be to hand them to the Minister of Police and to confide in him everything that had happened – including the alarming appearance of the young man and the handing over of the box.

Mademoiselle Scudery stood and slowly paced the room in silence, as if considering what should now be done. Then she told Baptiste to fetch a sedan chair, and Martinière to dress her: she wanted to go instantly to see the Marquise de Maintenon.

She had herself conveyed to the Marquise at a time when the latter, as Mademoiselle Scudery well knew, was alone in her apartments. She took the box of jewellery with her.

The Marquise wondered greatly when she saw Mademoiselle, usually the epitome of dignity, charm and grace, now enter pale, with face distorted and with faltering steps.

'What in heaven's name has happened to you?' she cried to the poor woman, who, quite beside herself and scarcely capable of standing, made for the armchair which the Marquise pushed towards her. At last, again able to speak, Mademoiselle explained what intolerable indignity that thoughtless jest with which she had responded to the plea from the imperilled lovers had caused her. The Marquise, after she had heard all in detail, thought that Mademoiselle Scudery was taking the extraordinary event much too much to heart, that insults of the rabble could never strike a noble spirit, and finally she asked to look at the jewels.

Mademoiselle Scudery gave her the opened box, and the Marquise could not suppress a cry of amazement when she beheld the gems. She took out the necklace and the bracelets and walked over to the window with them,

where she let the sunlight play on them and held the fine
gold-work up to her eyes to see clearly the marvellous craft
in each small link of the entwined chains.

Suddenly the Marquise turned to Mademoiselle and
cried: 'Do you realize, Mademoiselle, that these bracelets,
this necklace, can have been made by no one but René
Cardillac?'

René Cardillac was the most skilful goldsmith in Paris,
and one of the most artistically gifted and at the same time
strangest men of his age. Small in stature but broad-
shouldered and strongly built, though well advanced into
his fifties Cardillac still had the strength and agility of a
young man. He possessed a head of thick, curly red hair,
and a strange glance came from his deep-set, green-
flashing eyes. His familiarity with the nature of precious
stones was such that jewels rated as insignificant came out
of his workshop in glittering splendour. He took on every
order with a burning zeal, and fixed a price so low it
appeared to bear no relationship to the work he did. Then
he laboured without rest: he could be heard hammering in
his workshop day and night, and often the work would be
almost complete when the design would suddenly dis-
please him or he would have doubts about the elegance of
the setting – and that would be sufficient for the whole job
to be thrown back into the melting pot and started again
from scratch. Each item was thus an unsurpassable masterpiece. Now, however, it was scarcely possible to obtain
any finished work from him: on a thousand pretexts he put
his customers off from week to week, from month to
month. In vain he was offered double for the work: he
would take not a penny more than the agreed price. At
length he had to yield to the customer's insistence and
produce the jewellery: yet as he did so he could not
suppress signs of deep vexation, even of rage. If he had to
supply a particularly expensive work, worth perhaps

many thousands, he was capable of running round as if out of his mind, cursing himself and his work. But as soon as anyone came to him crying: 'René Cardillac! Won't you make a necklace for my bride, bracelets for my girl friend . . .' he would suddenly stand still, dart a fiery glance at him and ask, rubbing his hands together: 'What have you got, then?' The other would pull out a little case, and say: 'Here are some gems, they're nothing special, the usual thing, but in your hands . . .' Cardillac would not let him finish, but would snatch the little case from him, take out the gems, which really would not be worth much, hold them up to the light, and cry, full of delight: 'Ho ho! The usual stuff, eh! Not at all! Pretty stones, magnificent stones – just let me make them up! And if a few more Louis mean nothing to you, I will include a couple of little stones which will sparkle to your eyes like the dear sun itself!'

'I leave everything to you, Master René,' the other would say, 'and I will pay whatever you ask.' Cardillac would then throw himself impetuously at him, hug and kiss him, and say he was perfectly happy again and the work would be ready in a week. He would run headlong home and into his workshop, and hammer away, and in a week a masterpiece would be completed. But when he who had ordered it came to pay the small fee required and wanted to take the finished jewellery away with him, Cardillac would become rude and pig-headed.

'But Master Cardillac, just think, my wedding day is tomorrow.'

'What does your wedding matter to me, inquire again in a fortnight.'

'The jewellery is ready, here is the money – I must have it!'

'And I tell you I still have a lot of alterations to do and I will not release it today.'

'And I tell you that if you do not release the jewellery, for which I am willing to pay you double, you shall see me return straightaway with a couple of Argenson's men!'

'Now may Satan torment you with a hundred hot pincers and hang three hundredweight on the necklace so that your bride may choke!'

And with that, Cardillac would stuff the jewellery into the bridegroom's breast pocket, grip him by the arm, throw him out of the room and down the stairs, and would then stand at the window laughing at the poor young fellow limping out of the house holding a handkerchief to his bleeding nose.

It was a mystery why, when he had taken on work with enthusiasm, Cardillac would often suddenly beseech the customer, with every indication of deep agitation, with the most affecting protestations, even with sobs and tears and swearing by the Virgin and all the saints, to release him from it. He had thrown himself at the King's feet and begged not to have to undertake any more work for him. He had refused Madame de Maintenon's every order, too; with expressions of horror and disgust he had refused her proposal that he should produce a small ring, embellished with emblems of art, which she intended to give to Racine.

'I'll wager,' said Madame de Maintenon, 'that, if I send out to Cardillac to learn for whom he made this jewellery, he would refuse to come here because he would fear another order and he absolutely will not do anything for me, although he does seem to be desisting from his inflexible obstinacy, for I hear he is now working more industriously than ever and is delivering his work on time, though still with ill-humour and an averted face.'

Mademoiselle Scudery, who also set great store on returning the jewellery to its rightful owner if that were still possible, thought they might tell the strange master that it was not his work but only his opinion that was required. This the Marquise agreed to. A message was sent to Cardillac and, as if he had already been on his way, in a short time he entered the room.

When he saw Mademoiselle Scudery he seemed embarrassed and confused: he bowed low to the worthy lady, and then turned to the Marquise, who asked him abruptly whether the jewellery which sparkled on the dark green table was his work. Cardillac hardly glanced at it but, his eyes fixed on the face of the Marquise, he quickly packed the bracelets and necklace back into the casket and pushed it violently away from him. Then, with an unpleasant smile, he said: 'Indeed, Madame Marquise, one must have a very poor knowledge of René Cardillac's work to believe even for a moment that any other goldsmith in the world could set such jewellery. Certainly it is my work.'

'Tell me then,' the Marquise continued, 'for whom you made this jewellery.'

'For myself,' Cardillac replied. Madame Maintenon and Mademoiselle Scudery looked at him in amazement. 'Yes, you might find that rather strange, Madame Marquise,' he went on, 'but it is a fact. Desiring some beautiful work, I collected all my finest stones together and worked more diligently and carefully than ever before, purely for the joy of it. The jewellery inexplicably disappeared from my workshop some time ago.'

'Heaven be praised,' cried Mademoiselle Scudery, her eyes shining with joy. She jumped up from the armchair like a young girl, stepped across to Cardillac, and laid her hands on his shoulders. 'Take it,' she said, 'Master René, take back the property which those villains stole from you.'

Now she told how she came to possess the jewellery. Cardillac listened to everything in silence and with downcast eyes. Only now and then did he emit an inaudible 'Hm! So! Fancy! Oh!' now placing his hands behind his back, now stroking his chin. As Mademoiselle Scudery concluded, it was as if Cardillac were battling with his thoughts, as if some decision were refusing to be made. He rubbed his brows, he sighed, he passed his hand over his eyes as if to control impending tears. Finally, he grasped the little box which Mademoiselle Scudery offered him, dropped slowly on to one knee, and said: 'Fate has intended this jewellery for you, noble, worthy lady. Yes! I now realize for the first time that it was you I was thinking of while I worked. Yes! I was working for you. Do not disdain to take this from me and to wear it. This jewellery is indeed the finest I have made for a long time.'

'Now, now!' cried Mademoiselle Scudery, 'what are you thinking of, Master René? Does it become me at my age to dress myself in jewels? And how comes it that you wish to make me such a magnificent gift? If I were as beautiful as the Marquise de Fontange, and as rich, I would not let the jewellery out of my hands; but what will such splendour do for these wrinkled arms, what will this sparkling finery do for this scrawny neck?'

Cardillac had risen and, as if beside himself, with a wild look he extended the box to Mademoiselle Scudery and said: 'Have compassion on me, Mademoiselle, and take the jewels. You cannot believe what a profound admiration I have for your virtue, for your great merits! Accept my small gift if only to let me prove it to you.'

As Mademoiselle Scudery continued to hesitate, Madame Maintenon took the little casket from Cardillac's hands and said: 'Now, by Heaven, Mademoiselle, you are always talking of your great age; what have we to do with years, you and I, or with their burden? Do not behave like a young, bashful thing who would like to take the fruit if it could only be done without touching it. Do not reject honest Master René. Take as a gift what others cannot obtain for all the gold they have, for requests and supplications beyond number.'

Madame Maintenon had meanwhile forced the box on Mademoiselle Scudery. Now Cardillac dropped to his knees, kissed the hem of Mademoiselle Scudery's skirt, kissed her hands, moaned, sighed, wept, sobbed, and ran out upsetting the armchair and table, so that the porcelain and glasses rattled together. 'By all the saints, what has happened to the man?' Mademoiselle Scudery cried.

The Marquise emitted a shrill laugh, and cried: 'There we have it, Mademoiselle! Master René is desperately in love with you, and in accordance with practice and custom is with true gallantry beginning to storm your heart with rich gifts!'

She amplified the jest, admonished Mademoiselle Scudery not to be too cruel towards the desperate lover, and avowed that, if this was how matters stood, the world would soon behold the unexampled spectacle of a seventy-three years old lady of irreproachable aristocracy becoming the bride of a goldsmith. She volunteered to plait the bridal garland and to instruct Mademoiselle Scudery on the duties of a good housewife, for a young slip of a thing such as she was could certainly not know much about such matters.

When at last Mademoiselle Scudery rose to take leave of the Marquise, notwithstanding the jesting she became very serious again, since the jewel box was once more in her hands. She said: 'To be sure, Marquise, I shall never be able to wear this jewellery. It has been in the hands of those fiends who, with the cheek of the Devil and, indeed, even in association with him, commit robbery and murder. I shudder at the blood which seems to cling to these gems. And now even Cardillac's behaviour has, I must confess, for me something peculiarly unnerving and uncanny about it. I cannot resist a dark foreboding that behind all this there is some dreadful, terrible secret hidden. I cannot imagine how honest Master René, the model of a good, pious citizen, should have anything to do with such damnable evil. But this much is certain: I shall never dare to wear these jewels.'

The Marquise felt this was taking scruples too far. However, when Mademoiselle Scudery asked her, on her

conscience, what she would do in her place, she answered
seriously and firmly: 'Sooner throw the jewels into the
Seine than ever wear them.'

Mademoiselle Scudery penned some verses about her
meeting with Master René, which she read the following
evening to the King in Madame Maintenon's apartments:
the King laughed his sides sore, and swore that Boileau
Despréaux had met his match, Mademoiselle Scudery's
poem being one of the wittiest ever written.

Several months later Mademoiselle Scudery was driving
across the Pont Neuf in the glass coach belonging to the
Duchess of Montansier. The invention was still so new
that the gaping crowd encircling the coach almost blocked
the horses' path. Mademoiselle Scudery suddenly became
aware of a swearing and cursing, and observed someone
fighting and elbowing his way through the thickest part of
the crowd; as he came nearer, she met the penetrating gaze
of a deathly pale, grief-distorted youthful countenance.
The young man stared at her as he made his way through,
until he came within reach of the door of the carriage,
which he tore open, threw a note into Mademoiselle
Scudery's lap and, dealing and receiving cuffs and blows,
disappeared as he had come. Martinière, who was sitting
next to Mademoiselle Scudery, collapsed in a faint against
the cushions. In vain did Mademoiselle Scudery pull at the
cord and call to the coachman: as if driven by an evil spirit,
he whipped at the horses, which, foaming at the mouth,
veered round, reared up, and thundered on across the
bridge. Mademoiselle poured her smelling salts over the
unconscious woman, who at length opened her eyes and,
shaking and stammering and clutching hold of her mistress, stammered with difficulty: 'In the name of the Holy
Virgin, what did that dreadful man want? It was him, it
was him – the same who brought you the little casket that
awful night!'

Mademoiselle Scudery calmed the poor woman, and told her that nothing had happened and that it was only necessary to find out what the note contained. She unfolded the piece of paper, and read:

An evil fate which you can avert has hurled me into an abyss. I beseech you, take the necklace and bracelets which you received from me to René Cardillac under any pretext whatever – so as to have something improved or altered, perhaps. Your wellbeing, your life, depend on it. If you do not do this by the day after tomorrow, I shall force my way into your apartment and kill myself before your eyes.

'Now it is certain,' said Mademoiselle Scudery when she had read this, 'that though this mysterious man may belong to the band of villainous thieves and murderers, he harbours no evil designs against me. If he had succeeded in speaking to me that night, perhaps he would have given me the key to these mysteries, which I now seek for in my soul in vain. But let happen what will, what is asked of me I will do, if only to be rid of this unlucky jewellery. Cardillac will not so easily let it out of his hands again.'

Mademoiselle Scudery intended to make her way to the goldsmith's with the jewellery the next day, yet it was as if all the fine minds of Paris had agreed to besiege her that morning with poems, plays and anecdotes: hardly had La Chapelle finished the scene of a tragedy, and slyly assured her that he now believed he would conquer Racine, than the latter himself appeared and outdid him with a speech by some king or other. Noon was past, Mademoiselle Scudery had to visit the Duchess of Montansier, and Master René Cardillac had therefore to be postponed until the next day.

Mademoiselle Scudery felt tormented by a strange restlessness: the young man appeared constantly before her eyes, and an obscure memory seemed to want to rise from her innermost depths, as if she had seen that countenance, those features, before. Anxious dreams troubled the lightest slumber; it seemed to her that she had thoughtlessly failed to grasp the hand which the unfortunate fellow, sinking into the abyss, had stretched out to her, that she had failed to avert some ruinous event, some terrible crime. As soon as it was morning, she dressed and drove to the goldsmith's, bearing the jewel box.

People were streaming towards the Rue Nicaise, where Cardillac lived, gathering around the door, shouting, making an uproar, trying to storm inside and being with difficulty prevented by men-at-arms who surrounded the house. In a wild, confused uproar, angry voices shouted: 'Lynch him! tear the murderer to pieces!'

At length, Desgrais appeared with a party of men, who forced a way through the thickest part of the crowd. The main door burst open. A man weighed down with chains was brought out and dragged away under the curses of the furious mob. On the instant Mademoiselle Scudery, half fainting with terror and apprehension, became aware of all this, a wail of misery reached her ears.

'On! Keep going!' she cried to the coachman, who had with a rapid turn parted the crowd and stopped directly in front of Cardillac's door. There she saw Desgrais, and at his feet a young girl, as lovely as the day, with her hair loose, half undressed, wild anxiety and hopeless despair in her face, who gripped him about the knees and cried in a tone of mortal agony: 'But he is innocent! He is innocent!'

Desgrais's efforts, and those of his men, to pull her away and stand her on her feet were in vain. A strong, rough youth finally laid hold on the poor girl, and tore her away from Desgrais by force; then he stumbled and let go of the girl, who fell down the steps and lay, motionless and as if dead, in the roadway. Mademoiselle Scudery could restrain herself no longer. 'In Christ's name, what has happened? What is going on here?' she cried, and opened the door and climbed down. The people gave way to her; and she approached Desgrais and repeated her question.

'A terrible thing has happened,' said Desgrais. 'René Cardillac was found murdered this morning by a dagger. His apprentice, Olivier Brusson, is the murderer. He has just been led away to prison.'

'And the girl?' cried Mademoiselle Scudery.

'She', said Desgrais, 'is Madelon, Cardillac's daughter. The wicked man was her lover. Now she is crying that Brusson is innocent, quite innocent. But she knows about the deed, and I must take her to the Conciergerie too.'

As he spoke, Desgrais threw a malicious glance at the girl, at which Mademoiselle Scudery trembled. The girl was beginning to breathe, but she still lay incapable of sound or movement, with her eyes closed. Deeply moved, Mademoiselle Scudery gazed at the angelic child and shuddered at the thought of Desgrais and his men. There was a muffled rumbling down the steps: they were bringing Cardillac's body. With a sudden resolve, Mademoiselle Scudery cried: 'I am taking the girl with me. You can look after the rest, Desgrais!'

A murmur of approval ran through the crowd. The women lifted the girl, everyone pressed round, a hundred pairs of hands laboured to assist them and, as if floating on air, the girl was borne into the carriage.

Dr Serons, one of the most famous physicians in Paris, finally succeeded in reviving Madelon. Mademoiselle Scudery completed what the doctor had begun, until at last a flood of tears gave vent to Madelon's feelings. The overpowering pain of her words now and then choking her with great sobs, she tried to relate how everything had happened.

At about midnight she was awoken by a gentle knocking on her bedroom door, and she recognized Olivier's voice imploring her to get up immediately – her father was dying, he said. She sprang up and opened the door.

Olivier, pale, in disarray, and pouring with sweat, went with the light in his hand, reeling towards the workshop; she followed him. There lay her father in the throes of death. She threw herself upon him, and only then did she notice his bloodstained shirt. Olivier had gently drawn her away, and endeavoured to wash and bandage the wound in her father's left side. During this time her father's senses returned: he regarded her and then Olivier with a tender look, took hold of her hand, laid it in Olivier's and pressed them both firmly. Olivier and she had gone on their knees by her father's bed; with a piercing cry he raised himself up, but at once sank back again, and with a deep sigh passed away. Olivier had related how the master, on an errand which he had had to make with him that night, had been murdered in his presence, and how, with the greatest effort, he had carried the heavy man, whom he had not thought mortally wounded, back home. As soon as morning came, the occupants of the house, whose attention had been attracted by the banging, wailing and lamenting in the night, came up and found them, still quite inconsolable, on their knees beside her father's body. Now there was uproar. The constables burst in and hauled Olivier off to prison as his master's murderer. Madelon gave the most touching description of the virtue, piety and loyalty of her beloved Olivier: how he had held his master in high esteem, as if he had been his own father; how the latter had returned his love in full; how, in spite of Olivier's poverty, he had chosen him as his son-in-law, because his skill equalled his loyalty and noble spirit. All this Madelon related from the depths of her heart, and ended by saying that, even if Olivier had stabbed her father in her own presence, she would sooner regard it as a trick of Satan's than believe him capable of so dreadful and gruesome a crime.

Mademoiselle Scudery, deeply touched by Madelon's sufferings and inclined to regard the poor Olivier as innocent, made enquiries and confirmed everything Madelon had said as to the relations between master and apprentice. The other occupants of the house, the neighbours, all concurred in praising Olivier as a model of piety, loyalty and diligence; no one knew anything ill of him, and when the dreadful deed was mentioned, each shrugged his shoulders and said there was something incomprehensible about it.

Brought before the *Chambre ardente*, so Mademoiselle Scudery learned, Olivier steadfastly denied his guilt, and asserted that his master had been attacked in the street in his presence, and that he had dragged him back home still alive. This, too, accorded with Madelon's tale.

Mademoiselle Scudery had the details of the dreadful event repeated to her again and again. She inquired whether there had ever been any dispute between master and apprentice; whether perhaps Olivier was not entirely free of that violent temper which often overcomes even the most good-natured people and can lead to irrational deeds. The more Madelon spoke of the domestic happiness in which the three of them had lived, the more completely every shadow of suspicion against Olivier vanished away. Even discounting everything which spoke for his innocence, Mademoiselle Scudery could find not a single motive for the deed. 'He is poor, but gifted. He gained the affection of one of the most famous of master craftsmen and fell in love with his daughter; the master looked kindly on his love; happiness and prosperity opened to him!' Convinced of Olivier's innocence, Mademoiselle Scudery resolved to save the innocent youth whatever the cost.

Before appealing to the King's mercy, she approached La Regnie, to acquaint him with all the circumstances which spoke for Olivier's innocence, and thus perhaps to arouse in his soul a favourable disposition towards the accused which might communicate itself to the judges. La Regnie received Mademoiselle Scudery with the respect

due to a lady esteemed by the King himself; he listened in
silence to everything she said; but a thin, almost mocking
smile was the only indication he gave that her protestations, accompanied by frequent tears, did not fall on
completely deaf ears. As Mademoiselle, quite exhausted,
dried the tears from her eyes and at last fell silent, La
Regnie began: 'It is worthy of your splendid heart, dear
lady, that, touched by the tears of a young, lovesick girl,
you should believe everything she puts to you; indeed, that
you should be incapable of grasping the idea of so dreadful
a crime. But it is quite otherwise with the judge, who is
used to unmasking hypocrisy. It is not my office to
determine the course of criminal proceedings on behalf of
everyone who asks it, Mademoiselle! I do my duty. The
opinion of the world troubles me little. Evil-doers shall
tremble before the *Chambre ardente*, which knows of no
punishment other than blood and fire. But I should not like
you, dear lady, to take me for a monster of cruelty and
brutality. Therefore permit me to set out clearly before
you in a few words the guilt of this young scoundrel on
whom, Heaven be praised, vengeance has fallen. Your
own intelligence will then repudiate that kind heart which
does you credit but would not become me. So! René
Cardillac is found murdered by a dagger. Nobody is with
him except his apprentice, Olivier Brusson, and his
daughter. In Brusson's room there is found, among other
things, a dagger stained with fresh blood which fits the
wound exactly. "Cardillac," says Brusson, "was knocked
down and killed last night before my eyes." – "Did
someone want to rob him?" – "That I don't know." –
"You were with him and it was not possible for you to
ward off the murderer? to hold him? to call for help?" –
"The master went some fifteen or twenty paces in front of
me; I followed him." – "Why in the world so far behind?"
– "The master wanted it so." – "What was Master Cardillac about so late in the street?" – "That I cannot say." –

"Except on this occasion, however, he never went out of the house after nine o'clock in the evening?" – Here Brusson falters, he is dismayed, he sighs, he sheds tears, he protests by everything holy that Cardillac really did go out that night and meet his death. Now, however, pay great attention, Mademoiselle. It has been proved with absolute certainty that Cardillac never left his house that night; Brusson's assertion that he went out with him is therefore an insolent lie.

'The house-door is fitted with a heavy bolt which makes a resounding noise when it is drawn or shot; and then the door itself moves awkwardly, creaking and groaning on its hinges, so that – as tests carried out have shown – the din echoes even on the top floor of the house. Now, on the ground floor, close, that is to say, by the main door, lives old Master Claude Patru with his housekeeper, a person of almost eighty but still cheerful and active. These two heard how Cardillac, in his normal way as on every evening, punctually at nine o'clock came down the stairs, closed and barred the door, then went back up again, loudly read the evening prayers, and then, as could be heard from the closing of the door, went into his bedroom. Master Claude suffers from insomnia, as is often the case with old people. That night he was unable to close his eyes. His house-keeper – it must have been about half past ten – therefore went into the kitchen, crossing the hall to do so, kindled a light, and sat with Master Claude at the table reading an old news-sheet, while the old man, indulging his own thoughts, first sat in the armchair, then got up and, trying to induce tiredness and sleep, walked up and down the room. Everything was quiet and peaceful until after midnight. Then she heard sharp steps overhead, a hard thud as if something heavy had fallen on the floor and, immediately afterwards, a muffled groaning. They both felt a strange anxiety and a feeling of oppression. The horror of the dreadful deed which had just been done passed through them. Then, in the brightness of morning there came to light what had been done in the dark.'

'But', interrupted Mademoiselle Scudery, 'in Heaven's name, with all the circumstances which I have just related to you, can you envisage any reason for this hellish deed?'

'Hm,' replied La Regnie. 'Cardillac was not poor – he had many splendid stones.'

'But does not', continued Mademoiselle Scudery, 'the daughter get everything? You forget that Olivier was to be Cardillac's son-in-law.'

'Perhaps he had to murder only on behalf of others,' said La Regnie.

'Murder on behalf of others?' Mademoiselle Scudery asked in absolute amazement.

'You should know, dear lady,' continued La Regnie, 'that Brusson would have shed his blood long ago on the Place de Grève if his deed had not been connected with the impenetrable mystery which has had the whole of Paris in its grip. He obviously belongs to that accursed band which, in mockery of all effort and all investigation by the courts, has known how to pursue its activities with impunity. Through him everything will, must, become clear. Cardillac's wound is identical to those exhibited by all who have been robbed and murdered in streets and houses. And then, the most decisive thing: since the time of Olivier Brusson's arrest these murders and robberies have ceased. The streets are as safe by night as by day: sufficient proof that Brusson is, perhaps, the leader of that murderous band. He still refuses to confess, but there are ways of making him talk against his will.'

'And Madelon,' cried Mademoiselle Scudery, 'the loyal, innocent lamb!'

'Ah!' said La Regnie, with a smile, 'ah! who can guarantee that she is not in the plot? Whatever she may feel about her father, her tears are shed only for the murdering rogue.'

'What are you saying?' cried Mademoiselle Scudery. 'It is not possible! Her father! *This* girl!'

'Oh!' continued La Regnie, 'consider only the Brinvillier woman! You will have to pardon me if I perhaps am soon compelled to snatch your *protégée* from you and have her thrown into the Conciergerie.'

Mademoiselle Scudery shuddered. It seemed that loyalty and virtue did not exist for this dreadful man. She stood up. 'Be human' was all, her heart tightened and breathing with difficulty, she could utter. She was already on her way down the stairs, to which La Regnie had accompanied her with ceremonious courtesy, when a singular thought struck her. 'Would it be permitted for me to see the unfortunate Olivier Brusson?' she asked, turning suddenly. La Regnie regarded her with a thoughtful expression, then his face drew itself into that repellent smile peculiar to him.

'Certainly,' he said, 'certainly, dear lady. Trusting your inner voice more than what has happened before our eyes, you wish to test Brusson's guilt or innocence. If the dismal abode of crime does not frighten you, if you do not mind seeing images of depravity in every degree, then the doors of the Conciergerie shall be opened to you in two hours. This Brusson, whose predicament provokes your intervention, shall be brought before you.'

Mademoiselle Scudery could not convince herself of the young man's guilt. Everything spoke against him: no judge in the world would have acted otherwise than La Regnie in the face of such decisive evidence. Nevertheless, the image of domestic happiness which Madelon had conjured up in her outfaced every suspicion, so that she preferred to assume there was an inexplicable mystery here than to believe something against which her whole being rebelled. She intended to have Olivier relate once again everything that had happened on that fateful night; perhaps she could thus penetrate a mystery which was perhaps impenetrable to the judges because they thought the question was no longer worth pursuing.

Arrived at the Conciergerie, Mademoiselle Scudery was led into a large, bright room. Soon she heard the rattling of chains. Olivier Brusson was brought in. Yet at the moment he stepped through the door, Mademoiselle Scudery sank unconscious. When she revived, Olivier had disappeared. She demanded to be led out to her carriage: immediately, instantly, she wanted to leave this place. At first sight she had recognized Olivier Brusson as the young man who had thrown the note into her carriage on the Pont Neuf, who had brought her the casket of jewels. Now, indeed, every doubt was gone, La Regnie's dreadful suspicions were wholly confirmed. Olivier Brusson belonged to the frightful band of murderers; certainly he had murdered his master!

And Madelon? – Never before so bitterly deceived by her feelings, mortally crushed by the hellish power in whose existence she had not believed, Mademoiselle Scudery doubted all truth. She gave way to the awful suspicion that Madelon was an accomplice and might have participated in the terrible crime. And since, once a picture appears to the human mind, it seeks to paint it in more and more vivid colours, so Mademoiselle Scudery too, considering Madelon's behaviour in the minutest detail, found in each circumstance of the deed much to nourish that suspicion. Many things which before had seemed to her proof of innocence and purity now became a sure sign of outrageous evil and studied deceit. That heart-rending lamentation, those tears, could have been wrung forth by the fear of death – not from seeing her lover bleed, but from seeing herself fall under the hangman's hand. To rid herself of the viper she was nurturing in her bosom: it was with this decision that Mademoiselle Scudery alighted from her carriage. Once she was in her apartment, Madelon threw herself at her feet. The eyes of Heaven, an angel of God could not have seemed more true as, hands clasped before her heaving breast, she lamented and implored her help and consolation. Mademoiselle Scudery, pulling herself together with effort and trying to speak as calmly as possible, said: 'Go – go away – go and console the murderer who awaits a just punishment for his shameful deeds. I pray the Holy Virgin that you do not share in his guilt.'

'Oh, now all is lost!' – with this piercing cry Madelon fell to the floor in a swoon. Mademoiselle Scudery left the care of the girl to Martinière and went into another room.

Inwardly shattered, sundered from everything on earth, Mademoiselle Scudery no longer wished to live in a world full of such hellish deceit. She denounced the fate which in bitter mockery had granted her so many years in which to strengthen her belief in virtue and loyalty and had now, in her old age, shattered the beautiful image which had lighted her through life.

She perceived that Martinière was bringing out Madelon, who sighed and wailed: 'Oh! She too – she too has been deluded by those cruel men. I am so wretched – poor, unhappy Olivier!'

The cries pierced Mademoiselle Scudery's heart, and from the depths of her soul there arose again the presentiment of some unrevealed mystery and a belief in Olivier's innocence. Afflicted by contradictory feelings and quite beside herself, she cried: 'What spirit from Hell has involved me in these dreadful events which will cost me my life?'

Baptiste entered, white and terrified, with the news that Desgrais was outside. Since the dreadful trial of La Voisin, Desgrais's appearance in any house was the certain presage of some kind of painful accusation. Mademoiselle Scudery, however, asked him with a gentle smile: 'What is the matter, Baptiste? Has the name of Scudery been found on La Voisin's list?'

'Oh, in the name of Christ,' replied Baptiste, trembling

in every limb, 'how can you talk like that? Desgrais, the dreadful Desgrais, is so mysterious, so insistent; he did not seem to expect to be able to see you!'

'Now then, Baptiste,' said Mademoiselle Scudery, 'just show him in; the man who is so fearful to you cannot alarm me!'

'The president La Regnie', said Desgrais, when he had entered the apartment, 'sent me to you, Mademoiselle, with a request, the fulfilment of which he could hardly hope for, did he not know your virtue and your courage, if the last means of bringing an evil guilt to light did not lie in your hands, had you yourself not already intervened in the evil proceedings which are keeping the *Chambre ardente* and all of us in suspense. Olivier Brusson is, since he saw you, half crazy. Although he seemed almost ready to confess, he now swears again by Christ and all the saints that he is completely innocent of Cardillac's murder, though he is ready to suffer a death which he has deserved. Note, Mademoiselle, that the last statement obviously refers to other crimes which are burdening him. Yet all efforts to get another word out of him are vain: even threats of torture have achieved nothing. He beseeches and implores us to arrange an interview with you. To you, to you alone will he confess everything. Please condescend, Mademoiselle, to hear Brusson's confession.'

'What!' cried Mademoiselle Scudery indignantly. 'Am I to serve as an instrument of the bloody assize? Am I to abuse the trust of the unfortunate man to bring him to the scaffold? No, Desgrais! Brusson may be a murderer, yet never would I deceive him in such a way. I wish to know nothing of his secrets, which would in any case remain sealed in my heart like a holy confession.'

'Perhaps,' Desgrais said with a thin smile, 'Mademoiselle, you would change your mind if you had heard Brusson. Did you yourself not beg the president to be human? He is being so, by giving way to this foolish demand of

Brusson's and thus attempting a last expedient before inflicting the torture for which Brusson has long been ripe.'

Mademoiselle Scudery shrank back involuntarily. 'Look,' continued Desgrais, 'look, dear lady, you will not be expected to return to that dark place which fills you with such horror and disgust. In the quiet of the night, Brusson will be brought to you in your house like a free man. Not even spied upon, though well guarded, he may then tell you everything without constraint. That you have nothing to fear for yourself from the wretch I will answer for with my life. He speaks of you with fervent respect. He swears it is only the dismal fate which prevented him from seeing you earlier that is hurrying him to his death. And then you may tell as much as you please of what Brusson discloses to you. Can we compel you to do more?'

Mademoiselle Scudery stared before her, deep in thought. It was as if she must obey a higher power which was demanding from her the unravelling of this dreadful mystery, as if she could no longer evade the strange entanglements into which she had strayed. Suddenly resolved, she said with dignity: 'God will give me composure and steadfastness. Bring Brusson here, I will speak to him.'

As on the occasion when Brusson had brought the casket, there was a knock on the door of Mademoiselle Scudery's house at midnight. Baptiste, informed of the nocturnal visit, opened the door. An icy shudder ran through Mademoiselle Scudery as she perceived, from the soft steps and muffled muttering, that the guards who had attended Brusson were taking up their positions in the corridors of the house. Finally, the door of her apartment gently opened. Desgrais entered, behind him Olivier Brusson, free of his fetters and in ordinary clothes.

'Here,' said Desgrais, bowing respectfully, 'is Brusson, Mademoiselle!' and left the room.

Brusson dropped to his knees before Mademoiselle Scudery; beseechingly, he lifted his clasped hands; tears streamed from his eyes. She looked down at him, pale and incapable of speaking. Even with his features distorted and contorted by grief and pain, a pure expression of the trustworthiest nature shone from the youth's countenance. The longer she allowed her eyes to rest upon Brusson's face, the more vivid became the memory of some beloved person whom she was unable clearly to remember. All fear left her; she forgot that Cardillac's murderer was kneeling before her; she spoke in the tones of quiet kindness characteristic of her: 'Now then, Brusson, what have you to say to me?'

The latter, still on his knees, groaned with deep, fervent sorrow, and said: 'O most esteemed, most highly revered lady, has every trace of the memory of me gone?'

Mademoiselle Scudery, still regarding him attentively, replied that she found a resemblance in his features to some person beloved by her, and that he had only this resemblance to thank for her being able to conquer her deep disgust for the murderer and to listen to him calmly. Brusson, deeply hurt by these words, quickly rose and took a step backwards, gazing sullenly at the floor. Then he said in a muffled voice: 'Have you quite forgotten Anne Guiot? Her son Olivier – the child you often used to rock on your knee – now stands before you.'

'Oh, by all the saints!' cried Mademoiselle Scudery, covering her face with her hands and sinking back against the cushions. Mademoiselle had reason to be shocked. Anne Guiot, the daughter of an impoverished citizen, had lived with her from a small child and she had brought her up with the devotion and care of a mother. When she had grown up there appeared a handsome, upright young man called Claude Brusson, who courted her. As Anne had come to love him also, and as he was a skilled clockmaker who had to earn his bread in Paris, Mademoiselle Scudery had had no objection to giving him her foster-daughter in marriage. The young couple set themselves up, and lived in peaceful, happy domesticity; and their bond of love was tied still more firmly by the birth of a beautiful child, the image of his lovely mother.

Mademoiselle Scudery made an idol of the little Olivier, whom she kept from his mother for hours on end and whole days at a time to pet and pamper him; the boy grew altogether accustomed to her, and was just as happy with her as with his mother. Three years passed, and the jealousy of Brusson's fellow craftsmen had contrived to reduce his work day by day to the point at which he could scarcely feed himself. To this there was added a longing for his native Geneva, and so the little family moved thither – Mademoiselle Scudery's opposition, and her promise of every possible assistance, went unheeded. Anne wrote to her foster-mother once or twice, then there was silence, and Mademoiselle Scudery was left to believe that the happy life in Brusson's homeland no longer left room for memories of earlier days. It was now twenty-three years since Brusson and his wife and child had left Paris.

'Oh, how awful,' cried Mademoiselle Scudery, when she had recovered herself to some extent. 'Oh, how dreadful! You are Olivier? My Anne's boy? – And now!'

'Indeed,' Olivier said, calm and composed, 'dear Mademoiselle, you could never have had any presentiment that the child you used to pamper like the tenderest of mothers, whose mouth you used to fill with sweets and tidbits, whom you called the sweetest names, once grown to manhood would stand before you accused of a ghastly crime! I am not entirely blameless: the *Chambre ardente* can justly accuse me of one crime; but, as I hope to die blessed, even though by the hangman's hand, I am innocent of *that* guilt – Cardillac did not die by my hand, nor through my fault!'

As he said these words, Olivier broke into shivering and

trembling. Silently, Mademoiselle Scudery motioned him to a small armchair close by, and he slowly lowered himself into it.

'I have had sufficient time,' he began, 'to prepare myself for this interview with you, which I regarded as the final favour of a reconciled Heaven, and to gather as much calmness and composure as is needed to tell you the story of my terrible, unbelievable misfortune. Show compassion and listen to me calmly, however surprised, even filled with horror you may be at the disclosure of a mystery you have certainly not suspected. – If only my poor father had never had to leave Paris! – So far as my memory of Geneva goes, I find myself wet with my parents' sad tears, and by their lamentations, which I did not understand, myself too reduced to tears. Later there came to me a clear realization of the oppressive want and deep misery in which my parents were living. All my father's hopes were disappointed. Crushed by grief he died just as he had succeeded in apprenticing me to a goldsmith. My mother often spoke of you; she wanted to tell you of everything, but then she was overcome by that lack of courage which misery produces. And false shame, too, which often gnaws at the mortally wounded heart, also held her back. A few months after the death of my father, my mother followed him to the grave.'

'Poor Anne! Poor Anne!' cried Mademoiselle Scudery, overcome by grief.

'Thanks and praise be to Heaven that she has gone and cannot see her beloved son in the hands of the hangman, branded with shame!' cried Olivier aloud, with a wild, dreadful look.

The silence outside was broken by the sound of footsteps.

'Ha, ha!' said Olivier, with a bitter smile, 'Desgrais is waking his comrades – as if I could escape from *here*! Still, let us continue! – I was kept hard at work by my master, even though I soon worked best without supervision; indeed, I far surpassed him in the end. One day a stranger came into our workshop to buy some jewellery; when he saw a necklace I was working on, he clapped me on the back in a friendly fashion and, eyeing the jewellery, said: "Well, well, my young friend, that is really splendid work. I don't know who could do better except René Cardillac, who is easily the best goldsmith in the world. You ought to go to him: he would be delighted to take you into his workshop, for only you would be capable of helping him, and, on the other hand, only from him could you still learn something."

'The stranger's words left a deep impression on my soul. I no longer found any peace in Geneva. I longed to get away. At length I managed to leave my master. I came to Paris. René Cardillac received me coldly and roughly. I did not give up. I insisted he give me some work, however trifling it might be. He let me make a small ring. When I brought him the work, he stared at me fixedly with his flashing eyes as if he wanted to see into my heart. Then he said: "You are a skilful, stout-hearted fellow. You may join me and help in the workshop. I shall pay you well; you will be happy with me."

'Cardillac kept his word. I had been with him for several weeks without seeing Madelon, who, if I am not mistaken, was staying with an aunt of Cardillac's in the country. At last she came back. O eternal power of Heaven, how I was stirred when I beheld that angel! Was ever a man so in love as I? And now! – O Madelon!'

Olivier could speak no more. He hid his face in his hands and sobbed. At length, overcoming the sorrow which filled him, he continued: 'Madelon looked on me kindly. She came more and more often into the workshop. With joy, I became aware of her love. Closely though her father watched over us, many a stolen handclasp served as a sign of our sealed bond, and Cardillac seemed not to notice. I thought: if only I could first win his favour, and then attain my mastership, and thus win Madelon!

'One morning, as I was about to start on my work, Cardillac came up to me with rage and scorn in his eyes. "I no longer need your work," he began. "Get out of this house within the hour, and don't let me see you again. I need not tell you why I cannot have you here any longer. The fruit you desire is out of reach!" I was about to speak, but he set on me with his fists and threw me out of doors, so that I stumbled and injured my head and arm.

'Shocked, confused by the pain, I left the house and eventually found a good-natured acquaintance on the outskirts of the suburb of St Martin, who accommodated me in his attic. I had no peace, no rest. By night I crept around outside Cardillac's house, imagining that Madelon would hear my sighs and lamentations, that perhaps she would succeed in speaking to me from her window without being heard. All kinds of mad plans crossed my mind, which I hoped to persuade her to.

'Adjoining Cardillac's house in the Rue Nicaise is a high wall, with niches with old, half-disintegrated statues in them. One night I was standing close beside one of these stone figures and looking towards the house windows which give on to the yard which the wall encloses. Suddenly, I was aware of a light in Cardillac's workshop. It was midnight; Cardillac used never to be awake at this hour – he went to bed on the stroke of nine. My heart pounded with uneasy foreboding; I imagined there might be some incident or other which would help me to get into the house. Yet the light was immediately extinguished again. I pressed myself against the statue, inside the niche; then, horrified, I recoiled as I felt a counter-pressure, as if the statue had come to life. In the dimness of the night I realized that the stone was turning slowly round, and from behind it a dark figure slipped out and went softly down the street. I quickly examined the statue; it stood as before, close to the wall. Involuntarily, as if driven by some inner power, I crept after the figure. Close by an image of the Virgin the figure looked back; the light of the lamp burning before the shrine fell upon his face. It was Cardillac!

'An incomprehensible fear, an uncanny dread came over me. As if in thrall to some spell, I had to follow the ghostly sleepwalker – for that is what I took the master to be, though it was not the time of the full moon, when such spirits bewitch sleepers. At length, Cardillac disappeared sideways into the deep shadows. By a clearing of his throat, well-known to me, I perceived that he had stepped into the entrance of a house. What did it mean, what was he going to do? – wondering thus, and full of amazement, I pressed myself close against the house. It was not long before a man with glistening plumes and rattling spurs came along, singing and whistling. Like a tiger at his prey, Cardillac leaped from his hiding-place on to the man, who at the same instant dropped to the ground with a gasp.

'With a cry of horror I leaped across: Cardillac was bending over the man lying on the ground. "Master Cardillac, what are you doing?" I cried aloud. "Curse you!" Cardillac roared, and with the speed of lightning dashed past me and disappeared.

'Quite beside myself, hardly able to put one foot in front of another, I went up to the body. I knelt down by him: perhaps, I thought, he may still be saved, but there was no trace of life left in him. In my anguish I was scarcely aware that the officers had encircled me. "Well, well, another one laid low – hey! young man, what are you doing here? Are you one of the gang? Here with you!" – thus they cried together and lay hold on me. I was scarcely able to stammer that I was incapable of committing such a ghastly crime and that they should let me go in peace. Then someone held a lamp to my face and laughed: "This is Olivier Brusson, the goldsmith's apprentice, who works with our worthy Master René Cardillac! Yes – it is *he* who is killing people in the street! It's typical of an assassin to stay and lament by the corpse. – What happened, boy? Say without fear." – "Right in front of me," I said, "a man jumped out on to him, stabbed him, and ran away with lightning speed just as I cried out. I wanted to see if he could still be saved." – "No, my son," cried one of those who had lifted the body, "he's finished, stabbed through the heart, as usual." – "The Devil!" said another. "Again we are too late, as we were the day before yesterday" – and with that they went off with the body.

'How I felt I really cannot say. It seemed to me I was in a nightmare, and as if I would now wake up and be amazed at the mad illusion. Cardillac – the father of my Madelon – a murderer! I had fallen exhausted on the steps of the house. The morning glimmered towards dawn: an officer's hat, richly plumed, lay before me on the pavement. Cardillac's bloody deed, committed on the spot where I sat, rose clearly before me. Horrified, I ran away.

'Utterly confused, almost out of my mind, I sat in my attic. The door opened and Cardillac walked in. "In Christ's name, what do you want?" I cried. Paying no attention whatever, he came up to me and smiled at me calmly with a geniality which increased my loathing. He pulled up an old stool and sat down beside me, so that I was unable to rise from the straw mattress on to which I had thrown myself. "Now, Olivier," he began, "how are you, poor lad? I was badly over-hasty when I threw you out of the house. I miss you at every turn. Just now I have some work in hand which I really cannot finish without your help. How would it be if you came back and worked in my shop again? – You say nothing? – Yes, I know I have offended you. I didn't wish to conceal from you that I was angry at your flirtation with my Madelon. But I have carefully considered the matter since then, and I find that, with your skill, your diligence and your loyalty, I could wish for no better son-in-law than you. Come with me, then, and see how you may win Madelon for your wife."

'Cardillac's words pierced my heart. I trembled at his wickedness. I was unable to utter a word. "You are hesitating," he continued sharply, his eyes flashing. "You are hesitating? – Perhaps you cannot come with me today: you have other things to do! Perhaps you want to visit Desgrais, or introduce yourself to Argenson or La Regnie? Take care, my lad, that the claws you want to use to destroy others do not catch you yourself and tear you to pieces." At that my outraged feelings burst forth. "Let those," I cried, "who are conscious of gruesome crime feel the power of those names you have spoken; they do not affect me – *I* have nothing to do with them." – "Indeed, Olivier," continued Cardillac, "it would be to your honour if you were to work alongside me, the most famous master of his time, highly regarded everywhere for trustworthiness and honesty, so that any evil slander would rebound heavily on the head of the slanderer. As regards Madelon, I must confess that you have her alone to thank for my indulgence. She loves you with an ardour such as I could never have believed possible in the gentle child. As soon as you had left, she threw herself at my feet, clasped my knees, and confessed amid a thousand tears that she could not live without you. I thought she was imagining it, as is usual with infatuated young people, who are apt to want to die when the first baby face gives them a friendly look. But my Madelon did in fact become sick and ill, and when I tried to talk her out of the nonsense, she called your name a hundred times. What could I do if I did not want to see her give way to despair? Yesterday evening I told her I would consent to everything, and would fetch you today. Overnight she has blossomed like a rose and is now waiting for you, beside herself with love and longing."

'May the eternal power of Heaven forgive me, but I myself do not know how it happened that I was suddenly standing in Cardillac's house; that Madelon, crying aloud for joy: "Olivier – my Olivier – my love – my husband!" threw herself at me, flung both arms around me and pressed me to her bosom; that overwhelmed by ecstasy I swore by the Virgin and all the saints never, never to leave her!'

Deeply affected by the recollection of that moment, Olivier had to stop. Mademoiselle Scudery, filled with horror at the crime of a man she had regarded as virtue and trustworthiness itself, cried: 'It's dreadful! – René Cardillac belongs to the band of murderers who have made our city a den of robbers for so long?'

'Why do you say a band, Mademoiselle?' asked Olivier. 'There never has been such a band. It was Cardillac *alone* who sought and found his victims through the whole city. That it was he *alone* – therein lay the safety with which he attacked, and the insuperable difficulty of tracking down the murderer. – But let me continue: the sequel will explain to you the mystery of the wickedest and at the same time unhappiest of all men.

'The position in which I now found myself with the master is easy to imagine. I had taken the decisive step, and there was no going back. Sometimes it seemed to me as if I had even become Cardillac's assistant in murder; only in Madelon's love could I forget the pain which tormented me, only with her could I succeed in blotting out every trace of inexpressible grief. When I worked with her father in the workshop I could not bring myself to look him in the face; I could scarcely speak for the horror which filled me whenever I was near that dreadful man, who acted the virtuous role of a true and tender father, of a good citizen, while night concealed his crimes. Madelon, the gay, angelic, spotless child, clung to him with idolatrous love. It pierced my heart when I considered that, if ever revenge were to unmask the scoundrel, she, deceived by devilish cunning, must fall victim to the most atrocious despair.

That alone kept my mouth closed, even though I had to risk the death of a criminal for it.

'Although I was able to learn much from the talk of the constables, Cardillac's crimes, their motive, the way they were carried out, were still a puzzle to me; but the explanation was not far away. One day, Cardillac, who to my disgust normally worked in the gayest of humours, joking and laughing, was very serious and engrossed in his thoughts. Suddenly, he threw down the jewellery on which he was working; the gems and pearls rolled all over the place; he stood up violently and said: "Olivier! – things cannot go on like this between us; I find this relationship intolerable. What the cunning of Desgrais and his fellows could not discover, chance placed in your hands. You have seen me at my nocturnal work; my evil star drives me to it and resistance is useless. It was your evil star, too, which had you follow me, which enveloped you in an impenetrable veil, which gave your footsteps the lightness of the smallest beast which wanders unheard, so that I, who can see as clearly as a tiger in the darkest night, who can perceive the smallest sound, the humming of a gnat, did not notice you. Your evil star, my young comrade, led you to me. Betrayal, as you now stand, is out of the question. So you might as well know everything."

'"Never will I be your comrade, you hypocritical villain!" was what I wanted to cry; but the horror which gripped me at Cardillac's words choked me. Instead, I was able to utter only some incomprehensible sound. Cardillac sat down again on his work-stool. He wiped the sweat from his brow. Moved by the memory of the past, he seemed to have difficulty in pulling himself together. At length he began:

'"Wise men often speak of the strange impressions which afflict pregnant women, and of the strange influence these impressions from outside can have on the child. I have been told a strange story about my mother. In the first month in which she was pregnant with me, she was, together with other women, watching a brilliant court festival in the Trianon. There her glance fell on a cavalier in Spanish dress, with a glittering bejewelled chain about his neck from which she could scarcely tear her eyes away. Her whole being lusted after the sparkling stones, which seemed to her some heavenly treasure. Several years earlier, before my mother was married, this same cavalier had laid snares for her virtue, but had been rejected with horror. My mother recognized him, but this time he seemed to her, in the gleam of the sparkling diamonds, a being of a higher kind, the embodiment of everything beautiful. The cavalier noticed my mother's longing, fiery glances. Believing he might now be more fortunate, he found a way of approaching her, of enticing her away to a lonely place. There he clasped her passionately in his arms; my mother grasped the beautiful chain, but at the same instant he fell and dragged my mother with him to the ground. Whether it was a sudden heart attack or some other cause – suffice it to say that he was dead. My mother's efforts to free herself from the stiffened arms of the corpse were vain. His hollow eyes, their sight extinguished, fixed upon her, the dead man rolled on the ground with her. Her cries for help at last reached some distant passers-by, who hurried to her and rescued her from the arms of her gruesome lover.

'"The horror of it threw my mother on to a sick-bed. She, and I, were given up for lost; yet she recovered, and her delivery was better than anyone could have hoped for. But the fear of that terrible moment had got into *me*. My evil star had risen and had sent down fires which kindled in me one of the strangest and most pernicious of passions. Even when I was very young, sparkling diamonds, golden jewellery, meant more to me than anything else. It was held to be a normal taste for a child. But it showed itself in other ways: as a boy I stole gold and jewels wherever I could lay hands on them. As if I were the most experienced expert, I distinguished by instinct between paste and real gems. Only the latter enticed me; imitations I left untouched. This inborn urge had to be suppressed in face of the cruellest punishments by my father. It was only so as to be able to handle gold and precious stones that I turned to the goldsmith's trade. I worked with passion, and soon became the first master of the art.

'"Now there began a period in which my inborn urge, so long kept in check, burst forth and grew mightily, consuming everything around it. As soon as I had completed a piece of work and delivered it, I became agitated, I fell into a state of desperation which robbed me of my sleep, my health – of all my vital energies. The person for whom I was working stood before my eyes day and night like a ghost, adorned with my jewellery, and a voice whispered in my ear: It is yours really, it is yours really; take it, then – what do diamonds mean to a dead man? Then I set myself to the art of thieves. I had access to the homes of the great and I used every opportunity – no lock withstood my skill, and soon the jewellery I had made was again in my own hands.

'"But even that did not dispel my agitation. That sinister voice still made itself heard; it mocked me and cried: Ha, ha, a dead man is wearing your jewels! – I myself do not know how it happened, but I developed an inexpressible hatred for those for whom I made jewellery. Yes! Deep inside of me there grew a desire to murder them at which I myself quailed. – It was about that time that I bought this house. I had come to terms with the owner – we were sitting here in this room, pleased with the business we had transacted, and were drinking a bottle of wine. Night had fallen and I wanted to be going; then my vendor said: 'Listen, Master René, before you go I must let you into a secret about this house.' With that, he opened a cupboard let into the wall, pushed open the rear wall, stepped into a small chamber, bent down and lifted a trapdoor. We descended a steep, narrow stairway, came to a doorway which he opened, and stepped outside into the yard. Now the old gentleman walked over to the wall, pressed a piece of iron which projected only very slightly, and immediately a section of the wall swung out, so that a man could comfortably slip through the opening and get out into the street. You might like to see the device sometime, Olivier, which was probably made by the crafty monks of the cloister which used to be here so that they could slip in and out in secret. It is a piece of wood, mortared and whitewashed only on the outside, into which a statue has been fixed, again only of wood but looking like stone, and which turns together with the statue on concealed hinges.

'"Dark thoughts arose within me when I saw this contrivance. It seemed to me a preparation for such deeds as even to me still remained a secret. I had just delivered to a gentleman of the court some rich jewellery, which I knew was intended for a dancer at the Opéra. The mortal torments did not fail to appear – the spirit dogged my footsteps – the whispering Satan was at my ear! – I moved into my new house. Bathed in a cold sweat, sleeplessly I tossed and turned on the bed! In my mind's eye I saw the man gliding off to the dancer with my jewels. Filled with rage, I jumped up – threw on my cloak – descended the secret stairway – out through the wall, into the Rue Nicaise. He came. I fell upon him, he cried out, yet firmly seizing him from behind I stabbed him through the heart with my dagger – the jewels were mine! This done, I felt a peace, a happiness in my soul as never before. The ghost had disappeared, the voice of Satan was silent. Now I knew what my evil star desired: I had to give in to it or be destroyed!

'"Now, Olivier, you can understand all my actions! Do not believe that, because I must do what I cannot help doing, I have renounced all feeling of pity, of compassion, which adheres to the nature of man. You know how difficult it has become for me to deliver up jewellery, how for many whose death I do not desire I will not work, indeed how, even though I know that only bloodshed will banish my apparition tomorrow, I still settle tonight for a hard punch, which stretches the owner of my gems out on the ground and delivers them into my hands.''

'Having said all this, Cardillac led me into his secret vault and granted me the sight of his jewel cabinet. The King possesses nothing finer. On every piece of jewellery was hung a ticket marked with the name of the person for whom it was made and when it had been taken by theft, robbery or murder. "On your wedding day, Olivier," said Cardillac, gloomy and solemn, "you shall swear to me a sacred oath, with your hand on the image of Christ on the Cross, that as soon as I am dead you will reduce all these riches to dust by a means which I shall make known to you. I do not want any human being, least of all Madelon and you, to come into possession of a hoard which has been purchased with blood."

'Caught in this labyrinth of crime, torn between love and loathing, between delight and horror, I was like a man in Hell whom a lovely angel calls up on high with a gentle smile but Satan keeps firmly grasped with burning claws, so that the angel's loving smile, in which is all the blessedness of high Heaven, becomes for him the grimmest of his torments. I thought of running away – indeed, of suicide – but Madelon! Rebuke me, blame me, my dear Mademoiselle, for being too weak to conquer a passion which fettered me to the crime – but am I not making amends for it by a shameful death?

'One day, Cardillac came home in an unusually happy mood. He hugged Madelon, threw me the friendliest of glances, drank a bottle of fine wine at table – which he was wont to do only on high days and holidays – sang and

rejoiced. Madelon had left us alone; I was about to go into
the workshop. "Sit down, my boy!" cried Cardillac. "No
more work today. Let us have another drink to the health
of the worthiest, the most admirable lady in Paris." After I
had drunk a toast with him, and he had emptied a full glass,
he said: "Tell me Olivier! How do you like this verse?

> *Un amant qui craint les voleurs*
> *n'est point digne d'amour!"*

'He then told me what had transpired in the apartments
of Madame de Maintenon between you and the King, and
added that he had always respected you more than any
other human being, and that, gifted as you were with such
virtue that his evil star faded and was powerless before it,
even if you were wearing the most beautiful jewellery ever
made by him it would never raise any evil spirit or
murderous thought within him. "Listen, Olivier," he
said, "to what I have decided. Some long time ago I had to
make a necklace and bracelets for Henrietta of England,
and I even had to supply the stones for them. The work
succeeded like none other, but it tore me apart when I
thought of having to part with those jewels, which had
become my heart's treasure. You know of the princess's
unfortunate assassination. I kept the jewels, and now I
want to send them to Mademoiselle de Scudery as a token
of my respect and gratitude. I shall do so in the name of the
supposed band of murderers; thus I shall mock Desgrais
and his companions as they deserve. You shall bear the
jewels to her."

'As soon as Cardillac spoke your name, Mademoiselle,
it was as if a veil had been drawn away and the picture of
my happy childhood emerged in bright, shining colours.
A wonderful comfort crept into my soul, a ray of hope
dispelling the dark spirits. Cardillac must have noticed the
impression his words had made on me and interpreted
them in his own way. "My plan," he said, "seems to suit

you. I can confess that a deep inward voice – quite different from the one which demands bloody acts like a ravenous beast of prey – has commanded me to do this. Sometimes I get a strange feeling: an inner anxiety, the fear of something dreadful, the terror of which drifts in from the beyond and catches me in its grasp. It then seems to me as if what my evil star has done through me can be put right by my immortal soul, which has no part in it. It was in such a mood that I resolved to make a diamond crown for the Holy Virgin in the Church of St Eustace. But then that incomprehensible fear overcame me whenever I wanted to start the work, so that I left it altogether. Now it seems to me as if I am making a humble sacrifice to virtue and piety itself, and begging for its intercession, by sending to Mademoiselle Scudery the most beautiful jewellery I have ever made."

'Cardillac, who was aware of your mode of life, Mademoiselle, down to the last detail, now told me how and when I was to deliver the jewels, which he enclosed in a little box. My whole being was ecstatic, for Heaven itself was showing me through the sinful Cardillac how to save myself from the Hell in which I languished. So I thought. In quite another sense than Cardillac I wanted to get in to you. As Anne Brusson's son, as your foster-child, I thought to throw myself at your feet and reveal all to you. Moved by the unutterable distress which the poor, innocent Madelon was threatened with by its revelation, you would have kept the secret, but you would have found a sure means of restraining Cardillac's vile wickedness without its being revealed. Do not ask me what you would have done – I do not know; but that you would save Madelon and me, of this I was as firmly convinced in my soul as I was of the comfort and aid of the Holy Virgin.

'You know, Mademoiselle, that my intentions that night miscarried. I did not lose hope of being more fortunate some other time. Then Cardillac suddenly lost all his gaiety. He crept about miserably, stared in front of him, muttered incomprehensibly, fought with his hands as if parrying some enemy; his spirit seemed tormented by evil thoughts. He behaved in this way for a whole morning. Finally he sat down at the work-bench, leaped up again in an ill humour, gazed out of the window, and said in a serious and gloomy voice: "How I wish Henrietta of England could have worn my jewels!" – His words filled me with terror. Now I knew that his errant spirit was again in the grip of the dreadful murderous spectre, that Satan's voice was again loudly at his ears. I saw your life threatened by the murderous devil. If only Cardillac had his jewels back in his hands again, you would be saved.

'The danger grew with every moment. Then I met you on the Pont Neuf, managed to get through to your carriage, and threw you that note which begged you to take the jewellery you had received to Cardillac immediately. You failed to come. My anxiety turned to despair as the next day Cardillac spoke of nothing other than the jewels which had passed before his eyes in the night. I could only interpret that as meaning your jewels and I grew certain that he was brooding on some murderous plot which he was proposing to carry out that very night. I had to save you, even if it cost Cardillac his life.

'As soon as Cardillac had, as usual, shut himself away after evening prayers, I climbed through a window into the yard, slipped through the opening in the wall, and stationed myself in the shadows not far away. It was not long before Cardillac came out and slipped quietly down the street. I was behind him. He went towards the Rue St Honoré; my heart trembled. Suddenly he disappeared from my view. I decided to stand by your door. Then an officer came along, singing and whistling – just as on previous occasions when fate had made me a witness of Cardillac's murderous deeds – who passed by without being aware of me. In the same instant a black figure leaped out and fell upon him. It was Cardillac. I tried to prevent the murder: with a loud cry I reached the spot in two or three bounds. It was Cardillac – not the officer – who, stabbed to death, fell to the ground with a gasp. The officer let the dagger fall, drew his sword from its sheath and positioned himself, believing I was the assassin's accomplice, ready to fight me off; but he hurried quickly away when he realized that, unconcerned with him, I was only examining the body.

'Cardillac was still alive. After I had picked up the dagger the officer had dropped, I loaded him on to my shoulders and dragged him back home, through the secret passage, and up into the workshop. – You know the rest. You see, Mademoiselle, that my only crime is not turning Madelon's father over to the court and so making an end of his crimes. I am untouched by any blood-guilt.

'No torture will ever force from me the secret of Cardillac's crimes. I will not have, in defiance of the eternal power which has concealed from the virtuous daughter her father's gruesome guilt, the whole terrible past now break in upon her, earthly revenge disinter the body from the earth which covers it, the hangman brand the rotting bones with disgrace. No! – my beloved will mourn for me as for a fallen innocent; time will ease her pain; but she could never recover from grief at the hellish deeds of her beloved father!'

Olivier fell silent: then suddenly a stream of tears erupted from his eyes. He threw himself at Mademoiselle Scudery's feet and implored: 'You are convinced of my innocence! Have pity on me! Tell me how Madelon is!'

Mademoiselle Scudery called Martinière, and in a few moments Madelon flung herself about Olivier's neck. 'Now everything is all right, since you are here – I knew it, I knew that the noblest of women would save you.' So Madelon cried again and again, and Olivier forgot his destiny, everything which threatened him; he was free and happy. Tenderly they rehearsed to one another what they had suffered, and embraced again and wept for joy that they had again found one another.

Had not Mademoiselle Scudery already been convinced of Olivier's innocence, she must now have been compelled to believe in it as she saw the pair, in the bliss of their love, forgetting the world, and their misery, and their nameless suffering. 'No,' she cried, 'only a pure heart is capable of such blissful oblivion!'

The rays of morning broke through the window. Desgrais tapped on the door of the apartment, and told them it was time to take Brusson back to prison. The lovers had to part.

The forebodings which had filled Mademoiselle Scudery since Brusson's entry into her house had now become reality. She saw the son of her beloved Anne innocently ensnared in such a fashion it seemed impossible he could be saved from a humiliating death. She admired the youth's heroic spirit, which would rather die laden with guilt than betray a secret which would bring death to his Madelon. Within the whole world of possibilities she could see no way of rescuing the poor young man from the cruel court. And yet it was firmly fixed in her soul that she must shun no sacrifice to prevent the appalling injustice which was being done. She worried herself with plans and designs, some of which she discarded as quickly as she formed them. Every glimmer of hope began to disappear, until she was on the point of despair. But Madelon's childlike, innocent trust, the radiance with which she spoke of how her beloved, acquitted of all guilt, would soon make her his wife, deeply moved Mademoiselle Scudery.

Finally, to do *something*, Mademoiselle Scudery wrote a long letter to La Regnie, in which she told him that Olivier Brusson had proved to her his innocence of Cardillac's death; only his heroic decision to take with him to the grave a secret the revelation of which would destroy innocence and virtue itself prevented him from making a confession to the court which would free him from suspicion. All that burning zeal, that eloquence, could do, Mademoiselle Scudery summoned up to prevail over La Regnie's hard heart. In a few hours, La Regnie replied that he would be heartily glad if Brusson had justified himself to his most worthy benefactress; as regards his heroic decision to take with him to the grave a secret which had some bearing on the deed, he was sorry but the *Chambre ardente* could not respect such heroism, but would, rather, have to endeavour to break the same by the most forcible means. In three days' time he hoped to be in possession of the secret, which would no doubt bring to light many marvels.

Mademoiselle Scudery knew only too well what La Regnie meant. Now it was certain that torture was to be inflicted. In her mortal fear, it at length occurred to Mademoiselle Scudery that, merely to obtain a postponement, the advice of a legal expert would be of service. Pierre Arnaud d'Andilly was at that time the most famous advocate in Paris: his knowledge and understanding were equal to his integrity and virtue. Mademoiselle Scudery betook herself to him and told him everything, so far as that was possible without betraying Brusson's secret. She believed that d'Andilly would eagerly adopt the cause of the innocent, but her hopes were bitterly disappointed. He listened calmly to everything and then replied, smiling, with Boileau's words: *La vrai peut quelque fois n'être pas vraisemblable*. He demonstrated that the most obvious grounds for suspicion told against Brusson, that La Regnie's proceedings could in no way be called cruel or precipitate but were quite in accordance with the law – he could not, indeed, act otherwise without violating the duties of a judge. He, d'Andilly, did not believe he could save Brusson from torture even by the most skilful defence. Only Brusson himself could do that, either by a straightforward confession, or by a detailed account of the circumstances surrounding Cardillac's death, which would then perhaps offer some reason for fresh investigations.

'Then I shall throw myself at the King's feet and beg for mercy,' said Mademoiselle Scudery, quite beside herself and in a voice half choked with tears.

'No,' cried d'Andilly, 'in Heaven's name do not do that, Mademoiselle! Save that as a last resort: for if it should fail, it is lost to you for ever. The King will never pardon a criminal of *this* sort: the reproaches of the public would be levelled against him. It is possible that, by disclosing his secret, or in some other way, Brusson will find the means of dispelling the suspicion against him. Then will be the time to beg for the King's mercy: for then he will not ask what has or has not been proved before the court but will consult his own inner convictions.'

Mademoiselle Scudery had perforce to concur. Lost in the depths of grief, brooding and reflecting on what she should now attempt in order to save the unhappy Brusson, she was sitting in her apartment late in the evening when Martinière entered and announced Count Miossens, Colonel of the King's Guard, who urgently wished to speak to her.

'Forgive me, Mademoiselle,' said Miossens, bowing in a soldierly way, 'for disturbing you so late, at such an inconvenient time. We soldiers know no better, and besides, a few words shall be my excuse: Olivier Brusson brings me to you.'

Mademoiselle Scudery, tense as to what she should now learn, cried: 'Olivier Brusson? That most unfortunate of men? What have you to do with him?'

'I thought,' said Miossens, smiling, 'that your *protégé*'s name would succeed in procuring me a hearing. The whole world is convinced of Brusson's guilt. I know that you are of another opinion, though, as I have heard it said, your opinion is founded only on the protestations of the accused. With me it is different. No one could be more convinced than I of Brusson's innocence of Cardillac's death.'

'Go on! Oh, go on!' cried Mademoiselle Scudery, her eyes shining with joy.

'It was I', said Miossens with emphasis, 'who stabbed the old goldsmith in the Rue St Honoré, not far from your house.'

'By all the saints, you!' cried Mademoiselle Scudery.

'And,' Miossens continued, 'I swear to you, Mademoiselle, I am proud of my deed. Cardillac was the wickedest, most hypocritical scoundrel that ever existed, who murdered and robbed by night and for so long eluded all attempts at capture. I do not know how it happened that some suspicion arose within me against the villain when, visibly agitated, he brought the jewellery I had ordered, inquired precisely for whom I intended it, and then questioned my valet as to when I was accustomed to visit a certain lady. At length it occurred to me that the victims of the assassin all carried the same death wound. I felt certain that the murderer was practised in delivering a blow that would kill instantly, that he depended on it. If the blow failed, then the fight was even. This led me to adopt a precaution so simple I cannot understand how others did not think of it long ago. I wore a light breastplate under my waistcoat. Cardillac fell upon me from behind. He gripped me with great strength, but his dagger-stroke was deflected by the iron. In the same instant I wrested myself from him, and stabbed him in the chest with the dagger I held in readiness.'

'And you have kept quiet,' asked Mademoiselle Scudery, 'you did not tell the court of what happened?'

'Permit me, Mademoiselle,' Miossens continued, 'to point out that such a deposition could involve me in the most hideous proceedings, if not in immediate ruin. Would La Regnie, who scents criminals everywhere, have believed me if I had accused the honest Cardillac, the model of all piety and virtue, of being the sought-for murderer? What if the sword of justice had turned its point against me?'

'That would be impossible,' said Mademoiselle Scudery. 'Your birth, your rank . . .'

'Oh!' Miossens went on, 'think of the Duke of Luxembourg, who found himself under suspicion of poisoning, and was taken to the Bastille, because he had once had his horoscope cast by Le Sage. No, by Saint Denis, not one single hour of freedom, not the lobe of my ear, would I surrender to that lunatic La Regnie, who would like to put his knife to all our throats.'

'But you are thus bringing the innocent Brusson to the scaffold,' Mademoiselle Scudery interrupted him.

'Innocent?' Miossens replied. 'Innocent, Mademoiselle? Do you call the wicked Cardillac's accomplice innocent? Who stood by him in his deeds? Who has served death a hundred times? No: *his* blood will be justly spilled. I have disclosed to you, my esteemed Mademoiselle, the true state of affairs on the assumption that, without handing me over to the *Chambre ardente*, you would know how to make use of my secret in some way or another for your *protégé*.'

Mademoiselle Scudery, inwardly delighted at seeing her conviction of Brusson's innocence so decisively confirmed, did not hesitate to reveal all to the count, who already knew of Cardillac's crimes, and to invite him to go with her to visit d'Andilly. Everything would be disclosed to *him*, under the seal of secrecy, and *he* would then advise as to what should be done.

After Mademoiselle Scudery had related everything to him down to the last detail, d'Andilly again queried the most trifling circumstances. In particular, he asked Count Miossens whether he was convinced it was Cardillac who had attacked him, and whether he could again recognize

Brusson as the man who had dragged away Cardillac's body.

'Besides recognizing the goldsmith easily in the bright moonlight,' Miossens replied, 'I have even seen at La Regnie's the dagger with which Cardillac was killed. It is mine, recognizable by the decorative work on the hilt. As I was standing only a pace away from him, I perceived all the features of the youth, whose hat had fallen off, and I would certainly be able to recognize him again.'

D'Andilly sat silently for a few moments, gazing before him; then he said: 'Brusson cannot in any way now be saved from the hands of justice by the usual paths. He will not name Cardillac as the assassin for Madelon's sake. This makes no difference, for even if he were to succeed in proving it by revealing the secret exit and the stolen hoard, he would still face death as an accomplice. The same applies if Count Miossens discloses to the judges the incident with the goldsmith as it actually occurred. *Postponement* is the only thing we can consider. Count Miossens must go to the Conciergerie, have Brusson brought before him and identify him as the person who made off with Cardillac's body. He must then hurry to La Regnie and say: "I saw a man killed in the Rue St Honoré. I was standing close beside the body when another man sprang out, bent over the body, lifted him, as he seemed still to be alive, on to his shoulders, and carried him off. I recognized that man as Olivier Brusson." This statement will allow Brusson's hearing to be reopened and bring about a confrontation with Count Miossens. The torture will not be applied, and further investigations can be made. Then is the time to turn to the King himself. It must be left to your acumen, Mademoiselle, to find the best way of doing so. To my way of thinking, it would be a good thing to reveal the whole secret to the King. Brusson's confession is supported by this statement of Count Miossens. Secret investigations in Cardillac's house might do the same. No legal proceeding, but the King's decision, founded on the feeling that where the judge must punish mercy may pardon, must govern our actions.'

Count Miossens did exactly as d'Andilly had advised, and everything transpired as the latter had predicted.

Now came the time to go to the King, and this was the most difficult part, since, holding him alone to be the robber and assassin who had for so long kept all Paris in fear, he harboured such a horror of Brusson that, if reminded of the proceedings against him, he flew into a rage. Madame de Maintenon, true to her principle of never talking to the King of anything unpleasant, refused mediation, so Brusson's fate was laid squarely in the hands of Mademoiselle Scudery. After lengthy meditation she came to a decision and put it quickly into execution. She clad herself in a black dress of heavy silk, adorned herself with Cardillac's jewels, draped a long black veil over her shoulders, and appeared in this fashion in the apartments of Madame Maintenon at the hour when the King was present there. The noble figure of the worthy lady in this solemn garb possessed a majesty calculated to awaken awe even in those idle people used to drifting aimlessly in ante-rooms. Everyone stepped aside, and as she entered even the King stood up amazed and came towards her. The diamonds of the necklace and bracelets flashed before his eyes, and he cried: 'By Heaven, that is Cardillac's jewellery!' Then, turning to Madame Maintenon with a smile, he added: 'Look, Madame Marquise, how our beautiful bride grieves for her bridegroom.'

'Nay, gracious Lord,' Mademoiselle Scudery said, as if continuing the joke, 'how would it become a grief-stricken bride to bejewel herself so magnificently? No, I have severed all connection with that goldsmith and would think no more of him, did not the horrible sight of his body borne past me appear from time to time before my eyes.'

'What?' asked the King. 'You saw him?'

Mademoiselle Scudery now related how fate had brought her to Cardillac's house, just as his murder had been discovered. She described Madelon's wild grief, the deep impression which the angelic child had made on her, the way in which she had saved the poor girl from Desgrais's hands amid the cheers of the people. With ever growing fervour, she now began her scenes with La Regnie, Desgrais and Brusson himself. The King, carried away by the power of Mademoiselle Scudery's account, failed to notice that she was now speaking of the hateful proceedings against the evil Brusson; he could not utter a word, but occasionally gave vent to his emotions with an exclamation. He was quite beside himself at the scandal he was hearing of and incapable of putting everything in order; before he knew it, Mademoiselle Scudery was at his feet, begging for mercy for Olivier Brusson.

'What are you doing?' the King exclaimed, grasping her with both hands and compelling her to sit in the armchair. 'What are you doing, Mademoiselle? You amaze me! This is indeed a terrible story! Who can vouch for the truth of Brusson's remarkable tale?'

To which Mademoiselle Scudery replied: 'Miossens's statement, the investigation in Cardillac's house, inner conviction – oh, Madelon's virtuous heart, which recognizes the same virtue in the unfortunate Brusson!'

On the point of replying, the King turned at a sound from the direction of the door. Louvois, who was working in another apartment, looked in with a worried expression. The King rose and left the room, Louvois following. Both Mademoiselle Scudery and Madame Maintenon regarded this interruption with misgiving, for, having been surprised once, the King might be more wary a second time. But a few minutes later the King returned, paced the room quickly, then stood, his hands behind his back, before Mademoiselle Scudery, and, without looking at her, said, half aloud: 'I should like to see your Madelon!'

To which Mademoiselle Scudery rejoined: 'Oh, my gracious Sire, what great, great happiness you vouchsafe the poor, unhappy child! Ah, it needs only a sign from you to see the little one at your feet!'

And then she tripped to the door as quickly as she could in the heavy dress and called that the King wished to have Madelon Cardillac brought before him; then she returned and cried and sobbed for joy and emotion. She had anticipated such a favour and had therefore taken Madelon along with her, who had remained with one of the Marquise's chambermaids, holding a short petition which d'Andilly had drafted. In a few moments she lay speechless at the King's feet. Fear, bewilderment, awe, love and pain drove the blood through the poor girl's veins. Her cheeks glowed crimson, her eyes sparkled with tears, which now and then fell through the silky lashes on to the lily-white bosom. The King appeared touched by the beauty of the angelic child. He raised her gently, then made a movement as if he were going to kiss the hand he was holding. He let it go and regarded the child with moist eyes.

Madame Maintenon whispered quietly to Mademoiselle Scudery: 'Doesn't she look like Vallière, down to the last hair, the little dear? The King is wallowing in the sweetest of memories. Your gamble has paid off.'

Softly though Madame Maintenon said this, it seemed that the King had heard it. His face flushed, he glanced past Madame Maintenon, read the petition which Madelon tendered to him and then said gently: 'I can well believe that you, my dear child, are convinced of your loved one's innocence, but we shall hear what the *Chambre ardente* has to say about it.'

A gentle movement of his hand dismissed the girl, who was about to dissolve into tears. Mademoiselle Scudery was aware, to her dismay, that the memory of Vallière, salutary though it had seemed at the outset, had altered the

King's humour as soon as Madame Maintenon had mentioned her name. It might be that the King felt he was being reminded that he was on the verge of sacrificing justice to beauty; or perhaps he felt like a dreamer who, sharply awoken, sees the enchanted images disappear at the moment he thought to grasp them. Perhaps he now no longer saw his Vallière before him, but thought only on Soeur Louise de la Miséricorde (Vallière's name among the cloistered Carmelite nuns), who tormented him with her piety and penance. What else was there to do now but calmly await the King's decision?

Count Miossens's statement to the *Chambre ardente* had in the meantime become public knowledge, and, as the people are easily driven from one extreme to the other, it came about that he who had at first been execrated as the wickedest of murderers and threatened with lynching before he even reached the scaffold was now lamented as the innocent victim of barbaric justice. Only now did the neighbourhood remember his virtuous behaviour, his love for Madelon, the loyalty and devotion of body and soul he showed the old goldsmith. Processions, often in a hostile mood, appeared before La Regnie's palace, crying: 'Give us Olivier Brusson! He is innocent!' They even threw stones at the windows, so that La Regnie was forced to seek protection.

Several days passed without Mademoiselle Scudery's hearing anything about Olivier Brusson's case. Disconsolate, she betook herself to Madame Maintenon, who assured her that the King was silent on the matter, and that it did not seem advisable to remind him of it. She then asked, with a strange smile, what the little Vallière was doing, which convinced Mademoiselle Scudery that, deep down, the proud woman was annoyed at an event which could entice the susceptible King into a sphere whose charm she did not comprehend. From Madame Maintenon, therefore, she could hope for nothing.

Finally, with d'Andilly's help, Mademoiselle Scudery discovered that the King had had a long private conversation with Count Miossens, that Bontems, the King's trusted servant and *chargé d'affaires*, had been to the Conciergerie and spoken to Brusson; that, finally, one night the same Bontems had been to Cardillac's house with several others and had stayed there a long time. Claude Patru, the occupant of the ground floor, confirmed that there had been noises overhead all night long, and that Olivier had definitely been there with them, for he had clearly recognized his voice. It was thus certain that the King himself was having the case investigated, though the long delay in his decision remained incomprehensible. But La Regnie was doing everything he could to keep his teeth firmly on the sacrifice they were trying to wrest from him and that fact seemed to blight every hope.

Almost a month had passed before Madame Maintenon sent word to Mademoiselle Scudery that the King wished to see her that evening in her, Madame Maintenon's, apartments. Mademoiselle Scudery's heart leapt: she knew that Brusson's case would now be decided. Yet it seemed as if the King had forgotten the whole affair; for lingering as usual in pleasant conversation with Madame Maintenon and Mademoiselle Scudery, he said not a single syllable about poor Brusson. At last, Bontems appeared, approached the King, and spoke a few words so softly that the two women were unable to hear them. – Mademoiselle Scudery quaked inwardly. Then the King rose, stepped over to her, and said with eyes beaming: 'I wish you joy, Mademoiselle! Your protégé, Olivier Brusson, is free!'

Mademoiselle Scudery, her eyes welling over with tears and incapable of uttering a sound, was about to throw herself at the King's feet; but he prevented her, saying: 'Now, now, Mademoiselle, you ought to be a lawyer and fight my suits for me, for, by Saint Denis, no one on earth could withstand your eloquence. Yet', he continued more seriously, 'may he whom virtue itself takes under its protection be no less secure in the face of any evil accusation, before the *Chambre ardente* or any court in the world!'

Mademoiselle Scudery now found words, and she poured them forth in glowing gratitude. The King interrupted her, and told her that in her own house she could expect to receive far more ardent thanks than ever he could require from her, for probably at that very moment the happy Olivier was already embracing his Madelon.

'Bontems', the King concluded, 'shall pay you a thousand Louis, to be given to the girl in my name as her dowry. May she wed her Brusson, who certainly does not deserve such good fortune, but then both are to leave Paris. That is my will.'

Martinière hurried to meet Mademoiselle Scudery, Baptiste behind her, both with faces shining with joy, both jubilantly crying: 'He's here! He's free! Oh, the lovely young things!'

The happy pair threw themselves at Mademoiselle Scudery's feet. 'Oh, I knew that you, and you alone, would be able to save my husband,' cried Madelon.

'Ah, my faith in you, my mother, is firmly fixed in my soul!' cried Olivier, and both kissed the worthy lady's hands and wept a thousand burning tears. And then they embraced one another again, swore that the heavenly joy of that moment outweighed all the nameless sufferings of the past, and promised not to leave one another till death.

A few days later they were united by the blessing of the priest. Even if it had not been the King's will, Brusson would not have been able to stay in Paris, where everything reminded him of the dreadful era of Cardillac's crimes, and where any chance occurrence could reveal his secret, now known to many, and end for ever his life of happiness. Immediately after the wedding, he moved with his young wife, accompanied by Mademoiselle Scudery's blessings, to Geneva. There, equipped by Madelon's dowry, gifted with rare skill at his craft and with every civic virtue, he led a happy, carefree life. In him the hopes were fulfilled which had deluded his father.

A year had passed since Brusson's departure when a public proclamation appeared, signed by Harloy de Chauvalon, Archbishop of Paris, and by the lawyer Pierre Arnaud d'Andilly, which stated that a repentant sinner had, under the seal of the confessional, handed over to the church a rich hoard of stolen gems and jewellery. Anyone who had had jewellery stolen from him before the end of the year 1680, particularly by murderous attack in the open street, should apply to d'Andilly and, if his description of the jewellery stolen from him coincided with any of the gems found, and providing no doubt was otherwise found in respect of the rightfulness of the claim, the jewellery would be returned. Many who appeared on Cardillac's list presented themselves to the advocate and, to their no small surprise, received back the jewels that had been stolen from them. What was left fell to the treasury of the church of St Eustace.

THE SANDMAN

—◦❭ ❬◦—

Nathaniel to Lothario

You must all be very worried that I have not written for such a long time. I expect mother is angry, and Clara may think I am living here in a state of debauchery and altogether forgetting the dear angel whose image is imprinted so deeply into my heart and mind. But that is not the case. You are all in my thoughts every day and every hour, and in happy dreams my darling Clara's figure appears before me and smiles at me with her bright eyes as sweetly as she used to do whenever I came into the room. But, ah, how could I have written to you in the utter melancholy which has been disrupting all my mind? Something terrible has entered my life! Dark presentiments of a dreadful fate hover over me like black clouds impenetrable to any friendly ray of sunlight. I shall tell you what has happened to me – I shall have to do so, I can see that, even though only to think of it brings on a fit of insane laughter. Ah, my dear Lothario, how can I begin to make you feel in any way how what took place a few days ago might actually destroy my life? If only you were here, you could judge for yourself; as things are, you will certainly consider me a crazy spirit-seer.

In short, the terrible thing that has happened, and the deadly impression of which I strive in vain to eradicate, consists in nothing other than that a few days ago, namely on 30 October at mid-day, a dealer in barometers entered my room and offered me his wares. I bought nothing and threatened to throw him down the stairs. Whereupon he departed of his own accord.

You will understand that only some quite private association rooted deep in my life could bestow such significance upon this event that the mere person of that
unfortunate tradesman should produce an inimical effect.
And this is indeed the case. With all my strength I collect
myself together to tell you quietly and patiently as much of
my early youth as will suffice to make everything clear,
distinct and vivid to your lively senses. As I begin I hear
you laughing and Clara say: 'This is mere childishness!'
Laugh, I beg you, laugh at me as much as you like! I beg it
of you! But, God in Heaven! my hair is standing on end,
and it is as if, when I plead with you to laugh at me, I do so
in the madness of despair, as Schiller's Franz Moor pleaded
with Daniel. But now to the business in hand!

Except at lunchtime, we, my brothers and sisters and I,
saw little of our father all day. Perhaps he was very busy.
After supper, which was, in accordance with the old
custom, served as early as seven o'clock, all of us, our
mother as well, went into our father's study and sat around
a table. Our father smoked and drank a large glass of beer.
Often he told us strange stories and became so excited over
them that his pipe went out and I had to relight it for him
with a burning spill, which I found a great source of
amusement. But often he handed us picture books, sat
silent and motionless in his armchair, and blew out thick
clouds of smoke, so that we were all enveloped as if by a
fog. On such evenings our mother became very gloomy,
and the clock had hardly struck nine before she said: 'Now,
children, to bed, to bed! The sandman is coming.' On
these occasions I really did hear something come clumping
up the stairs with slow, heavy tread, and knew it must be
the sandman. Once these muffled footsteps seemed to me
especially frightening, and I asked my mother as she led us
out: 'Mama, who *is* this sandman who always drives us
away from Papa? What does he look like?'

'There is no sandman, my dear child,' my mother replied. 'When I say the sandman is coming, all that means is that you are sleepy and cannot keep your eyes open, as though someone had sprinkled sand into them.'

My mother's answer did not content me; and in my childish mind there unfolded the idea that she had denied the sandman's existence only so that we should not be afraid of him, for I continued to hear him coming up the stairs. Bursting with curiosity to learn more about this sandman, and of his connection with us children, I at last asked the old woman who looked after my youngest sister what sort of a man a sandman was.

'Oh Nat,' she replied, 'don't you know that yet? It is a wicked man who comes after children when they won't go to bed and throws handfuls of sand in their eyes, so that they jump out of their heads all bloody, and then he throws them into his sack and carries them to the crescent moon as food for his little children, who have their nest up there and have crooked beaks like owls and peck up the eyes of the naughty children.'

The image of the cruel sandman now assumed hideous detail within me, and when I heard the sound of clumping coming up the stairs in the evening I trembled with fear and terror. My mother could get nothing out of me but the cry 'The sandman! the sandman!' stammered out in tears. I was the first to run into the bedroom on the nights he was coming, and his fearsome apparition tormented me till dawn. I was already old enough to realize that the tale the old woman had told me of the children's nest in the moon could not be true; nevertheless, the sandman himself remained a dreadful spectre; and I was seized with especial horror whenever I heard him not merely come up the stairs but wrench open the door of my father's study and go into it. There were times when he stayed away for many nights; then he would come all the more frequently, night after night.

This continued for some years, but never could I accustom myself to the uncanny ghost: the image of the cruel sandman never grew paler within me. What it could be that he had to do with my father began to engage my imagination more and more. An invincible timidity prevented me from asking my father about it; but to investigate the mystery myself, to see the fabled sandman myself – this desire grew more and more intense as the years passed. The sandman had started me on the road to the strange and adventurous that so easily find a home in the heart of a child. I liked nothing more than to read or listen to gruesome tales of kobolds, witches, dwarfs, and so on; but over all of them there towered the sandman, and I used to draw the strangest and most hideous pictures of him on tables, cupboards and walls everywhere in the house.

When I was ten years old my mother removed me from the children's room into a little room which lay on the corridor not far from my father's room. We would still have to make off for bed at once when, on the stroke of nine, the unknown visitor was heard arriving. From my little room I would hear him go into my father's, and soon afterwards it would seem to me that a subtle, strange-smelling vapour was spreading through the house. As my curiosity grew, so did my courage, and I would resolve to make the sandman's acquaintance by some means or other. Often I would creep out of my room into the corridor when my mother had gone past, but I could discover nothing, for the sandman would always be already inside the door by the time I had reached the place from which I might have seen him. At length, impelled by an irresistible urge, I decided to conceal myself within my father's room itself and there await the sandman.

One evening, my father's silence and the gloominess of my mother told me that the sandman would be coming. I pretended to be very tired, left the room before nine o'clock, and concealed myself in a niche on the landing.

The housedoor creaked, and slow, heavy, thudding steps crossed the hallway towards the stairs. My mother hurried past me with my brothers and sisters. Softly, softly I opened the door of my father's room. He was sitting as usual, silent and motionless with his back towards the door; he did not notice me, and in a moment I was in and behind the curtain drawn across an open cupboard just beside the door where my father's clothes were hung. The footsteps thudded nearer and nearer, and there was a strange coughing, rasping and growling outside. My heart quaked with fear and anticipation. Close, close behind the door – a quick footstep, a violent blow on the latch and the door sprang open with a clatter! Taking my courage in both hands, I peered cautiously out. The sandman was standing before my father in the middle of the room, his face clearly visible in the bright illumination of the lamps! The sandman, the terrible sandman was the aged advocate Coppelius, who sometimes came to lunch with us!

But the most horrible of forms could not have aroused in me a more profound terror than did this Coppelius. Imagine a large, broad-shouldered man with a big mis-shapen head, an ochre-yellow face, grey bushy eyebrows from under which a pair of green cat's-eyes blaze out piercingly, and a large heavy nose drawn down over the upper lip; the crooked mouth often distorted in a malig-nant laugh, at which times two dark red blotches appear on the cheeks and a strange hissing sound comes from be-tween the clenched teeth. Coppelius always appeared in an ash-grey coat of old-fashioned cut and a similarly styled waistcoat and straight trousers, but in addition he wore black stockings and shoes with jewelled buckles. His little wig covered hardly more than the crown of his head, rolls of hair stood high over his big red ears, and a broad discoloured hairbag stuck out at the back of his neck, so that you could see the silver buckle which fastened the plaited cravat. The whole figure was altogether loathsome and repellent; but what we children found repugnant above all were his great knotty, hair-covered hands, and we lost all liking for anything he touched with them. He had noticed this, and took pleasure in touching, under this or that pretext, any little piece of cake or delicious fruit which our mother had secretly put on to our plate, so that the sweetmeats we were supposed to·enjoy then filled us only with disgust and revulsion. He did the same when, on special days, our father had poured for us a little glass of wine: he reached over quickly with his hand or even took the glass to his blue lips and laughed devilishly when we dared to express our anger only by gentle sobbing. He used always to call us the little beasts; when he was present we were not allowed to make a sound, and we cursed the malign and repellent man who deliberately sought to ruin for us even the most minute pleasure. Our mother appeared to hate the repulsive Coppelius as much as we did, for as soon as he showed himself her cheerfulness, her happy unaffected nature, was transformed into earnest gloom and sorrow. Our father behaved towards him as if he were a higher being whose ill-breeding one had to tolerate and who had to be kept in a good mood at all cost. He had only to drop the slightest hint and his favourite dishes were prepared and the rarest wines brought forth.

When I now saw this Coppelius, my soul was filled with fear, and with horror that it was he of all people who had turned out to be the sandman; the sandman was now no longer that bogeyman of the nursery tale who took children's eyes as food to his owl's nest in the moon: no! he was now a repellent spectral monster bringing misery, distress and earthly and eternal ruination wherever he went.

I stood as if rooted to the spot. At the risk of being discovered and, as I firmly believed, severely punished, I remained there listening, with my head stuck through the curtain. My father received Coppelius solemnly.

'Up! To work!' Coppelius cried in a hoarse, growling voice, and threw off his coat.

My father slowly and gloomily removed his dressing-gown, and both clad themselves in long black smocks. I did not see where they got them from. My father opened the folding doors of a wall-cupboard; but I saw that what I had for so long taken to be a wall-cupboard was, rather, a black cavern, in which there stood a small hearth. Coppelius approached it, and a blue flame flickered upon the hearth. All kinds of strange implements lay around. Good God! as my old father bent down to the fire, he looked quite different! A dreadful convulsive pain seemed to have distorted his gentle honest features into a repulsive devil-mask. He looked like Coppelius. The latter seized the glowing tongs and with them drew brightly gleaming substances out of the thick black smoke and began vigorously to hammer away at them. I seemed to see human faces appearing all around, but without eyes – instead of eyes there were hideous black cavities.

'Eyes, bring eyes!' Coppelius cried in a dull hollow voice.

Gripped by wild terror, I screamed aloud and fell out of my hiding-place on to the floor. Coppelius seized me.

'Little beast! Little beast!' he bleated, showing his teeth. Then he pulled me up and threw me on to the hearth, so that the flames began to singe my hair.

'Now we have eyes – eyes – a lovely pair of children's eyes!' Coppelius whispered and took a red-glowing dust out of the flame with his hands and was about to sprinkle it into my eyes. But my father raised his hands imploringly and cried: 'Master! Master! Let my Nathaniel keep his eyes – let him keep them!'

Coppelius laughed shrilly and cried: 'The boy can have his eyes then, and keep the use of them. But now let us observe the mechanism of the hands and feet.'

And with that he seized me so violently that my joints

cracked, unscrewed my hands and feet, and fixed them on again now in this way, now in that.

'They don't look right anywhere! Better where they were! The Old One knew what he was doing!' Coppelius lisped and hissed. But everything went dark around me, a sudden spasm shot through my frame – I felt nothing more.

A warm gentle breath passed across my face; I awoke as if from the sleep of death; my mother was bending over me.

'Is the sandman still here?' I stammered.

'No, my dear child, he has been gone a long, long time; he will not harm you!' my mother said, and kissed and embraced the child who had come back to her.

Why should I weary you, my dear Lothario, with all these minute details, when so much still remains to be said? Enough! I was discovered eavesdropping and was mishandled by Coppelius. Fear and terror had brought on a violent fever with which I lay sick for many weeks. 'Is the sandman still here?' were the first rational words I said: it was the sign that I was cured, that I was saved. The only thing I still have to tell you of is the most dreadful moment of my childhood, and then you will be convinced that it is not the weakness of my eyes which renders the world colourless to me, but that a dark destiny really has suspended a veil of gloom over my life – a veil which I shall perhaps rend asunder only in death.

Coppelius, however, was no longer to be seen and was said to have left the town.

It might have been a year later when, in accordance with our ancient custom, which was still unchanged, we were sitting at our round table one evening. My father was very cheerful and was telling us amusing things about the journeys he had made in his youth. Then, as nine o'clock struck, we suddenly heard the housedoor creak on its hinges, and slow, leaden footsteps thudded across the entrance hall and up the stairs.

'That is Coppelius,' my mother said, growing pale.

'Yes, it is Coppelius,' my father replied in a lifeless, broken voice. Tears started from my mother's eyes. 'But father, father!' she cried. 'Must it be so?'

'For the last time!' my father answered. 'He is coming for the last time, I promise you. Go now, go with the children! Go, go to bed! Good night!'

I felt as if crushed beneath a rock: I ceased to breathe! My mother took me by the arm as I stood there motionless.

'Come, Nathaniel, come along!' she said. I let myself be led away. I went into my room.

'It's all right, it's all right. Lie down in bed and go to sleep,' my mother called after me; but, tormented by an indescribable inner fear and anguish, I could not so much as close my eyes. The hated, loathsome Coppelius stood before me with his eyes blazing and laughed at me maliciously; I tried in vain to banish his image.

It might have been already midnight when there came a fearful detonation, like the firing of a cannon. The whole house rumbled; there was a clattering and rushing past the door of my room; the housedoor slammed with a crash. 'That is Coppelius!' I cried in terror, and leaped from the bed. Then I heard a piercing, despairing cry of woe and I rushed out to my father's room: the doors stood open, billows of choking smoke welled out towards me, the serving-maid was crying: 'Oh the master, the master!' Before the billowing hearth, his face blackened with smoke and hideously distorted, my father lay dead on the floor, my sisters lamenting and wailing all around him, my mother unconscious beside him. 'Coppelius, you infamous devil, you have killed my father!' I cried out, and my senses left me.

*

When my father was laid in his coffin two days later, his features had again grown mild and gentle, as they had been in life, and in my soul I experienced the consolation of knowing that his bond with the diabolical Coppelius had in any event not plunged him into eternal damnation.

The explosion had awakened the neighbours and the affair became public and was brought to the attention of the authorities, who wanted to call Coppelius to account over it; he, however, had disappeared without trace.

When I now tell you, my dearest friend, that the aforementioned dealer in barometers was none other than this same infamous Coppelius, you will not blame me for interpreting his reappearance as a herald of the heaviest misfortune. He was dressed differently, but Coppelius's form and features are too deeply imprinted in my innermost being for there to be any possibility of a mistake. He has, moreover, not even changed his name: I hear that he gives himself out here for a Piedmontese mechanician and calls himself Giuseppe Coppola.

I have resolved to get the better of him and, whatever the outcome may be, revenge my father's death.

Tell my mother nothing of the re-emergence of the vile monster. Greet for me my dear Clara; I shall write to her when I am in a calmer mood. Farewell.

Clara to Nathaniel

It is true you have not written to me for a long time, but I believe nonetheless that I am present in your thoughts. For you were certainly thinking of me when you intended to send off your last letter to brother Lothario but addressed it to me instead. I joyfully opened the letter and first became aware of the mistake at the words 'Ah, my dear Lothario'. I ought to have read no further but given the letter to my brother. You used to tease me that I had so calm and womanly self-possessed a nature that if the house was falling down I would, like the lady in the story, stop and smooth out the curtains before running, so it will be hard for me to convince you that the beginning of your letter affected me very deeply. I could hardly breathe and my head started to swim. Oh, my beloved Nathaniel, what dreadful thing had come into your life? To be separated from you, never to see you again: the thought pierced my heart like a fiery dagger. I read on and on! Your description of the repulsive Coppelius was horrible. Only now did I learn that your good father had died such a terrible violent death. Lothario, to whom I delivered up his property, tried to comfort me but could do so very little. The odious dealer Giuseppe Coppola pursued me everywhere, and I am almost ashamed to confess that he was able even to disturb my sleep, which is usually so sound, with all kinds of strange dreams. But soon – as soon as the next day – I saw everything differently. Do not be angry with me, my dearly beloved, if Lothario should tell you that, in spite of your strange presentiment that Coppelius is going to harm you in some way, I am now again as calm and cheerful as I always was.

Let me say straight out what it is I think: that all the ghastly and terrible things you spoke of took place only within you, and that the real outer world had little part in them. Old Coppelius may have been repulsive enough, but it was because he hated children that you children came to feel an actual revulsion for him.

The frightening sandman in the nursery tale naturally became united in your childish mind with old Coppelius; although you no longer believed in the sandman, Coppelius was still to you a spectral monster especially dangerous to children. The uncanny night-time activities with your father were no doubt nothing more than secret alchemical experiments they were making together, and your mother could hardly have been pleased about it, since a lot of money was undoubtedly wasted and, moreover, as is always supposed to be the case with such laboratory experimenters, your father, altogether absorbed in the deceptive desire for higher truth, would have become estranged from his family. Your father surely brought about his own death through his own carelessness, and Coppelius is not to blame for it. Yesterday I asked the learned chemist who lives next door whether such an instantly fatal explosion is possible with chemical experiments? He said: 'Oh, to be sure!' and described to me in his own way how it could happen, with all kinds of examples, and named so many strange-sounding names I was quite unable to remember them. Now I expect you will become annoyed with your Clara and say: 'No ray of the mysterious world which often embraces men with invisible arms penetrates that cold heart: she sees only the motley surface and, like a childish child, rejoices at the deceitfully gleaming fruit and does not think of the deadly poison within it.'

Ah, my beloved Nathaniel, do you not then believe that in cheerful, unaffected, careless hearts too there may not dwell the presentiment of a dark power which strives to ruin us within our own selves? Forgive me if I, who am only a simple girl, attempt to indicate in some way what it is I really believe about such inward struggles. I am sure that in the end I shall never find the right words and that you will laugh at me, not because what I think is stupid but because the way I go about saying it is so awkward.

Perhaps there does exist a dark power which fastens on to us and leads us off along a dangerous and ruinous path which we would otherwise not have trodden; but if so, this power must have assumed within us the form of ourself, indeed have become ourself, for otherwise we would not listen to it, otherwise there would be no space within us in which it could perform its secret work. But if we possess a firm mind, a mind strengthened through living cheerfully, we shall always be able to recognize an inimical influence for what it is; and then that uncanny power must surely go under in the struggle we must suppose takes place before it can achieve that form which is, as I have said, a mirror-image of ourself.

'What is also certain,' Lothario put in, 'is that this dark psychic power, once we have surrendered to it, often assumes other forms which the outer world throws across our path and draws them into us, so that the spirit which seems to animate those forms has in fact been enkindled by us ourselves. Through their inner affinity with us and their influence over our heart they have the power to cast us into Hell or transport us to Heaven, but that is because they are phantoms of our own ego.'

You will see, my beloved Nathaniel, that my brother and I have talked together very fully about dark powers and forces, and now I have set down our principal conclusions – not without effort – they appear to me extremely profound. I do not altogether understand Lothario's final words – I only sense what he means, and yet it seems to me all very true. I beg you, banish the repulsive Coppelius and the barometer-man Giuseppe Coppola from your mind altogether. Be assured that these forms from without have no power over you; only a belief that they have such a power can bestow it upon them. Were it not that every line of your letter spoke of the deep agitation you feel, were it not that the condition you are in strikes me to the very soul, I could laugh at the advocate sandman and the barometer-dealer Coppelius. Be cheerful, be cheerful! I have made up my mind to become your guardian spirit, and if the repulsive Coppola should presume to burden your dreams, I shall laugh him out of them. I am not afraid of him or his horrible hands: he can appear as advocate or sandman, but I shan't have him spoiling my cakes for me, or my eyes.

Ever yours, my most dearly beloved Nathaniel.

Nathaniel to Lothario

It happened through my own absent-mindedness, to be sure, but still I much regret that Clara opened that letter to you and read it. She has replied with a very profound philosophical letter, in which she proves at length that Coppelius and Coppola exist only within me and are phantoms of my ego which will vanish instantly into dust as soon as I recognize them for what they are. One would not have believed that the mind which so often shines out through such bright smiling eyes like a dear sweet dream could have been capable of so judicious and schoolmasterly an analysis. She appealed to you, and you talked about me. I suppose you gave her lectures in logic, so that she could sift and distinguish everything correctly. Let that be! It is virtually certain, moreover, that the barometer-dealer Giuseppe Coppola is by no means the old advocate Coppelius. I attend lectures with the newly arrived professor of physics, who is none other than the famous scientist Spalanzani and is an Italian. He has known Coppola for many years and says that you can in any case tell from his voice that he really is Piedmontese. Coppelius was a German. This has not, however, put me entirely at ease. Clara and you can go on thinking me a gloomy dreamer, but I cannot get rid of the impression which Coppelius's accursed face makes upon me. I am glad he has left the town, as Spalanzani tells me he has. This professor is an odd fellow: a little round man, with high cheekbones, a thin nose, turned-out lips, little piercing eyes. But Chodowiecki's picture of Cagliostro in a Berlin pocket calendar would give you a better idea of him than any description, for that is what Spalanzani looks like.

Recently I went upstairs in Professor Spalanzani's house and perceived that a curtain which was always drawn tight across a glass door up there was showing a chink of light. I don't know myself how I came to look through. A woman, tall, very slim, perfectly proportioned and gorgeously dressed, sat in the room at a little table, with her arms lying upon it and her hands folded. She was sitting opposite the door, so that I saw the whole of her angelic face. She seemed not to notice me, and her eyes had in general something fixed and staring about them, I could almost say she was sightless, as if she was sleeping with her eyes open. It made me feel quite uncanny, and I crept softly away into the neighbouring lecture-room. I afterwards learned that the figure I had seen was Spalanzani's daughter Olympia, whom, incredibly and reprehensibly, he keeps locked up so that no one may come near her. But there may, of course, be something peculiar about her – she may be weak-minded or something.

But why am I writing you all this? I could have told you about it better and at greater length face to face – for you must now learn that I shall be with you in a fortnight's time. I have to see my dear sweet angel, my Clara, again. The ill mood which (I confess it) threatened to overcome me after her annoying judicious letter will then be blown away. That is why I am not writing to her today either.

A thousand greetings . . .

Nothing stranger or more singular could be invented than that which happened to my poor friend, the young student Nathaniel, and which, indulgent reader, I have undertaken to tell you of. Have you ever, kind friend, experienced anything which completely filled your heart and mind and drove everything else out of them? Which made you bubble and boil and drove the blood glowing hot through your veins, so that your cheeks burned red? Which transfigured your gaze, as if it were seeking out forms and shapes invisible to other eyes, and dissolved your speech into glowing sighing? Your friends asked: 'What is the matter, honoured friend? What is wrong?' And you wanted to express your inner vision in all its colours and light and shade and wearied yourself to find words with which even to begin. You felt you had, as it were, to compress everything marvellous, glorious, terrible, joyful, harrowing that had happened to you into the very first word, so that it would strike your hearers like an electric shock, but every word, everything capable of being spoken, seemed to you colourless and cold and dead. You sought and sought, and stammered and stuttered; the sober inquiries of your friends struck the fire within you like a breath of icy wind until it threatened to go out. If, however, you had, like a daring painter, first thrown down in a few bold strokes an outline of the image you carried within you, you would then with little effort have proceeded to lay on the colours in more and more glowing tints, and your friends would be carried away by the lively tumult of multifarious forms, and would, like you, behold themselves in the midst of the picture which had come forth out of your heart! I must confess to you, kind reader, that no one has actually asked me for the story of young Nathaniel; but, as you no doubt know, I belong to the strange race of authors who, if they bear within them something of what I have just described, seem to hear everyone they encounter (and in due course more or less the whole world as well) asking: 'What is the matter? Tell us about it!' So it was that I felt a strong compulsion within me to speak to you about Nathaniel's unhappy life: my soul was filled with the strange and marvellous in it, but for just that reason, and because, O reader, I had to produce in you the right frame of mind for the reception of things of no ordinary degree of marvellousness, I tormented myself to begin Nathaniel's story in a significant, original, gripping fashion. 'Once upon a time' – the loveliest opening for any story, but too sober! 'In the little provincial town of S. there lived' – a bit better, at least going back to the beginning. Or, as it were, *in medias res*: '"Go to the devil!" cried the student Nathaniel, his eyes filled with rage and terror, as the barometer-dealer Giuseppe Coppola . . .' – I did in fact write that at a time at which it seemed to me I perceived something comical in the wild eyes of the student Nathaniel; his story is, however, in no way amusing. I could in the end find no form of expression whatever which reflected anything of the colours of my inner vision, so I decided not to begin at all. Accept, kind reader, the three letters which my friend Lothario was good enough to communicate to me as the outline of the picture into which I shall now in the course of narration strive to lay more and more colour. Perhaps, like a good portrait painter, I shall succeed in catching more than one figure in such a way that, although you never knew its original, you will nonetheless think it lifelike, that you had indeed seen the person many times with your living eyes. Perhaps you will then come to believe, O reader, that there is nothing more marvellous or madder than real life, and that all the poet could do was to catch this as a dark reflexion is caught in a dull mirror.

All that has to be added to these letters is that, soon after the death of Nathaniel's father, Clara and Lothario, the children of a distant relation who had likewise died and left them orphans, were taken into her house by Nathaniel's mother. Clara and Nathaniel conceived a warm attachment to one another, to which no one on earth raised the slightest objection; so that, when Nathaniel left the town to continue his studies in G., they were betrothed. And G. is where he is in his last letter, attending lectures by the famous professor Spalanzani.

I would now confidently go on with the story, were it not that Clara's image stands so vividly before my eyes at this moment that I cannot divert my gaze from it – as was always the case whenever she looked at me with her face sweetly smiling. Clara could not possibly be called beautiful: that was the opinion of all those whose office it was to understand beauty. But if the architects lauded the perfect proportions of her figure, if the painters found her neck, shoulders and breast almost too chastely formed, all were enamoured of her wonderful Magdalen hair and babbled about her complexion. One of them, however, a real visionary, had the very strange notion of comparing Clara's eyes with a lake by Ruisdael, with the pure azure of a cloudless sky, woodland and flowery meadow, the whole motley life of a rich landscape reflected in them. Poets and musicians, however, went further and said: 'What lake – what reflexion? When we behold her, we hear heavenly tones streaming towards us from out of her eyes; they penetrate our innermost heart, which then awakes and grows animated. If we are not then inspired to any truly accomplished song, that is because we are in general of very little account, and that fact we read unmistakably in the smile that plays about Clara's mouth whenever we venture to warble out before her something that presumes to think itself song, though it is indeed no more than a muddled confusion of notes.' That is how she affected them. Clara possessed the energetic imagination of a happy ingenuous child, a profound womanly-tender heart, a clear sharp understanding. Fantasists enjoyed little success with her: for, although she did not say very much – loquaciousness being in any case foreign to her reserved nature – her bright eyes and that subtle ironical smile told them: 'Dear friends! how could you believe of me that I should regard your transient poetic fancies as real beings, possessing life and action?' For this reason Clara was stigmatized by many as cold, unfeeling, prosaic; but others, who viewed life with clearer eyes, felt an uncommon affection for the cheerful, intelligent, childlike girl – and none felt it more than did Nathaniel. Clara, for her part, clung to her beloved with all her soul: the first clouds to pass over her life were those which appeared when he departed from her; with what a transport of joy did she fly to his arms when, as he had promised in his last letter to

Lothario, he returned home and appeared in his mother's room! And it was then as Nathaniel had believed it would be: at the first sight of Clara all thought of the advocate Coppelius and of Clara's letter was banished from his mind, all trace of the ill mood which had possessed him vanished away.

Nathaniel was right, however, when he told Lothario that his life had been influenced for the worse by the repulsive barometer-dealer Coppola – a fact apparent to everyone when in the very first days he exhibited a total change in his character. He would lapse into gloomy reveries, and he was soon behaving in a manner altogether foreign to his usual ways. Everything, the whole of life, had become for him a dream and a feeling of foreboding; he spoke continually of how each of us, thinking himself free, was in reality the tortured plaything of mysterious powers: resistance was vain; we had humbly to submit to the decrees of fate. He went so far as to assert that it was folly to think the creations of art and science the product of our own free will: the inspiration which alone made creation possible did not proceed from within us but was effectuated by some higher force from outside.

Clara found these mystical fancies in the highest degree antipathetic, but to attempt to refute them seemed pointless. Only when Nathaniel proceeded to demonstrate that Coppelius was in reality an evil force which had taken possession of him as he was hiding and listening behind the curtain, and that this repulsive demon was in a fearful fashion going to wreck the happiness of their love, did Clara become very serious, and say: 'Yes, Nathaniel, you are right; Coppelius is an evil, inimical force, he can do terrible things, he is like a demonic power that has stepped visibly into life – but only so long as you fail to banish him from your mind. As long as you believe in him he continues to exist and act – his power is only your belief in him.'

Incensed that Clara would grant the existence of the demon only as a force within him, Nathaniel was about to launch upon an exposition of his entire mystical theory of devils and cruel powers when Clara in vexation interposed some irrelevant remark and broke off the conversation. In his annoyance, Nathaniel consoled himself with the reflexion that such profound secrets as these were forever closed to cold, unreceptive hearts. Yet, failing to realize that he had thus numbered Clara among the subordinate natures, he did not cease his attempts to initiate her into these secrets.

Early in the morning, as Clara was helping to prepare breakfast, he stood beside her and read to her out of his mystical books, so that Clara asked: 'But, dear Nathaniel, suppose I were to call *you* the evil force which is having a bad influence on my coffee? For if, as you want me to, I neglected everything and stood and looked into your eyes as you read, the coffee would boil over and none of you would get any breakfast!' Whereupon Nathaniel shut the book violently and ran off to his room in a thorough bad humour.

In former days, he had had a great gift for lively and cheerful stories, which he would write down and Clara would listen to with the most heartfelt enjoyment; now his tales had grown gloomy, incomprehensible and formless, so that, even if Clara considerately refrained from saying so, he could nonetheless sense how little they appealed to her. Clara found boredom almost unendurable: when she was bored, the almost unconquerable weariness of mind she felt appeared in how she spoke and in the look in her eyes. Nathaniel's tales were indeed very boring. His annoyance at Clara's cold, prosaic disposition grew greater, Clara was unable to overcome the ill humour with which his obscure, gloomy and boring mysticism filled her, and thus without noticing it they became more and more estranged from one another. The figure of the

repulsive Coppelius had, as Nathaniel himself was constrained to admit, grown dim in his imagination, and in his
tales, where Coppelius appeared as a malign agent of
destiny, it often required an effort to bestow life and colour
upon him. At length he hit on the idea of making his
gloomy foreboding that Coppelius would disrupt the joy
of his love into the subject of a poem: he depicted himself
and Clara as united in true love; but now and then it was as
if a black hand reached out over them and erased their
feelings of joy; at last, as they were standing before the
marriage altar, the terrible Coppelius appeared and
touched Clara's lovely eyes, which sprang out like blood-
red sparks, singeing and burning, on to Nathaniel's breast;
Coppelius then seized him and threw him into a flaming
circle of fire which, spinning with the velocity of a tempest, tore him away with a rushing and roaring; there was a
commotion, as when the hurricane whips up the foaming
waves of the sea and they rear like white-haired giants in
furious combat, but through this commotion he heard
Clara's voice: 'Do you not see me? Coppelius has deceived
you: those were not my eyes which burned into your
breast; they were glowing-hot drops of your own heart's
blood – I still have my eyes; you have only to look at me!'
Nathaniel thought: 'That is Clara, and I am hers for ever' –
and the thought seemed to interpose itself into the circle of
fire, so that it came to a stop and the hubbub subsided into
the depths; Nathaniel looked into Clara's eyes, but it was
death which gazed at him mildly out of them.

While Nathaniel was composing this poem he was very
quiet and self-possessed: he polished and improved every
line, and the constraint of metre made it possible for him
not to rest until everything was clear and harmonious. Yet
when he had finished the poem and read it aloud to
himself, he was seized with horror and exclaimed: 'Whose
dreadful voice is this?' Before long, however, it again
seemed to him no more than a good poem, and he came to

think that Clara's cold disposition would certainly be inflamed by it, although at the same time he had no clear notion of what Clara's becoming inflamed might lead to or of what purpose could be served by distressing her with horrible images prophesying a terrible destiny and the destruction of their love.

Nathaniel and Clara sat in his mother's little garden; Clara was in a very cheerful mood, since for the three days previously, on which he had been working on his poem, Nathaniel had not plagued her with his dreams and premonitions. Nathaniel, too, was talking cheerfully of pleasant things, so that Clara said: 'Now at last I have got you back again. Don't you see how we have driven away the repulsive Coppelius?'

It was only then that Nathaniel remembered he had in his pocket the poem he wanted to read to her. He straightway brought out the pages and began reading from them; supposing it to be, as usual, something boring, but acquiescing in it, Clara began composedly to knit. But as the dark clouds arose blacker and blacker, she let fall the stocking she was knitting and gazed at Nathaniel in numbed amazement. The latter continued relentlessly on, inner fire coloured his cheeks bright red, tears welled from his eyes. At last he had finished and groaned with exhaustion; then he grasped Clara's hand and, as though dissolved in inconsolable misery, sighed: 'Ah! Clara, Clara!'

Clara pressed him gently to her bosom and said, softly but very slowly and earnestly: 'Nathaniel, my dear, dear Nathaniel! throw the mad, senseless, insane story into the fire.'

Nathaniel sprang up indignantly and, thrusting Clara away from him, cried: 'Oh, you lifeless accursed automaton!'

He rushed out, and Clara, deeply wounded, shed bitter tears: 'Alas, he has never loved me, for he does not understand me,' she sobbed aloud.

Lothario stepped into the arbour and Clara had to tell him what had happened; he loved his sister with all his heart and each word of her complaint struck into him like a fiery brand, so that the annoyance which he had for long secretly felt towards the dreamy Nathaniel was ignited into blazing anger. He ran to Nathaniel, in harsh words he reproached him for his senseless behaviour towards his beloved sister, and Nathaniel, provoked, replied in kind. Lothario called Nathaniel a crazy, fantastical coxcomb; Nathaniel retaliated by calling Lothario a wretched, commonplace fellow. A duel was unavoidable: in accordance with the academic custom there obtaining, they resolved to meet one another the following morning behind the garden with sharpened foils.

They crept about silent and with darkened brows. Clara had heard their violent contention and, as dusk fell, seen the fencing-master bring the rapiers. She sensed what was going to happen.

Arrived at the place of combat, Lothario and Nathaniel had at once thrown off their coats in gloomy silence and, with bloodthirsty belligerence in their burning eyes, were about to fall upon one another when Clara burst through the garden door. Sobbing, she cried aloud: 'You ferocious and dreadful men! Strike me down before you attack each other! for how should I go on living in the world if my beloved had murdered my brother or my brother had murdered my beloved?'

Lothario let his weapon fall and gazed at the ground in silence, and within Nathaniel all the love he had felt for his gentle Clara in their days of youth rose again in heart-rending sadness: the murder-weapon fell from his hand and he threw himself at Clara's feet. 'Can you ever forgive me, my only one, my beloved Clara? Can you forgive me, my beloved brother Lothario?'

Lothario was moved by his friend's profound pain, and the three, reconciled again, embraced one another with a thousand tears and vowed that, united in constant love and loyalty, they would never more be separated.

It seemed to Nathaniel as though a heavy burden pressing him to the earth had been lifted from him – as though, indeed, by resisting the dark power that had encompassed him he had saved his whole being from the destruction which threatened it. He spent three beautiful days with his dear friends before returning to G., where he intended to study for one more year but then to return to his home for ever.

Of all that concerned Coppelius his mother was told nothing, for they knew she could not think of him without dread because, like Nathaniel, she held him responsible for the death of her husband.

Nathaniel was very astonished when he arrived back at his lodgings and saw that the whole house had been burned down, so that only the naked charred walls still stood amid the rubble. Although the fire had broken out in the laboratory of the chemist who lived on the lower floor, and the house had thus burned from the ground upwards, his valorous and agile friends had succeeded in getting to Nathaniel's room, which lay on the upper floor, in time to rescue his books, manuscripts and instruments. They had transported everything, unharmed, to another house, and there taken a room, which Nathaniel straightaway proceeded to occupy.

It did not seem to him especially noteworthy that he now lived opposite Professor Spalanzani, nor did he think it anything remarkable when he noticed that the window of his room gave directly on to the room in which Olympia often sat alone, so that he could clearly recognize her figure, though the lineaments of her face remained indistinct. He was, however, finally struck by the fact that Olympia would often sit for hours on end, altogether unoccupied at a little table, in the same posture as that in which he had once discovered her through the glass door, and that she was quite clearly gazing across at him with an unmoving stare. He was also obliged to admit that he had never seen a lovelier figure. Nevertheless, with Clara in his heart he remained wholly indifferent to the stiff, rigid Olympia: only now and then did he glance fleetingly over his book across to the beautiful statue – that was all.

One day, he was in the act of writing to Clara when there came a gentle knocking at the door; it opened in response to his reply, and the repellent face of Coppola looked in. Nathaniel felt himself tremble in his innermost depths; recalling what Spalanzani had told him about his fellow countryman, however, and the sacred promise he had made to his beloved regarding the sandman Coppelius, he was ashamed of this childish fear, pulled himself together with all his might, and said, as gently and composedly as he could: 'I am not going to buy a barometer, my dear friend, so please be gone.'

At that, however, Coppola stepped bodily into the room and, his wide mouth distorted into an ugly grin and his little eyes blazing out piercingly from under long grey eyelashes, said in a hoarse voice: 'Not barometer, not barometer! – I also got lov-ely *occe*, lov-ely *occe*!'

Horrified, Nathaniel cried: 'Madman! how can you have eyes?'

But Coppola had already put aside his barometers and, reaching into his capacious coat pockets, brought out lorgnettes and pairs of spectacles and laid them on to the table. 'Here, here: glasses, glasses to put on your nose; they're my *occe*, lov-ely *occe*!'

And with that he fetched out more and more pairs of spectacles, so that the whole table began to sparkle and glitter in an uncanny fashion. A thousand eyes gazed and blinked and stared up at Nathaniel, but he could not look away from the table, and Coppola laid more and more pairs of spectacles on to it, and flaming glances leaped more and more wildly together and directed their blood-red beams into Nathaniel's breast. Unmanned by an un-governable terror, he cried: 'Stop! stop! dreadful man!'

Coppola was in the act of reaching into his pocket to fetch out more pairs of spectacles, although the whole table was already covered with them, but Nathaniel grasped him firmly by the arm. With a hoarse repulsive laugh, Coppola gently freed his arm, and with the words 'Ah! not for you, but here is lov-ely glasses' he collected together all the pairs of spectacles, put them away, and from a side pocket of his coat brought out a large quantity of telescopes of all sizes. As soon as the spectacles had disappeared, Nathaniel became quite calm and, mindful of Clara, realized that the spectre which so terrified him could have proceeded only from his own mind, and that Coppola might be a highly honourable optician and mechanician but certainly not the revenant and *Doppelgänger* of the accursed Coppelius. The glasses which Coppola was now laying on to the table had, moreover, nothing remarkable about them or anything sinister like the spectacles, and to make all well again Nathaniel now resolved actually to buy something from Coppola. He took up a small, very cleanly fashioned pocket-telescope and, in order to test it, looked out of the window.

He had never in his life before handled a glass which brought objects to the eyes so sharply and clearly defined. Involuntarily he looked into Spalanzani's room: Olympia was, as usual, sitting before the little table, her arms lying upon it and her hands folded. Only now did Nathaniel behold Olympia's beautiful face. The eyes alone seemed to him strangely fixed and dead, yet as the image in the glass grew sharper and sharper it seemed as though beams of moonlight began to rise within them; it was as if they were at that moment acquiring the power of sight, and their glance grew ever warmer and more lively. Nathaniel stood before the window as if rooted to the spot, lost in contemplation of Olympia's heavenly beauty.

An impatient scuffling and clearing of the throat awoke him as if from a deep dream. Coppola was standing behind him. '*Tre zechini* – three ducats.'

Nathaniel had completely forgotten the presence of the optician, and he quickly paid the sum demanded. 'It is so, eh? lov-ely glasses, lov-ely glasses?' Coppola asked in his hoarse repulsive voice and with his mocking smile.

'Yes, yes, yes!' Nathaniel replied in annoyance. 'Adieu, dear friend!'

Coppola left the room, but not without giving Nathaniel many strange sideglances, and Nathaniel heard him laughing on the stairway. 'Oh well,' Nathaniel thought, 'he is laughing at me because I must certainly have bought this little telescope at much too high a price – much too high a price!' As he softly spoke these words, it was as if a deep death-sigh echoed horribly through the room, and a wave of fear made Nathaniel catch his breath. But it was he himself who had sighed, he realized that well enough. 'Clara,' he said to himself, 'is surely right to consider me a tasteless spirit-seer; yet it is odd – no, more than odd – that the foolish idea I might have bought the glass from Coppola at too high a price still fills me with such strange trepidation: I can see no reason for it at all.'

Now he sat down to finish his letter to Clara, but one glance through the window convinced him that Olympia was still sitting there, and in an instant he sprang up, as if impelled by an irresistible power, and seized Coppola's telescope; he could not tear himself away from the seductive sight of Olympia until his friend and fellow-student Siegmund called him to come to Professor Spalanzani's lecture . . .

The curtain before the fatal room was tightly drawn and he could not observe Olympia through the door; nor, during the next two days, did he discover her in the room at all, although, hardly ever leaving his window, he gazed across unceasingly through Coppola's telescope. On the third day a curtain was even put up at the window. In utter despair and driven by burning desire, he rushed out of the town into the countryside. The figure of Olympia hovered before him in the air, and stepped out of the bushes, and peered out at him from the limpid brook with great gleaming eyes. Clara's image had been wiped clean from his mind; he thought of nothing but Olympia; and he wailed aloud and tearfully: 'Alas, my glorious star of love, have you risen over my life only straightway to vanish and leave me in black and hopeless night?'

As he was about to go back into his lodgings, he became aware of noisy activity going on in Spalanzani's house. The doors stood open, all kinds of objects were being carried in, the windows on the first floor had been re-moved, busy housemaids were dusting and sweeping with great brooms, and from inside there came the sound of the knocking and hammering of carpenters and upholsterers. Nathaniel halted in utter amazement; then Siegmund, laughing, came up and said: 'Well, what do you think of our old Spalanzani?'

Nathaniel assured him he thought nothing, that he knew nothing whatever about the professor, but that he perceived with great surprise that there was a tremendous bustle going on in the usually silent and gloomy house; he then learned from Siegmund that Spalanzani intended to give a great party with a concert and a ball the following day and that half the university had been invited. It was, moreover, noised abroad everywhere that Spalanzani's daughter Olympia, whom her father had kept anxiously concealed from every human eye, would there be making her first appearance.

Nathaniel later found an invitation card waiting for him; and, when the carriages were arriving and the lights beginning to gleam in the decorated rooms, he went to the professor's house with heart beating high. The company was numerous and glittering. Olympia appeared, very opulently but tastefully clad, and her face and figure compelled admiration. Her somewhat oddly bowed back and the wasp-like thinness of her body seemed to be the product of too tight lacing. Her pace and posture had about them something deliberate and stiff which many found unpleasing, but this was attributed to the constraint imposed upon her by the presence of company.

The concert began. Olympia played the piano with great accomplishment, and performed equally well a bravura aria in an almost piercingly clear, bell-like voice. Nathaniel was utterly entranced. He stood in the back row and, in the dazzling candlelight, could not quite perceive Olympia's features, so he took out Coppola's glass unnoticed and looked at her across the room. Ah! then he became aware how she was gazing across at him with eyes full of desire and how every note she sang merged with the look of love which was burning its way into his heart! The artificial roulades seemed to Nathaniel the heavenly rejoicing of a soul transfigured by love, and when at last, after the cadenza, the long trill shrilled out through the room, as though suddenly embraced by glowing arms he could no longer restrain himself and he cried aloud in pain and rapture: 'Olympia!'

Everyone turned and looked at him, and some laughed. The cathedral organist, however, pulled an even longer face than usual and said merely: 'Now, now!'

The concert was at an end, the ball began. 'To dance with her! with *her*!' – that was now to Nathaniel the goal of all desire, all endeavour; but how to raise the courage to ask *her*, the queen of the festivities, to dance with *him*? And yet – he himself knew not how it happened – as the dance was just beginning, he found himself standing close beside Olympia, who was still unengaged, and, hardly capable of stammering out the few words which did escape him, taking her by the hand. Olympia's hand was icy cold; he

felt a coldness as of death thrill through him; he looked into
Olympia's eyes, which gazed back at him full of love and
desire; and at that instant it seemed as though a pulse began
to beat in the cold hand and a stream of life blood began to
glow. And in Nathaniel's heart, too, the joy of love
glowed brighter; he embraced the lovely Olympia and
flew with her into the dancing throng.

He had hitherto thought of himself as an accomplished
dancer, but the singular exactitude of rhythm with which
Olympia danced, which frequently took him completely
out of his stride, soon compelled him to recognize how
defective his dancing was. Nonetheless, he no longer
wished to dance with any other woman, and he would
have liked to have murdered anyone who ventured to
approach Olympia with an invitation to dance. Yet this
happened only twice: to his astonishment, Olympia was
thereafter left sitting, and he did not fail to draw her on to
the floor again and again.

If he had been capable of noticing anything other than
the lovely Olympia, a disagreeable scene must necessarily
have taken place: the barely suppressed laughter which
arose among the observant young people in this and that
corner of the room was clearly directed at her. Enflamed
by dancing and by the amount of wine he had drunk,
Nathaniel had thrown off all his customary reserve. He sat
beside Olympia with her hand in his and spoke passionately of his love in words incomprehensible to either of them.
Yet she, perhaps, understood, for she gazed fixedly into
his eyes and sighed time after time: 'Ah, ah, ah!' – whereupon Nathaniel said: 'O lovely, heavenly woman! O beam
of light from the Promised Land of love! O heart in which
my whole being is reflected!' and much more of the same,
but Olympia merely sighed again and again: 'Ah, ah!'
Several times Professor Spalanzani passed by the happy
couple and smiled at them in a singularly contented way.

Although he now found himself in quite another world,

it suddenly seemed to Nathaniel that here below at Professor Spalanzani's it had grown noticeably darker: he looked about him and was not a little startled to see that the two lights left in the room had burned down and were on the point of going out. The music and dancing had long since ceased. 'Parting, parting!' he cried in wild despair; he kissed Olympia's hand, bent down to her mouth and his passionate lips encountered lips that were icy-cold! As he touched Olympia's cold hand, he was seized by an inner feeling of horror, and he suddenly recalled the legend of the dead bride, but Olympia had pressed him close to her; as they kissed, her lips seemed to warm into life.

Professor Spalanzani walked slowly through the empty room, his steps echoed hollowly, and his figure, played about by flickering shadows, had an uncanny ghost-like appearance.

'Do you love me? Do you love me, Olympia? Say but that word. Do you love me?' Nathaniel whispered, but as she rose to her feet Olympia sighed only: 'Ah, ah!'

'Yes, my glorious star of love,' Nathaniel said, 'you have arisen upon my life and you will illumine and transfigure my heart always!'

'Ah, ah!' Olympia repeated, moving away.

Nathaniel followed her and they found themselves standing before the professor. 'You have enjoyed an extraordinarily animated conversation with my daughter,' the professor said, smiling; 'well, then, dear Herr Nathaniel, if it is to your taste to converse with the witless girl, you will be welcome to visit her.'

Nathaniel departed with a whole radiant heaven in his breast. Spalanzani's party was the sole topic of conversation in the ensuing days. Notwithstanding the professor had done everything he could to make the affair an altogether splendid one, the local wits nonetheless told of all kinds of ineptitudes and oddities that had been in evidence, and assailed especially the deathly-rigid and

speechless Olympia, to whom, her lovely eyes notwithstanding, they ascribed total stupidity and thought to
discover therein the reason Spalanzani had kept her hidden
for so long. Nathaniel listened to this, not without inward
anger, but nonetheless kept silent: 'For,' he thought, 'what
would be the point of showing these fellows that it is their
own stupidity which stops them from recognizing Olympia's profound and glorious nature?'

'Do me the favour, brother,' Siegmund said one day, 'of
telling me how a clever chap like you could possibly have
been smitten with that wax-faced wooden doll over there.'

Nathaniel was about to flame up in anger, but he restrained himself and replied: '*You* tell *me*, Siegmund, how,
being as a rule so quick to perceive beauty wherever it
appears, you could fail to respond to Olympia's heavenly
charm. Yet I am grateful for the fact, since it means I do
not have you for a rival – for if I did, one of us would have
fallen bleeding.'

Siegmund saw very well what condition his friend was
in, skilfully turned the conversation in a different direction
and, after expressing the view that in love there was no
accounting for taste, added: 'Yet it is strange that many of
us hold more or less the same opinion of Olympia. Do not
take it ill, brother, but she has appeared to us in a strange
way rigid and soulless. Her figure is well proportioned; so
is her face – that is true! She might be called beautiful if her
eyes were not so completely lifeless, I could even say
sightless. She walks with a curiously measured gait; every
movement seems as if controlled by clockwork. When she
plays and sings it is with the unpleasant soulless regularity
of a machine, and she dances in the same way. We have
come to find this Olympia quite uncanny; we would like
to have nothing to do with her; it seems to us that she is
only acting like a living creature, and yet there is some
reason for that which we cannot fathom.'

Nathaniel restrained the feeling of bitterness which

threatened to take hold on him at these words, mastered his ill humour and only said very earnestly: 'Olympia may well seem uncanny to you cold, prosaic people. It is only to the poetic heart that the like unfolds itself! It was only for *me* that her look of love arose and flooded through mind and senses; only in Olympia's love do I find myself again. To you it may not seem in order that she refrains from the dull chatter which amuses shallow natures. She says but few words, that is true, but these few words appear as genuine hieroglyphics of an inner world full of love and a higher knowledge of the spiritual life in contemplation of the eternal Beyond. But for all of this you have no understanding, and all these words are uttered in vain.'

'May God protect you, dear brother,' Siegmund said very gently, almost sadly, 'but it seems to me you are set on an ill-fated course. You can depend on me if – no, I shall say no more!' To Nathaniel the cold, prosaic Siegmund suddenly appeared a very true-hearted friend, and he shook with much warmth the hand that was extended to him.

Nathaniel had clean forgotten that there existed a Clara whom he used to love. His mother, Lothario, all had vanished from memory: he lived only for Olympia. He sat with her every day for hours on end and fantasized over his love, the sympathy sprung up between them, their psychical affinity, and Olympia listened to it all with great devotion. From the profoundest depths of his writing-desk Nathaniel fetched up everything he had ever written: poems, fantasies, visions, novels, tales, daily augmented by random sonnets, stanzas, *canzoni*, and he read them all to Olympia without wearying for hours on end. And he had never before had so marvellous an auditor: she did not sew or knit, she did not gaze out of the window, she did not feed a cage bird, she did not play with a lapdog or with a favourite cat, she did not fiddle with a handkerchief or with anything else, she did not find it necessary to stifle a yawn with a little forced cough – in short, she sat motionless, her gaze fixed on the eyes of her beloved with a look that grew ever more animated and more passionate. Only when Nathaniel finally arose and kissed her hand – and no doubt her mouth, too – did she say: 'Ah, ah!' and then: 'Good night, my dear!'

'O you glorious, profound nature,' Nathaniel exclaimed when back in his room, 'only you, you alone, understand me completely.'

He trembled with inward delight when he reflected on the wonderful harmony which was day by day becoming ever more apparent between his nature and Olympia's: it seemed to him that what Olympia said of his work, of his poetic talent in general, came from the depths of his own being, that her voice was indeed the voice of those very depths themselves. And that must actually have been the case, for Olympia never said anything more than the words already mentioned. But even Nathaniel was able, in moments of sobriety – on awakening in the morning, for instance – to realize how passive and inarticulate Olympia really was; then, however, he would say: 'What are words? The glance of her heavenly eyes says more than any speech on earth. Can a child of heaven accommodate itself to the narrow circle drawn by the wretched circumstances of earth?'

Professor Spalanzani seemed highly delighted at the relationship which had grown up between his daughter and Nathaniel: he gave the latter many unambiguous signs of his goodwill, and when Nathaniel at last ventured distantly to hint of an engagement with Olympia, he smiled all over his face and said he would allow his daughter a completely free choice. Encouraged by these words, and with a burning desire in his heart, Nathaniel resolved to beg Olympia to say unreservedly in plain words what her look of love had long since told him: that she wanted to be his own for ever. He sought for the ring his mother had given him on his departure, that he might offer it to Olympia as a symbol of his devotion, of the dawning new life they were to share together. As he searched, he encountered Clara's and Lothario's letters; he threw them indifferently aside, found the ring, put it into his pocket and ran across to Olympia's room. As he mounted the staircase and arrived at the landing, he heard the sound of a strange uproar, which seemed to be coming out of Spalanzani's study. There was a stamping, a clattering, a pushing and thumping against the door, with oaths and curses intermingled: 'Let go! – Let go! – Wretch! – Rascal! – Is this what I staked my life on? – Ha, ha, ha, ha! – That isn't what we agreed! *I* made the eyes! – I made the clockwork! – Poor fool with your clockwork! – Damned dog of a clock-maker! – Away with you! – Devil! – Stop! – Puppet showman! – Beast! – Stop! – Get away! – Let go!'

The voices thus raised in contention were those of Spalanzani and the dreadful Coppelius. Seized by a nameless fear, Nathaniel burst in. The professor had hold of a female figure by the shoulders, the Italian Coppola had it by the feet, and transformed with rage they were tearing and tugging at it for its possession. Nathaniel recoiled in terror as he recognized the figure as Olympia; flaring into a furious rage, he went to rescue his beloved, but at that moment Coppola, turning with terrible force, wrenched the figure from the professor's hands and dealt him a fearful blow with it, so that he tumbled backwards to the table, on which retorts, bottles and glass cylinders were standing, and collapsed on to it – the glassware was shattered into a thousand pieces. Then Coppola threw the figure over his shoulder and, laughing shrilly, ran quickly down the staircase, so that the feet of the figure hanging down repulsively behind him thumped and clattered woodenly against the stairs.

Nathaniel stood numb with horror. He had seen all too clearly that Olympia's deathly-white face possessed no eyes: where the eyes should have been, there were only pits of blackness – she was a lifeless doll!

Spalanzani was rolling about on the floor: his head, chest and arms had been cut by pieces of glass and his blood was gushing as if from a fountain. But he gathered himself together with all the strength he possessed: 'After him, after him, what are you waiting for? Coppelius has robbed me of my finest automaton – it cost me twenty years' work! I have staked my life on it! The clockwork, speech, walk – all mine! The eyes, the eyes purloined from you! Accursed wretch, after him! Get Olympia back for me! – and here, here are the eyes!'

At this point Nathaniel saw that a pair of blood-flecked eyes were lying on the floor and staring up at him; Spalanzani seized them with his uninjured hand and threw them at him, so that they struck him in the chest.

Then madness gripped him with hot glowing claws, tore its way into him and blasted his mind. 'Ha, ha, ha! Circle of fire, circle of fire! Spin, spin, circle of fire! Merrily, merrily! Puppet, ha, lovely puppet, spin, spin!' – with this cry he hurled himself at the professor and took him by the throat, and would have strangled him if the uproar had not attracted a crowd, who burst in, wrenched the raging Nathaniel away and so rescued the professor, whose injuries were at once attended to. Strong though he was, Siegmund was unable to restrain the madman, who continued to cry in a fearsome voice 'Spin, puppet, spin!' and to flail about him with clenched fists. The united strength of several of them at last succeeded in overpowering him by throwing him to the floor and tying him up. The words he had been shouting dissolved into an awful animal bellowing. Thus, raging in hideous frenzy, he was taken to the madhouse.

Before I go on to tell you, kind reader, what further befell the unfortunate Nathaniel, I can assure you – supposing you take any interest in the fate of the clever mechanician and automaton-maker Spalanzani – that the latter recovered fully from his injuries, though he was in the meantime compelled to vacate the university, since the tale of Nathaniel had made a great stir and it was everywhere regarded as an altogether impermissible piece of deception to have smuggled into respectable tea-circles (which Olympia had attended with great success) a wooden puppet instead of a living person. The jurists even termed it a refined and all the more culpable deception in that it was practised upon the public and so cunningly conceived that no one (with the exception of extremely astute students) had detected it, notwithstanding that everyone now put on a show of wisdom and pretended to recall all kinds of things which had seemed to them suspicious. But they brought to light nothing of any real note: could it have seemed suspicious to anyone, for example, if, according to the testimony of an elegant habitué of the tea-circles, Olympia had, contrary to all custom, more often sneezed than yawned? The former, so the elegant gentleman asserted, had been the sound of the clockwork winding itself up; there had at the same time been a noticeable squeaking; and so on. The professor of poetry and rhetoric took a pinch of snuff, snapped the box shut, cleared his throat, and said solemnly: 'Esteemed ladies and gentlemen! Do you not see where the difficulty lies? The whole thing is an allegory, an extended metaphor! Do you understand me? *Sapienti sat!*' But the minds of many esteemed gentlemen were still not set at rest: the episode of the automaton had struck deep roots into their souls, and there stealthily arose in fact a detectable mistrust of the human form. To be quite convinced they were not in love with a wooden doll, many enamoured young men demanded that their young ladies should sing and dance in a less than perfect manner, that while being read to they should knit, sew, play with their

puppy and so on, but above all that they should not merely
listen but sometimes speak too, and in such a way that
what they said gave evidence of some real thinking and
feeling behind it. Many love-bonds grew more firmly tied
under this regime; others on the contrary gently dissolved.
'You really cannot tell which way it will go,' they said. To
counter any kind of suspicion, there was an unbelievable
amount of yawning and no sneezing at all at the tea-circles.

As already stated, Spalanzani had to leave so as to avoid a
criminal investigation into the deceitful introduction of an
automaton into human society. Coppola had also disappeared.

Nathaniel awoke as if from a dreadful oppressive dream:
he opened his eyes and felt an indescribable sensation of joy
flood with heavenly warmth through him. He was lying in
bed in his room in his father's house, Clara was bending
over him, and his mother and Lothario were standing not
far away.

'At last, at last, my beloved Nathaniel, you have recovered from your terrible illness! Now you are mine again!'
said Clara from the depths of her soul, and took Nathaniel
into her arms. He, however, wept hot glowing tears for
sheer delight and misery, and sighed aloud: 'My Clara!'

Siegmund, who had faithfully endured his friend's distress with him, came in. Nathaniel reached out his hand to
him: 'My faithful brother, you did not desert me.'

Every trace of madness had vanished, and soon Nathaniel grew stronger under the careful tending of his mother,
his loved ones and his friends. Good fortune had meanwhile entered the house: an old miserly uncle from whom
nobody had expected anything had died and had left
Nathaniel's mother, in addition to a not inconsiderable
sum of money, a small property in a pleasant region not far
from the town whence the mother, Nathaniel, his Clara,
whom he now wished to marry, and Lothario all intended

to move. Nathaniel had grown more gentle and childlike than he had ever been, and it was now he first really got to know Clara's glorious, innocent nature. No one alluded even in the remotest way to what had happened in the past. Only as Siegmund was about to depart did Nathaniel say: 'By God, brother! I was on a dreadful course, but when the time came an angel led me into the right way! Ah, that angel was Clara!' Siegmund would not let him go on for fear he would revive deeply wounding memories.

The time had come for the four happy people to move to the mother's little property. They were walking through the streets of the town at midday: they had done a large amount of shopping and the tall tower of the town hall threw a giant shadow over the market-place. 'Let us go up the tower just once more,' said Clara, 'and look across at the mountains!' No sooner said than done! Nathaniel and Clara climbed up together, the mother went home with the serving-maid, and Lothario, disinclined to clamber up the many steps that led to the top of the tower, remained waiting below. Then the loving pair stood arm in arm in the highest gallery of the tower and gazed out at the fragrant woodland and at the blue mountains that rose like a giant city beyond.

'Just look at that funny little grey bush that seems as if it is coming towards us,' said Clara. Nathaniel reached mechanically into his sidepocket; he found Coppola's telescope and gazed through it. Clara was standing before the glass! Then a spasm shuddered through him; pale as death, he stared at Clara, but soon his eyes began to roll, fire seemed to flash and glow behind them, and he started to roar horribly, like a hunted animal; then he leaped high into the air and, laughing hideously, cried in a piercing voice: 'Spin, puppet, spin! Spin, puppet, spin!' – and with terrible force he seized Clara and tried to throw her off the tower.

In mortal fear, Clara clutched at the railings of the

parapet; Lothario heard the raging of the madman, heard Clara's scream of fear; a dreadful presentiment flew through him and he ran up the stairs of the tower. The door to the second landing was shut; Clara's screams grew louder. Distracted with fear and rage, he threw himself against the door, which finally gave way.

Clara's cries were now getting more and more feeble: 'Help! Save me! Save me –' her voice died away in the air. 'She is lost – murdered by the madman!' Lothario cried.

The door to the gallery was also shut. Despair gave him strength, and he burst the door from its hinges. God in Heaven! Grasped by the raving Nathaniel, Clara was hanging in air over the parapet of the gallery; only one hand still kept hold on the iron railings. As quick as lightning Lothario seized his sister and drew her back in, and at the same instant dealt the raging madman a blow in the face with his clenched fist so that Nathaniel stumbled backwards and let go his prey.

Lothario ran down the steps of the tower, his unconscious sister in his arms. She was saved.

Now Nathaniel was running about on the gallery, raving and leaping high into the air, and screaming: 'Spin, spin, circle of fire! Spin, spin, circle of fire!' People came running at the wild screaming and collected below; among them there towered gigantically the advocate Coppelius, who had just arrived in the town and had made straight for the market-place. Some wanted to enter the tower and overpower the madman, but Coppelius laughed and said: 'Don't bother: he will soon come down by himself,' and gazed upward with the rest. Nathaniel suddenly stopped as if frozen; then he stooped, recognized Coppelius, and with the piercing cry: 'Ha! Lov-ely *occe*! Lov-ely *occe*!' he jumped over the parapet.

As Nathaniel was lying on the pavement with his head shattered, Coppelius disappeared into the crowd.

★

Several years later, you could have seen Clara, in a distant part of the country, sitting with an affectionate man hand in hand before the door of a lovely country house and with two lovely children playing at her feet, from which it is to be concluded that Clara found in the end that quiet domestic happiness which was so agreeable to her cheerful disposition and which the inwardly riven Nathaniel could never have given her.

THE ARTUSHOF

You have certainly heard, kind reader, of the remarkable old commercial town of Danzig. Perhaps you already know all that is worth seeing there, if only from descriptions; what I would like, however, is for you to imagine yourself actually present, and in an age earlier than this one, and regarding with your own eyes the extraordinary hall into which I now want to conduct you. The place I mean is the *Artushof* – the Court of King Arthur. In the middle of the day the Artushof resounded with the noise of commerce, people of all nationalities ran hither and thither, and the ear was deafened by their transactions; but when the exchange had finally closed for the night and the commercial gentlemen had retired for their dinner and only one or two of them were still pursuing their business in the hall (which, in fact, forms a thoroughfare linking two streets) – then, kind reader, would have been the time to visit it. A magical twilight then crept through the dusky windows, and the strange pictures and carvings with which the walls were hung – in too great abundance, perhaps – came alive and seemed to move. Stags with tremendous antlers gazed down at you with blazing eyes, so that you could hardly bear to look at them; and the deeper the twilight grew, the more awesome did the marble statue of the king in the middle of the hall appear. On one of the walls there was a great painting showing all the virtues and vices, with their names inscribed beside them; but as the hall became darker, the virtues, which were assembled at the top, gradually disappeared in the enveloping gloom, while the vices – beautiful women in lustrous gowns – stepped forth seductively and seemed to want to entice you towards them. If you averted your eyes, you might look up at the narrow band, passing around almost the entire hall, upon which was represented a long and brightly coloured procession of the militia of the imperial era: drummers, pipers, halberdiers, with grave-faced *Bürgermeister* at their head, and all so lively and lifelike you would almost believe you heard the music they were supposed to be playing and half expected to see them go marching on through the great window into the market-place outside. Such imaginings might well inspire you, kind reader – supposing you to be in any way gifted with pencil or pen and ink – to reproduce some of these splendid *Bürgermeister* and their handsome pages on your own account; for that purpose, indeed, paper, pen and ink were in those days placed throughout the hall at public expense, and the urge to use them might easily prove irresistible. Well, that would be a perfectly harmless occupation for *you*, kind reader! – but when the young merchant Traugott gave way to that temptation he got himself involved in all kinds of trouble.

'Give our friend in Hamburg a letter of advice on the business we have transacted, my dear Herr Traugott' – thus spoke Herr Elias Roos, merchant and businessman, who was Traugott's closest associate and whose daughter, Christina, he was going to marry.

Traugott found a place at a table – not an easy task, the hall was very crowded – took a sheet of paper, dipped his pen in the inkwell, and was about to begin his letter of advice with a bold flourish when, trying to assemble in his mind the exact wording of his first sentence, he happened to cast his eyes aloft. As chance would have it, he was standing right in front of one of the figures in the procession which, whenever he saw it, always filled him with a strange, incomprehensible feeling of melancholy. A serious, almost gloomy-looking man with a black, curly beard was riding richly clad upon a black horse, whose bridle was held by a wonderfully handsome youth (the abundance of his locks and the elegance of his dress made him look almost feminine); the man's form and visage aroused in Traugott a profound feeling of awe, but from the visage of the youth there seemed to radiate towards him a whole world of sweet presentiments. He always experienced the greatest difficulty in tearing himself away from the sight of these two faces, and so it was now: instead of getting on with Herr Elias Roos's letter of advice for Hamburg, he remained gazing at the marvellous picture and, without thinking what he was doing, began scrawling loops and lines on the paper in front of him. He had been doing this for some little time when he felt a hand descend on to his shoulder and heard a hollow voice cry: 'Good, very good – I like it, something can be made of that!' Awakening from his dream, Traugott span round; what he saw left him staring and speechless: he was gazing into the face of the gloomy-looking man whose picture had been before him. It was he who had spoken the words Traugott had heard, and beside him there stood the beautiful youth smiling at him with an expression of indescribable love. 'It is they,' Traugott thought. 'In a moment they will throw off those ugly coats they are wearing and stand before me in their own splendid garb!'

The crowd swirled about and the strange figures were soon lost in the thronging and bustle, but Traugott stood frozen to a statue, with his 'letter of advice' in his hand, long after the exchange had closed and only one or two people were left in the hall. At length he became aware that Herr Elias Roos was coming towards him in the company of two gentlemen he did not know.

'What are you doing ruminating here, my dear Traugott?' cried Herr Roos. 'It is getting late. Have you sent off the letter?'

Traugott, his mind a blank, handed him the sheet of paper; Herr Roos looked at it, then raised his hands in horror, stamped his foot, and cried: 'My God! My God! Scrawlings, childish scrawlings! Where is the letter of advice? O God, the post!'

It seemed as though Herr Roos would choke with annoyance. The strange gentlemen smiled when they saw the 'letter of advice', for it was in all conscience hardly usable: immediately after the opening words: 'In reply to your valued enquiry of the 20 inst . . .' Traugott had drawn, in bold outline, the figures of the gloomy-looking man and the beautiful youth. The gentlemen sought vainly to pacify Herr Roos, who tugged his wig back and forth, banged on the floor with his cane, and cried: 'Oh, the child of Satan! Drawings . . . ! Meanwhile, ten thousand marks go . . .' and he snapped his fingers and again wept: 'Ten thousand marks!'

'Calm yourself, dear Herr Roos,' the elder of the two gentlemen said. 'The post has left, to be sure, but in an hour's time I am sending a courier to Hamburg and he can take your letter of advice with him. It will get there earlier than it would have by post.'

The face of Herr Roos lit up. 'Most incomparable friend!' he exclaimed.

Traugott had recovered from his confusion, and was about to make for the table in order to write the letter of advice, but Herr Roos pushed him aside and, with a malicious glance, muttered between his teeth: 'No need, my son!'

While Herr Roos was busy scribbling away, the elder of the gentlemen approached Traugott, who was standing aside silent and abashed, and said: 'You seem to be in the wrong business, dear sir! It would never occur to a truly dedicated merchant to draw pictures instead of writing letters of advice.'

Traugott must have felt this reproach to be only too

justified and replied in confusion: 'Good God! I have written many excellent letters of advice; it is only now and then that these confounded ideas come into my head!'

'Oh no, my dear boy,' the stranger continued with a smile, 'I wouldn't call these ideas confounded: I believe, indeed, that none of your excellent letters of advice can have been better than these drawings. See how bold and clean-lined they are! You possess a real talent and a style of your own in these things.'

As he was saying these words, the stranger took the sheet, with its single line of text and pageful of drawings, out of Traugott's hand, folded it carefully, and placed it in his pocket. Within Traugott's soul there came into being the firm idea that he had just produced something much more glorious than a letter of advice; a spirit he had not known before flared up within him; and when Herr Roos, who had by then finished writing, turned to him and with a wicked expression exclaimed: 'Your childish pranks could have cost me ten thousand marks!' Traugott replied, in a louder and firmer voice than he had ever employed towards Herr Roos before: 'Do not adopt that tone towards me, my dear sir, or I shall never write you a letter of advice again as long as I live, but shall regard us henceforth as strangers to one another!'

Herr Elias set his wig correctly upon his head with both hands and stammered: 'My dear partner! My dear son! What expressions are these?'

The old gentleman again stepped forward, and a few words sufficed to restore perfect amity; then they all went off to dinner at Herr Roos's. The guests were greeted by Miss Christina, who was dressed in a very spick-and-span fashion and was soon skilfully brandishing the overflowing soup-ladle.

Of the five people at that dinner table I might, kind reader, offer you so lively a picture that you would believe you saw them before your eyes; but the meal lasted only a short while, and the strange tale of valiant Traugott which I have undertaken to indite for you urges me irresistibly forward, so that I must present them to you in only the most fleeting outline, in sketches far inferior, indeed, to those with which Traugott daringly covered that fateful letter of advice.

That Herr Elias Roos wore a little round wig, you know already, kind reader, from what has gone before, and I have nothing to add to it, since from the words he has spoken you will already have formed a picture of the little, round man in his liver-brown coat, trousers and waistcoat, with their gold-covered buttons. Of Traugott I have much to say (for this is, after all, his story), but if – as will not be denied – that strange harmony of the whole person to which we give the name Character, and which we cannot explain but only sense, originates within us and becomes perceptible only through our thoughts, actions and deeds, so, kind reader, will the figure of Traugott become perceptible to you of itself during the course of our narrative. If this does not occur, all the chatter and description in the world will be of no avail, and you may afterwards put our story aside as if you had not read it. The two strange gentlemen are uncle and nephew, formerly in commerce, now businessmen operating with the money they have acquired, and they are friends of Herr Elias Roos – that is to say, deeply involved with him in pecuniary transactions. They live in Königsberg, dress wholly in the English fashion, have with them a mahogany boot-jack from London, and are very artistically cultivated and altogether refined and educated people. The uncle possesses a cabinet of art-works and curiosities, and collects drawings (*vide* the purloined letter). But let these go: my real purpose at the moment is to present to you, kind reader, a picture of Christina, and to do so in as lively colours as possible, for I perceive that we shall not be enjoying her company for very long, and it would thus be as well if I set down a few of her characteristics straight away. Then let her go with our blessing! Imagine, dear reader, a medium-sized, well-nourished woman of about twenty-two or twenty-three years, with a round face, a short, slightly turned-up nose, and friendly, light-blue eyes which smile at everyone who looks into them the information: 'I'm soon to be married!' Her skin is snow white, her hair red but not too red – lips made for kissing – a mouth perhaps a little too wide which she also makes mouths with, though when she does so the teeth she reveals are like pearls. If the house next door were on fire and flames began to spread into her room she would do no more than quickly feed the canary and put away the clean washing before going along to her father's office and letting him know that his own house was on fire. No cake she has made has ever failed to turn out splendidly, and her butter-sauce always thickens to just the right consistency, because when she stirs it, she always stirs it clockwise! But I see that Herr Roos is already emptying the last bottle, and I will therefore add only that Christina is very fond indeed of Traugott, and she is so because he is going to marry her, for what in the world would she do if she never became a wife?

After the meal was over, Herr Roos proposed to his guests that they take a walk on the city ramparts. Traugott, who had that day experienced inward sensations stranger than any he had ever experienced before, would dearly have liked to slip away, but was unable to do so, for as he was about to exit through the door – without even having kissed the hand of his bride in farewell – Herr Roos seized him by the coat-tails, crying: 'My dear son-in-law, my valued partner! You aren't thinking of leaving us?' and he had no option but to stay.

A well-known professor of physics has given it as his opinion that the Universal Spirit, bold experimenter that it is, has somewhere or other constructed a thoroughly efficient electrical machine, from which there run cunningly hidden wires; these wires extend throughout all life and, elude and avoid them as we may, sooner or later we step on one; a lightning bolt then blasts its way through us – and suddenly everything has acquired a new shape. Now, Traugott must have stepped on one of these wires at the moment when the apparition of the two figures appeared before him and, without knowing what he was doing, he began to draw them; for the sight had flashed through him like a bolt of electricity, and it seemed to him he now possessed a clear perception of what had hitherto been only a presentiment and a dream. When people had spoken in conversation of those things which he treasured deep within him as if they were a holy mystery he had been embarrassed and tongue-tied; now that was all over, and so it happened that, when the uncle assailed the marvellous paintings and carvings in the Artushof as tasteless, and condemned especially the little portraits of the soldiers, calling them grotesque, Traugott boldy interposed that, though all this might well offend against strict canons of taste, his own experience of them had been what he confidently assumed that of others had also been: a marvellous world of fantasy had opened up before him in the Artushof, and certain of the figures there had even declared to him audibly that he, too, was a great master, and that he could form and create just as well as he out of whose mysterious workshop they had proceeded. Herr Elias looked even stupider than he normally did as the youth spoke these exaltant words; the uncle, however, said in a tone of mockery: 'I repeat, I do not understand why you want to be a merchant, and are not rather devoting yourself wholly to art.'

Traugott found the man highly repellent and therefore attached himself during their walk to the nephew, whose manner seemed remarkably friendly and familiar. 'O God,' said the latter, 'how I envy you your talent! If only I could draw like you! I do not lack genius, I have drawn really beautiful eyes and noses and ears, and even three or four entire heads, but, O God, business! Business!'

'I would have thought,' said Traugott, 'that when one is conscious of possessing true genius, a true inclination for art, one would then pursue no other business.'

'You mean become an artist,' the nephew replied. 'Oh, how can you say that? You see, my dear fellow, I have reflected more on these matters perhaps than many another, more indeed than many who count as noteworthy connoisseurs of art; I have delved into the nature of the thing more deeply than I am able to say; I can at this moment give you only the merest hint of it.' The nephew looked so learned and profound as he said these words that Traugott began to feel a genuine reverence for him. 'You will admit that I am right', the nephew went on, after taking a pinch of snuff and sneezing twice, 'to say that art wreathes flowers into our life – a sense of cheerfulness, a refreshment after serious business is done; *that* is the goal of all artistic endeavour, and the better the product the more completely is this goal attained. Life itself teaches us this lesson: only he who practises art with this goal in view will enjoy that ease and comfort which eludes him who, in oppugnancy to the true nature of the thing, sees in art the chief aim, the highest occupation of life. So, my dear fellow, do not take my uncle's suggestion to heart and desert the really serious business of life for an activity which, without some other support, can only totter about like a child that has not yet learned to walk.'

Here the nephew ceased, as if he anticipated some reply from Traugott; the latter, however, knew not what he should say, for all the nephew had said seemed to him indescribably silly. He therefore contented himself with asking: 'What, then, do you regard as the really serious business of life?'

The nephew seemed taken aback. 'Well, my goodness,' he finally exclaimed, 'you will allow that in life you have to live, which the artist by profession, oppressed as he is by want, almost never manages to do.'

He then proceeded to babble on at random, in affected words and phrases, and from out of this it emerged that by 'living' he meant no more than having plenty of money and no debts, eating and drinking well, possessing a pretty wife and well-behaved children whose Sunday clothes were never dirtied, and such things as that. Traugott listened with a feeling that he was about to choke, and he was glad when he had seen the last of the reasonable nephew and found himself alone again in his room.

'What a miserable life I lead!' he said to himself. 'It is a lovely morning in golden springtime, the gentle west wind is bringing even to the dismal city streets an air and breath of the woods and fields – and what am I doing? Dragging myself to Herr Roos's reeky office, where pallid faces sit before great shapeless desks and only the rustling of ledgers and the clatter of money being counted disturbs the gloomy silence in which all are sunk in work. And what work! What is all the cogitation and all the scribbling intended to achieve? Only the acquisition of more and more money for the cashbox, only the greater splendour of Fafner's baleful hoard! But how an artist such as I longs to leave the city and with head held high breathe in all the reviving odours of spring, so that his imagination is ignited and the liveliest pictures come into being within him! And then there emerge from the dark undergrowth all around those wonderful figures his spirit has created and which are his own – for in him there dwells the mysterious magic of light, colour, form, so that what his inner eye has seen he is able to hold and fix by giving it palpable shape.

'What stops me from tearing myself away from this hated way of life? The strange old man confirmed in me the knowledge that I am called to be an artist, but the fair youth with him did so even more: though he spoke not a word, yet his eyes seemed to tell me what for so long has lain crushed by a thousand doubts within me. Can I not put aside my present wretched existence and instead become a painter?'

Traugott fetched out everything he had ever drawn and inspected it. Much of what he saw now looked different – it looked, indeed, better than it had. What struck him most, however, was a drawing he had done in early boyhood which showed, in faltering but nonetheless recognizable outline, the old *Bürgermeister* and his beautiful page. He recalled very well how even in those days the figures had exercised a strange fascination, and how one evening he had been led as if by an irresistible force away from his games into the Artushof, where he had tried diligently to copy the picture. Gazing upon this drawing, Traugott was seized by the profoundest sense of sadness and longing! Normally he would have gone to the office for a couple more hours of work, but he found that impossible now, and instead he went to the Karlsberg. From there he gazed out over the surging sea: in the clouds of grey mist which had settled in strange forms and shapes over Hela, he endeavoured to descry, as in a magic mirror, the destiny awaiting him.

Do you believe, dear reader, that whatever descends to us from the higher realm of love must first reveal itself to us in an aura of hopelessness and pain, like the doubt that assails the heart of the artist? The lover beholds the ideal and feels he is powerless to grasp it – he sees it flee away and believes he will never recover it. But then a divine courage is restored to him; he struggles, he wrestles, and despair is dissolved in sweet desire: he acquires the strength to aspire to his beloved, he sees her draw closer and closer – though never, never does he attain her. Traugott was now seized with great force by just this same hopelessness and pain. When early the next morning he saw again his drawings, which still lay on the table, everything he had done seemed to him paltry and childish, and there came into his mind the words of an artistically gifted friend who had often told him that great mischief could be caused in the realm of art through mistaking a strong external stimulus for a true inner calling. Traugott was not a little inclined to regard the Artushof, with its strange figures of the old man and the youth, as just such an external stimulus; and he therefore condemned himself to a return to Herr Roos's office, where he worked on in disregard of the loathing which so often overcame him that he was frequently obliged to reckon up quickly and rush out into the fresh air. Herr Roos sympathetically ascribed this to a sickliness which seemed to him to have invaded the deathly pale youth.

Time had gone by and Blackfriars Fair had arrived, at the end of which Traugott was to wed Christina and, as Herr Roos's full partner, to enter formally into the world of commerce. These events would mean to him a farewell to all his hopes and dreams, and his heart sank as he beheld Christina in a whirlwind of domestic activity.

One day, he was standing among the thickest of the throng in the Artushof when he heard close behind him a voice whose familiar sound penetrated right to his heart. 'Are these bonds really worth so little?' the voice said.

Traugott spun round, and saw, as he had expected, the strange old man, who was speaking to a broker and trying to sell him a bond whose value had at that moment sunk very low. The fair youth was standing behind the old man, and he threw a friendly if melancholy glance in Traugott's direction. The latter quickly strode up to the old man and said: 'Excuse me, dear sir, but the bond you want to sell is worth no more than you have been told; but its value will quite certainly increase in a few days' time. If you will take my advice you will retain it now and dispose of it later.'

'Indeed, dear sir,' the old man replied with some acerbity, 'and what business is it of yours? Are you aware that a simple bond is at the moment quite useless to me, but ready money, on the contrary, an extreme necessity?'

Not a little disconcerted that the old man should have taken his friendly intervention so ill, Traugott was already on the point of departing when the youth, with tears in his eyes, cast a pleading glance upon him. 'I meant well, dear sir,' he quickly replied to the old man, 'and I still cannot allow you to sustain such a heavy loss. Sell me the bond, on the condition that I shall afterwards make up the price to the higher value which it will possess in a couple of days.'

'You are a strange fellow,' the old man said. 'Let it be so, then – though I cannot see why you should want to load me with wealth.'

As he spoke these words he cast a twinkling glance at the youth, who in turn lowered his lovely blue eyes modestly to the floor; both then followed Traugott to the office, where the money was counted out and handed to the old man, who, glowering darkly, put it into his purse. While this was taking place, the youth said softly to Traugott: 'Are you not the same person who several weeks ago was drawing such pretty figures in the Artushof?'

'That is so,' Traugott replied, the recollection of the ludicrous episode of the letter of advice sending the blood to his face.

'Oh, in that case,' the youth went on, 'none of this surprises me.' The old man glanced angrily at him and he fell silent.

Traugott could not help feeling a certain tightening of the heart in the presence of these two strange beings, and thus he let them go without having had the courage to inquire of them anything more as to where and how they lived. Their appearance was, indeed, sufficiently astonishing to arouse wonderment even in the personnel of the office. The morose book-keeper had stuck his pen behind his ear and, with hands clasped behind his head, sat staring at the old man. 'God help me,' he said when the strangers had gone, 'but he looks, with his curly beard and his black cloak, like a picture from St Johannis church, dated about fourteen hundred!' Herr Roos, however, blind, it seems, to the old man's noble bearing and the old German cast of his features, set him down definitely for a Polish Jew and cried with a smirk: 'Stupid animal! He sells now and in a week's time he could get at least ten per cent more!'

In mitigation of this remark it should be said that Herr Roos knew nothing of the private agreement Traugott had made with the old man – an agreement which, when he met him at the Artushof in the company of the youth a few days later, he proceeded to carry into effect.

'My son', the old man said, 'has reminded me that you are also an artist, and I shall therefore accept what I should otherwise have refused' – and he pocketed the money.

They were standing beside one of the four granite pillars which supported the roof of the building and close in front of the painted figures which Traugott had reproduced on his letter of advice; he now spoke unreservedly of the great similarity between these figures and those of the old man and the youth. The old man smiled a very strange smile, laid his hand on Traugott's shoulders, and said softly and with an air of circumspection: 'You do not know then, that I am the German painter Godofredus Berklinger, and that the figures you seem so much to admire were painted by me a long time ago when I was still a pupil? In the *Bürgermeister* I set down a memorial of myself, and that the page who leads his horse is my son you can easily see for yourself if you compare their forms and faces.'

Traugott was struck dumb with amazement; he quickly realized, however, that if the old man believed he had painted a picture which was at least 200 years old he must be the victim of a peculiar form of lunacy.

'It was in general a glorious and flourishing age of art,' the old man went on, raising his head and gazing around with an expression of pride, 'that age in which, in honour of the wise King Arthur and his Round Table, I decorated this hall with all these pictures. I believe it was the king himself – he looked very majestic – who once came to me as I was working here and exhorted me to the attainment of that mastery of which I did not yet have the command.'

'My father, sir,' the youth volunteered, 'is an artist of a rare kind, and you would not regret it if he granted you the privilege of seeing his work.'

The old man had been pacing the now empty hall, and he indicated to the youth that they ought to be going, whereupon Traugott asked him if he would show him his paintings. The old man looked at him penetratingly and at length replied in a very earnest tone: 'It is indeed somewhat rash of you to seek to enter the innermost sanctum even before your apprenticeship has begun. Yet – so be it! You may still be too purblind to see anything, yet you will at least sense something! Come to me tomorrow morning.'

He gave directions as to where he lived, and Traugott did not fail to keep his appointment the next day: freeing himself from the office as early as he could, he hurried to the distant street where the old man lived; the door was opened by the son, who was clad entirely in old German garb and who led him into a spacious room, in the middle of which the old man was sitting on a little footstool in front of a large canvas.

'You have come at a happy hour, dear sir,' the old man cried to him; 'I have just given the final touches to the large picture you see there, which has occupied me for more than a year and has cost me no little labour. It is the companion piece to an equally large picture representing Paradise Lost, which I completed last year and which you can also view. This, as you see, is Paradise Regained, and I should be much disappointed in you if you sought to extract some sort of allegory out of it. Only bad and bungling painters paint allegorical pictures; my picture is intended not to *signify* anything, but to *be*. Observe all these people, animals, these groups of fruit and flowers, these rocks, and see how they form a harmonious whole, how they create together a pure and heavenly chord, the music of eternal transfiguration.'

The old man then proceeded to extract individual groups and to draw Traugott's attention to the mysterious division of light and shade; to the varied glitter of flowers and metals; to the strange figures which, ascending from the calyxes of lilies, entwined themselves into the dance of divine youths and maidens; to the bearded men who, vigorous and youthful in eye and gesture, seemed to be conversing with all kinds of curious animals. His voice grew more and more forceful, yet at the same time what he said grew more and more incomprehensible and confused.

'Let your diamond crown shine forth, O exalted ancient!' he cried at last, his blazing eyes riveted to the canvas. 'Throw off the veil of Isis you draped upon your head when the unclean approached you! Why do you clasp your dark cloak so closely about you? I want to see your heart – it is the philosopher's stone, before which the Mystery stands revealed! Art thou then not I myself? Why do you appear so impudently, so valiantly, before me? Would you struggle against your master? Come on, then! Step forth! . . . I created you . . . for I am . . .' And with that the old man suddenly collapsed as if struck by lightning. Traugott lifted him up, the youth quickly fetched a small armchair, and they put the old man into it. He seemed to be sleeping peacefully.

'You now know', the youth said softly, 'what my good old father is like. A hard fate robbed him of all his powers, and for many years he has been dead to that art for which he once lived. He sits for whole days before the canvas, staring fixedly at it; this he calls painting, and into what exalted a condition he is transported by describing such a painting you have yourself just witnessed. It may help you to recover from this strange scene if you follow me into the next room, where you will find many paintings done by my father in earlier, more fruitful years.'

Traugott was astonished to find in the next room a row of pictures which might have been painted by the most celebrated of the Dutch masters: frequently representing scenes from life – a party returning from the hunt, engaged in singing and music, and so forth – they nonetheless breathed an air of profound seriousness, and the heads especially were of a quite exceptional strength and lifelikeness. Traugott was in the act of returning to the front room when he beheld close to the door a picture which transfixed him to the spot: it was a beautiful girl in old German costume, but her face was the face of the youth, only fuller and more highly coloured; and the figure appeared to be bigger than he. A shudder of unnamable delight trembled through Traugott at the sight of this wonderful woman: in force and truth to life it resembled a Van Dyck; the dark eyes gazed down at him full of desire; the sweet lips seemed to be opened in speech.

'My God,' Traugott sighed from the depths of his heart, 'where . . . where can I find her?'

'Let us go,' said the youth; then Traugott, as if in the grip of madness, cried: 'It is she, my soul's beloved! Where . . . where is she?'

Tears came into the eyes of young Berklinger and flowed down his cheeks; he seemed to be transfused with grief, and it was with an effort that he pulled himself together. 'Come along,' he said at last in a firm voice; 'the portrait is of my unhappy sister, Felizitas. She is gone forever! You will never see her!'

Almost bereft of his senses, Traugott allowed himself to be led into the other room. The old man was still lying asleep; suddenly, however, he leaped up, gazed at Traugott with eyes blazing in anger, and cried: 'What do you want? What do you want, sir?'

The youth went up to him and reminded him that he had just shown Traugott his new picture. At this, Berklinger seemed to recall everything, softened visibly, and said in a subdued voice: 'Forgive an old man such forgetfulness, my dear sir.'

'Your new picture, Master Berklinger, is altogether marvellous,' Traugott now put in; 'I have never seen anything like it; but much study and much labour must be needed before one can paint like that. I feel within me a great irresistible urge towards art, and I beg of you, my dear Master, to accept me as your industrious pupil.'

The old man became quite amicable and cheerful, embraced Traugott and promised him he would be his faithful teacher.

So it came about that Traugott went every day to the old painter and made great progress in the art of painting; his life at the office he now found wholly insupportable, and he neglected his work to such an extent that Herr Roos complained loudly and was in the end glad to see him stay away altogether, which he did under the pretext of suffering from a creeping sickness he could not shake off. As a result, the wedding was, to Christina's intense annoyance, postponed indefinitely.

'Your Herr Traugott,' a business acquaintance said to Herr Roos, 'seems to be labouring under an inner vexation, perhaps an old debt of the heart which he would like to liquidate before venturing on marriage. He looks quite pale and bewildered.'

'Well, and why not?' replied Herr Elias. 'I wonder,' he added after a pause, 'whether the roguish Christina has been playing tricks on him. The book-keeper is an enamoured ass and is always kissing and pressing her hands. Traugott is devilishly in love with my girl, that I know. Is there any jealousy there? I will sound him out.'

But carefully though Herr Roos sounded Traugott out, he failed to learn anything of value and said to his business acquaintances: 'He is a singular fellow, Traugott; but you just have to let him go his own way. If he didn't have fifty thousand thalers in my business, I know what *I* would do, since *he* no longer does anything.'

Traugott would now have been leading a truly sunny existence in the realm of art if his heart had not been torn by his burning love for the beautiful Felizitas, whose features he often beheld in delirious dreams. Her portrait had vanished: the old man had removed it, and Traugott dared not ask after it for fear of bringing on an outburst of wrath. In all other respects, however, the aged Berklinger had become more and more friendly, and instead of payment for his instruction he suffered Traugott to effect manifold improvements to his pitiful household. Through young Berklinger, Traugott learned that the old man was much in arrears with payments for a small cabinet he was buying, and that the bond he had exchanged constituted, not only the balance of the payments, but the entirety of their wealth. Only rarely could Traugott converse privately with the youth: the old man kept watch over him to an extraordinary extent and rebuked him sternly whenever it looked as if he were about to go off alone with Traugott. The latter found this all the more painful in that he was now thoroughly enamoured of the youth on account of the striking similarity he bore to Felizitas: it often seemed to him, indeed, as though the beloved portrait was standing vividly beside him and that he could feel its sweet loving breath, and then he would have liked to have pressed the youth to his glowing breast as if he were the beloved Felizitas herself.

Winter had departed; sweet spring was already blossoming in field and woodland. Herr Elias Roos advised Traugott to undertake a cure: a course of mineral waters or a diet of whey. Christina was again looking forward to the wedding, even though Traugott rarely put in an appearance and thought of their relationship even more rarely.

One day Traugott had been detained at the office with an account that absolutely had to be balanced, and it was not until evening was drawing on that he was able to escape to Berklinger's distant dwelling. On his arrival, he found the front room empty but heard the sound of a lute coming from the neighbouring room. It was an instrument he had never heard in the house before. He listened – a broken song crept through the chords like a gentle sigh. He pushed open the door – Heavens! With its back towards him there sat a female figure dressed in the old German mode, with a high lace collar, exactly like the figure in the portrait! At the sound of Traugott entering, the figure rose, put the lute down on the table and turned around. It was she!

'Felizitas!' Traugott exclaimed in delight, and was about to throw himself on his knees before the divine apparition when he felt himself seized violently by the collar and dragged out of the room.

'Wretch! Incomparable villain!' Berklinger screamed as he thrust Traugott along. 'Was that your love of art? You want to murder me!' – and with that he threw him from the house. A knife flashed in his hand; Traugott fled down the steps and, confused and half-mad with joy and horror, raced back home.

Sleepless he tossed back and forth on his bed. 'Felizitas! Felizitas!' he cried again and again, rent with pain and the torments of love. 'You are there, you are there, and may I not see you, may I not take you in my arms? You love me, ah, I know it! In the pain that pierces my heart so mortally I feel that you love me.'

Bright shone the springtime sun into Traugott's room, and he pulled himself together and resolved that, whatever the cost, he would fathom the mystery of Berklinger's house. He quickly hurried to the old man's – and was much taken aback when he beheld all the windows open and maids busy cleaning the rooms. His presentiment as to what had happened proved correct: Berklinger had left the house late the previous evening with his son and gone away, none knew whither. A cart drawn by two horses had removed a chest containing the paintings and the two small cases that contained all Berklinger's pitifully few possessions; he himself had left with his son half-an-hour afterwards. All inquiries as to where they could be proved fruitless; no carrier had rented cart and horses to such persons as Traugott described; even at the town-gates he could learn nothing definite – in short, Berklinger had vanished as if borne away on the cloak of Mephistopheles. In a torment of despair, Traugott ran back home.

'She has gone, she has gone, my soul's beloved – all, all is lost!' he cried, rushing past Herr Elias Roos, who happened to be standing in the doorway, and hurling himself into his room.

'God of heaven and earth!' cried Herr Roos, tugging at his wig; and again, so that the whole house resounded: 'Christina! Christina! – detestable person, misbegotten daughter!'

The office staff came running out with expressions of shocked alarm, and the book-keeper exclaimed in dismay: 'But Herr Roos!' The latter continued to cry without pausing: 'Christina! Christina!'

Mamsell Christina came in through the front door and, commencing to remove the wide-brimmed straw hat she was wearing, inquired with a smile why her dear father was bellowing in such a fashion.

'I will not stand this useless running away!' Herr Roos let fly at her. 'My son-in-law is a melancholy man and in jealousy a Turk. Stay indoors or there will be more trouble. He is in there now, howling and growling over his vagabond bride.'

Christina turned to the book-keeper with a look of

amazement; the latter, however, cast a meaningful glance into the office at Herr Roos's drinks-cabinet and said as he made off: 'Go in and console your bridegroom.' Christina repaired to her room, where she changed her clothes, distributed the linen, discussed with the cook the details of the Sunday dinner and heard from her some of the latest tidbits of news of the town, and then she went off to see what was ailing her bridegroom.

You know, dear reader, that in Traugott's position we all have to pass through certain definite stages and that there is no way of avoiding it. Despair was succeeded by a stage of dull brooding lethargy in which the crisis of his condition occurred, and this passed over into a stage of less intense agony in which nature could apply her healing balm. It was while he was in this last stage that Traugott was sitting a few days later on the Karlsberg and again gazing out at the waves of the sea and into the grey bank of mist lying over Hela, but now he had no desire to espy in them the fate that awaited him in the days ahead; all he had hoped for, all he had dreamed of, had vanished.

'Alas,' he said, 'my artistic calling was a bitter, bitter deception; it never existed except in the crazy fantasies of a fever patient; Felizitas was the phantom which lured me into believing in its reality. It is over! . . . I yield! . . . Back to prison! . . . It is decided!'

Traugott laboured again in the office and a new date was fixed for his wedding to Christina. On the eve of that day he was standing in the Artushof, and was gazing with heart-rending sadness at the fateful figures of the old *Bürgermeister* and his page, when his eye was caught by the broker to whom Berklinger had once sought to sell his bond. Without thinking, almost without realizing what he was doing, Traugott went up to him and asked: 'You remember the strange old man with the black curly beard who used to appear here in the company of a handsome youth – did you know them?'

'How should I not?' the broker replied. 'That was the crazy old painter Gottfried Berklinger.'

'Do you know where he is, where he is staying, at this moment?' Traugott asked further.

'How should I not?' the broker replied. 'For some time now he has been staying quietly with his daughter in Sorrento.'

'With his daughter Felizitas?' Traugott exclaimed so loudly and vehemently that everyone turned and looked at him.

'Quite so,' the broker answered calmly; 'she was the handsome youth who was always following the old man around. Half Danzig knew it was a girl, though the crazy old man believed no one would be able to guess it. It was prophesied to him that if his daughter contracted a love match he would thereupon die a shameful death, so he tried to prevent anyone knowing of her existence, and brought her up as his son.'

Traugott stood benumbed by this information, then ran out, through the streets and the town-gate, into the fields beyond, wailing loudly: 'O unhappy man! Unhappy man! It was she, it was she herself – I have sat beside her a thousand times, felt her sweet breath, pressed her tender hands, gazed into her eyes, listened to her sweet speech – and now she is lost! No! Not lost! I shall follow her into the land of art – fate has given me a sign! Away, away to Sorrento!'

He ran back home; there he encountered Herr Elias, seized him, and drew him forcibly into his room. 'I shall never marry Christina,' he cried; 'she looks like the *Voluptas*, and the *Luxurias*, and has hair like the *Ira* – in the picture in the Artushof. O Felizitas, Felizitas! Gentle beloved! How you reach out your arms to me in longing! I am coming! I am coming! – And let me tell you, Elias,' he went on, again seizing the merchant, who had become extremely pale, 'you will never see me again in your accursed office. What have your confounded ledgers and daybooks to do with me? I am a painter, and a good one; Berklinger is my master, my father, my everything, and you are nothing, nothing whatever!'

And with that he shook Herr Elias violently, and the latter cried at the top of his voice: 'Help! Help! Assist me! Help! My son-in-law has gone mad! my partner is raving! Help, help!'

Everyone came running out of the office; Traugott released Herr Elias and sank back exhausted into a chair. They all pressed round him; then he suddenly sprang up and, gazing wildly about him, cried: 'What do you want?' – whereupon they all ran out of the house, Herr Elias in the midst of them. Soon there came from without a sound as of the rustling of silk, and a voice asked: 'Have you really gone mad, dear Herr Traugott, or are you only playing?' It was Christina.

'I have certainly not gone mad, dear angel,' Traugott replied, 'but neither am I playing. Calm yourself, my dear: there will be no wedding tomorrow, or any other day. I shall not marry you, not now or ever.'

'That doesn't bother me in the slightest,' Christina replied calmly. 'I haven't liked you much for some time, and there are some people who wouldn't be so very delighted if pretty, wealthy Mamsell Christina were to become your bride! Adieu!' – and with that she rustled away.

'She means the book-keeper,' thought Traugott. Grown calmer now, he betook himself to Herr Elias and explained to him, briefly but conclusively, that he was of no use to him either as son-in-law or as business partner. Herr Elias agreed entirely; and sitting in his office he joyfully protested again and again that he thanked God he was done with the crazy Herr Traugott, who was now far away – far, far away from Danzig.

Life took on a wonderful new meaning for Traugott when he at last found himself in the land he had so long desired to visit. The German artists living in Rome accepted him into their circle, and it so happened that he remained there longer than seemed consistent with the desire to find Felizitas which had hitherto been propelling him on. But this desire had, in fact, grown somewhat cooler: he was now aware of it rather as a beautiful dream which permeated all his life, so that he felt that all he did, the practice of his art, was devoted to a higher, unearthly realm of things of which he had only a blissful presentiment. Every female figure he created bore a likeness to the lovely Felizitas. The young painters he was associating with were not a little struck by the wonderful countenance whose original they sought in vain in all Rome, and they assailed Traugott with a thousand questions as to where he had seen this beauty. Traugott drew back from narrating the strange experiences he had had in Danzig; until, when he had been in Rome for several months, an old friend from Königsberg named Matuszewski, who was also devoting himself wholly to painting, one day joyfully announced that he had seen the girl whom Traugott reproduced in all his pictures, and had seen her in Rome. Traugott's delight may be imagined, and, concealing no longer what it was that had drawn him so mightily towards art and so irresistibly to Italy, he told them everything that had passed, and they found the adventure so strange and fascinating they promised not to rest until they had discovered the whereabouts of Traugott's lost love.

Matuszewski's efforts were the most successful, and he soon unearthed where the girl lived; he learned, moreover, that she was in reality the daughter of a poor painter who was at that time engaged in daubing the walls of the Trinità del Monte church. Traugott at once hurried with him to the church, and was convinced that the painter he saw there standing on a very high scaffold was indeed old Berklinger. Unnoticed by the painter, the two then left the building and made for his house.

'It is she!' Traugott cried when he beheld the painter's daughter. She was standing on the balcony engaged in some domestic work or other. 'Felizitas!' he exclaimed, 'My Felizitas!' – and rushed into the room. The girl looked at him in horror. She possessed the features of Felizitas, but it was not she. Bitter disappointment pierced poor Traugott's wounded heart as if with a thousand daggers.

In a few words, Matuszewski explained everything. With cheeks flushed and eyes downcast in embarrassment, the girl presented a lovely picture to behold; and Traugott, who had at first wanted to depart as quickly as he could, remained standing where he was as if constrained by gentle bonds. His friend well knew how to chatter with Dorina in a pleasant way and so reduce the tension their extraordinary entry had caused. Dorina raised 'the fringèd curtains of her eyes' and regarded the strangers with a smile as she told them that her father would soon be home and would be delighted to find that two German artists, for whom he had a great regard, were paying him a visit. Traugott had to admit that, except for Felizitas, no girl had ever inwardly excited him so much as did Dorina. She was, indeed, almost Felizitas herself, only her features were stronger and more clearly defined, and her hair was darker. It was the same picture, painted first by Raphael, then by Rubens.

It was not long before the old man came in, and Traugott could then see that the height of the scaffold on which he had been standing in the church had been very deceptive: this aged painter was, unlike the vigorous Berklinger, diminutive, and wasted and disheartened by poverty. A black shadow falling across his clean-shaven face had bestowed upon it Berklinger's curly black beard. As they talked together, the old man proved to possess a thorough practical knowledge of the art of painting, and Traugott resolved to continue an acquaintance which, though it had begun so painfully, now promised to become more and more pleasant and beneficial. Dorina, the very image of innocence and charm, did not conceal that she felt drawn to the young German painter, and Traugott joyfully reciprocated; soon he was on such familiar terms with this lovely girl of fifteen that he found himself spending whole days in the company of the little family, at length transferred his studio to the spacious room that stood empty next to their house, and finally moved in with them. Thus in an inconspicuous way he effected improvements to their pitiable condition, and the old man was obliged to think that Traugott was going to marry Dorina – a thought which he frankly declared to him. Traugott was not a little taken aback, for it was only then that he realized clearly what had become of the goal of his journey to Italy. Felizitas appeared visibly before him, yet it seemed to him he could not desert Dorina.

In a strange way he found himself quite unable to imagine his vanished love as his wife. Felizitas was an image in his mind which he could never lose, yet never win: he imagined her dwelling with him for ever in spirit; he could never imagine possessing her physically. But he often thought of Dorina as his dear wife, and then a shudder of sweet desire passed through him, a gentle glow diffused itself within him – and yet it seemed that to let himself be fastened with indissoluble bonds would be a betrayal of his first love. Thus did the most conflicting feelings fight back and forth in Traugott's soul: he could come to no final decision, and he took to avoiding the old man. The latter, however, conceived the idea that Traugott was bent on robbing him of his beloved child, and so he came to speak of their marriage as of something fixed and definite – only thus could he bring himself to tolerate the intimate relationship which had developed between them and which would, on any other supposition, have brought ill-fame upon Dorina. His Italian blood surged up in him, and one day he declared to Traugott

without circumlocution that he must either agree to marry
Dorina or leave his house – that he would continue to
tolerate the state of affairs obtaining for not so much as
another hour. Traugott was seized by the greatest
annoyance and vexation: the old man appeared to him no
better than a common procurer, his own behaviour
seemed to him contemptible, his desertion of Felizitas
sinful and repulsive. It rent his heart to say farewell to
Dorina, but he steeled himself to break free from these
sweet bonds, and hurried away to Naples and to Sorrento.

He searched for Berklinger and Felizitas for a year, but
searched in vain: no one knew anything of them. A distant
suggestion, founded on nothing more substantial than a
legend, that an aged German painter had been seen in
Sorrento several years before, was all he acquired. He was
as if tossed back and forth on a stormy sea; at length,
however, he remained in Naples, and the more industriously he applied himself to his art, the more the desire
for Felizitas waned in his breast. But whenever he saw a
girl whose form or gait or bearing resembled those of
Dorina, even if in only the most distant way, he felt very
painfully the loss of the dear child. But Dorina's image
never appeared to him while he was painting – then it was
the image of Felizitas that stood before him as his constant
ideal.

At long last letters arrived from Danzig. Herr Elias
Roos, so the firm's representative reported, had departed
this life, and Traugott's presence was required so that he
might come to an agreement with the book-keeper, who
had married Mamsell Christina and taken over the business.

He stood again in the Artushof beside the granite pillar,
facing the *Bürgermeister* and his page, and thought about
the strange adventure which had obtruded itself so painfully into his life; in a mood of profound and hopeless sadness

he gazed at the youth, who seemed to be gazing back at him and to be whispering softly: 'So you were unable to get free of me!'

'Do I see aright? Are you really back again, honoured sir, fit and well, recovered from your evil melancholy?' – it was the familiar broker who spoke these words. He was standing close beside Traugott.

'I did not find them,' Traugott said involuntarily.

'Whom did you not find, honoured sir?' the broker inquired.

'The painter Godofredus Berklinger, and his daughter, Felizitas,' Traugott replied. 'I looked for them all over Italy; in Sorrento no one knew anything of them.'

At that, the broker stared at him with eyes amazed, and stammered: 'Where did your honour look for the painter and his Felizitas? In Italy? In Naples? In Sorrento?'

'Yes, there, to be sure!' Traugott cried in annoyance.

At that, however, the broker beat his hands together time and again, and cried as he did so: 'Oh my goodness! Oh my dear goodness! Herr Traugott, Herr Traugott!'

'What is so remarkable in that?' Traugott said. 'Cease these antics! For the sake of one's beloved one might well travel to Sorrento. Yes! I loved Felizitas and I went after her.'

But the broker continued to hop about and cry: 'Oh my goodness! Oh my goodness!' until Traugott took hold of him and with a stern face asked him: 'What is it you find so peculiar? For Heaven's sake, tell me!'

'But Herr Traugott,' the broker at last managed to bring forth, 'do you not know that our revered senator and guild chairman, Herr Aloysius Brandstetter, has a little villa, at the foot of the Karlsberg towards Conrad's Hammer, and that he calls it Sorrento? He bought Berklinger's pictures from him and took him and his daughter into his house – the one he calls Sorrento. They lived there for years, and if you had stood on the Karlsberg, my honoured sir, you could have looked down into their garden and seen Mamsell Felizitas strolling about in it, wearing the same ancient German dress you can see in these pictures here. You didn't have to go all the way to Italy. Afterwards, the old man . . . but it is a sad story.'

'Tell it,' said Traugott in a dull voice.

'Well,' the broker went on, 'young Brandstetter returned from England, saw Mamsell Felizitas, and fell in love with her. He surprised her in the garden, fell on both knees before her as they do in novels, and swore he wanted to marry her and free her from the tyranny of her father. The old man was standing, unseen by these young people, close behind them, and at the moment when Felizitas said: "I will be yours," he fell down with a dull cry and was as dead as a doornail. He is said to have looked very unpleasant – all blue and bloody; an artery had burst, no one knew why. After this, Mamsell Felizitas could no longer endure young Brandstetter, and in the end she married the lawyer, Hofrat Mathesius, from Marienwerder. Your honour can pay Frau Mathesius a visit for old times' sake: Marienwerder isn't far – not as far as Sorrento. The dear lady is said to be enjoying life and to have put a number of children into circulation.'

Traugott left the Artushof silent and benumbed. That his adventure should have had such an outcome filled him with horror. 'No, it is not she,' he cried, 'it is not she – not Felizitas, the heavenly image who ignited an unending longing in my heart, whom I pursued to a distant land, whom I saw always before me as my gleaming, beaming star of hope! Felizitas! Frau Mathesius! Ha, ha, ha! Frau Mathesius!'

Distracted by misery, Traugott laughed aloud and ran, as before, out of the town to the Karlsberg. He gazed down on Sorrento and tears welled from his eyes.

'O you eternal powers,' he cried, 'how deeply, incurably, you wound with your bitter mockery the tender breast of poor man! But no! Why does the foolish child complain of the pain it feels, if it puts its hands into the flames instead of enjoying their light and warmth? Fate came to me visibly, but my dull eyes failed to recognize a higher being: I thought in my presumption that what the ancient master had created had come, miraculously awakened, into life, and was a being such as I, and that I could draw it down into the wretched existence of the everyday world. No, no, Felizitas, I have never lost you, you will always be mine, for you yourself are the creative art which lives within me. Now, only now, do I know you as you are! What have you, what have I to do with Frau Mathesius? Nothing at all, I think!'

'I too cannot imagine what you have to do with the lady,' a voice interrupted at this point.

Traugott awoke as if from a dream: he found himself – how he got there he did not know – back in the Artushof and leaning against the granite pillar. It was Christina's husband who had addressed him. He handed Traugott a letter that had just arrived from Rome. Matuszewski had written:

Dorina is prettier and more charming than ever, only she is pale with longing for you, dear friend! She expects you hourly – for she is convinced to her very soul that you would never be capable of leaving her. She loves you deeply. When will you be with us again?

'I am very glad', Traugott said, after he had read the letter to Christina's husband, 'that we settled our affairs today, for tomorrow I am going to Rome, where a beloved bride is longing to see me.'

COUNCILLOR KRESPEL

The man I wish to speak of is none other than Councillor Krespel of H. . . This Councillor Krespel was one of the most astonishing people I have ever met in my life. When I went to H. . . the whole town was talking about him, for one of the maddest of all his mad tricks was at just that moment in full flower. Krespel was celebrated as a learned and skilful lawyer and a dextrous diplomat; a German prince – not a particularly significant one – had employed him in the acquisition of a piece of territory and had sought to reward him for his signal success in this transaction; and since Krespel had often complained that he had never been able to find a house comfortable enough for him, this prince had undertaken to meet the cost of one, which Krespel could have constructed entirely as he wished. The prince also wanted to buy for him the land on which the house was to stand, but Krespel preferred to build it in his own garden, which lay outside the town-gate in one of the fairest spots in the region. He purchased all the materials he could possibly need and had them brought out; and he was then to be seen in his peculiar garb (he had made it himself according to principles of his own) busying himself in sifting sand, slaking lime, piling up bricks and so forth. He had as yet not spoken with a builder or drawn up any plan or design. Then, one fine day, he went along to an excellent master-mason in H. . . and asked him to proceed to his garden the following morning with all his workmen and apprentices, under-workmen and handy-men, and to start building his house. The mason naturally asked for the architect's drawings and was not a little taken aback when Krespel replied that there was no need at all for such things and that all would go just as it ought to without them. When the mason and his men arrived they found in the garden a square trench, and Krespel said: 'Here is where the foundations of my house are to be laid; when that's done, I want you to start building the walls and to go on until I say: That's high enough.'

'Without doors or windows? Without cross-walls?' the mason interrupted, as though astounded at Krespel's madness.

'Just as I have told you, my good man,' Krespel replied with composure. 'We shall then see about all the rest.'

Only the promise of an ample fee could move the mason to undertake the senseless construction; but once it was begun no building work ever went forward more merrily: Krespel provided food and drink in abundance and the workmen never left the site as, to the accompaniment of their ceaseless laughter, the four walls rose into the heights with inconceivable rapidity, until one day Krespel cried: 'Stop!' Then trowel and hammer fell silent, the workmen descended from the scaffolding and, as they crowded around Krespel, there spoke from every laughing face the question: 'What now?'

'Make way!' Krespel cried; he ran to one end of his garden and then slowly paced towards his square of walls; when he had reached it, he shook his head in dissatisfaction, ran to the other end of the garden, again paced towards the square and did the same as before. He repeated this performance several times, until finally, with his sharp nose jabbing against the wall, he cried loudly: 'Come along, come along! Knock it in here, knock a door in here!' He gave them the height and width to the exact inch, and it took place as he had commanded.

Then he walked inside the walls and smiled complacently when the master-mason remarked that they were exactly the right height for an excellent two-storey house. Krespel paced thoughtfully around, the masons following him with hammer and mattock, and whenever he cried: 'Here a window, six feet high, four feet wide! There a small window, three feet high, two feet wide!' the required window-space was at once knocked through the wall.

It was while this operation was in progress that I came to H. . ., and it was highly amusing to see hundreds of people standing all around the garden and raising a loud cheer every time the bricks flew out and a new window appeared where you would least expect it to. The rest of the house was handled in the same way: Krespel gave the order and the work was done there and then. The comicality of the whole proceeding, the firm conviction that in the end everything would turn out better than could have been expected and, most of all, Krespel's generosity – which cost him nothing, to be sure – kept everyone in a good mood. The difficulties which this peculiar mode of construction could not fail to produce were thus overcome, and after a short while a completed house stood there: from the outside it possessed the craziest appearance, since none of the windows, for instance, was of the same size or shape as any other, but once inside you were filled with a quite unexampled sense of wellbeing and comfort. I myself experienced this when, after I had got to know him better, Krespel invited me in. For until then I had not so much as spoken to him: the building work kept him so busy he had ceased to come to lunch with Professor M. . . on Tuesdays, as had hitherto been his wont, saying that until his house was finally dedicated he would take not one step outside it. All his friends and acquaintances were looking forward to a mighty banquet, but Krespel invited only the master-builders, apprentices, workmen and under-workmen who had built the house. The feast was of the finest, and afterwards the wives and daughters came and a grand ball began. Krespel waltzed a little with the wives of the master-builders; then, however, he turned to the town musicians, seized a violin and conducted the music until dawn.

On the Tuesday following the festival I was delighted finally to encounter him at the home of Professor M. . . Krespel's demeanour was stranger than anything that could be invented. Stiff and awkward of movement, he gave the impression that at any moment he was going to bump against or damage something; but nothing of the sort happened, and you soon realized that nothing of the sort was going to happen, for the lady of the house maintained a perfect composure as he stumbled and stamped around the crockery-laden table, manoeuvered himself towards the floor-length mirror and even took up a painted porcelain flower-vase and waved it about in the air as if to watch the play of its colours. Before lunch he conducted a minute inspection of the professor's room and even took down a picture from the wall, examined it and put it back; he talked vehemently all the time as he did so, leaping from one subject to another or (this was especially noticeable at table) getting stuck on a single idea, returning to it again and again and in the end becoming utterly entangled in it – a predicament which continued until a new idea seized hold of him. The tone of his voice was sometimes rough and shrill, sometimes gentle and melodious, but whichever it was it was never appropriate to what he was saying: if music was the subject under discussion and someone praised a new composer, Krespel smiled and said in a gentle and melodious voice: 'I wish black Satan would hurl the infamous perverter of sounds ten thousand million fathoms into the abyss of Hell!' Or he would roar at the top of his voice: 'She is an angel of Heaven, pure God-hallowed sound and music! The light and constellation of all song!' – and tears stood in his eyes, and you had to remember that a celebrated singer had been spoken of an hour previously. We consumed a roast hare; I noticed how Krespel carefully cleaned all the meat from the bones, assembled them on his plate, and asked after the hare's feet, which the professor's five-year-old daughter brought him with a friendly smile. The children had been watching the councillor in the friendliest fashion throughout the meal; now they rose from the table and approached him – though they took care not to get closer than three paces away.

'What is this supposed to mean?' I asked myself.

Dessert was brought in; the councillor then fetched from his pocket a little chest in which there was a tiny lathe; he screwed this firmly to the table, took the hare's bones and, with incredible speed and dexterity, fashioned from them all kinds of diminutive boxes and pots and balls, which the children received with cries of joy.

Just as the meal had ended and we were leaving the table, the professor's niece asked: 'What is our Antonia doing now, dear councillor?' Krespel made a face – the kind of face a person might make if he had just bitten into a sour orange and was trying to appear to be enjoying it; but this face of his was suddenly distorted into an ugly mask from which angry and, as it seemed to me, really devilish mocking laughter proceeded.

'*Our? Our* dear Antonia?' he asked, in a long drawn-out, unpleasantly singing tone. The professor came up quickly; in the reproving glance he threw at his niece I read that she had touched a chord which was bound to set up dissonant vibrations in Krespel.

'How are things going with the violins?' the professor asked in a cheerful tone as he took Krespel by the hands. The latter's face brightened considerably and he replied: 'Excellently, professor; only today I received the splendid violin of Amati – I told you the other day what a piece of luck I had to get hold of it – only today I cut it open. I hope Antonia will have taken the rest of it to pieces carefully.'

'Antonia is a good child,' the professor said.

'Yes, truly, she is so!' the councillor cried, turned quickly and, seizing his hat and stick, leaped all at once through the door. In the mirror I saw that bright tears were standing in his eyes.

As soon as the councillor had gone, I urged the professor to explain to me what the talk about the violins, and especially about Antonia, had all meant.

'Ah,' the professor said, 'the councillor is an altogether strange man, and he makes violins in a way all his own.'

'Makes violins?' I asked in astonishment.

'Yes,' the professor went on. 'According to those who know about such things, Krespel makes the most splendid violins that can be obtained anywhere nowadays. When one of them turned out particularly well, he used to let other people play upon it, but he hasn't done that for some time now. When Krespel has made a violin he plays it himself for an hour or two and does so with all his energy and with ravishing expression, but then he hangs it up beside the others and never touches it again or lets anyone else touch it. If a violin by one of the great instrument-makers of the past comes on to the market, the councillor will buy it at any price you may ask. But again he plays it only once, then takes it apart to investigate its inner structure; if he fails to find within it what he imagines he is looking for, he throws the pieces into a great chest that is already filled with the wreckage of smashed violins.'

'But what about Antonia?' I asked.

'That is something', the professor went on, 'that would turn me against the councillor in revulsion, if I were not convinced that he is at bottom good-natured to the point of gentleness, and that in this matter there must therefore lie some special secret I am not aware of. When he first came to H. . . many years ago, the councillor lived like a hermit with an aged housekeeper in a gloomy house in . . . Street. The strangeness of his behaviour soon aroused the curiosity of the neighbours, and as soon as he noticed this, he sought and found acquaintances. Just as in my own house, people soon got so used to him he became indispensable. Notwithstanding his rough exterior, he was loved even by the children, and they never gave him trouble, for they felt a certain shy respect for him which protected him against any importunities. We all believed him to be a bachelor, and he did not contradict it.

'After he had been living here for some time, he travelled away, none knew whither, and after a few months returned. The evening after he had come back his windows were unusually bright – this alone attracted the attention of the neighbours – and soon there was heard the quite marvellous voice of a woman, accompanied by a pianoforte. Then the sounds of a violin arose and engaged in fierce contest with the voice. You could tell at once it was the councillor who was playing.

'I myself mingled with the large crowd which had gathered in front of his house to hear the concert, and I have to admit to you that, compared with the unknown voice I then heard, that of the most celebrated singers seemed to me dull and expressionless. I had never before imagined the possibility of such long-held notes, such nightingale trilling, such rising and falling, now as loud as an organ, now declining to the softest breath. There was not one who was not entranced by this sweet magic, and when the singer fell silent the stillness was broken only by gentle sighs. It would already have been about midnight when the councillor could be heard speaking very violently; another male voice was, to judge from its tone, offering him reproaches, and in the midst of it a girl was wailing in disjointed phrases. The councillor screamed more and more violently, until he fell into that long drawn-out singing tone which you know. He was interrupted by a loud scream from the girl, then it became deathly still; suddenly there was a clattering down the steps and a young man rushed out of the house sobbing, threw himself into a post-chaise standing nearby and drove rapidly away. On the following day the councillor seemed very cheerful, and no one had the courage to ask him what had been taking place the previous night. But when they asked the house-keeper, she said the councillor had brought with him a lovely young girl, whom he called Antonia, and that it was she who had been singing so beautifully. A young man had also come with them, who had acted very affectionately towards Antonia and who must be her fiancé. But the councillor had insisted that he leave immediately, and he had therefore done so.

'What the relationship is between Antonia and the councillor is still a mystery, but this much is certain, that he tyrannizes over the poor girl in the most odious fashion. He watches over her like Doctor Bartolo in the *Barber of Seville*; she hardly dares let herself be seen at the window. Whenever he accedes to pleas to take her into society, he follows her every move with the eyes of Argus and will not permit any music to be heard, much less that Antonia should sing, which she is in any case no longer allowed to do in his house. So it is that the singing of Antonia on that single night has become among the people of the town a fantasy and legend of a glorious miracle, and even those who have never heard her often say, when a singer ventures to perform here, "What is that commonplace squawking? The only one who can sing is Antonia."'

Now, you know that I am quite mad about fantastic things like this, and you may well believe how much I wanted to make Antonia's acquaintance. I had often heard these public observations about her singing, but I had not realized until then that the lovely girl was still in town and living under the tyrannical spell of the insane Krespel. It was only natural that I should that very night have heard Antonia singing wonderfully: when, in a glorious *adagio*, which, laughably enough, I imagined I had composed myself, she begged me in the most moving way to rescue her from the tyrant, I instantly resolved to get into Krespel's house like a knight storming a magic castle and liberate this queen of song from the shameful thrall in which she was held.

But everything worked out quite differently from how I had supposed it would: for hardly had I come to know the councillor and seen him two or three times and talked with him enthusiastically about the construction of violins than he himself invited me to visit him. I did so, and he showed me his treasury of violins. There must have been about thirty of them, hanging in a cabinet; and one of them, obviously of extreme antiquity – it had a carved lion's head and so forth – was suspended higher than the rest and hung with a wreath of flowers.

'This violin', said Krespel, when I asked him about it, 'is a very remarkable instrument by an unknown master, probably of the time of Tartini. I am convinced there is something special about the way it is constructed and that if I took it to pieces I should learn a secret I have long sought to discover, but – laugh at me if you will – this dead thing, upon which only I can bestow life and voice, often speaks to me of itself in the strangest fashion, and when I first played it, it seemed as though this instrument was a somnambulist and I only the mesmerizer who persuades her into speech. Do not think I am so foolish as to set any store by such fantasies; yet it is a strange fact that I have never been able to bring myself to dismember that foolish, lifeless object. I am now glad I didn't do so, for since Antonia has been here I have played to her sometimes on this violin. Antonia loves to hear it, she loves to hear it very much.'

The councillor spoke these words with obvious emotion, and that encouraged me to ask: 'Oh, my dear Herr Councillor, won't you do that while I am here?'

But Krespel pulled a wry face at this question and,

employing his long-drawn-out, singing tone of voice, replied: 'No, my dear Herr Studiosus!'

And that was that. I had to view numerous rarities he had collected, some of them quite childish, and finally he reached into a little chest and fetched out a folded piece of paper, which he pressed into my hand and said very solemnly: 'You are a friend of art; accept this gift as a dear memento. You must always value it more highly than anything else you possess.' He thereupon seized me by the shoulders and gently propelled me to the door, where he embraced me: symbolically he had thrown me out of the house.

When I opened the piece of paper I found a length of an E-string of a violin and an inscription: 'Part of the E-string of the violin on which the late Stamitz played his last concert'.

The snub I had received when I had mentioned Antonia convinced me I should never get to see her; but not so: when I visited the councillor a second time I discovered her with him, assisting him to put a violin together. Her appearance produced at first no very marked impression, but you were soon in thrall to her blue eyes and her rose-red lips; her face was very pale, but when something witty or funny was said she smiled sweetly and her cheeks were suffused with a fiery red, though they quickly grew pale again. I talked with Antonia quite unrestrainedly and noticed nothing of the Argus-eyes the professor had imputed to Krespel; on the contrary, he continued to behave with perfect normality and seemed indeed to approve my conversing with her. Thus it happened that I continued to visit the councillor, and as we grew accustomed to one another the three of us began to feel a sense of wonderful contentment in each other's company. I still found the councillor's strange scurrilities highly amusing, yet it was no doubt the irresistible charm of Antonia which drew me there and made me endure much that, as I was then constituted, I would otherwise have fled from. For the councillor's strange and singular observations were all too often interlarded with tastelessness and tedium, and what I found especially annoying was that, whenever I led the conversation in the direction of music, and in that of singing in particular, he would interpose something quite different, and as often as not something coarse, and would do so with a diabolical expression on his face and in that repulsive lilting tone. From the profound distress which then spoke out of Antonia's eyes, I realized well enough that he had done this only so as to cut short any suggestion I might have been about to make that she should sing something. But I did not desist. The obstacles the councillor placed in my way only increased my determination to overcome them: I had to hear Antonia sing in reality, so as not to dissolve away in my dreams of it.

One evening Krespel was in a particularly good mood. He had taken an old Cremona to pieces and discovered that the sound-post was set half a line more obliquely than usual, which he seemed to consider an important find. I succeeded in rousing him to a state of wild enthusiasm over the true nature of violin-playing. He spoke of the way in which the masters of former days would mould their phrasing after that of the great and true singers of the time, and this naturally led to the remark that today, quite to the contrary, song was modelled on the affected and artificial leaps and runs of our instrumentalists.

'What is more senseless', I cried, jumping up from my chair, running over to the pianoforte and opening it, 'than such distorted mannerisms which, far from being music, sound like peas being scattered all over the floor.'

I sang several pieces in the modern manner, with voice wobbling back and forth and humming like a spinning top, accompanying myself with occasional ugly chords. Krespel laughed immoderately and cried: 'Ha, ha! that sounds like some of our italianate Germans or germanic Italians!' Now, I thought, is the moment.

'Does Antonia', I said, turning to her I had named, 'not know any songs of this kind?' – and I intoned a lovely, soulful song of our old Leonardo Leo. Antonia's cheeks glowed, her eyes glittered in new animation, she ran to the pianoforte, she opened her lips – but as she did so, Krespel pulled her away, grasped me by the shoulders and cried in a shrill tenor: 'My son, my son, my son!' Then, seizing my hand in a posture of courteous deference, he continued in a soft singing tone: 'Indeed, most highly honoured Herr Studiosus, it would indeed offend against all good breeding if I were openly to express the wish that Satan would come from Hell at this moment and break your neck; but quite apart from that, you have to admit, my dear fellow, that it is getting decidedly dark; as there are no lamps lit today, even if I did not actually throw you down the steps, you could easily stumble painfully into something. Go home nicely and preserve the kindest possible recollection of your true friend if it should chance that you never again – do you understand me? – never again find him at home!'

Thereupon he put an arm around me and, grasping me firmly, turned towards the door and slowly drew me out, so that I lost all sight of Antonia.

You will agree that in the circumstances it was impossible for me to give the councillor a thrashing, which is really what should have happened to him. The professor was heartily amused and assured me I had now forfeited the councillor's trust for ever. I declined to play the languishing lover gazing forlornly up at his beloved's window: Antonia meant too much, she was too holy to me, for that. With a broken heart I left H. . ., but, as usually happens in such cases, the lurid pictures I took with me in my mind gradually faded and turned pale, and Antonia – and even the sound of her singing, which I had never heard – became a gentle consolation rather than a torment.

★

Two years afterwards I had already installed myself in B . . . when I took a trip to southern Germany. The towers of H . . . rose up in the sweet evening air; but as I drew nearer I was seized by an indescribable feeling of terror: it crept over me and now lay on my heart like an intolerable burden, so that I could not breathe. I had to leave the confinement of the carriage. But once I was in the open air the anguish I felt increased to the point of physical pain. Soon I seemed to be hearing the chords of a solemn hymn coming towards me through the air, then the notes became more distinct and I could distinguish the voices in the choir that was singing.

'What is it? What is it?' I cried, as the sound struck into my heart like a hot knife.

'Do you not see?' replied the postilion who had been travelling beside me. 'Someone is being buried in the churchyard over there.'

I then noticed that we were indeed close by a churchyard, and I saw a group of people clad in black standing around a grave which was about to be filled in. All at once my eyes filled with tears: it was as though all the joy of my life was being buried there. I had stepped down from the hillock on which I had been standing and I could no longer see the churchyard; the choir had fallen silent, and I watched as the black-clad company made its way out of the gate and back into the town. Dressed in deep mourning, the professor and his niece passed close by me without noticing my presence; the niece had a handkerchief pressed to her eyes and was sobbing violently.

I found it impossible to follow them; I sent my servant on in the coach to the inn I usually stayed at and ran into the familiar countryside in the hope of shaking off a mood which I thought had perhaps originated only in the physical discomforts of the journey. I had entered an avenue which led to a local pleasure-ground when I was presented with an astonishing spectacle: Councillor Krespel was being led along by two men in mourning garb, from whom he appeared to be making every effort to escape. He was dressed as I remembered him, in the odd-looking grey coat he had designed himself; but on his head he was wearing a little three-cornered hat which he had, in martial fashion, tilted down over one ear, and from which was suspended a long strip of mourning-crape; as he leaped and ran about, the crape fluttered back and forth in the air. Around his body he had fastened a black sword-belt, but instead of a sword he had put into it a long violin-bow. I felt an icy shudder pass through me. 'He is mad,' I thought as I followed slowly after them.

The men led the councillor to the door of his house; there he embraced them with a loud laugh. They left him and his glance fell on me. I was standing close to him, and he regarded me for a long time with a fixed stare; then he cried in a hollow voice: 'Welcome, Herr Studiosus! You realize what has happened' – and with that he took me by the arm and drew me into the house. We ascended the stairs to the room where the violins were hanging. They were all veiled in crape, but the ancient violin was missing and a wreath of cypress hung in its place. I realized what had happened. 'Antonia! O Antonia!' I exclaimed in utter misery.

The councillor stood beside me with his arms folded, as if turned to stone. I pointed to the cypress-wreath. 'When she died,' the councillor said in a very hollow and solemn tone, 'the violin shattered itself to pieces. It could live only in and through her: when she died, it died, and it is buried with her in her coffin.'

Profoundly moved, I sank into a chair, but the councillor began singing a merry song in a rough, coarse voice; it was hideous to see him hopping about on one foot in time to it, and the crape he was wearing (he had not removed his hat) flying about the room: it brushed against the violins, and I could not repress a cry as it fluttered over my head and settled upon me – it was as though Krespel wanted to draw me down with him into the abyss of madness. Then he suddenly stopped and said in his singing tone: 'My son! My son! Why do you exclaim so? Have you seen the angel of death? That always precedes the formalities!' – and with that he strode to the middle of the room, tore the violin-bow from his belt, held it with both hands over his head and broke it. Laughing loudly, he cried: 'Now the staff is shattered which hung over me – don't you think so, my son? Is it not shattered? Now I am free, free, free – ha, ha! Free! now I shall make no more violins – no more violins! Ha, ha! no more violins!'

He sang these words to a horribly cheerful melody, while again leaping about on one foot. Seized with horror, I made to rush from the room, but the councillor firmly restrained me and said very composedly: 'Stay, Herr Studiosus, do not regard these outbursts as madness: they spring from a grief which is tearing me to pieces, and it is all because a little while ago I made for myself a dressing-gown in which I wanted to look like Destiny or like God!'

The councillor continued to babble confused, mad and repellent nonsense, until he sank down exhausted; I called the old housekeeper to look after him and was glad when I found myself out in the street again.

I did not doubt for a minute that Krespel had become insane; but the professor denied that that was so. 'There are people', he asserted, 'from whom nature, or some special fatality, has drawn away the veil under the concealment of which the rest of us pursue our follies. Their inner workings are visible. What with us remains thought, becomes with Krespel – deed. The mad gestures and convulsive leaps are an acting out of the bitterness he feels within. They are his lightning-conductor. I thus believe that, his apparent follies notwithstanding, his inner consciousness is in good order. Antonia's sudden death may, to be sure, lie heavily upon him, yet I wager that tomorrow's dawn will see him back on his usual treadmill.'

It almost happened as the professor had predicted: the councillor appeared the next day quite as he had always been, only he declared that never again would he make or play upon a violin – a resolve to which, as I afterwards learned, he kept.

What the professor had said strengthened my conviction that Antonia's relationship with Krespel, which he had so carefully concealed, and even the circumstances of her death, were such as to set a burden of inexpiable guilt upon the councillor's head. Before I left H. . . I wanted to confront him with the crime I suspected him of and so compel him to confess it. The more I thought about it, the clearer it became that Krespel was a villain and the more impressive and heated grew the speech with which I intended to accuse him, until it had formed itself into a real masterpiece of rhetoric. Thus armed and equipped, and excited to the topmost pitch, I ran to the councillor's house. I found him quietly engaged in making little toys on his lathe. I flew at him in anger.

'How can your soul know peace for a moment,' I cried, 'when the recollection of your dreadful deed must be gnawing at you with serpent tooth?'

Laying aside his chisel, the councillor looked at me with amazement. 'How so, my dear man?' he asked. 'Take a seat, I beg you.'

But I continued to upbraid him and, growing more and more heated, accused him flatly of having murdered Antonia and threatened him with the vengeance of the eternal powers; indeed, in the newly acquired self-confidence of my judicial position and filled with pride in my profession, I went so far as to assure him that I would employ every possible means to unearth all the facts of the case and hand him over to his judges here below. When I had concluded, I was a little taken aback to see the councillor still sitting quietly and making no reply, but rather looking at me as if he expected me to continue. And I did, indeed, attempt to do so, but what I said now sounded so false and foolish to me that I quickly fell silent again.

Krespel enjoyed my discomfiture for a time, and a malicious, ironical smile passed across his face. Then, however, he grew very serious and said in a solemn voice: 'Young man! you may think me a fool or a lunatic; I forgive you for it, since we are both shut up in the same madhouse and you chide me for thinking I am God the Father only because you think you are God the Son; but how can you attempt to force your way into a life and take hold on its most hidden threads, when that life is and must always remain a mystery to you? She has gone and the mystery is resolved!'

Krespel ceased, rose and paced up and down the room several times. I ventured to ask for an explanation; he regarded me fixedly, took me by the hand and led me to the window, which he opened wide. Resting himself upon his arms, he leaned out and, gazing down thus into the garden, told me the story of his life. When he had finished I left him, greatly moved and much ashamed.

Twenty years before, his love of seeking out the finest violins and buying them – a love which had become a passion – drove Krespel to Italy. As yet he was not a violin-maker himself and was not acquiring these old violins in order to dismember them. In Venice he heard the celebrated singer, Signora Angela . . . i, who was at that time shining in the principal rôles at the Teatro di San Benedetto. Signora Angela was a first-rate artist, to be sure, but it was not her art alone that aroused Krespel's enthusiasm: her angelic beauty also played its part. He sought her acquaintance and, despite all the uncouthness of his manner, succeeded in winning her over to him, mainly through the boldness and expressiveness of his violin-playing. They grew very close to one another and in a few weeks they were married – though the marriage was kept secret, for Angela refused to be separated either from the theatre or from her own name, by which she was known and famous and to which she declined to prefix the ugly-sounding 'Krespel'.

With furious irony, Krespel went on to describe how, as soon as she was his wife, Signora Angela proceeded to make life a torment to him. All the self-will and capriciousness of every *prima donna* who ever sang was, according to Krespel, united in Angela's tiny frame; and if he ever showed any disposition to defend himself against her, she retaliated by surrounding herself with a crowd of *abbés*, *maestros* and academics who, not knowing who he was, snubbed him thoroughly as an unendurable and importunate admirer who knew no better than to abuse the Signora's good nature. After one such stormy scene, Krespel fled to Angela's country villa and there dispelled the sorrows of the day with improvisations on his Cremona; but it was not long before the Signora, who had hurried after him, came into the room. She was in a mood for amorous dalliance: she cast longing glances at Krespel, embraced him and laid her head upon his shoulder; but the councillor, lost in the higher realms of music, continued playing so that the room echoed, and it happened that his arm, and the violin-bow, brushed against her rather roughly. Signora Angela leaped away in fury; '*Bestia tedesca!*' she screamed, tore the violin from Krespel's hand, and smashed it into a thousand pieces on the marble table. The councillor stood before her frozen to a statue; then, however, as if awakening from a dream, he seized the Signora with fearful strength and threw her out of the window; thereupon, paying no further heed to her or to anything else, he fled back to Venice and thence to Germany.

It was only after a time that he realized fully what he had done: although he knew that the window was no more than five feet from the ground, and it was clear to him that in the circumstances he had had no alternative but to throw his wife through it, he nonetheless felt uneasy, especially as the Signora had given him to understand that she was in a certain happy condition. He hardly dared to make inquiries; and he was not a little surprised when, about eight months later, he received a charming letter from his beloved spouse which, while making not the slightest allusion to the events at the country villa, brought him the news that she had been delivered of the loveliest little daughter and the urgent request that the *marito amato et padre felicissimo* should see fit to come to Venice immediately. He refrained from doing this but wrote to a Venetian acquaintance, asking how things were in Venice, and learned that the Signora had fallen on to the soft grass below the window and that the 'accident' had had no effect at all except a psychological one: for, since Krespel's heroic deed, the Signora had been as if transformed – her moods and follies were a thing of the past – and the *maestro* who was composing for the coming carnival was the happiest man under the sun, as the Signora was going to sing his arias without the hundred thousand variations he usually had to put up with. For the rest, his friend said, there was every reason to keep silent as to the manner in which Angela had been cured, for otherwise *prima donnas* would go flying through the window every day. The councillor was now galvanized into action: he called for his horses, he sat himself in his carriage – and then: 'One moment,' he said to himself. 'Is it not certain that, as soon as she sets eyes on me, Angela will again fall back into her old, evil ways? And if she does, how would I behave? I have already thrown her out of the window: what else is there I might do?'

He descended from the carriage and wrote his wife a tender letter, in which he remarked how nice it had been of her to have noted especially, and with pleasure, that their little daughter had, like him, a little mole behind the ear, and – stayed in Germany.

Assurances of love, invitations, lamentations over the absence of the beloved, unanswered prayers, flew back and forth between Venice and H . ., H . . and Venice. At length, Angela came to Germany and, as is well known, scored a triumph at the theatre at F . . Though she was no longer young, her wonderful voice, quite undiminished by time, evoked universal rapture. Antonia had in the meanwhile grown bigger, and her mother wrote to her father all the time of how a singer of the first rank was coming into bloom – a judgement which was, in fact, confirmed by friends of Krespel in F . . ., who urged him to come there and witness the rare phenomenon of two quite sublime singers performing in concert (they had no suspicion how closely he was related to the pair). Krespel often dreamed of his daughter and he would dearly have loved to see her in reality; but when he thought of his wife, his feelings were such that he preferred to stay at home among his dismembered violins.

You will have heard of the promising young composer B . ., of F . ., who one day suddenly disappeared, none knew how or whither (or perhaps you even knew him). He was in love with Antonia and, since she returned his love, begged her mother to agree to a union in which art, too, would be hallowed. Angela had nothing against it, and the councillor assented all the more readily in that the young man's compositions had already found favour before his stern seat of judgement. Krespel expected to receive news that the marriage had taken place; instead there came a letter sealed in black and addressed in a strange hand. Doctor R . . . informed him that Angela had been taken ill as the result of a chill contracted in the theatre and that, on the night before the day of Antonia's intended wedding, she had died. Angela had revealed to him that she was Krespel's wife and Antonia was Krespel's daughter; would Krespel therefore come quickly to take care of the latter. Shaken though he was by Angela's death, the councillor could not help but feel that it had eradicated from his life a disturbing and uncanny element and that only now could he breathe freely. On the same day he departed for F. . . .

The heart-rending emotion of Krespel's account of the first moment he set eyes on Antonia is beyond my power to convey.

All Angela's charm and grace had been imparted to her, while the other, uglier qualities were lacking; she was Angela without the cloven hoof. The young bridegroom arrived, and Antonia – instinctively understanding the inner nature of her strange father – sang one of the motets of old Padre Martini which she knew Angela had had to sing to him ceaselessly when their love was at its height. The councillor overflowed with tears: even Angela had never sung so. Antonia's voice was unique, and its sound was now like the breath of an Aeolian harp, now like the warbling of a nightingale; it seemed impossible that the human breast could have room to contain it. Radiant with love and joy, Antonia sang all her loveliest songs, and B. . . played as though intoxicated with bliss. At first, Krespel was swimming in delight; then, however, he grew thoughtful and silent. Finally he leaped up, pressed Antonia to his breast and, in a quiet and hollow voice, said to her: 'Sing no more, if you love me; my heart is oppressed by it – I fear . . . I fear . . . sing no more!'

The next day he told Doctor R. . .: 'While she was singing, the flush which came to her pale cheeks collected itself together into two dark-red blotches, and I then knew it was no mere family likeness; it was what I had feared.'

The doctor, whose expression had been very grave throughout the conversation, replied: 'Whether it comes from over-exerting the voice too early, or whether nature is to blame, is all one: Antonia suffers from an organic defect in her chest. It is this which gives her voice its wonderful power and the strange tone which, I would almost say, resounds beyond the sphere of human song. But it could also kill her: for, if she goes on singing, I give her six months to live at most.'

The councillor felt as if he had been pierced with a hundred daggers. It was as though a lovely tree full of glorious blossom had for the first time hung its branches suspended over his life, and now it was to be sawn away at the roots and would no longer bloom and flourish. He came to a decision. He told Antonia everything, and that she had two choices: either to follow her bridegroom, give in to his and the world's enticements and die young; or to bestow on her father in his old age the joy and repose he had never known and live for many years. Antonia fell sobbing into his arms but, no doubt all too well aware of what she would say, he heard nothing clearly. He spoke with the bridegroom; notwithstanding the latter's assurance that not one musical sound should ever again pass Antonia's lips, the councillor was in no doubt that even B. . . would be unable to resist the temptation to hear her sing, even if only songs he had composed himself. And the world, the musical public, even if it knew of Antonia's illness, would not relinquish its claims on her, for these people are, when it comes to their enjoyments, cruel and egotistical.

Krespel disappeared from F. . . with Antonia and arrived in H. . . Wild despair seized B. . . when he learned of their departure; he followed them, overtook the councillor and arrived in H. . ., at the same moment.

'Let me see him once more,' Antonia pleaded. 'Then let me die.'

'Die? Die?' cried the councillor in furious rage. An icy shudder ran through him. His daughter, the only being in the whole wide world who had ever made him happy or reconciled him to life, had torn herself from his heart, and he wanted the worst to happen.

B. . . was made to play the pianoforte, Antonia sang and Krespel played merrily on his violin, until the red blotch appeared on Antonia's cheek. Then Krespel commanded a halt, but as B. . . was taking leave of Antonia she suddenly sank to the ground with a cry.

'I believed', Krespel told me, 'she was dead, as I had foreseen she would be. I therefore remained cool and composed. B. . ., looking altogether sheepish and stupid, stood as if numbed; I seized him by the shoulders and said to him (here Krespel fell into his singing tone): "Well now, most respected music-master, you have, you see, done what you wanted to do and murdered your bride; you may now leave quietly, unless, that is to say, you would prefer to stay until I have run this hunting-knife through your heart, so that my daughter – who, as you will observe, has grown a little pale – may acquire some colour through your valued blood. You may be a fast runner, but I could easily throw a knife after you!"

'I must have looked somewhat terrifying as I spoke these words, for he gave a scream of terror, tore himself loose from my grip and rushed out of the door and down the steps.'

When the councillor now made to lift Antonia from the floor where she lay unconscious, she gave a deep sigh and opened her eyes; but at once she closed them again and did indeed seem as though dead. Krespel let out a piteous wail. The housekeeper called a doctor, who declared that Antonia had sustained a severe but by no means mortally dangerous attack, and she did in fact recover more quickly than the councillor had dared to hope. Now she clung to Krespel with the most fervent, childlike love; she entered into all his interests and passions, into all his mad caprices. She helped him to dismember old violins and construct new ones. 'I don't want to sing any more, I want to live for you,' she would say, smiling gently at her father, whenever she was invited to sing and had declined. But the councillor sought to spare her such moments as much as he possibly could; that was why he disliked taking her into society and carefully avoided all music: for he knew well enough how painful it must be for her to renounce the art she practised to such perfection.

When Krespel had bought that marvellous and exceptional violin and was about to take it to pieces, Antonia regarded him very mournfully and said in soft, pleading tones: 'This one too?' The councillor himself did not know what power constrained him to leave the violin intact and to play upon it. Hardly had he sounded the first notes than Antonia cried aloud: 'Ah, that is I – I am singing again!' And the silver-bright bell-like tones that came from the instrument did indeed possess a wonderful and unique quality which seemed to have been engendered in the human breast itself. Krespel was moved to the very depths; he played better than ever before; and as he rose and fell, rose and fell again, with grand expressiveness and with full power of tone, Antonia clapped her hands together and cried in delight: 'Ah, how well I did! How well I did!'

From that time on, her life was suffused with cheerfulness and peace. Often she would say to Krespel: 'I should like to sing something, Father!' and Krespel would take the violin down from the wall and play Antonia's favourite songs; she would glow with happiness.

One night shortly before my arrival, Krespel thought he could hear the sound of his pianoforte coming from the next room, and soon he was able to make out clearly the distinctive style of B. . . He made to get out of bed but found he could move neither hand nor foot: he seemed to be fastened with bands of steel. Then he heard the voice of Antonia: beginning in tones that were hardly more than a breath, it rose and rose to a shattering *fortissimo*, then formed itself into the deeply moving song which B. . . had once composed for her in the solemn, pious manner of the old masters. The mood that came over him as he listened was, Krespel said, wholly incomprehensible: a joy he had never felt before seemed to be united with a fearful sensation of dread. Suddenly he was aware of a blindingly brilliant light, and within it he beheld B. . . and Antonia locked in each other's arms and gazing at one another in rapture. The sound of the singing and its accompaniment continued, though Antonia was not singing and B. . . was not playing. The councillor then fell into a kind of swoon, in which the image he had seen and the sounds he had heard sank down to nothing.

When he awoke, the sense of dread he had felt in his dream was still with him. He rushed into Antonia's room. She was lying on the sofa, with her eyes closed and a blissful expression on her face. Her hands were folded in an attitude of prayer, and she seemed to be asleep and dreaming of the joys of Heaven. But in fact she was dead.

THE ENTAIL

——◦❦◦——

Not far from the shore of the Baltic there stands Castle R., the ancestral seat of Baron von R. The district is wild and desolate; hardly anything grows, a blade of grass here and there in the bottomless quicksand; and, instead of a castle garden, a scanty pine-forest cleaves to the bare walls on the landward side – a place of eternal gloom in which there echoes only the croaking of ravens and the screams of storm-proclaiming seagulls. A quarter of an hour away – and nature is suddenly different: as if by magic one is transported to blossoming meadows and flourishing farmland and pasture. Here is the prosperous village and the spacious residence of the manager of the estate. At the head of a coppice of alder trees there can be seen the foundations of a large manor house one of the former owners intended to build. His successors, who made their home in Courland, neglected to continue it, and even Baron Roderich von R., who returned to live in the ancestral seat, did the same: the ancient, isolated castle appealed more to his dark, misanthropic nature. He restored the decaying structure as well as he could and shut himself up in it with a morose steward and a few servants. He was seldom seen in the village; he would walk and ride instead to the seashore, and people fancied they saw him addressing the waves and listening to the roaring and hissing of the surf, as if it bore the answering voice of the spirit of the sea. On the highest point of the watch-tower he had installed an observatory and fitted it out with telescopes and other astronomical apparatus; during the day he looked out to sea and watched the ships passing on the horizon like white seabirds; on starlit nights he practised his astronomy (the people regarded it as astrology), assisted by his ancient steward. He was in general suspected of knowledge of the so-called black arts, and it was rumoured that he had had to leave Courland because an unsuccessful operation of his in this realm had offended a high princely family in the most grievous way. The slightest allusion to his residence there filled him with horror; but whatever had disrupted his life, whatever had happened to him there, he ascribed to his forebears, who had wickedly abandoned the ancestral seat. To bind the head of the family at least to maintaining it in the future, he established it as an entail, and the crown confirmed it the more readily in that a wealthy and chivalrous family already drifting abroad would thereby be restored to the fatherland. Neither Roderich's son, Hubert, nor the present Lord of the Manor, also named Roderich, had wanted to live in the castle, and both had remained in Courland; it was presumed that, of a more cheerful disposition than the gloomy grandfather, they shunned the dreadful desolation of the spot.

Baron Roderich had allowed two old, unmarried and unprovided-for sisters of his father to dwell with him: they lived with an elderly maidservant in the warm little rooms of the adjoining wing and, except for them and the cook, who had a large room on the ground floor close to the kitchen, the only person who frequented the halls and galleries of the main building was an aged huntsman, who also acted as the castellan. The rest of the servants lived in the village with the estate manager. Only in late autumn, when the first snow started to fall and the wolf- and boar-hunts began, did the abandoned castle come to life: Baron Roderich arrived from Courland with his wife, relatives, friends, and numerous hunt-followers. The neighbouring nobility, and even hunt-loving friends from the nearby town, appeared, and the main building and adjoining wing were scarcely able to accommodate them all; fires crackled in every stove and hearth; from grey of dawn until late into the night the roasting-spits turned; upstairs, downstairs, ran the guests and servants; goblets were clashed together and hunting-songs resounded; there was music and dancing, jubilation and laughter everywhere – so that for over a month the castle was more like an inn on the highway than a manorial seat.

Baron Roderich devoted this time, so far as he could, to serious business: withdrawn from the social whirlpool, he attempted to run the estate. He had a complete account of income prepared, listened to any suggestions for improvements, heard the complaints of his tenants and endeavoured to put right any wrong or injustices. In this he was assisted by old Advocate V., who usually arrived at the estate at least a week before the baron did.

In the year 179– the time had come for Advocate V. to journey to Castle R. Vigorous though he still was at seventy, he must have thought that a helping hand would be of use to him; and one day he said to me, as if joking: 'Cousin!' – so he called me, though I was his great-nephew, since I had been given his forenames – 'Cousin! I have been thinking you ought to get a little sea air into your lungs and come with me to Castle R. You can give me some help with my often wearisome business, and you might also try the wild hunting life; after you have spent one morning drafting a contract, you can spend the next looking into the gleaming eyes of a long-haired wolf or a savage-toothed boar – or even learn how to bag one.'

I had heard so many strange things about the hunting season at R. that I was highly delighted that this time my great-uncle wanted to take me with him. Already fairly well acquainted with the business he had to deal with, I promised to relieve him of all his cares and worries. The next day we were sitting in the carriage, enveloped in warm furs and driving to Castle R. through thick flurries of snow that heralded the coming of winter.

On the way, the old man recounted to me all manner of strange stories about the old Baron Roderich, who had established the entail and, ignoring his youthfulness, had appointed him his legal adviser and the executor of his will. He spoke of the rough, wild character of the old baron, which seemed to have been passed on to the whole family: even the present master, whom he had known as an almost effeminate youth, seemed to become rougher and wilder with each passing year. He instructed me that I would have to be alert and unconstrained if I was to find favour with the baron, and he referred finally to the living quarters in the castle which he had, once and for all, chosen for his own: they were warm and comfortable and so situated that we could withdraw from the uproar of the company whenever we wanted to. He had two small rooms, hung with warm wall coverings, next to the courtroom in the side wing opposite the wing in which the aged aunts lived.

At last, after a quick though arduous journey, we arrived at R. late in the night. We drove through the village. It was in fact already Sunday; at the inn there was music and dancing and jubilation, the estate manager's house also resounded with music and was illuminated from top to bottom, and the desolation into which we now drove was all the more dreary. The wind howled piercingly from the sea and, as if awoken by it from a deep magic sleep, the gloomy pine-trees groaned back with a muffled wail. The naked black walls of the castle towered up from the snow-covered ground; we stopped at the closed gate. We called, cracked the whip, hammered and knocked, but to no avail: everything seemed dead and there were no lights visible in any of the windows. The old man called in his penetrating voice: 'Franz! Franz! Where are you? The devil take it, move yourself! We are freezing out here! The snow is lashing our faces bloody! Move yourself, the devil take it!'

Then a yard-dog began to whine, a light moved along on the ground floor, keys clattered and the heavy gate creaked open. 'Ay, welcome, welcome, Herr Justitiarius, in this terrible weather!' cried old Franz, lifting his lantern, so that the light fell full on his shrivelled face, drawn strangely into a smile.

The carriage drove into the yard, we climbed down and I saw for the first time the old servant's strange figure, dressed in ancient hunting livery marvellously adorned with braid. Over his broad, white forehead there were a few grey hairs, the lower part of his face bore the robust tan of the huntsman, and though the drawn muscles made it seem almost a mask, the geniality which shone from his eyes and played about his mouth restored to his face its humanity.

'Now then, old Franz,' began my great-uncle, knocking the snow from his coat in the hallway, 'is everything ready, have the carpets in my rooms been beaten, have the beds been brought in, has everything been properly heated, yesterday and today?'

'No,' Franz replied calmly, 'no, worthy Herr Justitiarius, none of that has been done.'

'Good God!' my great-uncle exploded. 'I wrote to you in good time, I have come at the right date; what stupidity! Now my rooms will be ice-cold.'

'Yes, worthy Herr Justitiarius,' said Franz, carefully removing a glowing ember from the wick with the lamp-trimmer and extinguishing it with his foot. 'Yes, you see, but all that, and especially the heating, wouldn't have been much use, because the wind and snow are blowing right in, through the broken windows and . . .'

'What!' my great-uncle interposed. 'What! The windows are broken and you, the castellan, have done nothing about it?'

'Yes, worthy Herr Justitiarius,' the old man calmly continued, 'not much can be done with them because of all the rubbish and all the stones from the walls lying around the room.'

'How, in the name of Heaven, have rubbish and stones got into my room?' my great-uncle roared.

'Bless you, bless you, young sir,' cried the old man, bowing politely, as I sneezed; then, continuing immediately, he said: 'It's the stones and plaster from the middle wall, which fell in with the great shaking.'

'Have you had an earthquake?' my great-uncle exploded.

'No, not an earthquake, worthy Herr Justitiarius,' replied the old man with a smile, 'but three days ago the heavy ornamented ceiling of the courtroom fell down with a tremendous crash.'

My great-uncle was about to give vent to a mighty oath; but as he pulled his fur cap from his head, he suddenly stopped, turned to me and said, laughing loudly: 'Truly, cousin, we must keep our mouths shut, we mustn't ask any more, or we shall learn of some still worse catastrophe, or the whole castle will fall on our heads. But,' he continued, turning to the old man, 'Franz, couldn't you have had the wit to get another room ready for me? Couldn't you have some other hall fitted out for the court hearing?'

'That's already been done,' the old man said, motioning us to the stairs and beginning to climb them.

'Bless me if this isn't a strange fellow!' said my uncle as we followed the old man. We went on through long, high-ceilinged corridors, Franz's flickering light casting an uncanny glow into the deep gloom. Pillars, capitals and coloured archways appeared, as if hovering in the air, our giant shadows strode along beside us, and the curious pictures on the walls past which they flitted seemed to shudder and tremble, with their voices whispering in the booming echo of our steps: 'Do not wake us, do not wake the mad enchanted beings who sleep in these ancient stones.'

At length, after we had passed through a row of cold, gloomy apartments, Franz opened the door to a hall in which a brightly blazing hearth welcomed us. I was restored to good humour as soon as I entered, but my great-uncle stood in the middle of the hall, looked around him and said in a very serious, almost solemn tone: 'Is this to be the courtroom?'

Franz, holding his lamp high, so that on the wide, dark wall a bright spot as large as a door met one's eyes, said gloomily: 'A court has already been held here!'

'What is that you say?' cried my uncle, throwing off his coat and stepping up to the fire.

'Nothing, nothing,' Franz replied. He lit the lamps and opened the adjoining room, which had been made comfortable for our stay.

It was not long before a table was set before the fire; the old man brought an excellent repast and – what gave us both real pleasure – a splendid bowl of punch, brewed in the true northern manner, followed it. Fatigued by the journey, my great-uncle sought his bed as soon as he had eaten; but the novelty and strangeness of the accommodation, even the punch, had aroused my spirits too much for me to be able to think of sleeping. Franz cleared the table, adjusted the fire and, with a friendly bow, left me.

Now I was sitting alone in the baronial hall. The snow had begun to ease off, the storm to cease its blustering, the sky had grown lighter and the bright full-moon shone through the arched windows, illuminating all the gloomy corners of the room, into which the candle and the firelight could not penetrate, with a magical light. The walls and ceiling were decorated in an antiquated manner, the walls with heavy panelling, the ceiling with fantastic pictures and gaily coloured painted and gilded carvings. Out of the

larger canvasses, most of them depicting the confusion of
bear- or wolf-hunts, there protruded the heads of men and
animals, carved in wood and set on to the painted bodies,
so that, especially in the flickering light of fire and moon,
the whole assumed a gruesome reality. Between these
paintings there hung lifesized portraits of knights striding
out in hunting dress – probably the hunt-loving ancestors.
Everything – paintings and carvings – bore the dark tinge
of the long passage of time; the bright bare patch on the
wall through which two doors led into the adjoining
apartments was therefore all the more striking, and I soon
realized that this patch must also have been a door, now
walled up. Now, we all know what power the unusual has
to grip the mind; even an idle imagination comes to life in a
valley surrounded by strange cliffs, within the gloomy
walls of a church; it anticipates experiences such as it has
never had. If I add that I was then twenty years old and had
drunk several glasses of strong punch, you will easily
believe that my baronial hall filled me with strange sensations. Imagine the stillness of the night, in which the
muffled murmur of the sea and the whistling of the wind
sound like the notes of a mighty organ played by invisible
spirits, the clouds flying past overhead seem to peer
through the rattling windows like giants – I was indeed
likely to have felt that a strange kingdom might now rise
up visibly and tangibly before me. Yet this feeling was like
the pleasurable chill one experiences at the vivid telling of a
ghost story; and it occurred to me that I had never been in a
better mood to read a book which, like so many others at
that time, I carried in my pocket. It was Schiller's *Ghost-
Seer*. I sat and read and heated my imagination more and
more. I had come to the gripping story of the wedding
feast at the Count von V.'s – just as Jeronimo's bloodstained figure entered, the door leading to the hallway
sprang open with a mighty crash. Terrified, I shot into the
air, the book fell from my hands. But everything was still,

and I was ashamed of my childish fears. The door might have been blown back by a draught. It was nothing – my over-excited imagination transformed everything into a ghost! Thus calmed, I picked the book up from the floor and threw myself back into the chair – something was walking quietly and slowly with measured tread across the hall, and there was a sighing and groaning, and in this sighing and groaning there lay an expression of the most profound human suffering, of the most inconsolable misery. Ha! a sick animal had been locked in on the ground floor – at night every distant noise seems close – who could be frightened by that? Thus I calmed myself again; but now there came a scraping, and louder, deeper sighs, as if emitted in the dread of death, and they came from behind the new wall.

'Yes, it is a poor animal locked up. I will call out, I will stamp on the floor, all will grow quiet' – was what I thought; but the blood was coursing through my veins, cold sweat stood on my forehead, and I sat frozen in my chair, incapable of standing, still less of calling out. The horrible scraping stopped at last, the footsteps again became audible; I seemed to come to life again, jumped up and took two steps forward – when an icy blast struck through the hall; in the same instant the moon threw a bright light on to the portrait of a very earnest-seeming man and, as if his voice were whispering through the roaring of the sea and the whistling of the night wind, I heard him say: 'No further, no further, or you will fall prey to the spirit world!'

Now the door slammed shut with the same heavy crash as before, I heard the footsteps in the hallway – they were going down the stairs – the door of the castle opened with a rattle and was closed again. Then it was as if a horse had been taken out of its stall and after a while led back in again – then everything was still! In the same instant, I perceived that my great-uncle in the adjoining apartment was sighing and groaning; this brought me to my senses; I grasped the lamp and hurried in. The old man seemed to be fighting an evil dream.

'Wake up, wake up!' I cried, taking him gently by the hand and letting the light of the candle fall on to his face. The old man woke with a muffled cry, then looked at me in a kindly way and said: 'You did well, Cousin, to wake me up. I was having a really bad dream, and this room and that hall is to blame for it, for I was thinking of past times and of the many strange things that have taken place here. But now let us get back to sleep again!' And with that, the old man pulled the bedclothes about him and seemed to fall asleep immediately; but as I extinguished the candle and laid myself down in bed, I heard the old man quietly praying.

Work started the next morning: the estate manager arrived with the accounts, and people came to have disputes settled and affairs put in order. At noon, my great-uncle went with me to call on the two aged baronesses. Franz announced us; we had to wait a few moments and then were led into the sanctuary by a bent little old woman of sixty who called herself the chambermaid. There the old ladies, eccentrically attired in a fashion long outmoded, received us with amusing ceremoniousness, and I especially was the object of their wonderment when my great-uncle introduced me as a young attorney assisting him. It was obvious from their expressions that they believed the wellbeing of R.'s inhabitants was endangered by my youth. The visit was very enjoyable, but the horror of the previous night still clung to me. I felt as if touched by some unknown power, or rather that I had already approached the circle to enter which means perdition. So it was that even the baronesses, with their strange, high-piled hair and their weird and wonderful clothes, seemed, not amusing, but quite dreadful and spectral. I wished I could read in their shrivelled faces and watery eyes, I wished I could hear in the bad French which came half through their pinched lips and half through their pointed noses, how the old ladies had got at least on to good terms with the uncanny beings which haunted the castle. My great-uncle, who was in a very merry mood, got the old ladies so entangled in his mad chatter that, had I been in a different mood, I would not have known how to control my laughter; but, as I have said, the baronesses remained spectral to me, and my great-uncle, who had thought the visit would give me especial pleasure, looked at me with amazement.

As soon as we were alone in our room, he burst out: 'Cousin, for Heaven's sake tell me what is the matter with you! You don't laugh, you say nothing, you eat nothing, you drink nothing! Are you ill? Are you in need of anything?'

I did not now hesitate to tell him all the horrific events of the previous night. I concealed nothing, and especially not that I had been drinking a lot of punch and reading Schiller's *Ghost-Seer*. 'I have to admit this,' I added, 'for it may be that it was my over-heated imagination that created all these apparitions.'

I thought my great-uncle would scoff at my ghost-seeing; instead of which, however, he grew very serious, gazed at the floor, then suddenly raised his head and, regarding me with a burning look, said: 'I do not know your book, Cousin, but you have neither it nor the spirit of the punch to thank for that ghost. You should know that I myself dreamt what happened to you. I was sitting, just like you (as it seemed to me) in the armchair by the fire, but what you only heard, I saw. Yes! I saw the gruesome fiend as he entered, as he crept to the walled-up door, how he scraped at the wall in despair until the blood spurted from under his torn nails, how he then went down the stairs, led the horse out of the stable and then brought it back. Did you hear the cock crow in the village? You woke me up just then, and I soon summoned up my resistance to that evil ghost.'

The old man fell silent and I did not like to question him: I knew he would explain everything to me if he thought fit. After a time, during which he was lost in his own thoughts, he continued: 'Cousin, have you the courage, now you know all the facts, to confront this ghost again, this time with me?'

I naturally declared I was quite capable of doing so. 'Then let us watch together tonight,' my great-uncle said. 'An inner voice tells me that, if I have the courage, the spirit must yield, and that it is no reckless undertaking but a religious work if I venture life and limb to banish an evil fiend which is expelling the sons from the seat of their ancestors. But do not let us think of danger: in such firmness of mind and devotion as exists within me, one is and remains a triumphant hero! Should it nonetheless be God's will that the evil power shall overcome me, then you, Cousin, must proclaim that I fell in Christian battle with the spirit of Hell. Keep well away! – then nothing will happen to you!'

Evening came. Franz had cleared away the meal and brought in the punch, the moon shone full through the clouds, the sea thundered and the night wind howled and rattled the windows. In spite of our excitement, we forced ourselves to sit and talk. My uncle had laid his repeater-watch on the table. It struck twelve. With a fearful crash the door sprang open and, as on the previous night, soft slow steps passed across the hall, and there came the sound of groaning and sighing. My uncle had turned pale, but his eyes shone with an uncommon fire, he rose from his chair, and as he stood, a tall figure with his arm raised towards the middle of the room, he looked like a commanding hero. The sighing and groaning grew louder, and then, even more horribly than before, there began the scraping on the wall. My uncle strode firmly to the walled-up door.

He halted before the spot where the scratching was growing more and more desperate and said in a solemn tone,
such as I had never heard from him: 'Daniel, Daniel! what
are you doing here at this hour?'

There was a terrifying scream and a heavy thud, as of a
burden falling.

'Seek mercy before the throne of the Most High. There
you should be! Away with you out of life, to which you
can never again belong!' – so cried my uncle, in an even
louder voice than before. And it was as if a gentle
whimpering floated through the air and died away in the
rising storm. Then my uncle went to the door and threw it
shut, so that the sound echoed through the empty hallway.
In his speech, in his bearing, there was something super-
human which filled me with awe. As he sat again in his
chair, his gaze was as if transfigured; he folded his hands, he
prayed silently. After a few minutes, he said in his gentle
voice, which penetrated so deeply into my heart: 'Well,
Cousin?'

Trembling with dread, horror and anxiety, with love
and awe, I fell to my knees and moistened the proferred
hand with hot tears. The old man embraced me in his
arms, and as he pressed me warmly to his heart he said very
gently: 'Now we can sleep in peace, dear Cousin!'

And so we did; and as nothing whatever uncanny
occurred the following night, we recovered our former
gaiety.

Some days later, the Baron at last arrived with the
Baroness and numerous hunt followers, the invited guests
collected and the castle now suddenly came to life in the
fashion already described. As soon as he had arrived the
Baron visited our apartments and seemed strangely surprised to find us there; he cast a baleful glance at the
walled-up door and, turning away, passed a hand over his
forehead as if to dispel some painful memory. My great-
uncle mentioned the devastation of the courtroom and the

adjoining apartments and the Baron exclaimed that Franz
should have found us a better alternative; my great-uncle,
he said, had only to ask if there was anything lacking for
his comfort. The Baron maintained an attitude of a certain
respect towards my uncle, as though he were an elder
relative, but this was the only thing which in any way
reconciled me to the man's generally rough and domineer-
ing manner. He seemed to regard me as no more than a
clerk; the very first time I undertook a transaction he
sought to find something wrong with it, and I was on the
point of an angry retort when my uncle interposed and
assured the Baron I had done all correctly. When we were
alone, I complained bitterly about the Baron, whom I was
coming to detest from the bottom of my soul.

'Believe me, Cousin,' replied the old man, 'the Baron,
despite his unfriendliness, is the most excellent, good-
natured man in the world. He has acquired this attitude, as
I have already told you, only since he became the head of
the house: before that he was a mild and modest man. But
really, he is not as bad as you make out, and I would like to
know why it is you dislike him so very much.'

As he said this, my uncle gave a mocking smile which
sent the blood rushing to my face and made clear to me my
innermost feelings: was it not obvious that this otherwise
unaccountable hatred originated in love, and specifically in
love of one who seemed to me the most wonderful being
that had ever walked the earth? This being was none other
than the Baroness herself. Immediately I saw her, her
dainty form enveloped in a Russian sable and her head in a
veil, she affected me with an irresistible magic. Even
though the aged aunts, in even stranger garb than I had
seen them in before, were tripping at her side when she
arrived, gabbling welcomes in French, as she gazed gently
around her, nodding to this person or that in a friendly
manner and speaking a few German words in her clear
Courland dialect – this first impression already produced

on me a strange effect, and I involuntarily associated it with that of the uncanny spectre, so that the Baroness was an angel of light before whom the powers of evil gave way. The lovely image remained in my mind's eye. She was then perhaps no more than nineteen years old; her face was angelic, and in her dark eyes there lay the indescribable magic of moonbeams suffused with melancholy yearning. Often she seemed lost in her own thoughts, and at such times dark clouds passed over her lovely brow: one might have thought that she was disturbed by painful memories, but to me it seemed rather that what was filling her mind was a presentiment of a future full of misfortune, and – I have no idea why – I connected this with the castle ghost.

The morning after the Baron's arrival everyone gathered for breakfast. My uncle introduced me to the Baroness; not surprisingly, I behaved in an indescribably foolish manner, became confused over the simplest questions the lady put to me and succeeded in giving the aged aunts the impression I was tongue-tied with awe, so that they found it necessary to come to my assistance and to assure the Baroness that in reality I was a *garçon très joli* and quite a gifted fellow. This annoyed me and, suddenly assuming control of myself, I spoke some witticism in much better French than the old ladies', whereupon they gazed at me with wide eyes and treated their long pointed noses to a good helping of snuff. From the look the Baroness then gave me, I realized that the intended witticism had failed of its effect, a fact which irritated me still further, and I damned the old women to the depths of Hell.

The period of sheepish longing and childish infatuation had long since been teased out of me by my great-uncle, and it was clear to me that the Baroness had taken more powerful a hold on my inner feelings than any woman had ever done. I saw, I heard only her; I was aware how mad it would be of me to risk any flirtation with her, yet I could not gaze from a distance like a lovesick calf; what I could do, however, was to approach her more closely without allowing her to suspect my feelings, absorb the sweet poison of her eyes and her speech and then, far away from her, carry her image forever in my heart. The idea of this romantic, almost knightly form of love, as it occurred to me during a sleepless night, set me childishly haranguing myself with great pathos; at length I sighed very lamentably: 'Seraphine, O Seraphine!' so that I awoke my uncle, who called out to me: 'Cousin! Cousin! Stop fantasizing out loud! Do so by day, if you want to, but do let me get some sleep at night!'

I was not a little concerned that my uncle, who had already noted my excitement at the arrival of the Baroness, should have heard me utter her name; I expected him to engulf me in ridicule, but the following morning he said nothing, except, as we went into the courtroom: 'May God give us sound understanding and keep us from making poltroons of ourselves.'

Thereupon he took his place at the great table and said: 'Write very clearly, dear Cousin, so that I can read it without a hitch.'

The respect, even reverence, in which the Baron held my great-uncle was evident in everything he did. Even at table he occupied the envied place next to the Baroness; chance determined where I sat, though a couple of officers from the capital usually succeeded in requisitioning me in order to unburden themselves of all the latest news from there – a recitation attended by much drinking. Thus it happened that I sat for several days at the far end of the table from the Baroness, until at last chance brought me into her proximity. As we were going into the dining room, a companion of the Baroness – a lady no longer exactly youthful but still presentable enough and not without wit – involved me in conversation; in accordance with etiquette, I had to offer her my arm, and I was overjoyed when she took her seat quite close to the

Baroness, who nodded to her amiably. You can well imagine that all I said from then on was intended less for my companion than for the Baroness. It may be that my inner tension gave a particular animation to everything I said: suffice it to say that my companion became more and more attentive, and soon our conversation sent out sparks in the direction I desired. I noted in particular that my companion cast several significant glances at the Baroness, and that the latter was endeavouring to hear what we were saying, especially when the conversation turned to music and I spoke rapturously of the sacred art and revealed that, notwithstanding my dry and tedious profession, I was quite a competent pianist, could sing and had even composed several songs.

We had gone into the drawing room to take coffee and liqueurs, and I found myself – I do not know how – standing before the Baroness, who was talking with my former companion. She turned to me at once and, speaking as though to an old acquaintance, repeated the questions she had asked on her arrival: whether I was enjoying my stay at the castle and so on. I assured her that in the first few days the dreariness of the region, even the ancient castle, had put me into a strange mood, but that this mood itself had conjured up many wonders and I only wished to be spared the wild hunts, to which I was not accustomed.

The Baroness smiled: 'I can imagine that cavorting through our forests would not be your idea of amusement,' she said. 'You are a musician and, if I am not completely mistaken, a poet too! I love both the arts passionately! I even play the harp a little, but I have to do without it here; my husband does not like me to bring it with me, and its gentle tones would certainly not go with the shouting and horn calls which is all that is allowed here! Oh my God, how I would like to hear some music here!'

I assured her I would do all I could to fulfil her wish: there must, I said, exist an instrument somewhere in the castle, even if only an ancient piano. But Fräulein Adelheid (the Baroness's companion) laughed aloud and asked whether I realized that in all human memory there had been heard in the castle no instruments but croaking trumpets, lamenting horns and the squeaking fiddles, out-of-tune basses and bleating oboes of itinerant players. The Baroness held fast to her wish to hear music, however, and she and Adelheid exhausted themselves in suggestions as to how a tolerable piano might be procured. At that moment, the servant Franz passed through the hall.

'Here's the answer!' Fräulein Adelheid cried. 'Franz will know what to do!'

Franz came across to us and Adelheid made him understand what was wanted; the Baroness, with folded hands, her head inclined forwards, listened to the old man and a gentle smile lit her eyes: she was like a pretty child eager to get her hands on some desired toy. After he had stated in his roundabout way the many reasons it was a sheer impossibility to procure so rare an instrument at short notice, Franz finally stroked his beard and said with a self-satisfied smirk: 'But the estate manager's wife over in the village plays the clavichord uncommon well, or whatever they now call it with their outlandish names, and she sings to it so well and lamentably that your eyes water like with onions and you want to skip about with both legs.'

'And possesses a fortepiano?' Fräulein Adelheid interrupted.

'Oh, indeed,' the old man continued. 'It came direct from Dresden. It's a –'

'Splendid!' the Baroness interjected.

'– lovely instrument,' continued Franz, 'but a little feeble, for when the organist recently wanted to play on it the tune *In allen meinen Taten*, he smashed it to bits, so that –'

'Oh my God!' cried the two ladies.

'– it had to be sent at great expense to R. to be repaired,' Franz said.

'Is it back again then?' Fräulein Adelheid asked impatiently.

'Oh indeed, Miss, and the estate manager's wife will count it an honour.'

At this moment the Baron came by; he glanced at our group with a look of some annoyance and whispered mockingly to the Baroness: 'Is Franz having to offer his advice again?'

The Baroness blushed and dropped her gaze, and old Franz, breaking off startled, stood with head erect and arms down stiffly to his sides, in the posture of a soldier.

The aged aunts swam over to us and led the Baroness away. Fräulein Adelheid followed them. I was left standing as if bewitched. My delight that I would now be able to approach my idol fought with my annoyance at the behaviour of the Baron: if he was not a despot, would his grey-haired servant have behaved so slavishly?

'Do you hear, can you see?' cried my great-uncle, clapping me on the shoulder. We went out into our apartment.

'Don't throw yourself at the Baroness so,' he said as we went in. 'Where could it lead to? Leave it to the young dandies who like paying court and whom there is certainly no lack of.'

I explained how everything had happened and invited him to tell me now whether I had earned his reproaches; but he only replied 'Hmm, hmm', put on his dressing-gown, lit his pipe and sat down in the armchair and talked about the previous day's hunt, teasing me about the shots I had missed. The castle had grown quiet, but the musicians with their fiddles, basses and oboes of whom Fräulein Adelheid had spoken had arrived; there was to be nothing less than a full-scale ball that night. My uncle, preferring sleep to such foolishness, remained in his room; but I had dressed myself for the ball when there was a light tap at the door, and Franz entered and informed me that the estate manager's wife's clavichord had been fetched by sleigh and taken to the Baroness; Fräulein Adelheid invited me to come at once. You can imagine how my heart beat, with what sweet trepidation I entered the room in which I found her. Fräulein Adelheid encountered me joyfully. The Baroness, already dressed for the ball, was sitting reflectively in front of the mysterious box in which there were slumbering the sounds I was supposed to awaken. As she stood, the radiance of her beauty made me gaze at her speechless.

'Now, Theodore' – she called everyone by his forename, after the pleasant practice of the north – 'the instrument has arrived; pray Heaven it may not be entirely unworthy of your skill!'

As I opened the lid, a number of broken strings sprang up at me; and when I struck a chord, it sounded as if all the remaining strings were out of tune.

'The organist has been at it again with his gentle touch,' Fräulein Adelheid laughed, but the Baroness, who was quite put out, said: 'What a misfortune! Again I shall find no pleasure or enjoyment here.'

I searched in the instrument's box and found a few rolls of strings but no tuning-key. Fresh complaints! Any key whose ward would fit the pegs could be used, I declared; whereupon the ladies ran hither and thither, and it was not long before a whole row of shining keys lay before me on the sounding board. Now I really got busy. Fräulein Adelheid and the Baroness herself endeavoured to assist me, testing this or that peg. Then one of the keys fitted. 'It works, it works!' they cried happily.

Then the strings began to become entangled and we fought together to unravel them. At length, however, some of them agreed to stay in place, and from the discordant noise there gradually emerged clear, pure chords. 'Ah, success, success! The instrument is in tune!' cried the Baroness, looking at me with a lovely smile.

This activity together swiftly banished all constraint between us; now that the pianoforte was tolerably in tune, I gave expression to my feelings, not in passionate fantasias, but in those sweet *canzoni* which come to us from the south. To the sound of *Seza di te, Sentimi idol mio, Almen se non poss'io, morir me sento, Addio* and *Oh dio*, Seraphine's eyes grew more and more radiant. She had placed herself at the instrument close beside me; I felt her breath on my cheek and a white ribbon which had come adrift from her gown fell over my shoulder and fluttered there like love's messenger, moved by the music and by Seraphine's sighs. It was amazing that I kept my senses! Then Fräulein Adelheid jumped up from where she had been sitting in a corner of the room, knelt before the Baroness and, taking her hands and pressing them to her breast, begged her: 'O dear Baroness, dear Seraphine, now you must sing too!'

'What are you thinking of?' the Baroness replied. 'How can I raise my wretched voice before our virtuoso here?'

Like a bashful child, with downcast eyes and blushing furiously, she fought with desire and shyness. I implored her and did not give up until she tried a few notes on the instrument as an introduction to a Courland folk-song. Now she began, in a soft, bell-like voice, a song whose simple melody bore the character of those folk-songs in which we can recognize our higher poetic nature. A mysterious magic lies in the insignificant words of the text: they become hieroglyphics of the inexpressible with which our heart is filled. Who cannot recall those Spanish *canzoni* whose words say not much more than: 'I sailed on the sea with my sweetheart, the storm blew up and my sweetheart was afraid. No! – I shall not sail again with my sweetheart on the sea!'? Thus the Baroness's song said nothing more than: 'When I was young I danced with my sweetheart at a wedding, a flower fell from my hair, he picked it up and gave it to me and said: "When shall we go to a wedding again?" '

As I accompanied the song, as I stole the melodies of the other songs straight from the lips of the Baroness, I seemed to her and Fräulein Adelheid as the greatest *maestro* of music. They heaped praise upon me. Then the shriek of out-of-tune trumpets and horns announced it was time to gather for the ball.

'Now I have to go, alas!' cried the Baroness. I jumped up from the instrument. 'You have given me a marvellous hour. These were the happiest moments I have ever spent here in R.'

With these words the Baroness gave me her hand; and as, in an ecstacy of delight, I pressed it to my lips, I felt the racing pulse in her fingers. I do not know how I got to my uncle's room and then the ballroom. A Gascon fears the battle because every wound must be fatal to him – he is all heart! I compared myself to him: every touch was fatal. The Baroness's fingers had struck me like poisoned arrows, my blood burned in my veins! My uncle heard the whole story early next morning and suddenly became very serious: 'I would ask you, Cousin, to resist the stupidity which has you in its grip,' he said. 'What you are doing, harmless though it may seem, can have the most dreadful consequences; you are standing on thin ice, and it will break under you before you know it. I shall take good care to keep you firmly attached to my coat-tails, for I know you will deceive yourself you have done no more than catch a cold, when in reality a fever is consuming you, and you will take years to recover. The Devil take your music if you don't know anything better to do with it than entice impressionable women.'

'But', I interrupted, 'is it in my mind then to flirt with the Baroness?'

'Fool!' cried my uncle, 'if I thought that, I would throw you through that window!'

The Baron interrupted this embarrassing conversation, and business then tore me out of my daydreams of love, in which I saw only Seraphine. In company, she said only a few friendly words to me now and then, but almost every evening a secret message came from Fräulein Adelheid, calling me to Seraphine.

Soon many other kinds of conversation mingled with the music, and many indications forced me to admit that the Baroness really did have some sort of mental disorder, as I had read in her look the first time I saw her. The harmful influence of the castle ghost came back to me: something dreadful had happened, or was to happen. I often felt moved to recount to Seraphine how I had encountered the invisible foe, and how my uncle had banished him for ever, yet an inexplicable shyness prevented me.

One day the Baroness was not at luncheon; she was said to be unwell and unable to leave her room. Asked whether the illness was serious, the Baron smiled disagreeably and said: 'Nothing more than slight catarrh caused by the raw sea air; it is hard on sweet voices and kind only to the harsh halloo of the hunt.'

He threw me a penetrating glance, and I realized that it was to me that he had been speaking. Fräulein Adelheid blushed scarlet and, staring down at her plate, murmured: 'And you will be seeing Seraphine again today, and again your sweet songs will console her injured heart.'

In that instant it seemed to me that I had entered into some forbidden relationship with the Baroness which could end only in something dreadful, in a crime. My great-uncle's warning lay heavily upon my heart. What should I do? See her no more? As long as I remained in the castle, that was impossible; and even if I was permitted to leave the castle and return to K., I was incapable of doing so. I felt only too well that I was not strong enough to shake myself out of the dream I was in. Adelheid almost seemed to me like a procuress, and I wanted to despise her – yet, on reflection, I was ashamed of my foolishness, for what had happened in those evening hours which could lead to any relationship with Seraphine other than that permitted by manners and decorum? Why should it occur to me that the Baroness felt anything for me? – and yet I was convinced I was in danger.

The table was cleared quickly: wolves had been spotted in the forest close to the castle. The idea of hunting appealed to me in my excited state of mind and I told my uncle I wanted to join in. He smiled happily and said: 'That's good. It will do you good to get out. I'll stay at home. You can take my gun and hunting-knife – it's a handy weapon in emergencies, provided you keep calm.'

The part of the forest in which the wolves were thought to lie was surrounded by the hunters. It was bitingly cold, the wind howled through the pines and drove the bright snowflakes against my face, so that, now dusk had fallen, I could scarcely see six paces in front of me. Quite numb, I left the spot appointed to me and sought cover deeper within the forest. There I leaned against a tree, the gun under my arm; I forgot the hunt; my thoughts bore me to Seraphine in her room. I heard the sound of distant firing; in the same instant there was a rustling in the thicket and not ten paces away there appeared a powerful wolf. I took aim, I fired – I missed, the animal sprang at me with blazing eyes and I would have been done for had I not had the presence of mind to draw the hunting-knife and stab it in the throat as it sprang. Its blood spurted over my hand and arm. One of the Baron's huntsmen, who was standing not far from me, came running up, and on his repeated hunting call the others gathered round us. The Baron hurried up to me: 'In Heaven's name, are you bleeding? You *are* bleeding! Are you wounded?'

I assured him I was not; then the Baron turned to the huntsman who had been standing closest to me and reproached him for failing to shoot after I had missed; the latter, however, maintained that he would probably have shot *me* instead, and the Baron, agreeing, conceded he should have taken more care of me himself. In the meantime the hunters had lifted the animal. It was the biggest of its kind seen for a long while, and there was general wonderment at my courage – though at the time I had given no thought to the danger I was in. The Baron was especially solicitous, and we went back to the castle arm in arm (one of the huntsmen had to carry my gun). He continued to speak about my heroic deed, so that in the end I too began to believe in it: I lost my self-consciousness, I had passed my examination and my anxieties had been wiped away. I felt I had acquired the right to try for Seraphine's favours. But then everyone knows what silly dreams an infatuated youth is capable of.

That evening, by the fire with the steaming bowl of punch, I was the hero of the day. Only the Baron had killed a wolf the equal of mine; the others had to content themselves with stories of other hunts and of dangers survived at other times. I now expected to amaze my uncle and recounted to him my adventure with great gusto and did not forget to emphasize the extreme savagery of the beast I had killed. My uncle, however, only laughed and said: 'God moves mightily in the weak!'

As I went along the corridor to the courtroom, tired of the drinking and the company, I saw a figure slip in before me with a lamp in its hand. Stepping into the room, I recognized Fräulein Adelheid.

'One has to wander around like a ghost, like a sleep-walker, if one is to find you, my brave wolf-hunter!' she whispered as she took me by the hand. The words 'sleep-walker' and 'ghost' weighed on my heart, spoken here in this spot: for a moment they brought to my mind the ghostly apparitions of those two gruesome nights; and, now as then, the sea-wind was growling like the deep notes of an organ, rattling and whistling shrilly through the windows, and the moonlight fell on to the wall where I had heard the scraping sounds. I thought I could see spots of blood upon it. Fräulein Adelheid must have felt the icy chill which shuddered through me.

'What is the matter?' she said softly. 'You are quite numb with cold. Now I will call you back to life. The Baroness can hardly wait to see you. She fears the wicked wolf has eaten you up. She is dreadfully worried. What have you done to Seraphine? I have never seen her like it before. Ha! Now your pulse is beginning to beat! How the dead man is suddenly awakened! Now, come along: we must go to our dear little Baroness!'

I allowed myself to be led away. Adelheid's manner of speaking of the Baroness seemed to me unworthy, especially the hint it contained of some secret understanding between us. As I entered her room, Seraphine came towards me with hurried steps and a gentle 'Ah!' Then she stopped, as if coming to her senses. I dared to take her hand and press it to my lips. She let her hand remain in mine as she said: 'But, dear God, is it your profession to take on wolves? Do you not know that the days of Orpheus are over and that the beasts have lost all respect for singers?'

This cheerful remark made clear the nature of the Baroness's interest in me and instantly restored me to discretion. I do not know how, but, instead of sitting at the instrument as usual, I placed myself next to the Baroness on the sofa. Her words: 'And how did you come to be in danger?' showed our mutual understanding that today it was to be not music but conversation. After I had related my adventure in the forest and referred to the lively interest evidenced by the Baron, hinting that I had not thought him capable of it, the Baroness began almost sadly: 'How violent and rough the Baron must seem to you! But, believe me, it is only while he is within these dark, inhospitable walls, only during these wild hunting trips in the dreary forest, that his nature, or at least his behaviour, changes. What puts him especially out of humour is the thought, which haunts him constantly, that something dreadful is going to happen here. That is why your adventure has shaken him so deeply. He will not allow the least of his servants to be exposed to the slightest danger, much less a newly-found friend; and I know for certain that Gottlieb, whom he blames for having left you unguarded, is to be punished with the most shameful punishment of having to follow the hunt in the rear, without knife or gun but armed only with a cudgel. Such hunts as we have here are never without danger, and the Baron constantly fears misfortune; yet he himself beckons on the evil demon. Many strange things are told of the ancestor who established the entail, and I know there is an evil family secret locked up in these walls, a dreadful ghost who drives the rightful owners away, so that they can endure this house only among a wild, noisy throng. But how lonely I am in this throng, and how troubled by the dread which seeps out of these walls! You, my dear friend, have with your music given me the first happy moments I have experienced here. How can I thank you?'

I kissed the hand she offered me and declared that I too had sensed the sinister atmosphere of the castle. The Baroness gazed fixedly at me as I went on to speak of the style of architecture, the decoration in the courtroom, the sighing of the wind, but – perhaps my tone and expression hinted that I meant something else – as I fell silent the Baroness cried vehemently: 'No, no! Something dreadful happened to you in that room, which I can never enter without a shudder. I beg you, tell me everything!'

Seraphine's face had grown deathly pale. I realized it would be better to tell her what had happened, rather than leave it to her imagination to conjure up some ghost which might be even more frightening than the one I had experienced. She listened to me with growing anxiety, and when

I spoke of the scraping on the wall, she cried: 'That is dreadful! Yes, yes: there *is* some dreadful secret hidden in that horrible wall!'

When I then related how my uncle had banished the ghost, she sighed deeply, as if released from a heavy burden. Leaning back, she held both hands to her face. Only then did I notice that Adelheid had left us. My tale had been finished for some time and, as Seraphine was still silent, I quietly stood up, went over to the piano and endeavoured with music to lead her out of the gloom into which my story had plunged her. I intoned softly one of the holy *canzoni* of Abbé Steffani; and to the melancholy tones of *Ochi, perchè piangete*, Seraphine awoke from her dreams and smiled gently, shining teardrops in her eyes. How did it then happen that I found myself kneeling before her, that she bent down towards me, that I embraced her in my arms, that a long glowing kiss burnt my lips? How did it then happen that I did not lose my senses, that I felt how tenderly she pressed me to her, that I released her from my arms and, rising quickly, went back to the piano? Turning from me, the Baroness took a few steps towards the window; then she turned again and came up to me with an almost proud bearing which was not at all like her. Looking me in the eyes, she said: 'Your uncle is the worthiest old gentleman I know. He is the guardian angel of our family. May he include me in his prayers!'

I was unable to utter a word: the poison which I had imbibed from that kiss seethed and burned in my veins, in every nerve. Fräulein Adelheid came in, and the rage of the battle going on within me poured out in hot tears which I could not hold back! Adelheid gazed at me in amazement – I could have killed her. The Baroness gave me her hand and said with indescribable gentleness: 'Farewell, my dear friend. Farewell, and think that perhaps no one has understood your music better than I. Ah, those sounds will long echo in my heart!'

With a few disjointed words I compelled myself to leave. I ran to my room. My uncle had already gone to bed. I fell to my knees, I cried aloud, I called out the name of my beloved – in short, I abandoned myself to the foolishness of infatuated madness, and only the loud complaining of my uncle, awoken by my ravings – 'Cousin, I think you have gone mad, or are you wrestling with the wolf again? Get off to bed, if you please' – drove me to bed, where I lay with the firm intention of dreaming only of Seraphine. It must have already been past midnight when, still not asleep, I thought I heard distant voices, a running hither and thither and the opening and shutting of doors. I listened: footsteps were coming closer in the corridor, and there came a loud knock on the door.

'Who's there?' I cried. A voice outside said: 'Herr Justitiarius! Wake up, wake up!'

I recognized Franz's voice; as I asked 'Is the castle on fire?' my uncle awoke and cried: 'Where's the fire? Are there ghosts loose again!'

'Get up, Herr Justitiarius!' said Franz. 'The Baron is asking for you.'

'What does the Baron want', my uncle asked, 'at this time of night?'

'Get up, sir!' Franz repeated. 'The Baroness is dying!'

I leaped out of bed with a cry of horror.

'Open the door for Franz,' my uncle cried to me. Half fainting, I tottered around the room, unable to find the door. My uncle had to help me; Franz entered, his face white, and lit the lamps. We had scarcely thrown on our clothes when the Baron was heard in the hall, calling: 'Can I talk to you, dear V.?'

'Why have you got dressed, Cousin? The Baron asked to see only me,' my uncle said as he went out.

'I must go down – I must see her and then die,' I murmured as though from the depths of pain.

'Indeed! You are right, Cousin,' my uncle said, slammed the door in my face so that its hinges rattled, and locked it from outside.

Enraged by this, I wanted at first to run against the door; but, quickly coming to my senses, I resolved to await my uncle's return and then give him the slip. I heard him talking energetically with the Baron and I heard my name mentioned several times, though I could not understand anything else. My position was becoming worse with every second that passed. At last, I heard someone run up to the Baron and the Baron quickly walk away. My uncle came back into the room.

'She is dead!' I cried as I rushed towards him.

'And you are a fool,' he said calmly as he forced me into a chair.

'I must go down!' I cried. 'I must go down and see her, even if it costs me my life!'

'Do that, dear Cousin,' said my uncle, locking the door and putting the key into his pocket.

Now I flared into rage. I made a grab for the loaded gun and cried: 'Here, before your eyes, I shall put a bullet through my head if you do not open the door for me immediately!'

My uncle stepped in front of me and said, as he held me with his glance: 'Do you think, boy, that you can frighten me with your threats? Do you believe your life is of any worth to me if you are capable of throwing it away like a discarded toy? What business have you with the wife of the Baron? What right have you to push your way in where you do not belong and where no one wants you? Do you want to play the sighing lover in the hour of death?'

Devastated, I sank down into the chair. After a while, my uncle continued in a more gentle tone: 'And to set your mind at rest, there is probably nothing at all to worry about. Fräulein Adelheid is beside herself over nothing, as usual. If a drop of rain falls on her nose she cries: 'What dreadful weather!' Unfortunately, the alarm penetrated as far as the aunts, who have rushed along with unseemly wailing and a whole arsenal of strengthening drops, elixirs of life and I don't know what else! A bad bout of the vapours.'

He ceased, walked back and forth a little, then halted before me, laughed heartily and said: 'Cousin! Cousin! What foolishness! Satan is haunting this place in many ways; you have run into his clutches and he is now having a little game with you.'

He again paced back and forth, then he continued: 'There is no chance of sleep now. I shall smoke a pipe and thus pass the few hours of night and darkness left.'

With that, he took a clay pipe from the cupboard and, humming a tune, slowly and carefully filled it, then looked among a pile of papers until he found a sheet, tore and folded it to make a spill, and lit it. Puffing thick clouds of smoke, he said: 'Now then, Cousin, how was it with the wolf?'

My uncle's calmness had a strange effect upon me: it was as if I was no longer at Castle R. and the Baroness was far, far away. But the question my uncle put to me annoyed me.

'Do you find my hunting adventure so very funny,' I asked him, 'so suitable for mockery?'

'By no means,' he replied. 'Not at all. But you would not believe how comical a figure you cut when Almighty God for once lets something special happen to you. I had an academic friend, a quiet, sensible, contented sort of person. Fate implicated him – who had never given cause for such a thing – in a matter of honour, and he, whom most of us took for a weakling, behaved with such decisive courage that everyone marvelled at him. But from that time on, he was a changed man: from an industrious, sensible youth, he turned into a boastful and intolerable bully. He drank, he shouted and fought and was at last killed in a duel. You can make whatever you like of that story,

Cousin. And now to return to the subject of the Baroness and her illness.'

Soft footsteps were heard in the hall, and a sound like a groan was borne through the air; 'She has gone!' was the thought which flashed through me. My uncle rose quickly and called: 'Franz, Franz!'

'Yes, dear Herr Justitiarius,' was the reply from outside.

'Franz,' my uncle continued, 'give the fire a poke, and if it can be done, would you make us a couple of cups of tea! It is devilish cold,' my uncle said, turning to me, 'and we would be better off outside by the fire.'

He opened the door and I followed him mechanically.

'What is going on downstairs?' he asked.

'Oh,' replied Franz, 'it really didn't amount to much. The Baroness is quite herself again and is blaming her fainting fit on a bad dream!'

I was about to shout for joy, but a glance from my uncle silenced me.

'Good,' he said. 'On the whole, I think it would be better if we were to lay our heads down for a couple of hours. Leave the tea for now, Franz.'

Franz left the hall, wishing us a peaceful night although the cocks were already beginning to crow.

'Cousin,' my uncle said, as he knocked his pipe out in the hearth, 'it is a good thing no misfortune happened to you with wolves or with loaded guns.'

I now understood everything and was ashamed I had given the old man reason to treat me like a naughty child.

'Be so good,' my uncle said next morning, 'dear Cousin, as to go downstairs and inquire how the Baroness is. You only need to ask Fräulein Adelheid, who will willingly give you a complete bulletin.'

You can imagine with what haste I hurried down; but as I was about to knock on the door of her antechamber, the Baron came out and bumped into me. He stood amazed and measured me with a penetrating glance.

'What do you want here?' he exclaimed.

Although my heart was beating wildly, I replied in a firm voice: 'On my uncle's instructions I am inquiring the state of health of your gracious wife.'

'Oh, it was nothing at all – one of her usual nervous attacks. She is sleeping quietly, and I know she will appear at table quite well again. Say that – tell him that.'

The Baron said this with a certain intensity which seemed to me to indicate he was more concerned about the Baroness than he wanted anyone to suspect. I turned to go, but the Baron suddenly grasped my arm and cried: 'I have something to say to you, young man!'

I thought I had before me an offended husband and feared a scene. I remembered the hunting-knife my uncle had presented to me and which I still carried in my pocket. I followed the Baron, determined to defend myself if need be; we entered his room, and he closed the door behind him. Now he paced rapidly back and forth with his arms folded; he halted before me and repeated: 'I have something to say to you, young man!'

With courage born of foolhardiness I replied: 'I hope it will be something I should like to hear.'

The Baron gazed at me in amazement, as if he did not understand me. Then he began marching up and down the room again. He took down a gun and examined it as if to see whether it was loaded. My blood tingled; I felt for my knife and stepped close to the Baron so as to make it impossible for him to take aim at me.

'A lovely weapon,' he said, replacing the gun in the corner. I took a few steps backwards and the Baron came over to me; then, clapping me on the shoulder a little more forcefully than necessary, he said: 'I must seem excited and disturbed to you, Theodore. After my night's vigil I am full of a thousand anxieties. My wife's attack was not serious, I realize that – but here in this castle, in which a dark spirit lurks, I feared something dreadful, and it is the first time she has been ill here. You – you alone are to blame.'

How that could possibly be the case I had not the slightest notion, I replied calmly.

'Oh,' continued the Baron, 'if only that damned box of misery belonging to the estate manager's wife had broken into a thousand pieces on the ice, if only you . . . but no – no! It has to be, it must be so, and I alone am to blame. As soon as you began to make music for my wife, I ought to have explained the whole thing, the whole matter of my wife's moods.'

I made as if to speak.

'Let me talk,' said the Baron. 'I must at the outset stop you from making any hasty judgement. You will take me for a rough Philistine. I am not so. But I am convinced that such music as moves everybody's soul, and certainly mine, must be forbidden here. My wife suffers from an excitability which must in the end undermine all her joy in living, and within these strange walls it is greatly stimulated. You will wonder why I do not spare her this dreadful place, this wild hunting life. But – you may call it weakness if you wish – I cannot leave her behind on her own. I would suffer a thousand anxieties and could concentrate on nothing. On the other hand, I feel that the regimen here ought to produce a strengthening effect. And now the sea breeze blustering its way through the trees, the bellowing of the hounds, the blaring of the horns, have to contend with a languishing strumming at the piano, such as no man ought to be able to play: you have set out methodically to torment my wife to death!'

The Baron spoke with a harsher voice and with wild, blazing eyes. My blood rose to my head, and I made a vehement movement with my hand. I made to speak, but he would not let me.

'I know what you want to say,' he went on, 'I know; and I repeat that you were on the way of killing my wife and, though I do not for a moment believe you intended to, you will understand that I must put a stop to it. In short: you have excited my wife with your playing and singing, and then, when she is floundering rudderless in an ocean of dream-like visions and forebodings which your music has conjured up, you thrust her further into the depths with tales of a ghost which is supposed to have haunted you. Your great-uncle has told me everything, but I would ask you to repeat to me all you saw, or did not see – or heard . . . or felt . . . or had a suspicion of.'

I pulled myself together and narrated calmly all that had happened. The Baron now and then interjected an expression of amazement. When I came to the point at which my uncle had banished the ghost, he clasped his hands together, raised them to Heaven and cried elatedly: 'Yes, he is the guardian spirit of our family! He shall rest in the grave of our ancestors!'

I had completed my story.

'Daniel, Daniel! What are you doing here at this hour?' murmured the Baron to himself, as he walked up and down the room with folded arms.

'Was there anything else, Baron?' I asked loudly, as I made as if to leave.

The Baron revived as if from a dream, grasped me amiably by the hand and said: 'Yes, dear friend. You must cure my wife, whom you treated so badly without meaning to. You are the only one who can do it.'

I felt myself blushing, and if I had been standing at a mirror I should certainly have seen in it a very childish, bewildered face. The Baron appeared to delight in my embarrassment and looked me in the eyes with an ironic smile.

'How on earth should I set about it?' I at last managed to stammer.

'Well,' the Baron said, 'you are not having to deal with a dangerous patient. I am now making a direct claim on your art. The Baroness is drawn into the magic circle of your music and to tear her away from it suddenly would be foolish and inhuman. Continue with the music. You will be welcome in my wife's apartments in the evenings. But you must gradually introduce more invigorating music; you must alternate the gay with the serious – and then, above all, you must often repeat the tale of the ghost. The Baroness will get used to it, then she will forget that it is lodged here in these walls, and the story will have no greater effect on her than any other fairy story. Do that, dear friend!'

With these words the Baron dismissed me. I was inwardly devastated, reduced to a mere child! I, who was mad enough to believe I could inspire jealousy in him! He had himself sent me to Seraphine, an instrument to be employed and then discarded! A few minutes before I had feared the Baron and the consciousness of guilt lay upon me, but this very guilt had made me feel that I was maturing to a man; now I saw only a foolish boy who in his folly had taken for gold the paper crown he had placed on his hot head. I hurried to my uncle, who was already waiting for me.

'Now then, Cousin, where have you been, where have you been?' he called to me.

'I have been talking to the Baron,' I replied quietly, incapable of looking at him.

'Good grief!' he said, as if amazed. 'Good grief! Yet I thought it must be something of the sort. The Baron has challenged you to a duel, eh, Cousin?'

The peal of laughter he emitted proved that he had completely seen through me again. I clenched my teeth: I did not want to utter a word, since I knew it would require no more to launch the thousand teasing quips already brimming on his lips.

The Baroness came to table in a morning gown whiter than newly fallen snow. She seemed tired, yet a sweet desire, a repressed ardour, shone from her eyes. She was more beautiful than ever. Who can number the follies of youth? I transferred the bitterness I felt towards the Baron to the Baroness; it all seemed to me a hopeless mystification. Like a sulky child, I avoided her and found a place at the end of the table between the two officers, with whom I began to drink and to talk loudly. A servant brought me a plate on which lay a few bonbons with the words: 'From Fräulein Adelheid'. I took them and saw that on one of them there had been scratched: 'and Seraphine!' My blood coursed through my veins. I looked towards Adelheid, who looked back at me with a sly expression, lifted her glass and nodded to me with a slight movement of her head. Almost involuntarily I murmured silently: 'Seraphine', took up my glass and emptied it in a draught. My glance flew across to her; she too had taken a drink at the same instant and was setting down her glass – her eyes met mine, and a malicious devil whispered in my ear: 'Unhappy man! She does love you!'

One of the guests rose and, in accordance with northern custom, proposed the health of the lady of the house. Glasses resounded in loud jubilation. Delight and despair – the wine flamed up within me, everything was going round, and I thought I should throw myself at her feet and breathe my last.

'What's the matter, dear friend?' – this question from my neighbour brought me to my senses. Seraphine had disappeared, the guests were rising from the table; I wanted to go, but Adelheid took hold of me; she spoke, but I understood nothing; she took me by the hands and, laughing loudly, shouted something into my ear. As if paralysed, I stood mute and motionless. Then, without thinking, I took a glass from Adelheid's hand and emptied it; I found myself alone at one of the windows; I staggered from the hall, down the stairs and into the forest. Snow was falling heavily, the trees were sighing in the storm;

like a madman, I laughed and cried wildly: 'Hey! the Devil is having a game with you!'

Who knows how it would have ended if I had not suddenly heard my name being called loudly in the forest? The storm had eased off, the moon was shining through the clouds; I heard the hounds starting up and saw a dark figure approaching. It was the old huntsman.

'Herr Theodore!' he began. 'You got lost in the storm, I see. The Herr Justitiarius is waiting for you very impatiently!'

I followed him in silence and found my uncle working in the courtroom.

'You did well to go outside to cool down,' he cried to me. 'Don't drink quite so much; you are still too young to take it. It is not good for you.'

I sat at the desk and said nothing.

'But now tell me, dear Cousin, what did the Baron want you for?'

I told my uncle everything, and ended by saying that I did not intend to lend myself to the dubious cure the Baron had suggested.

'There would be no time for it, in any case,' my uncle said. 'We are leaving early tomorrow.'

So it happened, and I did not see Seraphine again.

Hardly had we arrived back home in K. when my great-uncle complained that he felt more than usually exhausted by the journey. His silence, broken only by violent outbursts of temper, presaged the return of his gout. One day I was called for urgently. I found that the old man had been smitten by a stroke and was lying speechless on his bed. A letter was crushed in his hand. I recognized the writing as that of the estate manager at R. and in my anguish I dared not take the letter from his grasp. I did not doubt that he was close to death; yet even before the doctor had arrived his pulse had begun to beat again and he had begun to recover. A few days later the doctor declared him to be out of danger.

The winter was more tenacious than ever, and a bitter, gloomy spring followed; his gout, rather than the attack he suffered, kept my uncle to his bed. He had now retired from business and all hope of ever returning to Castle R. had thus disappeared. I alone was permitted to care for him and to entertain him with conversation. At length, even his gaiety returned, and there was no lack of jokes and humour; but even when it came to tales of hunting and I expected my heroic deed with the wolf to be again the subject of banter, never, not even once, did he mention our visit to Castle R., and I too forebore to remind him of it. The concern I felt for my uncle had almost banished the memories of Seraphine; but one incident served to recall her, and in such a way that ice-cold shudders ran through me. When I opened the briefcase I had carried at Castle R. a dark lock of hair tied with a white ribbon fell out of the folded papers. I recognized it instantly as Seraphine's. But as I looked at the ribbon more closely, I saw upon it a drop of blood! Perhaps it was Adelheid who had sent me this memento, but where did the bloodstain come from? and why did it seem to me like a fearful warning? The ribbon was that which, when I had first drawn close to Seraphine, had fluttered around me, but it now seemed to possess some dark power and to have become a symbol of fatality.

At last the storms gave up their blustering, summer asserted its rights, and by July it was the heat that had become unbearable. My uncle was visibly regaining his strength and, as was his custom, took himself off to a garden in the suburbs. One mild evening we were sitting together in the fragrant jasmine arbour; my uncle was unusually cheerful and in a gentle, almost mellow mood.

'Cousin,' he began, 'I don't know how it is, but today I feel a special wellbeing such as I haven't felt for years. I believe it is a forewarning of my death.'

I tried to turn him away from such gloomy thoughts.

'Let it be, Cousin,' he said. 'I shall not be remaining here below for much longer, and I therefore want to clear up a debt to you! Do you still think about the autumn at Castle R.?'

The question struck me like a bolt of lightning, but, before I could reply, he continued: 'Heaven willed that you should become entangled in the darkest secrets of that house. The time has come for you to learn everything. We have often spoken of things which you have guessed at rather than understood. They say that nature represents the cycle of human life symbolically in the changing seasons, but I think of it in a different way. The spring mists fall, the summer haze shimmers, and only in the clear ether of autumn can the distant landscape be seen clearly before the world is immersed in the night of winter. In the clear sight of old age the workings of the inscrutable power can be seen more clearly. The dark destiny of that house now stands clearly before my ancient eyes! Yet no tongue can express the heart of it. Listen, my son, to what I am going to tell you as to a remarkable story; keep within your soul the knowledge that the secrets into which you strayed – perhaps not accidentally – could have destroyed you! Yet – that is all in the past now!

The story of Castle R. which my uncle now recounted I have carried so truly in my memory that I can almost repeat it in his own words (he spoke of himself in the third person).

One stormy autumn night in the year 1760, a tremendous crash, as if the whole rambling castle had collapsed in a thousand pieces, awoke the servants in Castle R. from a deep sleep. In a moment everyone was on his feet; lamps were lit; and, with fear and anxiety on his deathly pale countenance, the steward came panting up with the keys. In a silence like that of the grave, he moved through the passages, halls and rooms, but nowhere was there the slightest sign of damage. A dark foreboding seized him. He went up to the big hall, in one of the side rooms of which Baron Roderich von R. used to rest when engaged on his astronomy. Between the door of this room and another small room there was an entrance which led through a narrow passage directly to the observation tower. But as Daniel (as the steward was called) opened this heavy door, the storm, howling and roaring, hurled rubble and broken masonry at him, so that he recoiled in terror and, as he dropped the lamp to the floor, cried aloud: 'O Lord of Heaven! The Baron has been dashed to pieces!'

At that instant, the sound of wailing was heard from the Baron's bedroom: Daniel found the servants gathered around the body of their master. Fully clad, he was seated in his chair as if resting. As daylight came, they saw that the top of the tower had collapsed, stones had crashed through into the astronomy chamber, and the heavy timbers, exposed by the fall, had broken through the lower vaulting and torn away part of the castle wall and the passage. To step through the doorway from the hall was to risk falling eighty feet into the abyss.

The Baron had foreseen his death to the hour and had told his son, so Wolfgang, Baron R., the eldest son of the deceased and hence holder of the entail, arrived the following day from Vienna, where he had been on a visit. The steward had had the large hall hung in black, and the dead Baron lay on a bier in the dress in which he had been found, surrounded by silver candelabra with burning candles. Silently, Wolfgang went up to the hall and stood gazing into his father's colourless countenance. At length, with a convulsive movement, he murmured: 'Did the stars compel you to make miserable the son you loved?'

Stepping back a pace, he gazed heavenwards and said gently: 'Poor deluded old man! Your game is now finished! Now you may learn that what we have here has nothing to do with what is beyond the stars. What will or power can reach beyond the grave?'.

He again fell silent – then he cried vehemently: 'No, not one atom of my earthly happiness, which you sought to destroy, shall I be robbed of now!'

With that, he drew a folded piece of paper from his pocket and held it to one of the candles: the paper flared up, and, as the reflexion of the flame flickered on the face of the corpse, it seemed as though the muscles were moving and the dead man speaking soundlessly, so that the servants standing at a distance were overcome by dread. The Baron calmly trod out the last piece of paper smouldering on the floor, then gave his father a final look and hurried from the hall.

The following day, Daniel told the Baron of the destruction of the tower and of all that had happened on the night of his father's death, and said that the tower should be rebuilt immediately – or the whole castle would be in danger.

'Rebuild the tower?' the Baron exclaimed, his eyes blazing with anger. 'Never! The tower', he continued more calmly, 'will not collapse further if there is no further cause. How if it was my father himself who destroyed the place where he carried on his uncanny astrology? How if he himself found certain contrivances which made it possible for him to destroy everything whenever he wanted to? Let it be as he wishes; and the rest of the castle can cave in too, for all I care. Do you think I intend to live here in this owl's nest? No, that wise ancestor who laid the foundations for a new house in the valley anticipated me and I shall follow him.'

'And so', said Daniel dejectedly, 'all the old faithful servants will have to take up their staves and go.'

'That I will not be served by doddering old men goes without saying,' the Baron replied, 'but I will throw nobody out. You shall eat the bread of charity.'

'Shall I be treated so?' the steward exclaimed.

The Baron, who had been on the point of leaving the hall, wheeled round, his face red with anger, and strode up to the old man. 'You hypocritical rascal,' he cried, 'you who carried on those sinister activities up there with my father, to whose heart you clung like a vampire, you who perhaps used his madness to drive him to the devilish decisions which brought me to the edge of the abyss – you, I ought to fling you out like a mangy dog!'

The old man had dropped to his knees in terror at this dreadful outburst, and so what happened may have been an accident; in anger, the body often mechanically follows the thought, and as he concluded his tirade the Baron struck out with his foot and kicked the steward in the chest, so that he fell with a muffled cry. As he then rose with difficulty he emitted a sound like the whimper of a dying animal and pierced the Baron with a look of rage and despair. The bag of money which the Baron threw to him as he went out he left untouched on the floor.

In the meantime, relatives had gathered, and the old Baron was interred in the family vault in Castle R. church with great ceremony. As the guests went their own ways again, the new Lord of the Manor, abandoning his gloomy mood, seemed highly delighted with what he had inherited. With V., the old Baron's legal adviser, to whom he seemed to have given his trust immediately on meeting him and whom he had confirmed in his office, he drew up accounts of the estate's income and considered how much could be used for improvements and for building the new house. V. believed the late Baron could not possibly have spent all his annual income, so that, as there were only a few insignificant sums in bank notes among the documents and as the cash found in an iron box was only just over a thousand thalers, there must be money hidden away. And who would know where it was if not the steward Daniel? The Baron was now worried that Daniel, whom he had seriously offended, would revenge himself by letting this hidden treasure rot away rather than disclose it. He recounted to V. all the circumstances of the case and ended by declaring his conviction that it had been Daniel who had nurtured in the late Baron an inexplicable horror of seeing his son in Castle R. The Justitiarius declared this conviction misguided: no human being in the world could sway the old Baron's mind in the slightest. He also undertook to discover from Daniel the secret of any money hidden away. This hardly needed doing, however, for scarcely had he begun: 'How is it, then, Daniel, that your former master left so little money in cash?' when Daniel replied, with an unpleasant smile: 'Do you mean the paltry few thalers you found in the box? The rest is in the vaulting next to my dear Master's bedroom! But the best of it', he continued, his smile changing into a fearful grimace and his bloodshot eyes flashing, 'is that there are thousands of gold pieces lying buried under the rubble!'

The lawyer at once called on the Baron, and together they went into the bedroom, in one corner of which Daniel shifted the wall panelling and revealed a lock. The Baron gazed at it greedily and drew a large bundle of keys from his pocket and prepared to try them. Daniel stood very upright, looking down at him as he crouched at the lock. With a quivering voice, he then said: 'If I am a dog, your excellency – I have the loyalty of a dog!'

With that he handed to the Baron a shining steel key. The latter tore it from his hand and easily opened the door. They stepped into a low vault, in which there stood a large iron trunk with its lid open. On the sacks of money there lay a note in the familiar hand of the late Baron:

One hundred and fifty thousand Reichsthaler in old Frederichsdor saved from the income of the Castle R. estate and intended for the upkeep of the castle. Further, the Lord of the Manor who follows me in ownership shall use some of this money for the construction of a high lighthouse tower for the benefit of seafarers on the highest hill to the east of the old castle tower, which he will find collapsed in ruins, and shall have it lighted each and every night.

Michaelmas Night in the year 1760, at Castle R.
Roderich Baron von R.

Only after the Baron had raised the bags of money one after another and allowed them to drop back into the chest, delighting in the jingling of the gold, did he turn to the steward, thank him for the loyalty he had displayed and assure him it was only slanderous gossip that had led him to treat him so badly at the outset: not only should he stay in the castle, but he would retain his post of steward with double the salary.

'I owe you full recompense,' he said. 'If you want gold, take one of these bags!'

The Baron indicated the chest and stood with downcast eyes. Suddenly the steward's face became a burning red, and he again emitted the dreadful sound as of a dying animal; as he did so he muttered between his teeth something that sounded like 'Blood for gold!'

The Baron, lost in gazing at the treasure, was oblivious to all else. Shaking in every limb, Daniel humbly approached him, kissed his hand and said in a tearful voice: 'Ah, my dear, gracious Master, what should a poor, childless old man like me do with gold? But the doubled salary – that I shall joyfully take, and will carry out my duties tirelessly!'

The Baron paid no particular attention to the old man's words, but let fall the heavy lid of the trunk, so that the vault resounded. Then, as he locked the chest and carefully withdrew the key, he said: 'That's good, that's good, old fellow! But', he continued when they had regained the hall, 'you also mentioned a quantity of gold pieces lying buried under the ruined tower.'

The steward went silently to the doorway and opened it with effort. The storm drove a thick flurry of snow into the hall; a frightened raven fluttered up, cawing and croaking, beat against the window with its wings and, having found the open doorway, plunged into the abyss. The Baron stepped into the passageway but took only a single glance into the depths before starting back.

'Hideous sight! I am giddy,' he stammered as he sank into the lawyer's arms. Pulling himself together, he eyed the steward sharply: 'And down there?'

The steward had closed the door again. He now turned to the Baron and said, toying with the great key and smiling strangely: 'Down there lie thousands upon thousands, the lovely instruments of my late Master – telescopes, quadrants, globes, reflectors – everything lies in ruins among the stones and rubble!'

'But money, actual money!' the Baron interrupted. 'You spoke of gold pieces, did you not?'

'I meant only objects,' the steward replied. 'Things which cost thousands of gold pieces.' And he would say no more.

The Baron was delighted that he had suddenly acquired the means of executing his favourite plan of raising a splendid new house. The lawyer V. pointed out that the will of the departed provided only for the repair and renovation of the existing castle and that it would be difficult to equal the simple grandeur of the old building in any new one, but the Baron stuck to his intention and asserted that in any matter not covered by the entail the wishes of the dead would have to yield to those of the living. He would improve the ancient castle to the extent the climate, ground and surroundings permitted; and he added that he would shortly be bringing home as his wife a creature for whom no sacrifice could be too great.

The way in which the Baron spoke of this union led the lawyer to suppose it had probably already been sealed and cut short any further questions on his part; but he was consoled by the feeling that the Baron's desire for riches was fuelled by a wish to provide for his beloved rather than by simple greed – though the sight of the Baron gloating over the Friedrichsdor made it rather hard to sustain this feeling. 'The old scoundrel is certainly not telling the truth,' the Baron said. 'But next spring I will have that rubble cleared away under my own eyes.'

Builders came and the Baron discussed with them at length how best to proceed with the new building. He discarded plan after plan; no design was sufficiently grand for him. He began to draft plans himself: this occupation, which kept the sunniest images constantly before his mind, put him into a mood that often touched on exuberance and expressed itself in generous, even opulent hospitality. Even Daniel appeared mollified, though it was clear the Baron still mistrusted him. What appeared wonderful to everyone was that the steward seemed to grow younger every day: perhaps the grief for his late master was wearing off, perhaps it was because he was no longer obliged to spend cold, sleepless nights in the tower; but whatever the cause, he had changed from a tottery old man to a robust, red-cheeked fellow who walked vigorously and laughed loudly.

The gaiety of life at Castle R. was now disrupted by the arrival of the noteworthy figure of Baron Wolfgang's younger brother, Hubert. When the Baron saw him he went deathly white and exclaimed: 'Wretch! What do you want here?'

Hubert threw himself into his brother's arms, but the latter led him away into another room and shut the door. The two were together for several hours; then Hubert reappeared with a wild demeanour and called for his horses. The lawyer tried to detain him, for he feared a fatal outcome to this quarrel; then the Baron also appeared and called loudly: 'Stay here, Hubert! You will come to your senses.'

Hubert mastered himself, and as he threw his coat to a servant he took V.'s hand and said with a mocking smile: 'The Lord of the Manor is, it seems, willing to have me.'

They went into a side room. V. said that whatever had arisen would only have been intensified if Hubert had left. Hubert took the tongs which stood by the hearth and poked the fire: 'You will note that I am a good-natured fellow and quite skilled in homely tasks,' he said. 'But Wolfgang is full of the most marvellous prejudices and inclined to be a skinflint.'

V. did not feel it advisable to pursue the subject further, as Wolfgang's behaviour indicated a man torn by emotions of every kind.

Late that evening he went to the Baron's apartment and found him pacing the room, his hands clenched behind his back. When he noticed the lawyer, he stopped and, looking him gloomily in the eyes, said in a broken voice: 'My brother is here. I know what you are going to say. But you know nothing about it. My wretched brother – I am right to call him so – crosses my path everywhere like an evil spirit and disturbs my peace. He has done everything possible to wreck my life. Since the promulgation of the entail he has pursued me with a deadly hatred. He begrudges me these possessions – though in his hands they would be dissipated like chaff. He is the maddest spendthrift there is. His debts more than exceed his share of his property in Courland, and now, pursued by creditors, he has come here for money.'

'And you, his brother, refuse him –' V. interrupted. The Baron took a step backwards. 'Yes!' he cried. 'I refuse him! I cannot and will not give away one thaler of the estate's income. But listen to the proposal I put to the madman a few hours ago and then judge me. Our possessions in

Courland are, as you know, considerable; I agreed that he should have the half which falls to me. Hubert has a wife and children, and they are starving. I proposed that the property be administered, the money needed for his keep given to him from the revenues, creditors satisfied. But what does an ordered life matter to him, what do wife and child matter to him? Money, cash in large sums, is what he wants, so that he can recklessly squander it. Some devil has told him the secret of the hundred and fifty thousand thalers, of which he is demanding half. I must and I shall refuse him. And I now feel he is plotting my destruction.'

V. tried to talk the Baron out of his suspicions against his brother, but to no avail. He was authorized to deal with Hubert and his monetary needs, and he performed this task with all discretion; at last Hubert agreed: 'Let it be so, then. I will accept the Lord of the Manor's proposals, but on the condition that, since I am on the point of losing my good name and honour for ever through the harshness of my creditors, he give me a cash advance of a thousand Friedrichsdor and allow me to make my home with him, for a time at least, in his beautiful castle.'

'Never!' the Baron exploded when V. transmitted these proposals to him. 'Never will I agree to Hubert's spending even a minute in my house once I have brought my wife here. Go, dear friend, and tell that disturber of my peace that he shall have two thousand Friedrichsdor, but not as an advance; no, it is a gift, and then he must be gone – gone from here.'

V. now suddenly realized that the Baron had married without his father's knowledge, and he guessed that the dispute between the brothers must have its origin here. Hubert listened composedly to what he had to say and then replied gloomily: 'I will think about it. For the moment I will stay a few more days.'

V. tried to prove to him that the Baron was in fact doing all he could to recompense him for the injustice inherent in an entail, which so greatly favours the first-born; there was, indeed, something hateful in the whole conception. As if suffocating, Hubert tore open his jacket, placed a hand on his hip and spun round like a dancer. 'Bah!' he exclaimed. 'Hatefulness is born of hatred.' Then he laughed loudly and said: 'How graciously the Lord of the Manor throws his gold pieces to the beggar!'

V. now realized there was no question of a reconciliation between the brothers.

Hubert installed himself in the side wing and, to the Baron's annoyance, seemed ready for a long stay. He often had long conversations with the steward, and they even went hunting together; but apart from this he was seldom seen and he avoided meeting his brother. Altogether, V. felt he understood the dread the Baron had evidenced on beholding Hubert's arrival.

One day, when V. was alone in his study, Hubert entered and said, in an almost melancholy tone: 'I will accept the most recent proposals of my brother. Can you manage it so that I receive the two thousand Friedrichs-dor today? I will then leave tonight – by horse – entirely alone.'

'With the money?' V. asked.

'Correct,' replied Hubert. 'I know what you are going to say. The weight! Make it out in notes to Isaac Lazarus in K. I will go straight to K. tonight. I am being driven from here: the old man has cursed this place with his evil spirits.'

'Are you speaking of your father, Herr Baron?' asked V., very seriously.

Hubert's lips trembled; he held firmly on to a chair so as not to fall, then cried: 'Today then, Herr Justitiarius!' and staggered from the room.

'He realizes he can do nothing once my mind is made up,' said the Baron, as he made out the notes to Lazarus. He felt a load had been lifted from his shoulders and as he sat at supper that evening was happier than he had been for a long time. Hubert had sent his apologies, and all were glad he was not there.

V. resided in a somewhat distant room whose windows looked out on to the courtyard. During the night he was awoken by what seemed to him a distant, plaintive wailing. He listened, but there was no repetition, and he had to dismiss it as a trick of some dream. Nonetheless, so strong a feeling of horror and anxiety had overcome him that he could no longer stay in bed. He rose and went to the window. Before long the castle door opened and a figure holding a burning candle stepped out and crossed the yard. V. recognized the steward, Daniel, and watched as he opened the stable door, went into the stable and emerged again, leading a saddled horse. Now a second figure appeared out of the darkness: it was wrapped in a fur coat and wore a fox-fur cap; V. recognized Hubert. He spoke earnestly with Daniel for a few minutes, then again disappeared. Daniel led the horse back into the stable, locked it and returned across the yard the way he had come. It was evident that Hubert had intended to ride off but had for some reason changed his mind; it was also evident he was involved with the steward in some kind of conspiracy. V. could scarcely wait for morning to come to inform the Baron of what had occurred.

But next morning, at the hour when the Baron was accustomed to rise, V. heard a running hither and thither, the sound of doors opening and shutting, confused talking and shouting. He stepped out into the corridor, and everywhere there were servants running. At length he learned that the Baron was missing: they had sought for him for hours in vain. He was known to have gone to bed; he must therefore have got up again and have wandered off with the candelabra in his hand, for that also was missing. Driven by a dark foreboding, V. rushed to the fateful hall where, like his father, Wolfgang had made his bedroom.

The door to the tower stood open; horror-struck, V. cried: 'There he lies, dashed to pieces!'

It was so. Snow had fallen, so that from above only one arm of the unfortunate man could be seen protruding from the stones. It was hours before workmen succeeded in climbing down and retrieving the body. In the convulsion of death, the Baron had clung to the silver candelabra, and the hand with which he still held it was the only part of his body uninjured: the rest had been shattered by the impact on the stones and rocks.

With a fury of despair in his countenance, Hubert rushed up to the body, which lay in the hall on a wide table just where the old Baron had lain a few weeks earlier. Crushed by the sight, he wailed: 'Brother! O my poor brother! No, this is not what I desired from the devils who were driving me!'

V. shuddered at this insidious language, for he believed he would have to proceed against Hubert as his brother's murderer. Hubert lay unconscious on the floor; he was put to bed, but recovered fairly quickly with a strengthening tonic. Pale and with grief in his eyes, he then went to V. in his room and said as he slowly lowered himself into a chair: 'I have wished my brother dead, because my father bestowed on him the best part of his estate through that evil entail. Now he has met his death in a dreadful way. I am Lord of the Manor. But my heart is crushed. I shall never be happy again. I confirm you in your office. You shall have the widest powers to administer the estate, on which I shall not be living.'

In a few hours Hubert was on his way back to K. It appeared that the unhappy Wolfgang had risen during the night, had probably made for the library, but, bemused by sleep, had mistaken the door. This explanation did not satisfy V. If the Baron could not sleep, he could not have been bemused by sleep and thus could not have mistaken the door. The tower doorway was, moreover, firmly locked and must have been difficult to open. He expressed his doubts to the assembled servants.

'Ah,' said Franz, the Baron's huntsman, 'my dear sir, indeed it never happened like that.'

'How else, then?' V. asked him.

Franz declined to speak in front of the others; he desired to say what he had to say in confidence. V. now learnt that the Baron had often spoken to Franz about the treasure which lay buried under the rubble and that, as if driven by an evil spirit, he often went at night to the doorway, to which Daniel must have given him the key, and looked down longingly into the depths for these supposed riches. What was probable was that, on that fateful night, the Baron had again made his way to the tower and had there been seized by a sudden dizziness and had thus fallen. Daniel, who also appeared very shaken by the Baron's death, proposed that the dangerous doorway be walled up, and this was done.

Baron Hubert von R., now Lord of the Manor, returned to Courland. V. received unrestricted authority for the administration of the estate: the building of the new house was discontinued and the old building put in as good condition as possible.

Many years passed. Late one autumn, Hubert again appeared at Castle R. and spent several days closeted with V. Then he returned to Courland; on his journey through K. he deposited there his last will and testament. During his visit he had spoken much of forebodings of an early death, and these forebodings were fulfilled, for he died a year later. His son, also named Hubert, came quickly from Courland to take possession of his inheritance. His mother and sister followed him. The youth seemed from the first moment to combine all the evil qualities of his forebears: he wanted many changes on the spot, he threw the cook out of the house, he tried to thrash the coachman (but did not succeed, for the fellow was as strong as a tree) – in short, he was well on the way to making himself thoroughly unpopular when V. stepped in firmly to assure him that not so much as a chair should be moved before the reading of the will.

'You are subordinate here to the Lord of the Manor,' the Baron began. V. did not allow him to continue. 'No hastiness, Baron!' he said. 'You may not hold sway here before the will is read. For the moment I, and I alone, am master here and well know how to meet force with force. I have the power of my authority as executor of your father's will and am authorized by the power of the court to prohibit your stay in Castle R. I advise you to take yourself back to K.'

The decisive tone in which he spoke gave his words suitable weight, and the young Baron retreated with derisive laughter.

Three months passed, and the day arrived on which, according to the wishes of the late Baron, the will was to be opened at K., where it had been deposited. In addition to the court officials, the Baron and V., there was also in the courtroom a younger man, of noble appearance, whom V. had brought with him and whom everyone assumed to be V.'s clerk, as a sealed document was sticking out of his pocket. The Baron looked askance at him, as he did at almost everybody, and demanded that the tedious ceremony be disposed of quickly. He recognized the hand and seal of his late father, and as the clerk prepared to read the will aloud he gazed indifferently out of the window, an arm thrown carelessly over the back of his chair. After a brief preamble, the deceased Baron Hubert von R. declared that he had never possessed the entail as true Lord of the Manor, but had only administered it on behalf of the only son of the deceased Baron Wolfgang von R., named Roderich after his grandfather: it was to him, accordingly, that the inheritance fell. Detailed accounts of income and expenditure would be found at his estate. Wolfgang von R. – so Hubert recounted – had in Geneva made the acquaintanceship of Miss Julie von St Val and taken so passionate a liking to her that he had resolved never to be parted from her. She was very poor, and her family was of the people: he could, therefore, never hope for the consent of old Roderich, whose whole endeavour had been to enhance the status of his house in every way; and when he had, in fact, disclosed to his father what his intention was, the old man had specifically declared that he had already chosen a bride for the Lord of the Manor of R. and that there could never be any question of another. Wolfgang had then, in the name of Born, married Julie; after a year she had borne him a son, and it was he who was now to become Lord of the Manor.

The Baron stared at the clerk as if thunderstruck. As the clerk finished reading the catastrophic document, V. arose, took the young man by the hand and said, as he bowed to those present: 'Here, my Lords, I have the honour to present to you Baron Roderich von R., Lord of the Manor of R.'

Hubert stared at the youth who, as if fallen from Heaven, had robbed him of everything. With rage in his burning eyes and clenched fists, he ran from the court without a word. Baron Roderich now handed over to the court the documents which proved he was who he claimed to be. V. perused them and said, as he put them back in order: 'Now God will help.'

At once on the following morning, Baron Hubert submitted a complaint to the authorities at K., in which he applied for immediate possession of the entail. Neither by testament, nor in any other way, his lawyer asserted, could the deceased Baron Hubert von R. dispose of it. On the death of the father, ownership passed automatically to the son: there was no need for any declaration of accession; the terms of the entail could not be waived. What reasons the deceased may have had for appointing a different Lord of the Manor were quite immaterial. It should also be noted that the former Baron had himself had a love affair in Switzerland, and his alleged brother's son was perhaps his own.

Though the probability that the facts asserted in the testament were accurate was very strong, and though the judges were particularly incensed that the son did not shrink from accusing his father of a crime, yet the son's view of the case was correct, and it was only the tireless efforts of V. which succeeded in having the transfer of the entail postponed to give him time to establish the legitimacy of the youthful Roderich.

He realized only too well how difficult it would be. He had been through all old Roderich's correspondence without finding any trace of a letter, or even a paragraph, connecting Wolfgang with Mlle de St Val. He was sitting in old Roderich's bedroom in Castle R. and working on a letter to a notary in Geneva, who had been recommended to him as sharp-witted and who was to produce notices for him which might clarify the case of the young Baron. It was midnight and the moon shone brightly into the adjoining hall, the door of which stood open. It seemed as if someone was slowly climbing the stairs, rattling and jingling keys. V. rose and went into the hall; now he heard someone approaching the door of the hall from the passageway. It was opened, and there entered a man with a deathly white face, dressed in night attire and holding a candelabra in one hand and a large bunch of keys in the other. V. at once recognized the steward and was on the point of calling out to him when he was gripped by an icy chill: in the whole attitude of the old man there was something sinister and ghostly. He realized he had a sleepwalker before him. The steward went with measured tread through the hall and up to the walled-up door which had formerly led to the tower; in front of it he stopped and emitted a howling sound which echoed so dreadfully throughout the hall that V. trembled in horror. Then, placing the candelabra on the floor and hanging the bundle of keys on his belt, Daniel began to scratch at the wall with his hands, so that blood was soon spurting out from under his nails, while groaning as if tormented by the pangs of death. Now he put his ear to the wall as if listening to something; then he motioned with his hand as if silencing someone, bent down, picked up the candelabra and paced quietly back to the door. V. followed him warily, lamp in hand. The steward went down the stairs, opened the main doors, proceeded to the stable and, to V.'s amazement, fetched saddle and harness and with great care saddled a horse. After brushing back a lock of hair from its forehead and patting it on the neck, he took it by the bridle and led it out. In the courtyard he stood still for a few seconds as if receiving orders, to which he responded with a nod of the head. Then he led the horse back into the stable, unsaddled it and tied it up. Now he took the candelabra, closed the stable door, returned to the castle and disappeared into his room, which he carefully bolted.

V. was deeply disturbed by this scene: a foreboding of some dreadful deed reared up before him like a black ghost.

Filled with a sense of the dangerous position his protegé was in, he believed he must employ what he had just seen to his own advantage. The following day, as dawn was breaking, Daniel came to his room to receive instruction about some domestic matter. V. seized him and made him sit down.

'Now listen, Daniel, my old friend!' he said. 'I have been wanting to ask you what you think about the muddle Hubert's strange will has got us into. Do you believe the boy is really Wolfgang's son, born in wedlock?'

Avoiding V.'s gaze, the steward said peevishly: 'He

might be and he might not be. Why should I care? Let whoever wants be master here now.'

'But I mean,' continued V., drawing closer to the old man and laying a hand on his shoulder, 'as you had the old Baron's complete confidence, surely he didn't keep silent about his son's relationships? Did he tell you of the alliance Wolfgang had made against his wishes?'

'I can't remember anything of the sort,' replied the steward, yawning.

'You are tired, old fellow,' said V. 'Did you have a restless night?'

'Not that I know of,' replied the other coldly. 'But I will now go and prepare food.'

With this, he rose wearily from the chair, rubbing his back and yawning again.

'Just wait a moment,' said V., taking him by the hand and indicating that he wanted him to sit down. The steward remained standing, supporting himself on the desk. 'Why should I care about the will? Why should I care about the dispute over the entail?' he exclaimed.

'Let us not talk about that any more,' interrupted V., 'but about something completely different. You are being cantankerous, you are yawning, and I almost believe it really was you last night.'

'What was I last night?' asked the steward.

'Last night, at midnight,' continued V., 'as I was sitting in the old Baron's chambers next to the great hall, you came in through the door, quite stiff and pale, you walked to the walled-up door, scratched on the wall with both hands and moaned as if you were suffering great agony. Are you a sleepwalker, Daniel?'

The steward dropped back into a chair which V. quickly pushed towards him. He made no sound, his face was hidden in shadow, but V. heard him breathing and his teeth chattering.

'Yes,' continued V. after a short silence, 'it is a strange

thing with sleepwalkers. The next day they don't remember the slightest thing.'

Daniel remained motionless.

'I have experienced something similar,' continued V. 'I had a friend who, as soon as the moon was full, regularly began nocturnal wanderings. Many a time he would sit and write letters. The most amazing thing, however, was that if I began to whisper in his ear I soon managed to make him start talking. He answered all my questions pertinently; what, awake, he would have been careful to keep secret flowed from his lips. I believe that if a moon-struck person has kept silent about a crime, you could get it out of him in that strange condition. He who has a clear conscience, like we two, my dear Daniel, has, of course, nothing to fear. But listen, Daniel; you were certainly wanting, trying to go up into the observatory tower when you were scratching away at that walled-up door so horribly. Did you want to go on with the work of old Roderich? Well, I shall get that out of you next time!'

As V. was speaking, the steward began trembling more and more; now his body was in the grip of convulsions, and he burst into a shrill, incomprehensible babbling. V. rang for the servants. Lamps were brought. The old man could not get up and was lifted like an automaton and carried to his bed. After almost an hour in this dreadful condition he fell into a deep sleep; when he awoke, he demanded wine to drink, and when this was brought him he sent out the servant who had brought it and locked himself in.

V. had really decided to try the experiment the moment he spoke of it to Daniel, though he had to admit to himself that Daniel, perhaps only now aware of his sleepwalking, would do all he could to avoid him and that any confession made in that state would be hard to build upon. Nevertheless, he went to the hall towards midnight, hoping that Daniel would sleepwalk in spite of himself. Soon there was a commotion in the courtyard; V. heard a window being broken, hurried down and, as he rushed along the corridors, was met by the stench of fumes which, he soon realized, were streaming out of the steward's room. Daniel was in the act of being carried out, stiff as death, to be laid in another room. One of the grooms – so the servants recounted – awakened by a strange muffled knocking, believed something had happened to the steward and was about to get up when the watchman in the courtyard cried: 'Fire! Fire! The steward's room is ablaze!'

At this cry, several other servants came running, but all efforts to break down the door were vain. They hurried into the yard, but the watchman had already broken the window of the room and had pulled down the burning curtains; a few jugs of water served to put out the flames. The steward was found unconscious on the floor in the middle of the room, still holding the candelabra which had set light to the curtains. The old man's eyebrows and hair were singed, and if the watchman had not noticed the fire he would have been burned to death. To their surprise, the servants found the door of his room secured by two recently fitted bolts which had not been there the previous evening; V., however, understood their purpose – the steward had wanted to make it impossible to sleepwalk out of the room.

The steward was seriously ill, he did not speak, he took little nourishment and he stared before him as if in anticipation of death. V. believed the old man would never get to his feet again. He had done everything he could for his protegé and had to await the result calmly; he now wanted to go back to K. His departure had been fixed for the following morning. Late that evening he was packing his manuscripts when there fell into his hand a small packet which Baron Hubert had addressed to him with the inscription: 'To be read after the opening of my will'. V. could not understand how he had come to neglect this packet, and he was in the midst of opening it when the door opened and Daniel entered with quiet, ghostly steps. He laid a black document case, which he was carrying under his arm, on to the writing table; then, sinking to his knees with a deathly sigh, he grasped V.'s hands frantically and said, in a voice that seemed to come from the depths of the tomb: 'I do not want to die on the scaffold; He above judges'; he then rose with difficulty and much fearful gasping and left the room as he had come.

V. spent the night reading all that was contained in the black document case and in Hubert's packet, and what he read determined what he then did. As soon as he arrived in K. he visited the younger Baron Hubert, who received him disdainfully; the outcome of their ensuing discussion, however, was that the Baron declared before the court on the following day that he recognized the pretender to the entail as the legitimate son of Baron Wolfgang and consequently as the rightful heir. He then drove quickly away; to his mother and sister, whom he left behind, he had written that they would probably never see him again.

Roderich was amazed at the turn events had taken, and begged V. to explain how this wonder had been brought about. V. put him off until after he had taken possession of the entail. The transfer of the estate was now further delayed by the court's demand for, in addition to Hubert's declaration, documentary proof of Roderich's legitimacy. V. offered him an apartment in Castle R., and added that Hubert's mother and sister, embarrassed by his sudden departure, would probably prefer to stay there too, rather than return to the noisy city. The delight with which Roderich accepted the notion of living under the same roof as the Baroness and her daughter was evidence of the deep impression the child Seraphine had made on him; within a few weeks he had gained Seraphine's love in return and her mother's assent to their marriage. This was much too precipitate for V.; Roderich's legitimation as Lord of the Manor was still in doubt. Letters from Courland now interrupted the idyll: Hubert had not returned to his property there but had gone to Petersburg, where he had entered military service, and was now in the field against the Persians, with whom Russia had just commenced hostilities; this made it necessary for the Baroness and her daughter to depart for Courland, where disorder and confusion reigned. Roderich, who already regarded himself as an adopted son, accompanied his beloved; and so it was that, when V. also returned to K., the castle was deserted as before. The steward's illness became worse, and it was thought he would not recover; his duties were transferred to the old huntsman, Franz.

At last, after long delay, V. received the desired news from Switzerland. The priest who had officiated at Wolfgang's wedding had long since died, but an annotation in his hand had been discovered in the church register, to the effect that the person whom he had joined in holy wedlock in the name of Born with Mlle Julie St Val had proved to him his legitimacy as Baron Wolfgang von R., the eldest son of Baron Roderich von R., of Castle R. Moreover, there were two witnesses to the marriage, a merchant in Geneva and an old French captain who lived in Lyons; Wolfgang had disclosed his identity to both of them, and their sworn statements confirmed the annotation in the church register. Nothing now stood in the way of the transfer of the estate, which was to take place the following autumn. Hubert had fallen in his first battle, and the property at Courland thus fell to Baroness Seraphine von R. It made a fine dowry for the overjoyed Roderich.

November had arrived when the Baroness and Roderich with his bride-to-be arrived in Castle R. The transfer of the estate followed, then Roderich's marriage to Seraphine. Many weeks passed in revelry, until at length the satiated guests departed – to the great delight of V., who did not want to take his leave of Castle R. without having initiated the new master into all the affairs relating to his new property. Since Daniel had appeared to him as a sleepwalker, V. had elected to sleep in old Roderich's bedroom, so as to be close by if there should be any more sleepwalking. It was thus in this apartment and the adjoining hall that the new Baron and V. met to transact their business. They were sitting there at the great table beside the blazing fire making their way through accounts and documents and oblivious to the muffled thundering of the sea, the shrieking of the gulls, the storm whistling through the castle and awakening evil echoes in the chimneys and narrow corridors. Suddenly a loud gust of wind resounded through the castle and the hall was filled with the light of the full moon. V. said merely: 'What terrible weather!'

The Baron, immersed in the prospect of wealth which had opened up before him, replied, as he turned over a leaf of the cash book with a satisfied smile: 'Indeed, very stormy.'

But now he started up in terror as the door of the hall sprang open and a white, ghostly figure came into view! It was Daniel – whom everyone supposed to be lying incapable of motion – again on his nocturnal wanderings. Dumbstruck, the Baron stared at the steward as he scratched away at the wall, groaning piteously. His face as white as death and his hair standing on end, the Baron jumped from his seat and approached the steward, crying loudly, so that the whole hall echoed: 'Daniel! Daniel! What are you doing here at this hour?'

The steward emitted the wailing howl that had burst from him on the occasion Wolfgang had offered him gold for his loyalty, and collapsed to the floor. V. called the servants; they lifted the steward, but all efforts to revive him were vain. Then the Baron cried, as if beside himself: 'Dear God, have I not heard that sleepwalkers may be on the threshold of death if one calls them by name? O wretch! I have killed the poor old man! I shall not know another moment's peace.'

When the servants had carried the body away and the hall was empty again, V. took the Baron by the hand and led him to the walled-up doorway. 'He who has just died at your feet, Baron Roderich,' he said 'was the wicked murderer of your father.'

The Baron stared at him as if he were a ghost from Hell. V. continued: 'Now it is time to reveal the secret which burdened that wicked man and drove him to walk in his sleep. The Almighty Power has seen to it that the son has revenged his father's murder: the words you shouted in the sleepwalker's ear were the last spoken by your unhappy father.'

Trembling and unable to utter a word, the Baron sat beside V. as the latter told him of the contents of the package which Hubert had left behind. Hubert blamed himself, with expressions which were proof of the deepest regret, for the implacable hatred of his brother which had taken root in him from the moment old Roderich had established the entail; when Wolfgang had begun his courtship of Julie von St Val in Geneva, he believed he had acquired the means to destroy him. In collusion with Daniel, he sought to compel the old man to a decision which would reduce Wolfgang to despair. Old Roderich was obsessed with the idea of uniting his family with one of the oldest families in the kingdom: he believed he had read this union in the stars. He thus regarded Wolfgang's union with Julie as nothing less than a crime against the eternal powers, and every attempt to destroy it seemed to him justified. In this Hubert had seconded him. But Heaven had decreed that Wolfgang should prosper, and his actual marriage, and the birth of his son, remained a secret from Hubert. With the premonition of the nearness of death, there also came to old Roderich the premonition that Wolfgang had in fact united himself with the detested

Julie; in a letter summoning him to Castle R. he had pronounced his son cursed if he did not destroy that union. It was this letter that Wolfgang burned beside his father's bier.

Roderich had written to Hubert that Wolfgang had married Julie, but that he would break up that union. Hubert took this for imagination and was not a little startled when Wolfgang himself not only confirmed the old man's suspicion but added that Julie had borne him a son and that very shortly he would inform her (who still held him to be a merchant) of his real standing. He intended to go to Geneva to fetch his beloved wife, but before he could do so death had claimed him. Hubert had kept silent as to the existence of a son and stolen the birthright for himself. But after a few years he began to feel regret. Shame prevented him from revealing his deceit, but he did not wish to take another penny from the rightful owner, made inquiries in Geneva and learned that Frau Born, inconsolable at the incomprehensible disappearance of her husband, had died, but that young Roderich Born was being brought up by a foster-father. To him, Hubert announced himself under an assumed name and forwarded sufficient money to raise the young Lord of the Manor in a fitting way.

How he had husbanded the income of the estate and how he had disposed of it in his Will was already known. As for the death of his brother, Hubert wrote in such strange, enigmatic terms that it appeared likely he was at least indirectly responsible for it. The contents of the black document case had made all clear. It contained the treacherous correspondence between Hubert and Daniel; there was also a page which Daniel had written and signed: a terrible confession at which V. felt his whole being tremble. Hubert had come to Castle R. at Daniel's request; it was Daniel who had written to him telling him of the hundred and fifty thousand gold thalers. Within the steward there seethed a rage which had to discharge itself on the young man who had wanted to throw him out like a dog. He fanned the flames consuming the disappointed Hubert, and at meetings in the forest, in storm and snow, they agreed on Wolfgang's destruction.

'We must get rid of him,' Hubert had said, fingering his gun. 'Yes, we must get rid of him,' Daniel had agreed, 'but not like that.'

This inspired Hubert to dare greatly – he would murder the Baron, and no one would know of it; but when he at last received some money, he regretted the idea and intended to leave. Daniel himself had saddled the horse and led it from the stable, but when the Baron had made to mount it, Daniel had said in a scornful voice: 'The estate belongs to you, Baron Hubert, for its proud lord lies crushed in the tower's abyss. Perhaps you would now prefer to stay.'

Daniel had observed that, in his greed for gold, Wolfgang often rose at night, went to the door which formerly led to the tower and peered down with avaricious looks into the depths, which, he believed, concealed a great treasure. On the fateful night, Daniel had concealed himself behind the hall doors; as he heard the Baron open the door leading to the tower, he ran up behind him. The Baron, standing at the edge of the precipice, turned as he became aware of the presence of the mad servant in whose eyes murder was already gleaming and cried out in terror: 'Daniel! Daniel! What are you doing here at this hour?'

Daniel then shrieked wildly: 'Down with you, you mangy dog!' and hurled the Baron into the depths with a single blow.

Shattered by these revelations, the young Baron Roderich could find no peace in the castle where his father had been murdered. He lived on his property in Courland and went to Castle R. only in the autumn. Franz affirmed that Daniel still haunted the castle at the full moon and described the ghost just as he was when V. later saw and banished him. The discovery of these events, which shamed the memory of his father, had also driven the young Baron Hubert forth into the world.

Thus my great-uncle related all that had occurred. Then he took my hand and said very gently, his eyes filled with tears: 'Cousin, Cousin, even she, that gentle lady, has fallen victim to the evil power which resides in that place. Two days after we left Castle R. the Baron arranged a sleighride; he himself was driving with his wife, and as they were heading down the valley the horses, shying suddenly, bolted furiously away. "The old man, the old man is behind us!" the Baroness shrieked, and in that instant she was flung from the sleigh. She was found lifeless. She is dead. The Baron is inconsolable, and he too is near to dying. We shall never return there, Cousin.'

My uncle fell silent. Heartbroken, I took leave of him, and only the universal healer, Time, could soothe the pain in which I thought I should perish.

Years passed. V. had long been resting in his grave. I had left my homeland. The storm of battle blowing across Germany drove me to Petersburg. On my return, I was driving one dark summer night along the coast when I saw in the sky a great shining star. Approaching nearer, I saw that what I had taken for a star was a red flickering flame, though I did not understand how it could be so high in the sky.

'Coachman, whatever is that fire over there?' I asked.

'Oh,' he replied, 'that isn't a fire; that is the Castle R. lighthouse.'

Castle R.! As the coachman uttered the name, the image of those fateful autumn days sprang vividly to life within me. I saw the Baron, Seraphine, the strange old aunts; I saw myself, an infatuated youth, sighing like a furnace, with woeful ballad made to his mistress's eyebrow! Thus, moved by pain and a strange longing, I climbed out of the coach in the early morning at R., where it had stopped to take on mail. I recognized the house of the estate manager and asked after him.

The postal clerk took the pipe from his mouth and pushed back his nightcap. 'There is no estate manager here,' he said. 'This is a government office, and the officer is still asleep.'

On questioning further I learned that some sixteen years previously Baron Roderich von R., the last Lord of the Manor, had died without issue, and ownership had, in accordance with the terms of the entail, passed to the state. I went up to the castle. It lay in ruins. Many of its stones had been used to build the lighthouse, an old farmer assured me. He also had knowledge of the ghost: even now, he said, at the time of the full moon wailing could be heard from among the stones.

Poor, ill-advised Roderich! What evil power did you conjure up to poison in its first youth the race you thought to have planted for eternity?

DOGE AND DOGARESSA

This, according to the catalogue of the September 1816 Exhibition of the Berlin Academy of the Arts, was the title given to a painting by the excellent C. Kolbe, Member of the Academy, which so fascinated visitors to the salon that the space before it was rarely empty. A Doge of Venice, in sumptuous robes, the equally splendid Dogaressa by his side, is striding towards a balustrade. He is an old man, a greybeard, whose bronzed and russet face reveals a strange mixture of traits, suggesting now strength, now weakness, now pride and impetuosity, but also kindness. His consort is a young creature, whose expression, whose very bearing convey a blend of sorrow and of yearning, of reverie and desire. Behind them stand an elderly woman and a man with an open sunshade. To one side of the balustrade, a young man is blowing a horn like a triton shell, and on the water at his feet floats a richly accoutred gondola flying the Venetian flag, while two oarsmen stand by in attendance. The wide expanse of sea in the background is covered with hundreds of sails, and beyond them, rising from the waters, can be seen the towers and palaces of Venice the Magnificent. To the left, one can make out the basilica of San Marco; to the right and more in the foreground is the church of San Giorgio Maggiore. The following words are carved into the gilt frame of the picture:

Senza amare
Andare sul mare

Col sposo del mare
Non può consolare

One day, a somewhat futile argument arose among a group standing in front of this picture about what had been the artist's intentions. Had he been painting a mere picture, as it were, an illustration prompted by the verse, capturing a moment in the life of an old man long past his prime who, in spite of all his pomp and splendour, could do nothing to gratify the desires of a girl's longing heart? Or did it represent a real historical occasion? The argument must have grown tedious, for one by one the crowd drifted away until presently there remained only two friends, both high-minded admirers of the noble art of painting.

'I cannot understand,' began one of them, 'how people can spoil their own pleasure by such endless hair-splitting and quibbling. Besides, although I believe I have a shrewd idea as to how matters must have stood between this Doge and his Dogaressa in real life, I am also deeply impressed by the aura of wealth and power that emanates from the work as a whole. Look at the banner with the winged lion, see how imperiously it flutters in the breeze, proclaiming Venice the Magnificent to the world!' And here, he began reciting Turandot's riddle concerning the Lion of the Adriatic, starting: *Dimmi, qual sia quel terribil fera* . . . Hardly had he ceased when, to his astonishment, a pleasing male voice immediately replied with Calaf's answer: *Tu quadrupeda fera* . . . Unnoticed by the two friends, they had been joined by a gentleman of most distinguished appearance, his grey cloak draped artistically over one shoulder, who was surveying the painting with glittering eyes. The three men fell into conversation, and the stranger told the friends in almost reverent tones: 'The artist has a unique and secret power, whereby a picture is conjured up within the depths of his being, so that figures hitherto

imperceptible and disembodied, mere shreds of mist drifting in empty space, first take shape and then come to life,
as if they find their true abode within that artist's soul. And
all at once, these images fuse with the past – or indeed,
with the future equally well – until they portray an event
that has actually happened, or even one that is yet to come.
It could very well be that Kolbe himself did not know that
these two figures painted by him in the picture before our
eyes are none other than the Doge Marino Falieri and his
wife Annunziata.'

The stranger fell silent, but the two friends pressed him
to say more and to tell them the answer to this riddle too,
just as he had already solved that of the Lion of the Adriatic
for them. The man hesitated and then he spoke. 'Since you
have expressed your curiosity, gentlemen, and provided
you have the patience to hear me out, I will gladly explain
the painting to you by telling you Falieri's story here and
now. But have you such patience? For I warn you that I
shall not be brief, since I would not care to skimp the
telling of matters that are as vivid in my mind as if I had
witnessed them myself. And that could well have been the
case, for every historian such as I is in truth a kind of
phantom, speaking to the present with the voice of a
bygone age.'

The three men then withdrew to a remote chamber
where, without further preliminaries, the stranger began
his tale.

Many years ago – in August 1354, if I am not mistaken –
the intrepid Genoese admiral Paganino Doria dealt the
Venetians a severe blow when he stormed their city of
Parenzo. Pressing ever closer to Venice itself, his well-
manned galleys sailed hither and thither across the gulf,
racing up and down like hungry beasts of prey, with a keen
eye for booty that could be taken with least risk to
themselves. The people of Venice and the Signoria too

were seized with panic, believing their last hour had come. Every man who still had use of his limbs buckled to with a will, grasping a weapon here, an oar there. In the port of San Nicolò the citizens assembled in small groups. Ships, tree-trunks and heavy iron chains shackled together were sunk in order to block the entrance to the lagoon and thus keep out the enemy. While there was frenzied activity here, with the clatter of weapons and the thunderous roar of heavy barriers being pushed into the foaming waves, there was a different scene on the Rialto. There one could see the distorted faces of the Signoria's brokers, as they mopped the cold sweat from their livid brows, hoarsely offering unheard-of rates of interest for the loan of hard cash, for the threatened Republic was also short of ready money.

It was at this moment of greatest distress and direst need that the eternal powers, in their inscrutable wisdom, decided to snatch the faithful shepherd from the sore-pressed flock. Overwhelmed by the burden of imminent catastrophe, the Doge of Venice, Andrea Dandolo, died suddenly. His people had called him affectionately *il caro contino*, their dear little count, because the pious kind-hearted Doge had never crossed the Piazza San Marco without stopping to bestow either money or good advice on those in need, words of comfort for one, for another a few ducats to slip in his pocket. As happens so often when misfortune has already sapped men's courage, any fresh blow seems doubly painful, even one that would other-wise be scarcely felt. And so it was that when the bells of San Marco tolled the death of the Doge in sombre spine-chilling strokes, the people were beside themselves with lamentation and grief. Now that their stay, their only hope was gone, they needs must bow their necks to the Genoese yoke and they cried aloud their woe, with scant regard for the fact that, so far as the necessary war measures were concerned, the loss of Dandolo might not be such a calamity after all. For the dear little count had been a man whose only desire was to live in peace and tranquillity, following the marvellous paths of the constellations in the heavens rather than dealing with the devious intricacies of statecraft; someone who was far better at organizing the order of procession during Holy Week than leading an army into battle. Now the time had come to find a Doge endowed equally with bold generalship and expert states-manship, so that Venice, shaken to its very foundations, might be rescued from the menacing might of an ever more daring enemy.

When the senators assembled, there were nothing but clouded brows, eyes fixed on the ground and heads leaning on hands for support. Where could they find the man with strong hands to grasp the unmanned tiller of state and steer it on its true course? At last the eldest councillor, Marino Bodoeri by name, uttered what was in his mind. 'Here in our midst you will not find such a man,' he declared, 'but turn your eyes to Avignon, to Marino Falieri, whom we sent thither to congratulate Pope Innocent on his en-thronement. Now he can rise to even greater heights. If we elect him as our Doge, he will save us from disaster. No doubt you will object that Marino Falieri is already nearing eighty, that his hair and beard have turned to silver, that, as his detractors maintain, his lively mien, his burning eye, the ruddiness of his nose and cheek owe more to good Cyprus wine than to inner strength, but pay no attention. Remember the shining bravery Falieri displayed as *prov-veditore* to the Fleet in the Black Sea, consider how out-standing his services to the state must have been to induce the Procurators of San Marco to reward this same Falieri with the rich lands of Valdemarino and the title of count?'

Thus did Bodoeri extol Falieri's services with lavish praise and find an answer to every objection raised, until in the end the councillors were unanimous in their choice of Falieri. True, some mentioned his ungovernable temper, his lust for power and his stubbornness, but soon the word went round: It is for these very reasons that we elect him as our Doge now that he's old rather than when he was in his prime. The carping voices died away completely once the people learned of the Council's election, and the new Doge was acclaimed amid unrestrained rejoicing.

Is it not a well-known fact that in times of danger, unrest and tension, any decision, provided only that it is firmly taken, always appears as a Heaven-sent inspiration? And so it happened that the piety and good works of the old Doge, Andrea Dandolo, were all forgotten and now everyone cried: 'By San Marco, if we had had Marino as our Doge long ago, the overweening Doria would not now be breathing down our necks.' And the crippled old soldiers painfully waved their crippled arms and shouted. 'This was the Falieri who defeated Morbassan, the same Falieri who led our troops and whose banners flew victoriously over the Black Sea!'

And wherever people gathered, someone was sure to have a tale to tell of one brave deed or other performed by old Falieri, and the air rang with wild jubilation as if Doria had already been defeated. In addition, the Venetian admiral Nicolò Pisani who, Heaven alone knows why, had sailed the fleet to Sardinia instead of giving battle to the Genoese, returned at last to home waters. Doria at once withdrew from the gulf, and although he did this because of the approach of Pisani's warships, credit for the outcome was given to the awesome name of Marino Falieri. Then people and Signoria went almost delirious with delight at the happiness of their choice, and it was decided, against all custom, that the newly elected Doge should be received like a messenger from heaven bringing honour, victory and riches in abundance. Twelve noblemen, each with a train of liveried servants, were sent by the Signoria to Verona, where, on Falieri's arrival, the republic's envoys solemnly reaffirmed his elevation to the office of

Head of State. Fifteen state barges equipped with costly trappings by the *podestà* of Chioggia and commanded by his son, Taddeo Giustiniani, arrived at Chiozza, where they welcomed on board the Doge and his retinue. Like the triumphal procession of some mighty royal conqueror, the flotilla made its way to San Clemente, where the *Bucentoro* was waiting.

At the very moment Marino Falieri was about to board the *Bucentoro* – that is, about sunset on the evening of the third of October – a poor unfortunate man was lying full length on the hard marble slabs in front of the columns of the Dogana. A few rags of striped linen, so faded that their colour was no longer recognizable but probably once part of some garment worn by the humblest of porters or gondoliers, hung from his emaciated body. No shirt was visible beneath these rags; only here and there one could see the poor wretch's skin showing through, but so white and delicate was it that it would not have disgraced or humiliated the noblest in the land. His very thinness served only to accentuate the pure harmony of his well-knit limbs, and if one examined the light chestnut locks whose tangles overshadowed his fine forehead, the blue eyes now clouded with despair and misery, the aquiline nose and the fine-drawn mouth of the unfortunate youth, who appeared to be at most twenty years old, it became clear that some hostile fate must have struck this well-born stranger and flung him down among the dregs of humanity.

As has been said, the young man lay in front of the columns of the Dogana. His head rested on his right arm. He neither stirred nor moved, but with a glazed and vacant look he stared down into the sea. One might very well have thought that life had left his body, that the death agony had turned him to stone like a statue, if not for the fact that every now and then, as if in the grip of some indescribable suffering, he had sighed deeply. Very likely this was due to the pain in his gravely injured left arm, which was wrapped in bloody rags and which he rested on the pavement. All work had come to a halt, the noise of commerce had been silenced, the whole city of Venice was afloat in a thousand boats and gondolas, making their way towards the wildly acclaimed Falieri. That was how it came to pass that the poor youth moaned aloud in his pain uncomforted and unaided. However, at the very moment when his weary head sank to the ground and he seemed about to faint, a hoarse voice was heard calling to him most plaintively again and again: 'Antonio! My dear Antonio!' At last, with a great effort, Antonio half raised himself; as he turned his head in the direction of the columns of the Dogana from which the voice seemed to come, he whispered barely audibly: 'Who calls me? Who has come to cast my corpse into the sea, for my end is very near?' A shrivelled little old woman leaning on a stick hurried towards the injured youth panting hard, and as she bent down beside him, she broke into a horrible peal of laughter. 'Foolish child,' she tittered, 'foolish boy, do you want to perish here just because your golden luck has forsaken you for a while? Look there! Look into the blazing sunset; there are ducats shining for you there! But you must eat, dear lad, eat and drink; it is only hunger that has brought you so low here on the cold pavement. Your arm has already healed, it is well again, I tell you.'

By now, Antonio had recognized the hag for the weird beggarwoman who used to solicit alms on the steps of the church of San Francesco, who was always giggling and chuckling, and to whom he himself, driven by some inexplicable impulse, had often thrown a hard-earned quattrino he could not really spare.

'Leave me in peace,' he said, 'leave me alone, you witless old crone; of course it is hunger rather than my wound which makes me so weak and wretched. I wanted to cross the water to see if the brothers at the convent had a few mouthfuls of broth for me, but all my fellow oarsmen have gone – there is no one left to take me in his boat for mercy's sake, and that is why I have collapsed here and do not think I shall ever rise again.'

'Hee, hee, hee,' chortled the old hag, 'why do you yield to despair so soon? Why lose heart so quickly? Here are some dainty little dried fish, bought this very day in front of the Zecca, here is lemon juice, here is a piece of fine white bread. Eat and drink, my son; then we will tend your injured arm.' And indeed the woman had already produced from the sack-like hood that hung down her bent back the fish, bread and lemon juice she had mentioned. The moment Antonio's burning shrivelled lips had been moistened by the cool drink, his hunger doubled in force and he wolfed down the fish and the bread.

The woman, meanwhile, was busily unwinding the rags from his injured arm, and she discovered that, although the boy must have been attacked savagely, the open wound was all but healed. She took ointment from a small box, warmed it with her breath and as she applied it she asked: 'Who was it who beat you so ferociously, my poor child?'

Antonio, now completely refreshed and with the desire to live glowing through his veins, sat up straight. 'Ha!' he cried, fiery-eyed and raising his clenched right fist, 'it was that rascal Nicolò. It was out of envy that he beat me senseless; he grudges me every quattrino thrown my way by some charitable hand. You must know that I used to labour hard for my bread loading goods from ships and boats at the warehouses used by the German merchants, the Fondaco dei Tedeschi. I'm sure you know the building I mean.' But as soon as Antonio had pronounced the word Fondaco, the old woman giggled again and burst into hideous laughter, babbling over and over again: 'Fondaco! Fondaco! Fondaco!'

'Stop that crazed laughter of yours if you want to hear my tale!' exclaimed Antonio angrily. The harridan was silent again immediately and Antonio continued: 'When I had earned a nice little sum, I bought myself a new doublet; I cut quite a dash and became a gondolier. And since I was always cheerful and hard-working, and knew many a beautiful song, I earned much more than the other gondoliers. But that aroused their envy. They told lies about me to my employers, who soon chased me away. Everywhere I went, everywhere I stopped, they called after me: "German dog! Accursed heretic!" And three days ago, as I was helping to beach a boat in San Sebastiano, they attacked me with sticks and stones. I defended myself lustily, but the treacherous Nicolò struck me with an oar, which brushed against my head and severely gashed my arm, felling me to the ground. Now you have stilled my hunger and I can feel that your salve has worked wonders on my sore arm. See! I can swing it again! I shall be able to go back to my rowing again and do it as well as ever.'

Antonio had risen to his feet and swung his injured arm back and forth with powerful movements. The old woman, however, was tittering again and squealing with laughter, and as she did so, she danced an amazing kind of jig with small springy steps, calling out to Antonio: 'Son of mine, son of mine, row stoutly, row stoutly! He is coming, he is coming! See how the gold gleams in the flames – row stoutly, stoutly! But only once more. One last time, then never again.'

Antonio paid no more attention to the crone's antics, however, for in front of him the most splendid spectacle was beginning to take shape. From the direction of San Clemente emerged the state barge, the *Bucentoro*, the Lion of the Adriatic fluttering from the masthead, while the resounding strokes of the oars were like the powerful wing-beats of a golden swan. Surrounded by a thousand boats and gondolas, with its bold majestic head raised aloft, it seemed to command a jubilant army whose shining helmets were newly risen from the depths of the sea. The setting sun cast its burnished rays across the water, across Venice, so that all was enveloped in flickering flames. But as Antonio watched in rapture, forgetting all his woes, the reflection turned to the colour of ever darkening blood. A dull roar ripped through the air and a terrifying echo reverberated from the depths of the waters. The tempest came riding high on blackest clouds, shrouding everything in utter darkness, while the waves foamed higher and higher, rising from the seething lagoon like hissing monsters threatening to devour everything. Scattered to the four winds like a flock of bedraggled birds, gondolas and boats drifted helplessly across the sea. The flat-bottomed *Bucentoro*, not designed to withstand the storm, swayed ominously back and forth. Instead of the joyous cheering of cornets and trumpets, all one heard through the storm were the cries of terror of those in distress.

Antonio, frozen with horror, became aware of a noise close by him, as if a chain were rattling. When he looked down, he saw that a small rowing boat was moored to the landing stage and rocking up and down on the waves. A thought flashed through his very soul. He jumped down into the boat, unhitched it, seized the oar that was lying there and with stalwart courage struck out across the lagoon, making straight for the *Bucentoro*. The closer he came the more clearly he heard the cries for assistance from aboard the barge: 'Help! Help! Hurry and save the Doge!'

It is well known that, during a storm, small fishing boats are safer and more easily handled in the lagoon than larger craft, and by now boats like Antonio's were scurrying from all quarters in an attempt to save the precious head of the distinguished Falieri. But in real life, Destiny always grants the successful accomplishment of a bold deed to one person only, so that all other efforts are rendered vain. On this occasion, it was the poor youth Antonio who was fated to save the newly elected Doge and, unaided, he came alongside the *Bucentoro* with his flimsy little boat. Old Marino Falieri was no stranger to such perils and without a moment's hesitation he stepped from the magnificent but treacherous *Bucentoro* into Antonio's small craft. Lightly skimming the seething waves like a dolphin, the skiff bore Falieri to the Piazzetta in a matter of minutes. With his robes drenched, and great drops of water oozing from his grey beard, the old man was led forward to the basilica of San Marco, where the pale-faced aristocracy concluded the ceremonial entry. The populace, as disturbed by the unfortunate end to the procession as the Signoria – and to make matters worse, during the hurry and confusion the Doge had been inadvertently led towards the church between the Piazzetta's two columns, the traditional place of execution for common criminals – fell silent amid the rejoicings; thus the day which had begun with such festivity ended in sadness and gloom.

No one, not even Antonio himself, gave a second thought to the Doge's saviour. He lay exhausted on the paving stones beneath the portico to the Doge's Palace, half unconscious with the pain of his newly re-opened wound. So he was the more astonished when, as night fell, a ducal envoy took him by the shoulder and with the words: 'Come, my dear friend!' ushered him into the palace, to the Doge's private apartment. Old Falieri came towards him with a benevolent expression on his face. Pointing to some purses lying on the table, he said: 'You behaved with valour, my son. Here, take these three thousand ducats. If you need more, you have only to ask. But in return you must do me a favour. Never appear before my eyes again.' As he spoke these last words, the old man's eyes flashed and the end of his nose grew redder. Antonio had no idea what the old man meant, but he did not take his hasty dismissal too much to heart; he had all his work cut out to carry away the heavy purses – which, however, he firmly believed were no more than his deserts.

Next morning, radiant in the glory of his newly won power, Marino Falieri looked out from the tall pointed window of the palace on the people below engaged in all kinds of vigorous weapon drills. Into the room walked Bodoeri, who had been bound to the Doge with bonds of eternal friendship ever since they were boys together. And when Marino, preoccupied with his thoughts and his own dignity, seemed not even to notice his friend, Bodoeri clapped his hands smartly and exclaimed: 'Why, Falieri! What exalted notions are hatching and thriving in that head of yours since you were given the right to don the Doge's cap?'

As if waking from a dream, Falieri walked towards his visitor with feigned friendliness. In his heart, he knew that it was Bodoeri he had to thank for the privilege of sporting the cap of office, and such words served to remind him of it. By now he felt that every obligation pressed like a burden on his proud ambition, and since he could not dismiss his old and trusted friend as summarily as the poor youth Antonio, he forced himself to utter a few words of thanks and immediately passed to talking of the measures needed to counter the foes of Venice, who were rising on every side. Bodoeri interrupted him with a sly smile. 'This and all other matters the state demands from you we shall reflect on and discuss in thorough detail in a few hours' time, when we meet in the assembly of the Great Council. But affairs of state are not the reason I have come to you so early in the day. I am not here to devise with you ways to defeat the presumptuous Doria or bring to his senses the Hungarian Ludwig, who is once again casting an envious eye on our Dalmatian ports. No, Marino, I have been thinking about you personally, and reflecting on a subject that would probably never have occurred to you. It is about your marriage.'

'How can you,' retorted Falieri, rising to his feet, turning his back on Bodoeri and staring out of the window, 'how can you think of such a thing? It is a long time until Ascension Day. By then, I hope, the enemy will have been defeated, and I shall have won victory, honour, new wealth and glorious might to offer the sea-born Adriatic Lion. On that day, the chaste bride will find the bridegroom worthy of her.'

'Oh nonsense!' Bodoeri broke in impatiently. 'You mean that quaint ceremony on Ascension Day when the Doge throws a golden ring from the *Bucentoro* into the waves, in token of his marriage to the Adriatic Sea. But, Marino, kinsman of the sea, is the only bride you are to know to be the cold, wet, treacherous element which you are pleased to believe you command, but which only yesterday rebelled against you and threatened your very life? What pleasure lies in the arms of such a wife, the wayward headstrong maiden, who, the moment you glide up in the *Bucentoro* to stroke those ice-blue cheeks, turns on you in fury to pick a quarrel with you? Would the glowing heat of Vesuvius itself suffice to warm the chilly bosom of such a deceitful faithless female, who weds and weds again, not receiving the rings of the Doges of Venice as a precious pledge of love, but seizing them rather as the tribute of her slaves? No, Marino. My idea was for you to marry one of the most beautiful of earthly maidens it is possible to find.'

'What ravings are these?' muttered Falieri, still staring out of the window. 'You must have taken leave of your senses, my friend. I, a greybeard of eighty years, burdened with responsibility and cares, a man who has never married — indeed, one who is scarcely capable any more of loving . . .'

'Stop!' cried Bodoeri. 'Do not decry yourself. Does not the rawest winter, as he comes to the end of his days, stretch out longing arms towards the sweet goddess of spring floating thither on the warm west wind? And when at last he presses her to his frozen bosom, when the tender glow runs through his veins, what remains of all his ice and snow? You say you are nearing eighty and that is true, but is old age to be measured merely in a span of years? Do you not hold your head as high as ever, do you not walk with the same firm step that you did forty summers ago? Or do you indeed feel that your strength is failing, that you must carry a lighter sword, that you tire if you walk too fast, that you gasp for breath when you mount the steps of the Doge's Palace?'

'No, by Heaven,' Falieri answered his friend. And with a quick strong movement he turned from the window and stepped towards him. 'No, by Heaven, I feel nothing of the kind.'

'Well then,' continued Bodoeri, 'now that you are an old man, enjoy to the full all the earthly happiness that is your destiny. Make the woman I have chosen for you your Dogaressa. And where beauty and virtue are concerned, the women of Venice will immediately acknowledge her as a paragon, just as the men see in you the epitome of bravery, spirit and strength.'

Bodoeri now presented Marino with a portrait in words, and so skilfully did he mix his colours, so life-like was his rendering of the girl's picture, that Falieri's eyes sparkled, his face grew more and more flushed, his lips smacked as if relishing glass after glass of the fiery wine of Syracuse. 'Mmm!' he said, smiling at last. 'Who is this feast of feminine delights of whom you speak?'

'None other,' answered Bodoeri, 'than my own dear niece.'

'Your niece?' protested Falieri. 'Surely she was already married to Bertuccio Nenolo during the time I was *podestà* of Treviso?'

'Oh no, it is not my niece Francesca,' Bodoeri went on.

'It is her daughter whom I wish to be your bride. You know that Nenolo, ever rough and impetuous, was lured from home by the fighting at sea, where he met his untimely death. Francesca was so stricken with sorrow that she cloistered herself in a nunnery, so that I myself brought up the child Annunziata in my villa at Treviso in complete isolation.'

'What's that?' objected the Doge, all impatience once more. 'You want me to marry your niece's daughter? Why, it is no time at all since Nenolo's wedding. Annunziata can be no more than ten years old at most. When I was first appointed to Treviso, the marriage was not even thought of, and that was . . .'

'That was twenty-five years ago,' Bodoeri corrected him, smiling. 'Time must indeed have passed swiftly for you if you have so misjudged the span of years. Annunziata is now nineteen years old, as beautiful as the sun, modest, obedient, and quite innocent of love, for she has hardly seen a man in all her life. She will cling to you with childlike affection and undemanding devotion.'

'I wish to see her!' cried the Doge, conjuring up again before his eyes the portrait of the fair Annunziata painted by Bodoeri. His wish was granted that very day, for hardly had he returned to his apartment after the meeting of the Great Council, when the cunning Bodoeri, who may have had any number of reasons for wishing to see his niece as Falieri's consort, secretly presented the lovely maiden to him.

As soon as the old man saw her angelic face, he was quite overwhelmed by the miracle of her beauty, and he stammered so incomprehensibly that he was scarcely able to woo his bride. Annunziata, with flaming cheeks, who must surely have been instructed in advance by her great-uncle, curtsied low before the princely figure. She took his hand, pressed it to her lips and whispered softly: 'Oh my lord, do you really wish to honour me thus by raising me to reign by your side on your princely throne? If so, I will honour you from the depths of my soul and remain your faithful handmaid until my last breath.' Old Falieri was beside himself with rapture and delight. When Annunziata took his hand, a thrill ran through his limbs, and his head and whole body began shaking and trembling to such a degree that he was compelled to sit down hastily in the great chair of state. It seemed as though Bodoeri's favourable opinion of the octogenarian's sturdiness might still have to be revised. Indeed, Bodoeri could not quite control an enigmatic smile that played about his lips, although the innocent and unselfconscious Annunziata noticed nothing, and fortunately there were no others present. Could it have been that, on reflection, the old Doge himself felt the embarrassment of showing himself to the people as the new bridegroom of a girl of nineteen? Did he perhaps feel in his bones that it might be better to avoid provoking the mockery of the Venetians, who were always ready to jeer at such things? Would it not be better to suppress the exact date of the wedding? With Bodoeri's agreement, the ceremony could take place in the greatest secrecy, and a few days later, pretending that the marriage had taken place some time before, Annunziata would be presented to the people and the Signoria, as if she had just arrived from Treviso, where she had been staying during Falieri's mission to Avignon.

Let us now return to that neatly dressed and most handsome youth sauntering up and down the Rialto with a purse of ducats in his hand, making conversation with Jews, Turks, Armenians and Greeks. Now and again he would turn away his furrowed brow and then stroll on, stop, and turn back once more, until at last he hailed a gondola to convey him to the Piazza San Marco, where, with uncertain steps, arms folded and eyes on the ground, he paced up and down, not noticing, nor even suspecting, that the many whispers from this or that window, the many throat-clearings from this or that richly draped balcony, were tokens of love intended especially for him. Few would have found it easy to recognize this youth as the ragged impoverished Antonio who only a few days before had lain on the marble paving stones outside the Dogana.

'My son, my golden boy, Antonio! Good day, good day to you!' The greeting came from the ancient beggar-woman seated on the steps of San Marco, whom Antonio had almost passed without seeing. Turning swiftly, he recognized the old crone and, taking a handful of ducats from his purse, he would have thrown them to her. 'Oh keep your gold,' tittered the hag, and laughed: 'What do I need with your gold? Am I not rich enough? But if you would care to do me one favour, have a new hood made for me, since this one is too worn to keep out wind and weather. Yes, do that, my son, my golden lad! But stay away from the Fondaco – the Fondaco!'

Antonio stared into her faded yellow countenance, where deep furrows twitched in a curiously loathsome way. She clapped her withered hands loudly, and half giggling, half moaning, rambled on: 'Stay away from the Fondaco!'

'What!' exclaimed Antonio. 'Will you never cease your witless babbling? You old witch!' No sooner had Antonio spoken than the old woman collapsed, as if struck by lightning, and would have rolled down the marble steps had not Antonio leaped to her side, caught her in his arms and prevented a serious fall.

'Oh my son,' keened the old woman in a softly plaintive voice, 'oh my dear son, what fearful word did you use? Kill me, Antonio, rather than call me that again. If you but knew how deeply you have wounded me, I who cherish you so faithfully in my heart. And yet – no, you do not know.' The woman stopped abruptly, covered her head with the brown rag that hung like a cape about her shoulders, and sighed and whimpered as if afflicted by a thousand pains. Antonio, strangely moved, picked up the old woman and carried her to the porch of San Marco, where he placed her on one of the marble benches.

'You did me a good turn, old lady,' he began, having removed the ugly cloth from her head. 'You did me a good turn; in fact I owe all my present prosperity to you, for had you not stayed with me when I was at death's door, I would long ago have been lying at the bottom of the sea, would never have saved the Doge's life and never received these solid ducats. But even had you not done so, I feel some special inclination to remain with you as long as I shall live, although your senseless ramblings and your odious laughter make my very soul shudder. Indeed, when my life was a hard one and I could barely keep body and soul together by carrying loads and rowing boats, even then I had a feeling that I must strive harder than ever, so as to be able to spare you a few quattrini for yourself.'

'O my heart's dearest, my beloved Tonino, I knew it, I knew it! No matter what you pretend or do, you are indeed drawn to me, utterly and completely, for . . . but no! Silence, silence!'

The old woman bent down painfully to try and retrieve her stave, but Antonio was quicker and passed it back to her. With her pointed chin resting on its handle, her eyes staring at the ground, the old woman spoke again, but this time in a dull restrained voice: 'Tell me, child, do you really choose not to remember the old days, the life you led before you sank into poverty and misery and could scarce keep yourself alive?'

With a deep sigh, Antonio seated himself beside the old crone and began: 'Ah, Mother, I know all too well that I was born of parents who lived in great prosperity, but of who they were and how I came to be separated from them, not the faintest trace or recollection remains in my mind or soul. I remember most clearly a tall, good-looking man who often held me on his arm, clasped me fondly and fed me with sweetmeats. I also call to mind a gentle, sweet-faced woman who dressed and undressed me, laid me to rest in a soft bed every evening and who was invariably kind and loving to me. Both of them spoke to me in a foreign tongue and, baby-fashion, I too repeated many words after them in the same language. When I was still a boatman, the other lads who made life hard for me used to say that from my hair, my eyes and my whole build, I must be of partly German origin. I believe that too, for the language of my guardians (the man, I am convinced, was my father) was certainly German.

'My most vivid memory of that time is the horror of being awakened one night from deep sleep by terrible wailing and lamentation. People were running hither and thither, doors were opened and slammed to. Seized by a fear too awful to describe, I began crying loudly. Then the woman I think of as my nurse dashed into my room, snatched me from my bed and, keeping her hand over my mouth, wrapped me in blankets and ran with me out of doors. From that moment on, I can remember nothing until I found myself once more in a fine house situated in a most delightful neighbourhood. Another man stands out in my mind, someone I called "Father", who was a distinguished gentleman of noble yet kind-hearted appearance. He, like all the others in that house, spoke Italian. Then several weeks passed during which I did not see this new "Father" of mine, until one day strange people of hideous appearance came to the house, creating much noise and searching through everything. When they caught sight of me, they asked me my name and what I was doing there. "I am Antonio, the son of the house," I replied, but they laughed in my face, tore my fine clothes from my body and thrust me out of doors with the threat that, if I dared show myself there in future, they would give me a thrashing and throw me out again. Weeping loudly, I ran away. Hardly a hundred paces from the house, however, an old man came towards me whom I recognized as one of my foster father's servants. "Come, Antonio," he said, "come, poor lad. The house is forever closed against us both. We must try and find some means of obtaining our bread." The old man took me with him, and I quickly noticed that he was not as poor as his shabby clothes suggested. There were ducats in the lining of his torn doublet and he spent the days on the Rialto, acting sometimes as a broker, sometimes as a merchant. I always had to keep close beside him, for when he had concluded a deal, he made the habit of asking for a trifle over and above the agreed sum for me, whom he called his *figliuolo*, his son. I looked his customers impudently in the eye and they willingly parted with a few quattrini, which he pocketed shamelessly, stroking my cheeks the while and assuring me that he was putting the money aside to buy me a new doublet.

'I was well treated by this old man, whom everyone – I don't know why – called Papa Blaunas. But this life did not last long. You must surely remember that day of terror barely seven years ago when the earth trembled, when towers and palaces swayed as if the arms of invisible giants were tearing at their very foundations. The old man and I were fortunate; we escaped from the house where we were lodging just as it collapsed behind us. Everything came to a standstill, commercial life on the Rialto was stunned. But this terrifying event was but the harbinger of the approaching monster, soon to breathe its poison over town and country alike. We knew that the plague had reached Sicily first of all from the Levant, but it was already raging in Tuscany by then. So far, Venice had not been affected. Then one day Papa Blaunas concluded some business with an Armenian on the Rialto. They agreed on terms and shook hands heartily. Papa Blaunas had sold the

Armenian some good quality wares at a modest price and, as usual, he asked for a trifle for his *figliuolo*. The Armenian, a tall strong man with a thick curly beard – I can still see him – looked at me kindly. Then he kissed me and pressed a ducat or two into my hand, which I hastily pocketed. We then went by gondola to San Marco. On the way, Papa Blaunas asked me for the money and, although I myself cannot explain why I did it, I insisted on keeping it for myself, for this was what the Armenian had wished. The old man became angry, but as we quarrelled, I observed that his face was acquiring a livid hue horrible to behold and that his speech was growing blurred and incoherent. When we reached the Piazza, he swayed back and forth like a drunken man, and as we reached the Doge's Palace, he fell down dead. I threw myself on his corpse with loud cries of grief. The people ran up, but once the dread cry arose: "The plague! The plague!" they scattered like dust in sheer horror. At that moment, I felt I was fainting and I knew no more. When I came to, I found myself in a large room, lying on a thin pallet and covered by a woollen blanket. Around me lying on similar mattresses were some twenty or thirty pale wretched figures. As I discovered later, kind-hearted monks, who were leaving San Marco when I collapsed, had discovered that I was still alive. They took me in a gondola to the convent of San Giorgio Maggiore, on the Giudecca, where the Benedictines had improvised a makeshift hospital. How can I possibly convey to you how I felt at the moment of my awakening? The severity of my illness had robbed me completely of all my memories of the past. Now it was as if the spark of life had ignited a dead statue. For me there was only the present, unconnected to any previous existence. You can imagine the misery, the despair I felt, for this my life was no more than a shifting swirling consciousness in a bare room. The monks could tell me nothing but that I had been found beside Papa Blaunas, whom they had assumed was my father. Gradually I collected my thoughts and recalled something of my previous life, but all I know is what I have told you today, isolated fragments of events with no links to bind them. Ah, it is this hopeless sense of being quite alone in the world that prevents me from being cheerful, no matter how well I may be faring now.'

'Tonino, my dear Tonino,' said the old woman, 'be content with those bright gifts the present moment bestows upon you.'

'Silence, woman,' said Antonio impatiently. 'There is something else saddening my life, pursuing me inexorably, something which must surely destroy me sooner or later. Some inexpressible desire, a longing that tears at my innermost heart, a yearning for what I can neither name nor dwell on, has encompassed my whole being since my return to life in that hospital. When I was at my most wretched and, exhausted by fatiguing labours, rested at night on a hard pallet, a dream came to haunt me, fanning my hot brow with its gentle breeze, of the total bliss of a happy moment when the powers above allowed me a glimpse of the glory of Heaven. And the knowledge of it lies deep within me, locked in my soul. Now I sleep on soft cushions and no labours sap my strength, and yet if I wake from a dream or, lying awake, the awareness of that moment slips into my mind, I feel that my life is as aimless and as oppressive a burden as it was then, so that I would gladly be rid of it. All my brain-racking, all my searching is in vain; I cannot discover what supremely wonderful experience happened in my past life, whose dark unfathomable echo fills me with such ecstasy. But will not this very ecstasy turn into searing pain to torture me to death, when I must acknowledge in the end that all hope of finding that unknown Eden is in vain, nay, even to search for it is fruitless? Can there really be traces of something that has vanished without trace?'

Antonio stopped and heaved a deep sigh. As he told his tale, the old woman followed his words like someone completely absorbed in another's suffering, who takes it all to heart and like a looking-glass reflects every spasm occasioned by another's pain. 'Tonino,' she began in a tearful voice, 'my dear Tonino, do you mean to say you despair because of some wondrous past event whose memory now escapes you? Foolish child, listen to me! Tee, hee, hee!' The old woman began teetering and laughing in her usual maddening fashion and jigging up and down on the marble pavement. When people passed, she crouched on the ground and they threw her alms. Then she croaked: 'Antonio, take me hence – let us go to the waterfront.' Almost involuntarily, and as if he was hardly aware of what he was doing, Antonio took her by the arm and led her slowly across the Piazza San Marco. As they went, the old woman muttered softly in a solemn voice: 'You see these dark bloodstains on the ground, do you not? Yes, there is blood, much blood, everywhere there is blood. But, tee, hee, hee! From blood do roses spring, wreaths of beautiful red roses for you and for your love. O Lord of all life, who is this sweet angel of light walking towards you with such grace, with such a radiant smile? Her lily-white arms are outstretched to embrace you. O Antonio, child of fortune, keep a stout heart! And in the pleasant hour of sunset you may pick myrtles, myrtles for your bride, the virgin widow. Tee, hee, hee, myrtles picked at sunset that blossom only at midnight. Do you not hear the night wind whispering, the yearning, lamenting surge of the sea? Go forward, my bold mariner, row stoutly on!'

A feeling of horror gripped Antonio as he listened to the old woman's wondrous utterances, which she mumbled aloud in a strange inhuman tone amid constant giggling. By now they had arrived at the foot of the column on which stands the Lion of the Adriatic. The crone would have shambled past, still muttering away, but Antonio, embarrassed by the old woman's behaviour and the stares of the passers-by, stopped and said severely: 'Sit down on these steps and cease your chattering, which is enough to drive me mad. It is true you saw my ducats in the flaming sunset, but all the same, what are you babbling about now? Angels of light, a bride and a virgin widow? Red roses and myrtles? Are you trying to turn me insane, horrible hag, to tempt me to some hare-brained endeavour that will hurl me into the abyss? You shall have your new hood, bread in plenty and ducats too, everything you wish. But you must leave me alone.'

Antonio would have made off very quickly, but the woman caught him by his cape and cried with a cutting edge to her words: 'Look at me one last time, Tonino, look at me hard; otherwise I must take myself to the water's edge and throw myself into the lagoon in sheer despair.'

Antonio, anxious to avoid drawing even more attention to himself, did indeed pause. 'Sit down by my side, Tonino. I must tell you what is weighing on my heart. Do sit down beside me – here.'

Antonio obeyed, but he sat in such a way that his back was towards the old woman, and he pulled out the account book he kept in his pocket whose white pages were witness to the zeal with which he conducted his business on the Rialto.

'Tonino,' breathed the old woman very softly, 'when you look into my withered face, does not some faint recollection stir within you, do you not feel that long, long ago, you may very well have known me?'

'I have told you so already,' replied Antonio equally softly, but without turning his head. 'I told you before that I feel inexplicably drawn to you, although not because of your ugly shrivelled face. Rather when I look into your weird, black, darting eyes, when I observe your pointed nose, your blackened lips, your long chin and bedraggled grey hair, and when I hear your odious giggling and incoherent mumblings, I want to turn from you in disgust. And instead, you appear to lure me to you, as if you have at your command some nefarious means to do so.'

'Lord in Heaven,' cried the old woman, as if under the spell of some unspeakable anguish, 'what evil spirit prompted such horrifying thoughts in you? O my sweet Tonino, the woman you remember, the one who cared for you and tended you so gently in childhood and who rescued you from imminent death during that night of terror, that woman was I.'

The shock of this disclosure was so great that Antonio spun round, but now as he stared into the old woman's repulsive face, he cried out angrily: 'So this is how you try to drive me out of my wits, madwoman! Those few pictures of my childhood still present in my mind are as lively and fresh as ever they were. That sweet kind woman who nursed me, oh I see her vividly before my eyes. She had a full rosy face, tender kindly eyes, beautiful dark brown hair and delicate hands. She could hardly have been more than thirty at the time, while you – why, you're an old harridan of ninety . . .'

'O ye saints in Heaven!' interjected the woman, sobbing as she spoke. 'How can I convince my Tonino that it is indeed I, his faithful Margareta?'

'Margareta?' murmured Antonio. 'Margareta? The name slips into my ear like music heard long ago and long forgotten. But it is not possible. It cannot be.'

'It is so indeed,' the woman continued more calmly, her head bent, her eyes fixed on the ground, scratching in the dust with her stick. 'Yes, that tall handsome man who took you on his arm, who fondled you and fed you sweetmeats, was your father, Tonino. And when we spoke to each other, it was indeed in the rich full-bodied tones of the German language. Your father was a respected and wealthy merchant in Augsburg, whose beautiful young wife died giving birth to you. He could no longer bear to go on living in the land where his dearest love was buried, so he came to Venice and brought me here with him, to be your wet-nurse and to look after you. The night when your father met his ghastly end was also an imminent threat to your own life, and I was able to rescue you. A noble Venetian gave you shelter, but, friendless and homeless, I found myself compelled to remain here in Venice.

'My father had been a surgeon, whom some accused of trafficking in forbidden realms of knowledge. But from my earliest childhood he had made me familiar with the secret healing powers of nature. From him, wandering through forest and meadow, I learnt how to distinguish many soothing herbs and inconspicuous mosses, when to pluck and gather such plants and how to mix sundry juices. But hand in hand with this knowledge has gone another special gift which Heaven, for its own inscrutable purpose, has bestowed on me. I often see future events, as in a dark, distant looking-glass, and whether I will or no, I have to utter aloud what I see, often using words that do not make sense even to me, compelled by an unknown but irresistible power. When, all alone, I was forced to stay in Venice, I thought I would earn my bread with my well-tried art, and in a short time I had cured many people of the gravest ills. And, moreover, my very presence produced a beneficial effect on the sick, so that often, in a few moments, the soft stroking of my hand overcame the crisis. Thus it needs must happen before long that my reputation became known throughout the city and money flowed into my purse. This awakened the envy of the doctors and charlatans who were wont to sell their pills and elixirs in the Piazza San Marco, on the Rialto or beside the Zecca, and who used to poison the sick rather than cure them. They spread the word that I was in league with Satan, with the Evil One himself, and the superstitious people believed them. Soon I was arrested and brought before the Inquisitors. O my Tonino, with what hellish tortures did they try to make me confess my abominable association! I stood firm. My hair turned white, my body shrank to that of a mummy, my feet and hands were crippled. The most ghastly torments, the most ingenious inventions of the spirits of Hell were now applied and at last they wrung a confession from me with means which still make me tremble at the thought, even today. I was condemned to be burnt at the stake, but then there occurred the great earthquake you mentioned, which shook the foundations of the palace in which was the great prison. The doors of the underground cell where I was held opened of their own accord; I staggered out through the ruins, like a ghost rising from the depths of the grave. Ah Tonino, you said you thought I was an ancient crone of ninety, yet I am scarcely fifty years old. This emaciated body, this unsightly shrunken face, this white hair and these crippled feet . . . No, they are not due to the weight of years, but to the unspeakable tortures that changed a healthy woman into this hideous scarecrow within the space of a few moons. And all this giggling and laughter you find so abhorrent – it was the last torment inflicted on me, at the memory of which my hair still stands on end and my whole body blazes as if encased in a white-hot suit of armour, that had this terrible effect on me. From then on, spasms sweep over me like uncontrollable seizures. But do not shrink from me in horror any longer, Tonino. Your heart, I know, has already told you that when you were a babe in arms I held you to my breast.'

'Woman,' replied Antonio dully, deep in thought, 'my heart tells me I must believe you. But who was my father? What was his name? What grisly fate did he meet during that night of terror? Who was it who took care of me afterwards? And – what happened in the course of my life that still rules it inexorably like a powerful spell from an exotic unknown world, so that all my thoughts melt into a dark nocturnal sea? You must answer all my questions, you enigmatic woman. Only then will I believe you.'

'Tonino,' replied the old woman, sighing, 'it is for your own good that I must hold my peace, but soon, soon the time will come . . . The Fondaco! The Fondaco! Stay away from the Fondaco!'

'Oh!' cried Antonio in a passion. 'No nefarious arts of yours can lure me now. My whole being is torn asunder, rent into a thousand pieces! You must speak or else . . .'

'Stop!' the old woman interrupted. 'No threats! Am I not your devoted nurse?'

Without waiting to hear more, Antonio sprang to his feet and rushed hence, calling as he ran: 'But you shall have your new hood, I promise you, and ducats too, as many as you wish!'

It was indeed a remarkable spectacle to see the old Doge Marino Falieri and his youthful bride. True, he was still strong and robust, but with his grizzled beard and a thousand wrinkles in his rubicund face, it was a sad thing to see him striding back and forth, to see the effort it cost him to hold his head erect, whereas she was vivacity itself, with angelic sweetness in a countenance divinely fair, winsome magic in her eager look, nobility and dignity on her open, lily-white brow over-shadowed by dark locks, sweet smiles on cheeks and lips, with her head a little bowed in chaste humility, her slim body so light she might have been floating. Yes, it was a superb portrait of womanhood that might not have been considered out of place in another loftier world. For I am certain you have seen the figures of angels painted by old masters, who knew so well how to capture and represent such beings. This was how Annunziata looked. How could anyone who saw her fail to be both amazed and enraptured? How could any hot-blooded young member of the Signoria help but be consumed with ardour for her and, taking the old man's measure with mocking glances, not swear in his heart to play Mars to the Doge's Vulcan, cost what it may? Annunziata soon found herself beset by petitioners, whose flattering and treacherous speeches she listened to in gracious silence, without suspecting any ulterior motive. Her innocent spirit had accepted her relationship with the agèd prince as one in which she must honour him as her lord and master, to whom she must be faithful with the unconditional fidelity of a submissive maidservant. He was kind, even tender to her. He pressed her to his icy bosom, he called her his darling, he showered her with all the costly gifts he could think of. What other wishes had Annunziata, or what rights could she claim from him? Thus it was that the very idea of betraying him was incapable of taking shape in her mind, and anything beyond the narrow circle of their restricted relationship was foreign territory, whose forbidden frontiers lay shrouded in dark mist, unseen, nay unsuspected, by the piously dutiful child.

The courtier who burned most passionately with love for the fair Dogaressa was one Michele Steno. In spite of his youth, he was a member of the important and influential Council of Forty. Relying on his prestige, and also on his handsome appearance, he had no doubts about his ability to conquer Annunziata. He was certainly not frightened of Falieri, and indeed, from the earliest days of his marriage, the old man seemed to have abandoned his violent surges of rage, his crude and uncontrollable violence. Swaddled in the richest and gaudiest of robes and arrayed in all his finery, he sat beside his charming consort, smirking and smiling, with fond looks in his grey eyes, from which there trickled many a tear, challenging those present and swearing that none of them could boast such a paragon of a spouse. Instead of his previously brusque and commanding tones, he now lisped his words, hardly moving his lips, calling all and sundry his dearest friends and granting the most preposterous petitions. Who would have recognized in this feeble, infatuated dotard the same Falieri who, in a fit of fury, had struck the Bishop across the face in Treviso on Corpus Christi, and who had defeated the intrepid Morbassan? This increasing weakness incited Michele Steno to undertake the most daring ventures. In spite of his incessant allusions and his constant pursuit of her with ardent looks and fiery words, Annunziata simply did not understand what Steno wanted from her. She remained as calm and courteous as ever, and it was her frank and even manner that convinced him that his suit was hopeless and brought him to desperate measures. He therefore devised dishonourable means to secure his end. He inveigled Annunziata's most trusted maidservant, Luigia, with amorous advances, who in the end yielded and granted him nightly visits to her bed. This, he believed, would soon enable him to have access to Annunziata's inviolate couch, but the powers of Heaven willed it that such deceit recoil on the head of its wicked instigator.

One night it happened that the Doge, having just received the ill tidings that the Doria had defeated Nicolò Pisani at the battle of Portolongo, was pacing the corridors of his palace, too grief-stricken and concerned to sleep. Presently he glimpsed a shadow, apparently gliding away from Annunziata's apartments and tiptoeing towards the staircase. In rapid pursuit, Falieri recognized Michele Steno, who had at that moment left his mistress. An appalling thought struck the old man. With a cry of 'Annunziata!' he ran at Michele, dagger drawn. But the stronger and nimbler Steno easily dodged aside, felled Falieri with one well-aimed blow and, cackling loudly: 'Annunziata, Annunziata!' fled down the staircase. The old man picked himself up and, with all the torments of Hell burning in his heart, crept towards Annunziata's room. All was as silent as the grave. He knocked; a maid he had never seen before opened the door to him. 'What does my princely consort command so late at night?' Annunziata herself had quickly slipped on a filmy robe and emerged from her own room. Hearing her sweet unruffled tones, the old man stared at her and, raising both hands in the air, cried: 'No, no. It is not possible! It cannot be!'

'What does your lordship mean? What is not possible?' asked Annunziata, bewildered at her husband's sombre tones. But, without answering, Falieri turned to the maid-servant. 'Why are you sleeping here tonight? Why is not Luigia with her mistress, as is her custom?'

'It was Luigia herself who made me change places with her tonight,' replied the girl. 'She is sleeping in the ante-room near the staircase, where I usually sleep.'

'Beside the staircase?' cried Falieri, overcome with joy. He strode swiftly towards the antechamber the girl had mentioned. In response to his loud knocking, Luigia opened the door; when she saw the Doge's face crimson with anger and his eyes flashing, she fell on her bare knees and confessed her shame, although her guilt was already plain to see, for an ornate pair of men's gloves lay on an upholstered chair, whose amber perfume betrayed their careless owner, the dandy Steno.

Next day, furious at Steno's outrageous insolence, Falieri wrote to him forbidding him to enter the palace or to come within the sight of the Doge or Dogaressa again, on pain of banishment from the city. Michele Steno was beside himself with anger at the failure of his well-laid plans, as well as the humiliation of being barred from the presence of his idol. Compelled to watch from afar how the Dogaressa, as cordial and gentle as usual, conversed easily with other young men from the Signoria, the envy within him and the passion of his guilty conscience gave him the notion that Annunziata had spurned his advances only because others had preceded him in her favours with greater success, and he made no bones about saying so loudly and clearly in public. Whether this kind of shame-

less talk also came to old Falieri's ears, or whether the
image of that night appeared to him to be a warning sign
from Fate, no one knows. In spite of all his calm and
complacency, and his utter confidence in his wife's fidelity, the danger of the unnatural and false relationship with
his consort had been brought sharply to his attention, and
he grew gloomy and bad-tempered; the devil of jealousy
pinched him black and blue, and he locked Annunziata in
the innermost chamber of her apartments in the heart of
the Doge's Palace and allowed no one to see her. Bodoeri
took his great-niece's part, spoke up for her boldly and
rated Falieri roundly, but the old man would neither budge
nor change his conduct.

This happened shortly before the carnival due to take
place on the last Thursday before Lent, which was known
as *giovedì grasso*. It was the custom for such festivals to be
held in the Piazza San Marco, and the Dogaressa, with the
Doge by her side, would watch the festivities from beneath a canopy placed over one of the hanging balconies
overlooking the Piazzetta. Bodoeri reminded Falieri of this
and declared that if, contrary to all use and custom,
Annunziata were to be excluded from this honour because
of the old man's misplaced jealousy, the people and the
Signoria would undoubtedly scoff and laugh the Doge to
scorn. Falieri was suddenly offended, as if his honour had
been slighted. 'Do you take me for such a stupid dotard',
he retorted, 'that I would hesitate to display my most
precious jewel for fear of thieving hands, or that I could
not guard against such a theft with my drawn sword? No,
no, old friend, you are wrong. Tomorrow I shall lead the
glittering procession across the Piazza San Marco with
Annunziata by my side, in order to show the people their
Dogaressa. And on *giovedì grasso* she will receive the
bouquet from the hands of the daring young man who will
swoop down from the Campanile.'

Here the Doge was thinking of an old and popular

tradition. On the Thursday before Shrove Tuesday, some bold young boatman, a man of the people, would be hauled up by ropes from the edge of the lagoon to the top of the Campanile in a contrivance shaped like a small shallop and from that dizzy height would descend at lightning speed to the balcony where the Doge and Dogaressa were seated and present a bunch of flowers to the Dogaressa, or to the Doge if he were sitting there alone.

The next day, Falieri was as good as his word. Annunziata had donned her most magnificent robes and with an escort of the Signoria, noble pageboys and attendants, Falieri stepped forth with her into the crowds gathered in the Piazza San Marco. The people jostled and pushed, half trampling one another to death, in order to see the beautiful Dogaressa, and the lucky ones who managed to catch a glimpse of her believed they had looked into Paradise and seen the fairest angel imaginable, radiant and splendid. The Venetians, however, are as they are. In the midst of their most extreme expressions of delirious rapture, there could also be heard now and again much mockery and many scurrilous rhymes, referring coarsely to the aged Falieri and his young wife. Yet Falieri seemed to notice nothing. Although he saw from every quarter looks of ardent longing and desire cast towards his sweet consort, he strode ahead, smirking and grinning, a painfully pathetic figure by Annunziata's side. In front of the main portico to the palace the attendants, not without difficulty, had cleared a path through the throng, so that when the Doge entered with his Dogaressa, there were only small groups of well-dressed citizens standing here and there, people who could not very well be excluded from access even to the inner courtyard of the palace. It so happened that at the very moment when Annunziata entered the precincts, a young man, standing with a few others near the colonnade, let forth a loud cry: 'O God in Heaven!' and fell

headlong to the hard marble pavement. Everyone rushed
to screen the dead man from the Dogaressa's sight, but at
the very instant when the young man collapsed, a red-hot
stab of pain suddenly pierced her breast, she turned pale
and swayed, and only the smelling-salts of her women
who hurried to her aid prevented her from swooning
away. Old Falieri, alarmed and upset by the accident,
heartily wished the devil would take the unfortunate
young man and his apoplectic stroke, and he felt bitter
resentment at the occurrence as he carried his Annunziata
up the stairs and into their private apartments, her eyes
closed and her dear head drooping like that of a sick dove.

Meanwhile, before the eyes of the populace, who had
come crowding in ever growing numbers into the inner
courtyard of the palace, a curious spectacle was being
enacted. They were about to lift and carry away the youth,
who was assumed to be dead, when amid the cries and
lamentations an ugly old ragged beggarwoman came
limping along, elbowing her way to where the crowd was
thickest. When at last she stood by the unconscious figure,
she called out: 'Let him be, you fools. You must be mad.
Can't you see he isn't dead?' She squatted down, took the
lad's head in her lap and, softly stroking his brow and
rubbing his temples, called him by the sweetest names.
Anyone seeing the hideous gargoyle face of the ancient
dame, how it loomed over the marvellously beautiful
countenance, whose gentle features seemed frozen in the
pallor of death, while the muscles in the old woman's face
twitched grotesquely; anyone seeing her dirty rags fluttering against the youth's rich clothing, the sallow withered
arms and bony hands trembling over his forehead and bare
breast, could not help shuddering in sheer horror. Was it
not as if the grinning figure of Death itself held the young
man in its strong embrace? One by one the onlookers
slipped away and when the lad, with a deep sigh, at last

opened his eyes, only a few remained to do the woman's bidding and carry him to the Canal Grande, where a gondola then took them both to the house which she said was the young gentleman's residence. Is it necessary to say that the youth was Antonio and the old woman the beggarwoman from the steps of the church of San Francesco, who had never wavered in her claim to have been his nurse?

When Antonio was completely himself again and Margareta, having administered a few drops of some reinvigorating potion, was watching him as he lay on his couch, he began to speak in a muted, weary voice, staring at his old nurse the while with sombre despondent looks. 'How good it is to have you here beside me, Margareta! What more faithful nurse could a man have? Only forgive me, Mother – I was indeed a fool to have doubted for a moment that what you told me was the truth. Yes, I know you are the Margareta who used to feed, tend and care for me. I always knew it, but some evil spirit confused my thoughts. And now I have seen her! It is she, it is she! Did I not tell you that some dark magic lies within me and rules my life inexorably? Today it flashed from the darkness like a streak of lightning, to ruin me in nameless delight. I know everything now, everything. Was not my foster-father Bertuccio Nenolo, who took me to live in his villa near Treviso?'

'Ah yes,' replied Margareta. 'Bertuccio Nenolo it was, the great naval hero who was drowned at sea in an attempt to win the laurel wreath of victory.'

'Let me say on without interruption,' Antonio continued. 'Be patient while I tell you. Life was good in Nenolo's house. I wore fine clothes, whenever I felt hungry servants spread a table for me, and once I had dutifully recited my three prayers a day I was free to wander where I wished through wood and meadow. Not far from the villa stood a cool dark pinewood, fragrant and loud with birdsong. One evening, when the sun was already setting and I was tired of running and of jumping, I lay down there under a tall tree, staring into the blue of the sky. It could have been the spicy scent of the flowering herbs on which I lay that dulled my senses, but be that as it may; suffice it to say that willy-nilly I closed my eyes and sank into a reverie, until a swishing sound, like that of a heavy blow through the thick grass close beside me, roused me to full wakefulness. Near me stood a sweet child with a face that seemed divine, smiling down at me in innocent mischief, who spoke to me in a gentle voice. "O my dear lad, you were sleeping so peacefully, yet death, ugly death, was very close to you." Hard by my chest lay a small black snake with its head crushed, a venomous creature the child had killed with a blow from a walnut twig at the very moment it would have coiled around me and killed me. A delightful shudder ran through me. I knew that often angels descend from heaven for the purpose of saving human beings from the threat of evil and I sank to my knees, lifted my folded hands and said: "O angel of light, you have been sent by our Lord to save me from death!" The innocent maid, her cheeks aglow with a sudden blush, stretched out both her arms to me and whispered: "I am no angel, dear lad, I am a girl, a child like you." Then the shudder yielded to an indescribable ecstasy, suffusing me with tender warmth. I stood up; we embraced. Our lips met and we did not speak. And we both wept, in the grip of a sweet mysterious sorrow. Then a silvery voice could be heard calling through the wood: "Annunziata! Annunziata!" "I must go now, dearest boy. My mother is calling me." So she lisped, and an unspeakable pain shot through my breast. "Ah, but I love you so!" I sobbed, the girl's hot tears still burning on my cheeks. "And you are dear to me too!" exclaimed the girl, pressing one last kiss on my lips. "Annunziata!" Again the call rang out and the maid disappeared into the bushes. That,

Margareta, that was the moment when the powerful spark of love ignited my soul, kindling flames that were to glow within me from that day on ever and anew. A few days later, I was turned out of that house. Unable to contain my silence, I talked to Papa Blaunas of the angel child who had appeared to me and whose dulcet voice I heard in the rustling of the leaves, the murmur of the fountains and the beating of the waves of the sea. Then Papa Blaunas told me the girl could be no other than Nenolo's daughter Annunziata, who had been staying at the villa with her mother Francesca, but who was said to have left it the day after we met. O Margareta, may Heaven help me! That girl Annunziata is none other than the Dogaressa!' Weeping in the unbearable turmoil, Antonio hid his face in the pillows.

'Come, Tonino, be a man!' answered the old woman. 'Resist bravely such foolish pangs. Should a man despair in the throes of love? For whom else blossoms the golden bud of hope, if not for a lover? When evening falls, no one knows what the morrow will bring; the things seen in a dream become reality at daybreak. The castle that appears to be floating in the clouds is suddenly there on the ground, shining and splendid. Listen, Tonino. I know you pay little attention to what I say, but I feel it in my bones – and probably so does someone else – that the radiant banner of love is waving joyfully in the breeze, beckoning you across the water. Patience, my child, have patience!'

Thus did the old crone try to comfort Antonio, and to such good effect that her words soothed him like the sweetest melody. He refused to allow her to leave him. The ragged beggarwoman from the steps of the church of San Francesco disappeared, and she became a soberly clad matron, housekeeper to Signor Antonio, who used to limp across the Piazza San Marco every day to purchase the daily requirements for her master's table.

★

Giovedì grasso had arrived and the celebrations were to be more lavish than ever. In the middle of the Piazzetta a huge framework had been erected for letting off fireworks, one far bigger than anyone had ever seen before, the work of a Greek who was well versed in such arts. In the evening, the Doge and his beautiful spouse appeared on the balcony, the old man basking in the glory of his splendour and happiness, his looks transfigured as he claimed the astonishment and admiration of the throng. He was about to take his seat on the Doge's throne when he caught sight of Michele Steno standing on the same balcony, and in such a position that not only could he keep his eyes fixed on Annunziata, but she needs must notice him too. Consumed with wrath and insane jealousy, Falieri's strong masterful voice could be heard shouting to his men to remove Steno instantly. Michele raised his arm to strike Falieri, but attendants rushed in and compelled him to leave the balcony, which he did, gnashing his teeth in anger; using the most terrible oaths, he swore he would have his revenge.

Meanwhile, quite beside himself at having seen his adored Annunziata once again, Antonio had forced his way through the crowd. A thousand torments rent his heart as he paced up and down alone beside the lagoon in the darkness. Might it not be better, he mused, to extinguish the fiery glow within him in the iciness of the sea, rather than be slowly tortured to death by inconsolable pain? Little more was needed to persuade him to plunge into the water; he was already on the last step of the landing-stage, when a voice called to him from a small barque tied up beside him. 'A very good evening to you, Signor Antonio!'

In the reflected light from the Piazza, Antonio recognized a merry fellow, Pietro, one of his fellow oarsmen from the old days, who was now standing in his boat. The young man wore a cap shining with tinsel and feathers, his new striped jerkin was gaudily beribboned and he clasped a large bouquet of sweet-scented flowers. 'Good evening, Pietro,' replied Antonio. 'Who is the noble lord you will row tonight, who merits such finery?'

'Aha,' answered Pietro, with a sudden leap of excitement which made the boat sway. 'Tonight I am going to earn myself three ducats, Signor Antonio. I am the one who will go to the top of the Campanile and then slide down in order to hand this bouquet to the fair Dogaressa.'

'But is not this a very hazardous venture, friend Pietro? Might you not break your neck?'

'Oh well,' replied the latter, 'I suppose you could say that. And today there is a special risk, for I have to pass through the fireworks being set off by the Greek. True, he declares he has arranged things in such a way that not a hair of my head will be singed. All the same . . .' Pietro shook his head doubtfully. By now Antonio had climbed down in Pietro's barque, and only then did he realize that close by it was the small shallop ready to be hauled aloft to the Campanile; the ropes, however, that made this possible could not be made out in the surrounding darkness.

'Listen, Pietro,' said Antonio after a pause, 'listen my friend. If you could earn yourself ten ducats tonight without endangering your life, would you not rather do that?'

'Yes, of course,' laughed Pietro heartily.

'Very well then,' Antonio continued, 'take these ten ducats, let us exchange clothes and you will allow me to take your place. I will go to the top of the Campanile instead of you. Do me this favour, my faithful comrade Pietro!'

The boatman bowed his head thoughtfully as he weighed the gold in the palm of his hand. 'How gracious you are, Signor Antonio, to greet a poor devil like me as your comrade and to be so generous into the bargain. The money is important to me, I admit, but to place these flowers in the lovely Dogaressa's hands, to hear her soft voice . . . ! Ay, ay, things like these make a man eager to risk his life! Ah well, since it is you who ask, Signor Antonio, I agree.'

They quickly exchanged clothes and hardly was Antonio ready when Pietro cried: 'Hurry! Climb into the machine! The signal has been given!' As he spoke, the sea was lit up by the flaming reflection of a thousand shooting flames, and the whole of the waterfront, the very air, resounded with the whirling rush of thunder. With the speed of a hurricane, Antonio was hoisted into the air through the crackle and hiss of the fireworks and descended from the top of the Campanile to the balcony, where he hovered before the Dogaressa. She had risen and stepped forward; she felt his breath on her cheeks as he handed her the flowers. But in the indescribable bliss of that single moment, the burning pain of hopeless love gripped him in its searing arms. His mind unhinged, maddened with longing, delight and torment, he raised the girl's hand to his lips and rained burning kisses on it, before exclaiming in the piercing tones of hopeless sorrow: 'Annunziata!' Then the shallop, like the blind instrument of Fate itself, tore him away from his beloved and he was carried down to the barque in the lagoon where, stunned and exhausted, he sank into Pietro's waiting arms.

In the meantime, on the balcony where the Doge was seated everything was in a state of uproar and confusion. A slip of paper had been found attached to the throne on which were the following words in the Venetian dialect:

Il Dose Falier	(The Doge Falier
della bella mujer	has a fair Dogaressa)
I altri la gode	(He keeps her in style
é lui la mantien!	while others caress her!)

Old Falieri flew into a white-hot rage and swore that the author of this wicked outrage would pay the most severe penalty for it. Looking wildly about him, his eye fell on the spot beneath the portico where Michele Steno was standing in full candlelight, and he at once ordered his men to arrest Steno as the perpetrator of the crime. This command of the Doge's aroused universal protest. By allowing his anger to get the better of him, Falieri was insulting both the Signoria and the people, the former by infringing their acknowledged rights and the latter by spoiling the innocent pleasure of the carnival.

The Signoria left their places and only Marino Bodoeri could be seen mixing with the crowd, whipping up great indignation at the grave affront to the head of the state and attempting to divert all the hatred against Michele Steno. Falieri was not wrong in attributing the deed to Steno himself. Driven from the Doge's balcony, he had run home, written the malicious doggerel and, when all eyes were focused on the firework display, had left the scrap of paper on the Doge's throne, after which he had slipped away, again unobserved. It was a cunning plot intended to wound both Doge and Dogaressa at their most sensitive. Michele freely admitted his authorship, but he placed the blame squarely on the Doge himself, who had been the first to offend. The Signoria had for some time past been growing dissatisfied with a Head of State who, instead of fulfilling the Republic's justifiable expectations, showed every day that martial ire in a decrepit greybeard's cold heart resembled nothing so much as the Greek's fireworks, a sizzling display of soaring rockets that dwindled into useless blackened fragments. Furthermore the old man's marriage with the beautiful maiden (it had long been known how recent it was, and that it had taken place since he was elected Doge) made Falieri's jealousy look not so much like the stout war-hero defending his honour as the ridiculous protests of the *vecchio Pantalone*. It was inevit-

able that, with such poison fermenting within their vitals, the Signoria were more inclined to take Michele's part than that of the deeply insulted Head of State. The matter was referred by the Council of Ten to that of the Forty, of which Michele was a leading member. Their verdict was that Steno had already suffered sufficiently, and that a month's exile would be enough reproof. As a result, the embittered Falieri's grudge against the Signoria was reinforced, since, instead of rising to their Doge's defence, they had had the impudence to punish the insult he had endured with the mildest penalty at their disposal.

As for the sighing lover, who, having once been blessed with a single ray of love's happiness, spent days, weeks, nay months, bathed in its golden gleam, Antonio could not recover from the stunning effect of that blissful moment and could hardly breathe for the sweetness of his sorrow. Margareta scolded him roundly for his daredevil venture, ceaselessly muttering and mumbling about starting such an unnecessary enterprise. One day, however, she entered the room in a curious fashion, leaning on her stick and prancing and hopping as was her wont when she came under the spell of that strange magic. Ignoring Antonio's remarks and questions, she tittered and laughed, and having kindled a fire on the hearth, she placed on it a small pan containing ingredients poured from a number of small bottles. She boiled these into a salve and ladled it into a little jar, which she took with her as she limped away, giggling and chortling. She did not return until late that evening, and she sat herself down in an armchair, gasping and coughing. At last, as if she had recovered from her exhaustion, she began speaking. 'Tonino, my child, whom have I been to see? From whom have I come? Can you guess?' Antonio gazed at her in the grip of a weird intuition. 'Yes,' chortled Margareta, 'from seeing her, from your own dear dove, the fair Annunziata!'

'Do not drive me mad!' cried Antonio. 'What are you saying?'

'No, no, I think of you all the time, my Tonino,' the woman went on. 'This morning, as I was haggling for some nice fresh fruit beneath the colonnade of the palace, I heard a murmur about some misfortune that had befallen the Dogaressa. I asked first one, then another, until after a while a tall red-faced boor, who was yawning and sucking a lemon as he leant against a column, answered me. "It's the little finger of her left hand. A baby scorpion was trying out its new teeth, and the poison has worked its way into her blood. Now my master, the worthy Doctor Giovanni Basseggio, is upstairs in the palace, and I expect he'll soon have chopped off her hand and the little finger with it." At that very moment, a great cry went up from the broad staircase, and a mannikin came rolling down the steps, kicked by the attendants as if he were a ball. He landed right at our feet, screaming and wailing. The people flocked round laughing most heartily, while the little fellow struggled and thrashed with his feet like a baby who has fallen and cannot get up again. The red-faced lout sprang to his side, picked up the woebegone doctor in his arms and, with the man still bawling at the top of his voice, ran off to the water's edge as fast as his legs could carry him, where he promptly put him in a gondola and rowed him away. I could well imagine the scene. The doctor must have been about to take his knife and cut off that beautiful hand, when the Doge intervened and had him kicked downstairs. And I thought quickly. Hurry, hurry home, Margareta. Prepare a salve and take it immediately to the Doge's Palace. Soon I was standing on the great flight of stairs with the shining little jar in my hand, just as Falieri was coming down. He shot me a swift glance and said in a blustering voice: "What does the old woman want here?" But I made him my deepest curtsey and said I had a goodly unguent, one that could cure the fair Dogaressa in a

very short time. As soon as the Doge heard that, he stared
at me hard with terrifying eyes. Then, taking me by the
shoulders, he pushed me towards his wife's apartments,
but so roughly that I almost fell. Ah Tonino, there was the
sweet maid stretched out on a couch, pale as death,
groaning with pain and sighing softly: "Ah me, I am
poisoned through and through!" But at once I hastened to
her side and removed the stupid poultice the simpleton of a
doctor had applied. O Heavens, her dainty little hand was
dark red and so swollen! "There, there," I told her. "My
ointment cools, relieves the pain." "Yes, that feels better
already, much better," whispered the sick little dove. At
this, Marino exclaimed with delight: "A thousand ducats
are yours, old woman, if you save my Dogaressa for me!"
And he stalked out of the room. For three hours I sat there,
holding her tiny hand in mine, stroking it and nursing her.
And when she awoke from the soft slumber into which she
had fallen, all the pain had gone. After I had bandaged her
hand afresh, she looked at me, her eyes shining with joy.
Then I spoke: "Ay, gracious lady, you once saved the life
of a boy by killing the black snake that would have bitten
him to death while he slept." Tonino, you should have
seen how swiftly her pale face flushed as if touched by a ray
of the setting sun, how her eyes glistened! "Oh yes, I was a
child then, in my father's country villa. He was such a dear
delightful boy. When I remember him, it seems as if those
moments with him were the happiest I have ever known."
Then I told her that you were here in Venice, that you still
treasured in your heart the love and glory of those minutes, that for the sake of looking once more into the blue
eyes of your guardian angel, you had dared the dangerous
flight on *giovedì grasso* and handed her the bunch of flowers.
At that she cried out in great excitement: "I knew it, I
knew it! When he pressed my hand to his lips, when he
called me by my name, although I could not describe what
flashed through my heart so mysteriously, I know now

that it was rapture and also pain. Bring him here to me, bring me that charming young man!'' '

As Margareta said those words, Antonio sank to his knees and prayed like one distraught: 'O Lord in Heaven, do not allow any monstrous fate to overwhelm me now, not until I have seen her again, until I have clasped her to me!' He wanted the old woman to take him to the palace the very next day, but she quickly discouraged him, telling him that, at present, old Falieri was in the habit of visiting his sick bride at any hour of the day.

Several days passed and, thanks to the old woman's nursing, the Dogaressa's hand was completely healed, yet it remained impossible for her to conduct Antonio into Annunziata's presence. Margareta comforted the impatient lover as best she could, repeating that she always spoke to Annunziata of the boy whose life she had saved and who loved her so passionately. Antonio, in an agony of longing and desire, used to go out in a gondola or wander through the piazzas. Willy-nilly, his steps invariably led him back to the Doge's Palace. Near the bridge opposite the prison at the rear of the palace, he discovered Pietro, leaning on a brightly painted oar. Tied to a post and rocking up and down in the water was a small but luxurious gondola, with a delicately worked awning and painted carvings, and as it also flew the Venetian flag, it reminded one of the *Bucentoro*. As soon as Pietro caught sight of his former comrade, he called out to him. 'Welcome a thousand times, Signor Antonio! The ducats you gave me have brought me good fortune!' Almost absent-mindedly, Antonio asked him what good fortune he meant, only to learn the important tidings that Pietro was hired almost every evening to ferry the Doge and his lady across to the Giudecca, where Falieri had a fine house not far from San Giorgio Maggiore. Antonio eyed Pietro intently. 'Comrade,' he blurted out impetuously, 'let me

take your place and row the Doge across the lagoon in
your stead.'

It was Pietro's opinion, however, that that would not do
at all. The Doge knew him by now and would trust no
other boatman. Antonio flew into a passion, occasioned by
the manifold torments of love in the turmoil of his soul. He
would not take no for an answer, swearing like a man
possessed that he would jump into the gondola and drag
them both into the canal, until Pietro protested laughingly:
'Aha, Signor Antonio, I see that the Dogaressa's lovely
eyes have turned your very wits!' He agreed, however,
that Antonio should pretend to be his assistant, saying that
the weight of the vessel really needed two oarsmen,
especially as he wanted to save the fragile old man from too
prolonged a journey, since Falieri was always complaining
that the crossing by gondola was painfully slow. Antonio
dashed away and in no time he was back again at the bridge
– clad in the poor garb of an ordinary boatman, with his
face stained brown and a long, drooping moustache – just
as the Doge and Dogaressa, in brilliant gleaming robes,
took their places in the gondola. 'Who is this stranger?'
exploded Falieri, turning to Pietro; it was only when the
latter swore by all the saints that he needed an assistant that
day that the old man was persuaded to allow Antonio to
accompany them.

It can indeed happen that, when rapture is overflowing,
the bliss in one's soul may be fortified by the power of the
moment, so that one can still exercise self-control and
subdue the flames that blaze within one. That was how
Antonio, although so close to the fair Annunziata that the
hem of her dress brushed against him, concealed his fiery
love as he plied the oar with powerful strokes and, avoiding any undue risk, did not so much as look at his beloved,
except for a rare fleeting glance. Falieri meanwhile chuck-
led and laughed, stroked and kissed Annunziata's little
white hand and placed his arm about her slender waist.

Half way across to the Giudecca, when the Piazza San Marco and the splendid city of Venice with all her proud towers and palaces was spread out before them, the old Doge raised his head and, gazing round him with pride, said: 'Well, my dearest, is it not a fine thing to sail the sea with the lord of the Adriatic, with the husband of the sea? But do not be jealous, my love, of my other spouse, who bows her neck so humbly beneath us. Only listen to the sweet plash of the waves; are they not fond words of love that she whispers to her lord and master? Yes, yes, beloved, you wear my ring on your finger, but the wedding ring I threw to her she cherishes in her bosom.'

'Ah, my prince,' replied Annunziata, 'how can the cold and unkind waters be your consort? The very notion of you as the husband of such a proud overbearing element makes me shudder.'

This remark made Falieri laugh so much that his chin and beard both shook. 'Pray do not alarm yourself, my dove,' he answered. 'Of course it is more comfortable to lie in your white arms than the ice-cold lap of my wife below. All the same, is it not a fine thing to sail the sea with the man who is her overlord?'

As the Doge was speaking thus, a faint strain of music arose in the distance. As the boat skimmed the waves, the soft notes of a man's voice came nearer and nearer; these were the words he sang:

> Ah! senza amare
> Andare sul mare
> Col sposo del mare
> Non può consolare.

Other voices joined in and the verse was sung in canon with each word repeated over and over again, until at last the melody died away like a breath of wind.

The old man seemed to pay not the slightest attention to the singing; he was far too busy telling the Dogaressa in great detail the significance of the splendid ceremony on Ascension Day, when the Doge sets out in the *Bucentoro* to cast a ring into the water, thus celebrating the wedding of the Republic to the Adriatic. He spoke of the Republic's victories under the regency of Pietro Orsoleo the Second and how the ceremony had its origin in his conquest of Istria and Dalmatia. But if Falieri ignored the singing, his entire narrative was equally lost on Annunziata. She sat in silence, her whole mind dwelling on the sweet notes hovering above the water. When they ended, she sat staring before her with a strange look on her face, like someone awakening from deep sleep who gazes still at the images seen in a dream, trying to grasp their meaning as they flutter in the air. *Senza amare, senza amare . . . non può consolare*, she whispered softly, and the tears in her blue eyes shone like pearls, while her breast rose and fell with anguish and heartfelt sighs. The Doge, still smirking and smiling in the full flow of his story, disembarked with his bride and stepped towards the balustrade before his house near San Giorgio Maggiore, and had no idea that the silent Annunziata by his side was lost in a dream, stirred by mysterious dark emotions, her tear-filled eyes turned towards some distant land. A young man clad as an oarsman blew a horn shaped like a triton shell, so that the blast could be heard far out at sea. At this signal, another gondola approached. Meanwhile, a man carrying a sunshade and a woman had arrived and, thus accompanied, the Doge and the Dogaressa moved towards Falieri's palace. The second gondola now drew up at the landing stage; Marino Bodoeri was among those who alighted, most of them merchants and artists, but also humbler citizens, who all followed in the Doge's footsteps.

Antonio could hardly wait until the following evening, hoping to receive the joyful summons from his beloved. It seemed an eternity until at last the old woman returned limping to the house and sat down in the armchair, gasping for breath and beating her withered hands together in despair. 'Ah, Tonino, what has happened to our poor dear dove?' she exclaimed. 'When I went to see her today, she was lying on her couch, her eyes half closed, her little head resting on her arm, not sleeping, not waking, not sick, not well. I stepped near her and said: "O my lady, what evil has befallen you? It is surely the pain from your so recently healed wound, is it not?" But she gazed at me with eyes . . . with eyes, Tonino, I had never seen before. Hardly had I looked into those moist moonbeams when their light was hidden again behind her silken lashes, as if covered by dark clouds. Then she sighed from the depths of her being and, turning her dear pale face to the wall, whispered softly but so sorrowfully that my heart was stabbed with grief: *Amare, amare! Ah senza amare!* I fetched a low chair and sat down beside her. She buried herself deeper in her cushions, she breathed faster and faster, until the breathing turned to sighs. I told her frankly that you had been close to her in the gondola in disguise, that you were languishing with love and longing and that I was ready to lead you to her without delay. Then she started from her pillows and, with the hot tears coursing down her cheeks, cried out passionately: "No, no, for Jesus' sake! By all the saints I implore you! I cannot see him! I beg you, old lady, tell him he must never, never come near me again. Tell him he must leave Venice; he must go, and go quickly." "In that case," I interrupted her, "my poor Tonino must die." She fell back on her cushions as if racked by indescribable pain and, in a voice choked with tears, sobbed: "And must not I die too? Ay, and the bitterest of deaths!" At this point, Falieri entered her chamber and immediately dismissed me with a wave of his hand.'

'She has rejected me! Away, away! I shall throw myself into the sea!' cried Antonio in utter despair.

At this, the old crone chortled and laughed in her usual

fashion. 'Simple child!' she scolded him. 'Do you not understand that the charming Annunziata loves you with all the passion, with all the pangs of love, that ever encompassed a woman's heart? Foolish boy, tomorrow, when night falls, you may slip unnoticed into the Doge's Palace. I shall be there waiting for you at the end of the second corridor to the right of the great staircase. Then we shall see what happens.'

Next evening, when Antonio, a-quiver with longing, crept silently up the great staircase, he had a sudden feeling that he was about to commit some monstrous crime. He trembled and swayed as if benumbed, and he found he could scarcely muster the strength to mount the stairs. As he neared the spot described by the old woman, he had to pause and lean against a pillar. All at once, strong torch-light bathed him from top to toe and, before he could stir, Marino Bodoeri was standing before him, accompanied by several torchbearers. Bodoeri scrutinized the youth's face and then he spoke. 'Ha, it is you, Antonio. I know you have been sent for. Follow me.' Convinced that someone had betrayed his tryst with the Dogaressa, he did as he was bid, although not without hesitation. He was all the more astounded when Bodoeri led him to a distant chamber, where he embraced him warmly and told him about an important mission to be carried out that very night with courage and resolution. But his astonishment turned to fear and horror when he learned that, for many weeks, a conspiracy led by the Doge himself had been planned against the Signoria. The arrangements had been made in Falieri's house on the Giudecca; this very night the whole of the Signoria would be wiped out and Marino Falieri proclaimed sole and sovereign ruler of Venice. Antonio gaped at Bodoeri, speechless, and the latter, taking the youth's silence as a refusal to take part in the nefarious plot, shouted in disappointment: 'Coward and fool! You will never leave this palace again! Either you die here and now, or else you will take up arms in our cause. But first, speak to this man!'

From the shadowy background emerged a tall, noble figure. As soon as Antonio discerned the man's lineaments, which hitherto he had merely glimpsed by candlelight, he recognized them. He sank to his knees, beside himself at such a totally unexpected appearance. 'God in Heaven!' he cried. 'It is Bertuccio Nenolo, my dear foster-father!' Nenolo raised the boy to his feet and clasped him in his arms.

'I am indeed Bertuccio Nenolo, whom you believed drowned,' he declared in a quiet voice. 'But I was captured by the savage Morbassan, and it is only now that I contrived to escape from his infamous prison. Yes, it was I who brought you up and could not guess that stupid servants, dismissed by Bodoeri when he bought the villa after my supposed death, would turn you out of the house. Misguided youth! Are you not ready to take up arms against the despotic and cruel class who robbed you of your father? Yes, go to the Fondaco dei Tedeschi; you can still see the stains of your father's blood on the paving stones in the yard. When the Signoria took possession of the premises, everyone who used them was ejected, told to remove their goods and forbidden to retain their keys. They had to be left with the superintendent. Your father disobeyed this law and was ultimately made to pay the supreme penalty. On his return to Venice, his storerooms were opened and a coffer containing forged Venetian coins was found among his goods. In vain did he protest his innocence; it was only too obvious that some cunning devil, perhaps the superintendent himself, had planted the coffer there in order to ruin your father. The ruthless judges, satisfied with the evidence that the chest had been found with your father's wares, condemned him to death. He was executed there in the courtyard of the Fondaco, and you, his son, would have suffered a similar fate had not the faithful Margareta saved you. I had been your father's dearest friend and so I adopted you. To make it impossible for you to betray your identity inadvertently, your father's name was kept a secret from you. But now, Anton Dalbirger, the moment has come for you to take up your sword and avenge your father's shameful death on the heads of the Signoria.'

Antonio, inspired by the spirit of revenge, took an oath of loyalty to the conspirators and vowed he would fight to the death in their cause.

It is well known that Bertuccio Nenolo had been aggrieved because the naval command had been given not to him, but to Dandolo, who had struck him in the face during a quarrel; this moved him to conspire with his ambitious son-in-law against the Signoria. Both Nenolo and Bodoeri believed that, once Falieri ruled Venice, they would share power with him. The plot devised by the conspirators was this. Rumours were to be spread that the Genoese fleet was lying at anchor outside the lagoon. During the night, the great bell in the Campanile would ring a tocsin and the citizens would be summoned to defend the city stoutly. At this signal, the conspirators, whose numbers were considerable and who had a footing in all parts of the town, would occupy the Piazza San Marco, capture the main strongholds, execute the leaders of the Signoria and proclaim the Doge Prince of Venice. However, it was not Heaven's will that this murderous plan should succeed, nor that the foundations of the sorely pressed Republic should be trampled in the dust, merely because of the angry Doge's injured pride and over-weening ambition. The meetings at Falieri's house on the Giudecca had not escaped the notice of the Council of Ten, although they could not discover the precise details of the plot being hatched. One of those involved, however, a certain Bentian, who was a fur-dealer from Pisa, was moved by his conscience to try and save the life of his friend and neighbour, one Nicolao Leoni, himself a member of the Council of Ten. He betook himself at twilight to Leoni's house and implored him not to go out that night, no matter what might happen. Leoni was immediately suspicious. He seized the fur-dealer and would not let him leave until he had forced him to reveal all. Together with Giovanni Gradenigo and Marco Cornaro, he summoned the Council of Ten to meet at San Salvatore, and in less than three hours they had taken measures to ensure that the entire enterprise would be smothered the moment the attempt was made.

Antonio had been assigned the task of taking a troop of men to the Campanile in order to ring the bells. When he arrived, he found the tower strongly guarded by soldiers from the Arsenal; at his approach, they rushed towards him, their halberds raised. His men panicked and took to their heels in fear of death, while he himself escaped into the darkness of the night. He soon heard footsteps close behind him, a hand reached out and grabbed him, and he was about to strike his pursuer to the ground when by good luck an unexpected glimmer of light enabled him to recognize Pietro. 'Save yourself, Antonio,' shouted the latter. 'My gondola is waiting. The plot has been betrayed. Bodoeri and Nenolo are in the hands of the Signoria. The gates of the palace have been locked and the Doge is a prisoner in his own apartments, guarded like a common criminal by his own treacherous attendants. Away, away!'

Half unconscious, Antonio allowed himself to be dragged into the gondola. There was a sound of muffled cries, the clash of blade on blade, single screams of fear. Then, at the darkest hour of night, a noiseless, spine-chilling silence set in. Next morning, the crushed and terrified mob saw for themselves the grisly spectacle, which curdled the very blood in their veins. The Council of Ten had carried out the death sentence on the conspirators during the night.

They had been strangled, and now their bodies swung over the Piazzetta, suspended from the very balcony of the palace from which the Doge had been accustomed to watch the festivities below, the selfsame spot where Antonio had presented the bouquet of flowers to the fair Annunziata, after his daring descent from the top of the Campanile. Among the corpses were those of Marino Bodoeri and Bertuccio Nenolo. Two days later, Marino Falieri was himself condemned to death by the Council of Ten and executed on the so-called Giants' Staircase within the Doge's Palace.

Antonio slunk through the streets of Venice like a man in a dream. He was not arrested, for no one knew that he had been one of the conspirators. When he saw Falieri's grey head fall to the ground, the shock suddenly brought him to his senses, like a man shaking off a nightmare about death. With a wild cry of horror, he rushed through the corridors of the palace shouting 'Annunziata!'; the attendants stared at him as if they were wholly stunned by the dreadful deed to which they themselves had been parties. Margareta limped towards him. She took his hand and, with tears and groans, led him to Annunziata's chamber. The poor girl lay unconscious on her cushions. Antonio dashed to her side, covered her hands with scorching kisses, calling his beloved by the sweetest, tenderest names. Then she slowly opened her lovely blue eyes, staring at Antonio as if she did not know who he was. After a few moments, however, she sat bolt upright, clasped him in her arms and held him to her breast. Her scalding tears fell on his face; she kissed his cheeks, his lips. 'My Antonio, I love you more than words can say. Yes, Heaven on earth is still possible. What is a father's, an uncle's, a husband's love compared to the bliss of yours? Let us flee together, let us leave this bloody city of murderers.'

Thus wept Annunziata, torn between bitterest grief and

passionate love. With a thousand kisses, a thousand tears, the lovers plighted their everlasting troth, forgot the terrifying events of those dreadful days and turned their gaze from earth to Heaven, now opened to them through the spirit of love.

Margareta advised them to make for Chiozza. From thence, Antonio planned to use devious routes to return to the land of his fathers. His friend Pietro obtained a small barque for him and moored it by the bridge just behind the palace. When night fell, the heavily veiled Annunziata crept down the stairs with her beloved, followed by Margareta, who had a casket of rich jewels concealed in her hood. They reached the bridge unobserved and climbed into the boat. Antonio seized the oar and rowed them away with swift vigorous strokes. The bright moonlight danced on the waves before them like a joyful messenger of love and they soon reached the open sea. Then a weird whistling sound arose, a roaring high in the air, dim shadows drifted past, dark veils shrouded the shining countenance of the moon. The dancing moonlight, that joyful messenger of love, sank into the inky depths, whence could be heard the dull roll of thunder. A storm sprang up and chased the sombre massed clouds before it, violent in its fury. 'Oh help us, heavenly Father!' shrieked the old woman. The barque rose and fell. Antonio found the oar was useless. He embraced Annunziata who, roused by his burning kisses, held him in her arms in rapturous ecstasy. 'O my Antonio!' 'O my Annunziata!' Thus did they address each other, oblivious of the storm that raged and howled with ever increasing ferocity. Thereupon, the jealous widow of the beheaded Falieri lifted foam-capped waves like enormous arms, grasped the pair of lovers and, together with the old woman, dragged them down into the bottomless abyss.

No sooner had the man in the cloak concluded his tale

with these words than he sprang to his feet and, with firm swift strides, left the room. The two friends watched him depart in astonished silence and then returned to the salon for another look at the picture. The old Doge still smirked as he flaunted his foolish splendour and senile vanity, but when they studied the Dogaressa's face, they could sense the hint of a shadow on her lily-white brow, a presentiment of suffering as yet unknown but not far away, as well as the yearning dreams of love, lustrous beneath her dark lashes and playing round her charming lips. From the distant sea, from the clouds billowing round San Marco, the powers of evil appeared to be threatening death and destruction. The deeper meaning of this delightful picture was now evident to them, and whenever they chanced to see it again, they were invariably moved afresh at the love story of Antonio and Annunziata, so that the sweetest anguish filled their innermost souls.

THE MINES AT FALUN

⸻ ❦ ⸻

One bright, sunny July day, everyone had gathered at the roadstead in Göteborg. A rich East-Indiaman, happily home from foreign lands, lay at anchor in the harbour. Its long pennants, its Swedish flags, streamed out gaily, and hundreds of boats and skiffs, filled with jubilant sailors, raced hither and thither across the mirror-bright waters, while the cannon of the Masthuggetorg thundered their greetings over the wide sea. The gentlemen of the East India Company paced up and down the harbour calculating, with pleased expressions, the rich gains their valiant undertakings were bringing them and how Göteborg was flourishing more and more with every year that passed. Everyone thus regarded the said gentlemen with warm approval, for it was their profits which gave life and strength to the whole town.

The crew of the East-Indiaman – they numbered close on 150 men – came on shore and set about their *Hönsning* – the feast celebrated by a ship's company on such occasions and often lasting several days. Performers in wonderful gay costumes appeared with fiddles, pipes, oboes and drums, while others sang all kinds of merry songs in time to them. They were followed by the sailors, two by two; some wore gaily beribboned jackets and hats and waved fluttering pennants, others danced and leaped about, and the laughing and rejoicing echoed far and wide. Thus the happy procession wound its way across the dockyard and through the suburbs to the Haga district, where there was to be feasting and drinking.

Now the finest drink flowed in rivers, and flagon after flagon was emptied; as always happens when sailors return home from long journeys, they were soon joined by the local ladies, dancing began and all grew ever louder and wilder.

Only one solitary sailor, a slim, handsome youth hardly twenty years old, had slipped away from the din and had sat alone outside on a bench which stood close to the door of the tavern. Two sailors came up to him, and one of them called out loudly, with a laugh: 'Elis Fröbom! Elis Fröbom! Are you playing the fool again and sulking out here? Listen, Elis, if you stay away from our Hönsning, you had better stay away from the ship too! You will never be a sailor the way you are going. You have courage enough and are plucky when there's danger, but you can't drink and would rather keep your ducats in your pocket than spend them. Drink, lad! or the trolls will get you!'

Elis Fröbom leaped up hastily from the bench, gave the sailors a fiery glance, took a glass filled to the brim with brandy and emptied it in a single gulp. Then he said: 'You see, Joens, I can drink as well as any of you, and whether I am a good seaman, the Captain can decide. Now shut your trap and be off. What I'm doing out here has nothing to do with you!'

'Now, now,' Joens replied, 'I know you are a Neriker and that they are all gloomy and melancholy and don't really like the sailor's life! Well, wait there, Elis, and I'll send someone out to you who will soon get you off that bench.'

Before long a girl came out of the inn and sat next to the melancholy youth. Her whole appearance betrayed the occupation to which she had sacrificed herself, but it had not yet destroyed her beauty, and a quiet grief lay in the glance of her dark eyes.

'Elis!' she said, 'don't you want to share in the joy of

your comrades? Aren't you happy to have braved the perils of the sea and to be home again?'

The girl spoke in a quiet voice and put an arm around the youth. As if awakened from a dream, Elis looked into the girl's eyes, took her hand and pressed it to his breast. 'Ah,' he began at length, as if coming to himself, 'alas, I no longer know joy or happiness. At least, I cannot share in the revels of my comrades. Go back inside, my dear child, and enjoy yourself; leave me out here, I would only spoil your pleasure. But wait! I like you and would want you to think well of me when I am again at sea.'

So saying, he took two shining ducats from his pocket, drew forth from his jacket an East Indian kerchief and gave them to the girl. Bright tears welled up in her eyes; she rose, placed the ducats on the bench and said: 'You shall keep your ducats – they only make me sad – but I will wear the beautiful kerchief for you as a memento, and you will certainly not find me next year if you hold your *Hönsning* here in Haga.'

With that the girl slipped away, not back into the tavern but across the street, with her hands pressed to her face.

Elis again sank back into his gloomy daydreaming, and as the noise in the inn grew louder and more riotous, he cried: 'Oh, if only I were lying at the bottom of the sea – for in life there is no one with whom I can be happy!'

A rough, deep voice said close behind him: 'You must have had bad luck indeed, young man, if you are wishing for death when your life is only just beginning.'

Elis looked round and beheld an old miner leaning against the wooden wall of the tavern with his arms folded and looking down at him with a serious, penetrating glance.

The longer he gazed at the old man, the more it seemed to him as though a friend was coming to meet him in his desolate loneliness; he pulled himself together and told of how his father, a fine steersman, had been lost in a storm at sea, how his two brothers had been killed in battle and how he alone had been left to keep his mother, which he did with the rich rewards of the East India service. For he had been destined to be a sailor from the first and had thought himself fortunate in being taken on by the East India Company. Profits this time had been higher than ever before, and every sailor had received a large sum in addition to his pay, so that, his pockets full of ducats, he had run home joyfully to the cottage where his mother lived. But strange faces had peered at him through the windows, and a young woman who had finally opened the door to him had told him in cold, rough tones that his mother had been dead for three months and that he could collect from the town hall the little of her property that was left after the burial had been paid for. The death of his mother had broken his heart: he felt abandoned by the whole world, as if dashed on a barren reef, helpless and wretched. His whole life at sea seemed to him a pointless drifting; yes, when he considered that his mother had died alone and comfortless, it seemed to him dreadful that he should have gone to sea at all instead of staying at home to care for her. His comrades had dragged him to the *Höns-ning*, and he had believed that the rioting and drinking would ease his pain, but, instead of that, it seemed to him as if all the veins in his chest were bursting and he must bleed to death.

'Soon', said the old miner, 'you will be back at sea again, Elis, and then your pain will pass. Old people die, that is something that does not change; and your mother has left behind only a hard, wearisome life.'

'Alas!' replied Elis. 'That no one believes how I suffer, that I am considered foolish, *that* is what is driving me out of this world. I cannot go to sea again, the life disgusts me. In former times my heart leaped when the ship, sails spread like stately wings, rode out the sea and the waves splashed and roared and the wind whistled through the rigging.

Then I was happy to cheer with my comrades on deck and then – during my watch in the quiet darkness of the night – I would think about the homeward journey and my dear mother and how happy she would be when I again returned. Ha! then I could rejoice at the *Hönsning*, when I had poured ducats into my mother's lap, when I had given her kerchiefs and all kinds of other rare goods from far-off lands; when her eyes had lit up for joy, when she had clasped her hands together with pleasure and joy, when she had brought out the best ale she had been saving for me, when I spent my evenings sitting with her and telling her of the strange people I had met, of their customs and habits, of all the strange things which had happened to me on the long voyage. She took great pleasure in all this and told me again of the wonderful voyages my father used to make to the far north, and many dreadful sailors' tales which I had heard a hundred times and which I still could not hear enough. Oh, who will give me such joy again? No, never back to sea! What should I do among men who would only mock me, and how could I take pleasure in work which would seem to me only wearisome labour?'

'I am listening to you with pleasure, young man,' said the old man as Elis fell silent, 'just as I have been observing with pleasure your whole behaviour over the past couple of hours without your being aware of me. Everything you have done, all you have said, shows that you have a deep, introspective, pious, childlike disposition, and Heaven could not have conferred a finer gift upon you. But the life of a sailor is not the life for you. How should you, a melancholy-inclined Neriker – I can tell you are one – how should you be suited to the unsettled life of the sea? You would do well to give it up for ever. But you won't want to sit doing nothing. Take my advice: go to Falun and become a miner. You are young, hale and hearty, and would soon be a skilful pitman, then a hewer, then a foreman, and so on upwards. You have a good sum in your pockets; invest it, earn some more; you will soon own a home of your own and have shares in the mine. Take my advice: become a miner!'

Elis Fröbom was almost terrified by the old man's words. 'What are you advising me to do?' he cried. 'Am I to leave the beautiful earth and the sunlit sky and go down into the dreadful depths and burrow like a mole, grubbing for ores and minerals, for the sake of vile profit?'

'People despise what they want to know nothing about!' the old man cried angrily. 'Vile profit! As if the horrors perpetrated on the face of the earth by trade and commerce were nobler than the work of the miner, whose indefatigable industry opens up nature's most secret treasure-houses. You speak of vile profit, Elis Fröbom! – well, something higher than that might be involved. If the blind mole burrows by blind instinct, it may be that the eyes of man acquire more penetrating sight in the deepest depths of the earth, until they can recognize in the wonderful stones they find a reflection of that which is hidden above the clouds. You know nothing about mining, Elis; let me tell you about it.'

With these words, the old man sat on the bench next to Elis and began to describe in detail and the liveliest colours how things were done in a mine. He came to the mines at Falun, in which, he said, he had worked since his early youth; he described the huge crater with its blackish brown walls to be found there; he spoke of its immeasurable wealth of precious stones. His speech grew more and more lively, his eyes brighter and brighter. He wandered through the galleries as though along the paths of a magic garden. The rocks came to life, the fossils stirred, the pyroxenite and almandite sparkled in the light of the lamps – the rock-crystals glowed and flickered.

Elis listened intently: the old man's strange way of speaking of these subterranean wonders as if he were standing in the midst of them gripped his whole being. He felt as though his chest were constricted and it seemed to him that he was already in the depths with the old man and that a powerful magic was keeping him there, so that he would never again look on the light of day. Yet it seemed to him too as if the old man had revealed to him a new and unfamiliar world in which he nonetheless belonged and whose magic had been known to him from earliest boyhood in strange, secret presentiments.

'I have shown you all the splendour of a situation which nature really intended you for,' the old man said at last. 'Take counsel with yourself and then do as your spirit bids you!'

With that he rose quickly from the bench and walked away, without another word and without even looking back, and soon disappeared from sight.

In the meantime, the tavern had grown quiet: the power of beer and brandy had triumphed. Many of the seamen had slipped away with their girls; others lay in the corners and snored. Elis, who could no longer return to his usual shelter, asked for and obtained a tiny room in which to sleep.

Hardly had he stretched out on his bed, worn out and weary as he was, when dreams touched him with their wings. It seemed as if he were floating in a ship under full sail on a mirror-bright sea with a vault of dark clouds above him. Yet as he looked down into the water, he realized that what he had taken for the sea was a solid transparent sparkling mass into whose shimmering light the whole ship dissolved away, so that he was standing on a crystalline floor and above him was a vault of glittering black rock. It was this which he had at first taken for clouds. Propelled by an unknown power, he took a step forward, but at that instant everything around him stirred, and there arose from the ground like rippling waves strange flowers and plants of flashing metal whose blossoms and leaves climbed upwards from the profoundest depths and twined themselves about one another. The ground was so clear that Elis could distinguish the roots of the plants, but soon, his gaze penetrating even deeper, he saw at the very bottom countless lovely maidens embracing one another with white shining arms; it was from their hearts that the roots, the flowers and plants shot up; and whenever the maidens smiled, a sweet, melodious sound echoed through the vault and the strange metallic flowers climbed higher. An indescribable feeling of pain and pleasure seized the youth, a world of love, yearning and passionate desire rose up in his soul.

'Down – I will come down to you!' he cried, and threw himself on to the crystal ground with outstretched arms. But it gave beneath him, and he found himself floating as if in shimmering air.

'Well, Elis Fröbom, how do you like this grandeur?' a voice called loudly to him. Elis became aware of the old miner, but as he looked at him, he began to grow into a giant figure made of molten ore. Before he had time to be terrified, a burst of light broke from the depths within which Elis beheld the face of a huge woman. He felt the rising ecstasy in his breast turn into annihilating fear. The old man had laid hold of him and cried: 'Take care, Elis Fröbom, that is the Queen.'

Involuntarily he turned his head and saw the stars of the night sky shining through a crack in the vaulting. A gentle voice called his name in a tone of inconsolable sorrow. It was his mother's voice. He thought he could see her above him – but it was a beautiful young woman who stretched her hand down to him through the vaulting and called his name.

'Lift me up,' he cried to the old man. 'I belong to the upper world and its friendly sky.'

'Take care!' said the old man. 'Take care, Fröbom! Be true to the Queen, to whom you have yielded.'

As the youth then looked down again into the stern face

of the mighty woman, he felt his being dissolve into the shining rock. He screamed out in unspeakable terror and awoke from the dream, its joy and horror still echoing deep within his soul.

When he had pulled himself together with difficulty, Elis said to himself: 'It must have been a dream. But the old miner told me so many things about the splendour of the underground world that my whole head is still full of it. Never in my life have I felt as I do now. Perhaps I am still dreaming. No, no – I am only sick. Out into the open air! The fresh sea breeze will cure me.'

He rose quickly and ran down to the harbour, where the *Hönsning* was again starting up. But he soon realized that all the enjoyment was passing him by, that he could keep his mind on nothing, that presentiments and desires to which he could not put a name flitted through his soul. He thought sadly of his dead mother; then it seemed to him that he desired to meet once more the girl who had spoken to him so kindly the previous evening, but he feared that even if the girl should step out of this or that alleyway, it would turn out to be the old miner, who filled him with fear, though he could not really say why. And yet he would have dearly loved the old man to tell him more about the wonders of the mines.

Driven hither and thither by all these thoughts, he gazed down into the water. It seemed to him as if the silver waves were stiffening into a sparkling light, into which the great ships were dissolving, as if the dark clouds drawing across the bright sky were sinking down and forming a rocky vault. He was again in his dream, he again gazed into the face of the mighty woman and the fear and passionate longing again seized hold of him.

His comrades shook him out of his daydreams and he had to go along with them. But now it was as if an unknown voice was whispering incessantly in his ear: 'Why are you still here? Away! Away! Your home is in the mines at Falun. There you will find all the splendour of which you dreamed. Away, away to Falun!'

For three days Elis Fröbom wandered the streets of Göteborg, pursued by the strange images of his dream, incessantly admonished by the unknown voice. On the fourth day, he stood at the gate through which led the road to Gefle. A large man was passing through in front of him. Elis thought he recognized the old miner and, drawn irresistibly, hurried after him without being able to catch up. Tirelessly, he went on and on. Elis knew clearly that he was on the road to Falun, and this reassured him, for it seemed to him that the voice of Destiny had spoken through the old miner and was now leading him on. And indeed, several times, especially when the way was uncertain, he saw the old man step out of a ravine, out of thick undergrowth, out of the dark rock, and walk on in front of him, then quickly disappear again.

At length, after many wearisome days of walking, Elis saw in the distance two great lakes, between which there rose a thick fog. As he climbed further and further up the rising ground to the west, he distinguished amid the smoke a number of towers and black roofs. The old man stood gigantically before him and pointed with outstretched arm towards the fog, then disappeared again amid the rocks.

'It is Falun!' cried Elis. 'It is Falun, the goal of my journey!'

He was right: for people coming up behind him confirmed that there, between the Runn and Warpann lakes, lay the town of Falun, and told him he was climbing the Guffrisberg, where the entrance to the mine was to be found.

Elis Fröbom went forward in good heart, but when he stood before the great chasm of Hell, his blood froze in his veins. As is well known, the great opencast working of the Falun ore mine is twelve hundred feet long, six hundred feet wide and a hundred and eighty feet deep. The black-ish-brown side walls begin for the most part vertically, then level off about half way down through the tremendous deposits of rubble and debris. Among these, and in the side walls, there could be seen the props of old shafts: strong, thick tree trunks laid one against the other and fitted together at the ends, in the manner of a log-cabin. No tree, no blade of grass grew in the barren, rocky chasm, but jagged cliffs and boulders towered up in strange forms, some like gigantic animals turned to stone, some like colossal humans. In the abyss there lay in wild confusion rocks, slag, burnt-up ore, and an everlasting choking sulphurous haze rose out of the depths, as if a hellish brew were being cooked whose vapours poisoned all nature. You could well believe it was here that Dante climbed down and gazed into the Inferno, with all its inconsolable torment and all its horror.

As Elis gazed down into the enormous crater, there came into his mind what an old steersman had told him long ago. He had imagined, as he had been lying in a fever, that under him an immeasurable chasm had opened, so that he saw all the monsters of the deep struggling among the rocks until, with opened jaws, they stiffened into death. Such a vision, the old sailor had said, signified an early death amid the waves – and in fact he had soon afterwards fallen from the deck into the sea and dis-appeared. Elis remembered this now, for the chasm did indeed resemble the seabed when the waves have rolled back, and the black rock and blueish-red ore slag looked like horrific monsters stretching out their hideous arms towards him. It happened that several miners were at that moment climbing up out of the depths: with their dark pit-clothes and their black, scorched faces, they resembled hideous fiends wearily making their way out of the earth to the surface.

Elis felt a sense of profound dread and – what never

happens to the sailor – was seized by a fit of giddiness: it seemed to him as though invisible hands were drawing him down into the abyss. He closed his eyes and ran a few steps; only when he was away from the pithead and climbing down the Guffrisberg again and gazing up at the bright sunlit sky did the fear of that dreadful sight leave him. He breathed freely again and cried from the very bottom of his soul: 'Oh, Lord of my life, what are all the terrors of the sea against the horror which lives within these desolate rocky chasms? Let the storm rage, let the black clouds dip in the foaming waves, soon the majestic sun will shine again and before its friendly countenance the wild tumult will be stilled; but down there its eye never penetrates the black cavern, and no fresh spring breeze quickens the heart. No, never can I be one of you, you black earthworms; never could I live your dismal life!'

Elis intended to stay the night in Falun and then make his way back to Göteborg early the following morning. When he reached the market-place, which is called the Helsing-torget, he found a crowd gathered. A long procession of miners dressed in finery, with miner's lamps in their hands and musicians leading the way, had just stopped before an imposing house. A tall, thin man of middle years stepped out and looked about him with a smile; in the freeness of his manner, in the open brow, in the dark-blue shining eyes, you could recognize at once the true lowlander. The miners formed a circle around him and shook him by the hand in turn; he had a friendly word for everyone. On inquiring, Elis learned that the man was Pehrson Dahlsjö, senior foreman and owner of a fine *Bergsfrälse* at Sotra-Kopparberg. *Bergfrälse* are lands let out for copper and silver mining in Sweden. The owners of such lands have shares in the mines and are responsible for their operation.

Elis was further informed that the *Bergthing* – the sitting of the court – had ended that day: the miners were now paying a round of visits to the mine-master, the works supervisor and the guild officials, and would everywhere be hospitably entertained.

As he regarded these handsome people, with their frank, friendly faces, Elis forgot the earthworms in the great funnel: the gaiety which started up afresh as Pehrson Dahlsjö stepped out and spread through the whole circle was something different from the wild jubilation of the *Hönsning*. The way in which these miners celebrated made a deep impression on the quiet, serious Elis. He felt indescribably happy and could hardly hold back tears of emotion when some of the younger men began an old song whose simple melody, penetrating the soul and heart, praised the blessings of mining.

As the song ended, Pehrson Dahlsjö opened the doors of his house and the miners filed in. Elis followed involuntarily, stood on the threshold and viewed the spacious hall in which the miners were taking their places on benches. A splendid banquet was spread out.

Now the door opposite him opened, and a beautiful young woman entered in festive dress. Tall and slim, with her dark hair arranged in plaits on the crown of her head and a neat bodice fastened with brooches, she was the very picture of blossoming youth. All the miners rose and a murmur ran through the room: 'Ulla Dahlsjö! Ulla Dahlsjö! How God blessed our brave guildsman with such an angelic child!'

The eyes of even the most aged miners sparkled as Ulla offered them all her hand in friendly greeting. Then she brought out silver tankards, filled them with the excellent ale that is brewed in Falun and handed them to the guests. Her face was suffused with innocent beauty, and as Elis gazed upon her it seemed as if a flash of lightning had struck through him and enkindled all the passion, love and ardour locked up inside him. It was Ulla Dahlsjö who had proferred him her hand in that fateful dream; he now believed he divined the meaning of that dream and, forgetful of the old miner, lauded the fate that had drawn him to Falun.

But then, standing as he was on the threshold, he felt a neglected stranger, miserable, disconsolate and deserted, and wished he had died before he had looked on Ulla Dahlsjö, for now he would surely pine away with love and longing. He could not take his eyes from the lovely girl, and as she passed close to him, he spoke her name in a quiet, tremulous voice. Ulla looked around and beheld poor Elis, who, his face burning scarlet, stood transfixed, with downcast eyes, incapable of another word.

Ulla went up to him, and said with a sweet smile: 'You must be a stranger, dear friend! I can tell from your sailor's dress! Well – why are you standing on the threshold? Come in and enjoy yourself with us!'

With that she took him by the hand, led him into the hall and handed him a full tankard of ale. 'Drink,' she said. 'Drink, my dear friend, and believe yourself welcome!'

To Elis it seemed as if he was in a paradisial dream from which he would soon awake to a feeling of inexpressible misery. He emptied the tankard mechanically. At that moment Pehrson Dahlsjö came over to him and, after shaking him by the hand, asked whence he had come and what had brought him to Falun.

Elis felt the warmth of the ale in all his veins and, looking Pehrson in the eye, he recounted how, the son of a sailor, he had been at sea since childhood; how, returned from the East Indies, he had found his mother no longer of this earth; how he now felt utterly abandoned in the world; how the wild life of the sea had now become completely repugnant to him; how his inner inclinations were driving him towards mining; and how here in Falun he would make every endeavour to find work as a pitman. This last statement – so completely contrary to all he had resolved only a short while before – came out quite involuntarily, but it seemed to him as though he could not have said anything different, as though he had expressed his innermost desire, of which he had not until that moment been aware.

Pehrson Dahlsjö regarded the youth with a grave expression, as if he wanted to see right into him, then said: 'I would not like to think that you had lightly abandoned your former profession, or that you had not weighed all the toil and discomfort of mining before deciding to devote yourself to it. It is an ancient belief with us that the mighty elements in which the miner boldly rules will destroy him if he does not exert his whole being to assert his mastery over them, if he leaves room in his mind for other thoughts which diminish the strength he must exert undivided on his work in earth and fire. But if you are sufficiently sure of your inner calling, then you have come at the right time. We are short of workers. If you would like to, you may stay here with me and then go tomorrow morning with the foreman, who will instruct you in the work.'

Elis's heart leapt at Pehrson Dahlsjö's words. He thought no more of his horror at the fearful Hell-mouth into which he had gazed: that he would now see the beautiful Ulla every day, that he would be living under the same roof as her, filled him with joy and delight; he gave way to the most delicious hopes.

Pehrson Dahlsjö announced to the miners that a new young pitman had just joined them and introduced Elis Fröbom. They all seemed to approve of the robust youth who, with his slim and powerful build, seemed born to be a miner and would no doubt not be lacking in industriousness and piety. One of the miners, already advanced in years, approached him and shook him heartily by the hand; he said he was head foreman at Pehrson Dahlsjö's pit and that he would make it his business to instruct Elis in everything he should know. Elis had to sit beside him, and even while they were still drinking the old man began to tell him what his first duties would be. Elis then recalled the old miner from Göteborg and, strangely enough, could repeat almost all the old man had told him.

The head foreman cried out in astonishment. 'How did you come to know all that?' he exclaimed. 'Now, indeed, you can hardly fail; you will surely become the best pitman we have.'

The lovely Ulla, passing among the guests and filling their glasses, often glanced at Elis. Now, she said, he was no longer a stranger but belonged with them. No longer the treacherous sea – no, Falun with its ore-laden mountains would be his home! A whole Heaven of bliss opened up to the young man at Ulla's words. It was noted that she liked to linger near him, and Pehrson Dahlsjö too regarded him with visible pleasure.

But Elis's heart nonetheless pounded when he again stood at the smouldering crater and, enveloped in his miner's suit and with the heavy iron-shod boots on his feet, he clambered with the foreman down into the deep shaft. Hot fumes seemed to choke him, the miner's lamp flickered in the biting winds which blew through the endless depths. Deeper and deeper they went, descending finally on iron ladders scarcely a foot wide. Elis soon realized that all the climbing he had learned as a sailor would be of no help to him here, but at last they stood in the deepest shaft, and the foreman assigned to Elis the work he was to do there.

Elis thought of the lovely Ulla; he saw her hovering over him like an angel of light and he forgot all his fear of the abyss and all his labour was as nothing. It was now firmly fixed in his soul that only when he had, with all his courage and all the effort he was capable of, come to devote himself wholly to Pehrson Dahlsjö's mine, might he realize one day perhaps his sweetest hope – and so it happened that in an unbelievably short time he was the equal of even the most skilled miner.

Pehrson Dahlsjö grew fonder and fonder of the indust-
rious Elis with every day that passed, and he often told him
frankly that he had gained in him not so much a new
workman as a new son. And that Ulla felt a strong
affection for him became more and more evident: often
when the work he was leaving to do had anything dangerous about it, she would plead with him, with tears in her
eyes, to take the greatest care of himself; and when he
returned safe and sound, she would run to meet him and
always had the finest ale or a fine meal ready for him. Elis's
heart beat with joy when Pehrson Dahlsjö one day told
him that, as he had brought with him a good sum of
money, he could hardly fail in due course to become
part-owner of a mine and that when that happened no
mine-owner at Falun could possibly refuse him if he were
to ask for the hand of his daughter. Elis would now have
liked to have said how unspeakably in love he was with
Ulla and how all his future hopes depended on his possessing her, but he was restrained by an unconquerable
shyness and even more by the doubts which assailed him as
to whether Ulla loved him in return.

It happened that Elis was one day working in one of the
deepest shafts, where the sulphurous smoke made it hard
for him to see his way, when he heard coming from an
even deeper region of the mine a sound as of someone
tapping with a little hammer. But since no work was ever
done in the shafts that involved this kind of hammering,
and as he also knew that no one but he had descended
this far on that day, he wondered very much what the
sound could mean and so put down his tools and listened
to the hollow tapping, which seemed to be coming
nearer and nearer. Suddenly he was aware of a dark
shadow close beside him and, as a blast of air bore away
the sulphurous smoke, he recognized the old miner of
Göteborg.

'God speed you!' the old miner cried. 'God speed you,

Elis, down here among the rocks! Well, how do you like the life, fellow worker?'

Elis was about to ask him by what strange path he had got down into the mine, but the miner at that moment struck the rock so violent a blow with his hammer that sparks of fire flashed all around and the sound echoed in the shaft like distant thunder; then he said in a terrible voice: 'There is a glorious trap-vein here, but you, you base rogue, can see nothing but an end hardly thicker than a straw. Down here you are a blind mole who will never find favour with the Prince of Metals; and up above, capable of nothing, you set traps for the Mine King in vain. Ha! you seek to win the daughter of Pehrson Dahlsjö for your wife, so you work down here without true love of the work. Take care, false traitor, that the Prince of Metals whom you mock does not seize you and hurl you down, so that your limbs shatter on the sharp rocks. And Ulla will never be your wife, I tell you that!'

Elis felt anger well up in him at the old man's insolent words. 'What are you doing here,' he cried, 'in my master Pehrson Dahlsjö's mine, in which I am working with all my strength and as it is my calling to do? Be off with you the way you came, or we shall see who first gets his brains knocked out!' Thereupon he confronted the old man and raised high the huge miner's hammer he had been working with. The old man laughed mockingly and, to Elis's horror, slipped up the narrow ladder with the agility of a squirrel and vanished into the dark crevices above.

Elis felt weak in every limb, could no longer work and came back to the surface. When the old head foreman saw him, he cried: 'In God's name, what has happened to you, Elis? You look as pale as death! Is it the sulphur, which you are not yet used to? Drink this, my boy, it will do you good.'

Elis took a deep draught of brandy from the bottle the head foreman handed him; then, his strength restored, he told of all that had just happened down in the mine and of how he had first met the old miner back in Göteborg.

The head foreman listened quietly, then, shaking his head in a thoughtful fashion, said: 'The man you met was old Torbern, and I now see that what we tell of him here is something more than a fable. Over a hundred years ago there lived here in Falun a miner named Torbern. He is supposed to have been one of the first to make mining flourish in Falun, and in his day the amount of ore they got out was much greater than it is now. At that time no one understood mining as well as Torbern did and, deeply learned in the subject, he was in charge of the whole undertaking. As if he were endowed with special powers, the richest veins seemed to open up to him of their own accord, and since he had neither wife nor child – he was a gloomy kind of man and had no regular dwelling-place either – he spent almost all his time working in the darkness of the mine, so that it could hardly fail to be said of him that he was in league with the hidden powers which rule in the womb of the earth. Torbern used ceaselessly to admonish the other miners that ill fortune would befall them if they worked the mine without having within them a true love of the precious stones and metals they dug out, but no one paid him any heed, and, inspired only by greed, they drove the shafts further and further into the ground, until at last, on St John's Day in the year 1687, it finally gave way and produced the tremendous crater you see now. The mine was wrecked, and it was only with great effort and great skill that they were able to sink new shafts. Of Torbern there was nothing to be seen or heard, and it seemed that, working in the mine when the collapse took place, he had been buried alive.

'Soon afterwards, as the work of reconstruction was beginning to get really under way, the miners declared they had seen Torbern down in the shafts and that he had pointed out to them the best veins of rock. Others had seen

him wandering about up on the crater, sometimes lamenting, sometimes raging in anger. And there were young
men who came here as you did, saying an old miner had
urged them to take up mining and had directed them
hither; it always happened when we were short of workmen.

'If it was really old Torbern you had a dispute with in the
shaft, and if he spoke of a glorious trap-vein, then we can
be sure there is a rich vein of ore down there, and tomorrow we shall go and look for it.'

When, his mind in a state of confusion, Elis entered
Pehrson Dahlsjö's house, Ulla failed to come hurrying to
greet him as she usually did: she was sitting with downcast
eyes and, as Elis believed, tear-stained cheeks beside an
elegant young man who was holding her hand in his and
trying to entertain her with conversation, though she did
not appear to be paying much attention to him. Elis was
disturbed by this sight, but Pehrson Dahlsjö drew him into
another room and began: 'Now, Elis, you will soon be
able to demonstrate your love and loyalty to me; I have
always treated you as my son, now you will become my
son in reality. The man you see in my house is the wealthy
merchant Eric Olavsen, from Göteborg. I shall give him
my daughter's hand in marriage, as he has desired; he will
return with her to Göteborg, and you will remain here
alone with me, Elis, my only support in my old age. You
do not speak, Elis? – you are growing pale. I hope you do
not dislike my decision, or that, now my daughter is to
leave me, you will leave me too! But I hear Herr Olavsen
calling my name – I must go in!' – and with that Pehrson
went back into the other room.

Elis felt as though he were being torn to pieces by a
thousand glowing pincers. He could not speak, he could
not weep. In wild despair he ran out of the house to the
great opening of the mine. If the crater had presented a
fearful spectacle by day, now by the light of the moon it

seemed as though countless hideous monsters spawned from Hell were writhing together down there on the smouldering floor and reaching upwards with their claws to prey on human kind.

'Torbern! Torbern!' Elis cried in a fearful voice that re-echoed among the desolate gorges. 'Torbern! Here I am! You were right: I was a base rogue to give way to foolish hopes up here on the surface! It is down there that my treasure lies, my life, my all! Torbern! Climb down with me, show me the richest veins and I will dig and bore and labour and behold the light of day no more! Torbern! Torbern! Climb down with me!'

He took out his tinder-box, lit his lamp and clambered down into the crevice he had travelled through the previous day, but the old man did not appear. When he reached the deepest shaft, he beheld – to his amazement – the rich trap-vein of which the old man had spoken; yet as he gazed upon the wonderful vein of ore it was as though a blinding light filled the whole shaft and the walls grew as transparent as pure crystal. That fateful dream in Göteborg returned to him: he beheld the glorious metal trees and shrubs standing in paradisial fields, with fiery flashing jewels hanging from them like fruit; he saw the young girls, he saw the noble face of the mighty Queen. She seized hold on him, drew him down, pressed him to her breast – a beam of heat transfixed him, and all he was aware of was of floating among the waves of a blue transparent sparkling mist.

'Elis Fröbom! Elis Fröbom!' – a voice called down loudly, and the reflection of a torch fell into the shaft. It was Pehrson Dahlsjö, who had come with the foreman to look for the youth, whom they had last seen running towards the mine as if out of his mind. They found him standing as though turned to stone, his face pressed against the cold wall of the shaft.

'What are you doing down here at night?' Pehrson cried

to him. 'Pull yourself together and come back to the top with us; who knows what good news there may be for you up there!'

In profound silence Elis climbed back up, in profound silence he followed Pehrson Dahlsjö, who reprimanded him severely for having placed himself in such danger.

Morning had dawned by the time they reached the house. Ulla ran to Elis with a loud cry and threw herself on to his breast. Pehrson said to him: 'What a fool you are! Do you suppose I have not long been aware that you are in love with Ulla and that it is only for her sake that you labour so zealously in the mine? Do you suppose I have not long been aware that Ulla loves you from the depths of her heart? Could I desire a better son-in-law than an indust-rious and pious miner – than you, my dear Elis? It was your silence that annoyed and upset me.'

'But did we ourselves know how much we loved one another?' Ulla interposed.

'Be that as it may,' Pehrson went on, 'I was annoyed that Elis did not speak openly and honestly to me of his love, and because I wanted to test your feelings, I arranged that little scene with Herr Olavsen. What an effect it had on you! You foolish fellow, Herr Olavsen has been married for years, and to you, Elis, I give my daughter for wife – for I repeat that I could not wish for a better son-in-law.'

Elis wept for joy – the turn of events was so unexpected that he was almost afraid he was dreaming again.

At Pehrson's command the miners assembled at midday for a joyful feast. Ulla had dressed herself in her finest clothes and looked more charming than ever, so that all who were there cried time and again: 'Oh, what a glorious bride our valiant Elis has won for himself! May Heaven bless them both in their piety and virtue!'

Elis's pale countenance was still filled with the terrors of the night just gone, and he often sat staring before him as if far away from everything around him.

'What is it, my Elis?' Ulla asked. Elis pressed her to his breast and said: 'Yes, yes – you are really mine and now everything is well!'

But in the midst of all his joy it sometimes seemed to him as though he was suddenly gripped by an ice-cold hand and a dark voice said: 'Is winning Ulla now the highest thing you know? You poor fool – have you not beheld the countenance of the Queen?'

He was almost overwhelmed by an indescribable fear and tormented by the idea that one of the miners would suddenly rise up gigantically before him, reveal himself as Torbern and admonish him in terrible tones to remember the subterranean realm of metals and precious stones to which he had surrendered himself. Yet he still could not see why the spectral old man should be so hostile towards him, nor why his work in the mine should have anything to do with his love for Ulla. Pehrson could not fail to notice how disturbed and distracted Elis was, but attributed it to the shock he had had and to his nocturnal flight to the mine. Not so Ulla: seized with a secret presentiment, she begged Elis to tell her what terrible thing had happened to him that was tearing him away from her. Elis felt as if his chest were bursting asunder. He struggled in vain to tell his beloved of the wonderful vision that had come to him in the depths: it was as though an unknown power were closing his mouth, as though the fear-inspiring face of the Queen were rising up within him and as though everything would turn to stone about him, as at the glance of Medusa, if he spoke her name. All the splendour that had filled him with supreme delight down in the depths of the mine now seemed to him an Inferno of inconsolable torments, disguised so as to lure him to destruction.

Pehrson demanded that Elis should stay at home for a few days to recover from the sickness into which he appeared to have fallen; and in this time Ulla's love banished from his mind all recollection of his fateful adventure in the mine. Elis recovered his faith in his good fortune and believed no evil power could ever lay hands on it again.

When he once more descended into the mine, everything seemed different to him: the richest veins lay open before him, he worked with redoubled zeal, he forgot everything – and when he again came to the surface he had forcibly to direct his thoughts to Pehrson Dahlsjö and even to his Ulla. He felt himself split into two: the better half, his real being, descended with him into the bowels of the earth and reposed in the arms of the Queen, while in Falun all was dull and gloomy. If Ulla spoke of her love and of how happy they would be living together, he began to speak of the splendours of the depths, of the immeasurably rich treasure which lay hidden there, and became so confused and incomprehensible that the poor child was seized with fear and anguish and could not imagine how Elis had suddenly become so utterly changed. The youth ceaselessly declared to the foreman, and to Pehrson himself, how he had discovered the most ore-laden veins, and when they then found nothing but hollow rock he laughed mockingly and maintained that he alone knew how to read the secret signs, the meaningful inscriptions the hand of the Queen had inscribed on the rocky crevices, and that it was sufficient to understand these signs without also bringing forth what they proclaimed. The aged foreman gazed sadly at Elis as, with wildly blazing eyes, he spoke of the paradise which shone in the womb of the earth.

'Alas,' he whispered softly into Pehrson's ear, 'it is the wicked Torbern who has done this to the poor boy!'

'Do not believe such miner's fables, old man,' Pehrson replied. 'Love has turned the deep-thinking Neriker's head, that is all. Once we get the wedding over with, we shall hear no more of these trap-veins and treasures and paradises under the earth.'

The day of the wedding at last arrived. A few days before, Elis had become more silent and withdrawn than ever, but never had he evidenced so much love for Ulla: he refused to leave her side for a moment and ceased to go to the mine or even, so it seemed, to think about his life as a miner – for he ceased to speak of the subterranean realm at all. Ulla was filled with joy: all her fears that the powers under the earth of which she had heard might lure her Elis to his destruction had vanished away. And Pehrson, too, said to the foreman with a smile: 'You see, Elis was only lightheaded with love for my Ulla!'

Early on the morning of the wedding day – it was St John's Day – Elis knocked gently on the door of his bride's room. She opened it – and started back in alarm as she saw him, clad already in festive dress, deathly pale, dark fire darting from his eyes.

'I only want to say, my dearly beloved Ulla,' he began, 'that we now stand close to the summit of all human happiness. Last night all was revealed to me. Down in the mine there lies, encased in metals and minerals, the pink sparkling almandine on which is engraved the record of our life, which you have to receive from me as a wedding gift. It is more lovely than the most glorious blood-red carbuncle, and when, united in true love, we gaze into the light that streams from it we shall behold how our inner being is intertwined with the wondrous branches which rise up out of the heart of the Queen at the mid-point of the earth. All that is needed is that I should bring this stone up to the light of day, and that I shall now do. Farewell now, my beloved Ulla. I shall soon return.'

With hot tears, Ulla pleaded with her lover to desist from this visionary undertaking, which she felt would end only in great ill-fortune; but Elis assured her that he would never know another quiet hour until he possessed that stone and that there was no danger at all involved in getting it. He pressed his bride warmly to his breast and departed.

The guests were assembled to conduct the bridal pair to the Koppaberg Church, where the betrothal was to take place after a service. A whole host of dainty maidens who were, according to the custom of the country, to precede the bride as her bridesmaids, were laughing and joking around Ulla; the musicians were tuning their instruments and practising a cheerful wedding march. It was already nearly midday – but still Elis had not arrived. Then a group of miners suddenly came running up, fear and terror inscribed in their pallid faces, and told how a fearful land-slide had just overwhelmed the quarry in which Dahlsjö's mine was situated.

'Elis – my Elis, you are gone – gone!' Ulla screamed, and fell down as though dead. It was only now that Pehrson learned from the foreman that, early that morning, Elis had gone to the great crater and descended into it; he had been alone, since everyone else had been invited to the wedding. Pehrson and all the miners that were there hurried out to the mine, but, though they searched even at the greatest risk to their own lives, they searched in vain. Elis Fröbom was not found. It was certain that the fall of earth had buried the unfortunate youth; thus misery and woe descended upon the house of Pehrson Dahlsjö at the moment when he thought he had secured peace and repose for his old age.

Pehrson Dahlsjö had long been dead, his daughter Ulla had long since vanished, and no one in Falun knew any-thing of either of them, for fifty years had passed since Elis Fröbom's unhappy wedding-day. Then it happened that, as the miners were attempting to dig a passage-way be-tween two shafts, they found in a pool of vitriolic water at a depth of three hundred ells the body of a young miner. The body appeared to be petrified when they brought it to the surface. The lines of the face were so well preserved, the clothes and even a flower attached to the jacket were so completely free of decomposition, that the youth might have been merely sleeping. Everyone in the neighbourhood assembled about the body, but none of them knew who it was and none of the miners could recall any of their number having been buried in an accident. They were about to take the body to Falun when an ancient woman appeared out of the distance, gasping as she made her way on her crutches.

'Here comes the St John's Day woman!' cried some of the miners. It was a name they had given her on account of her habit of appearing once a year, on St John's Day, when she would approach the crater, gaze down into its depths, wring her hands, weep and wail in the most melancholy way and then disappear again.

The old woman had hardly set eyes on the motionless youth when she let her crutches fall, raised her hands to Heaven and cried in heart-rending tones: 'O Elis Fröbom! O my Elis! My dear bridegroom!' And with that she knelt down beside the body and took the rigid hand in hers and pressed it to her aged breast. 'Alas!' she cried, gazing around at the assembled company, 'alas! none, none of you can recognize poor Ulla Dahlsjö, who was the happy bride of this youth fifty years ago! When in misery and woe I departed for Ornäs, I was consoled by old Torbern, who told me that one day I would see my Elis – buried alive on his wedding day – again on this earth; since then I have come here, year in, year out, and, filled with desire and faithful love, gazed down into the depths. And today this happy reunion has been granted me! O my Elis, my beloved bridegroom!'

Again she clasped her thin arms about the body of the youth as though she never wanted to let him go. All who stood around were deeply moved. But at length the old woman's sobs and sighs grew softer and softer, and finally they ceased. Then the miners came forward and made to lift her from the ground, but Ulla had breathed her last on the body of her bridegroom. It was then, too, that they noticed that the body had not petrified but was beginning to dissolve into dust.

In the Koppaberg Church, where, fifty years before, the couple were to have been married, they laid the ashes of the dead youth, and with them the body of his bride, Ulla, who had been faithful to him unto death.

THE CHOOSING OF THE BRIDE

*A story in which several altogether improbable
adventures take place*

—◦❧ ❦◦—

I

On the night of the autumnal equinox, Chancellery Private Secretary Tusmann was returning from the coffee-house, where he was accustomed to spend a couple of hours each evening, to his home in the Spandauerstrasse. In everything he did, the chancellery private secretary was punctual and precise, and he had made it his practice to get out of his coat and boots as eleven o'clock was chiming from the towers of the Marienkirche and the Nikolai-kirche, so that, his capacious slippers on his feet, he could pull his nightcap down over his ears with the final boom of the bell.

The clocks were already preparing to strike eleven and he was hurrying (you might almost say running) out of the Königsstrasse into the Spandauerstrasse when a strange knocking sound close beside him rooted him to the ground. At the base of the tower of the old Town Hall he perceived in the bright lamplight that a tall, thin figure shrouded in a dark cloak was hammering at the closed shop-door of the merchant Warnatz, who, as is well known, offers his hardware for sale there; the figure, having hammered louder and louder, stepped back, emitted a deep sigh and looked upwards at the dilapidated windows of the tower.

'My dear sir,' the chancellery private secretary turned to the man and said good-naturedly, 'you are making a mistake: no human soul dwells up in that tower, nor indeed, if I exclude a few rats and mice and a couple of little owls, no living creature of any kind. If you wish to purchase any of Herr Warnatz's excellent ironware or steelware you will have to put yourself to the trouble of coming back tomorrow.'

'My esteemed Herr Tusmann –'

'Chancellery Private Secretary Tusmann for many years now,' Tusmann involuntarily interposed, notwithstanding that he was somewhat taken aback at the stranger's knowing who he was.

The latter, however, paid not the slightest attention to this interruption but began again: 'My esteemed Herr Tusmann, you are altogether mistaken in your conjecture of the reason for my presence here. I require neither ironware nor steelware, and have indeed no business whatever with Herr Warnatz. Today is the autumnal equinox and I have come to behold the bride. She has already heard my passionate knocking and my amorous sighs and will shortly appear up there in the window.'

The hollow tone with which the man spoke these words had something strangely solemn, even spectral, about it, so that the chancellery private secretary felt an icy trickle pass through every limb. Then, as the first stroke of the eleventh hour boomed down from the tower of the Marienkirche, there came a clattering and rustling from the dilapidated window of the Town Hall tower, and a female figure became visible. As the full glare of the lantern fell upon her face, Tusmann moaned dolefully: 'O great God in Heaven, O all you heavenly host, whatever is that?'

On the final stroke – the very moment when Tusmann usually thought to put on his nightcap – the figure vanished.

The chancellery private secretary seemed to become completely beside himself at the sight of the astonishing apparition: he sighed, he groaned, he stared up at the window, he whispered to himself: 'Tusmann! Tusmann! Chancellery secretary! Come to your senses! Beat not so wildly, my heart! Do not let the Devil deceive you, O my soul!'

'You seem', the stranger began, 'to be very much affected by what you have seen, my good Herr Tusmann. I wanted merely to behold the bride, but to you, honoured sir, something quite other must have appeared.'

'Please, please,' Tusmann whined, 'won't you allow me my simple title? I am a chancellery private secretary and at this moment an extremely excited one. May I humbly state, most worthy sir, that if I do not give you your appropriate rank, that is entirely because I am utterly unacquainted with your worthy person; but I will call you Herr Privy Counsellor, for there are so remarkably many of them in our dear Berlin that if one employs that dignified title one rarely goes wrong. Therefore, Herr Privy Counsellor, would you please no longer conceal from me what kind of a bride it was you thought to behold here at this uncanny hour?'

'You are', the stranger said in a raised voice, 'a peculiar man, with your titles and ranks. If one can call oneself a privy counsellor if one is privy to many secrets and is also able to give good counsel, then I possess every right to that title. I am seized with wonder that a man as well read in ancient writings and rare manuscripts as you, most worthy Herr Chancellery Private Secretary, should not know that if an initiate – mark that well! – an initiate knocks on the door or even only on the wall of this tower at eleven o'clock on the night of the equinox there will appear to him in the window above the girl who by the vernal equinox will be the happiest bride in Berlin.'

'Herr Privy Counsellor,' Tusmann cried, as if suddenly inspired with a transport of joy, 'most honoured Herr Privy Counsellor, can that really be so?'

'It is nothing but the truth,' replied the stranger; 'but

why do we remain standing here in the street? You have already missed your usual hour of retirement; let us betake ourselves immediately to the new wine-house on the Alexanderplatz. The purpose is simply for me to tell you more about the bride, if you wish it, and for you to be restored to the composure which, I really don't know why, you seem altogether to have lost.'

The chancellery private secretary was an extremely abstemious man. His sole relaxation consisted, as has already been indicated, in spending a couple of hours each evening in a coffee-house, where he ran through the papers and pamphlets or read a book he had brought with him, and enjoyed a glass of beer. He almost never drank wine: only on Sundays after church did he go to a wine cellar and take a small glass of Malaga with a few biscuits. He loathed roaming about at night; it therefore seemed incomprehensible that he should have allowed himself unresistingly, indeed without so much as a word, to be conducted away by the stranger, who with firm step resounding through the night hurried off to the Alexanderplatz.

When they entered the wine-house there was only one other person there: a man sitting alone at a table with a large glass of Rhine-wine standing before him. The deep lines that furrowed his brow witnessed to his great age. His glance was sharp and piercing, and only the majestic beard betrayed the Jew still faithful to ancient custom and tradition; he was, moreover, clad in the kind of dress worn about 1720 to 1730, and this was no doubt why he gave the impression of one returned to the world from an age long past.

But even more curious to look at, surely, was the stranger Tusmann had encountered: he was a large and lean but strongly built man, apparently in his fifties; his face might once have been accounted handsome, and his large eyes still flashed with youthful fire from under black bushy eyebrows; a free, open brow, a strongly arched aquiline nose, a delicately formed mouth, an arched chin – none of this would have distinguished the man from a hundred others, but while his jacket and trousers were cut according to the latest fashion, his coat, cape and cap belonged to the end of the sixteenth century; the singular glance of the stranger, however, which seemed to rise from the depths of night, the hollow tone of his voice, his whole appearance, which contrasted strongly with that of all his contemporaries – all this may have been the main reason why anyone who came into his presence felt a strange, almost uncanny sensation.

The stranger nodded to the old man seated at the table as to an old acquaintance. 'It is a long time since I have seen you,' he called. 'Are you still well?'

'I cannot complain,' the old man replied morosely. 'Fit and well, and up and about again, as you can see, and prepared to be busy if needs be!'

'I am glad to hear it,' the stranger called, laughing aloud, and ordered from the waiter a bottle of the oldest French wine they had in the cellar.

'My good, most worthy Herr Privy Counsellor!' Tusmann began when he heard the order.

But the stranger interrupted him quickly: 'Let us forget all about titles, my good Herr Tusmann. I am neither a privy counsellor nor a chancellery private secretary, but nothing more nor less than an artist who works in noble metals and precious stones, and my name is Leonhard.'

'He is a goldsmith, a jeweller, then,' Tusmann murmured to himself. He also reflected that his first sight of the stranger in the brightly lit wine-house ought to have told him that the man could not possibly be a genuine privy counsellor, since he was clad in an old-fashioned German coat, cape and cap, which was not customary among privy counsellors.

The two of them, Tusmann and Leonhard, then sat down at the table with the old man, who greeted them with a grin. When, after much prompting by Leonhard, Tusmann had drunk a couple of glasses, his pale cheeks began to acquire some colour; gazing before him, cheerfully consuming the wine, he smiled and smirked in the friendliest way, as if the most pleasant images were passing before his mind's eye.

'And now', Leonhard began, 'tell me frankly, my good Herr Tusmann, why you behaved so very strangely when the bride appeared at the tower window, and what it is that is now engrossing your attention so completely. You and I are, whether you believe it or not, old friends, and you need not be afraid to speak before this good man.'

'O God,' replied the chancellery private secretary, 'most respected Herr Professor – allow me to bestow on you this title, for since you are, I am convinced, an absolutely first-rate artist, you could with every right and justification be a professor at the Academy of Arts – how can I possibly keep silent? Of what the heart is full the mouth speaketh. Hear, then! – I am, to use a common expression, courting and expect at the next vernal equinox to lead home a happy little bride. How could I then fail to be profoundly stirred when you, most respected Herr Professor, were pleased to display to me such a happy bride?'

'What?' the old man interposed in a shrill, croaking voice, 'What? You intend to get married? But you are much too old for it and as ugly as a baboon.'

Tusmann was so startled at the old Jew's dreadful coarseness he was bereft of speech.

'Do not mind the old man, my dear Herr Tusmann,' Leonhard said, 'he doesn't mean to be half as rude as he sounds. But, to speak honestly, I too cannot help feeling you have left it rather late to think of marriage: you seem to me to be almost in your fifties.'

'On 9 October, on St Denis's Day, I shall attain my forty-eighth year,' Tusmann put in somewhat irritably.

'Be that as it may,' Leonhard went on, 'it is not age alone

that speaks against you. You have hitherto lived the simple, solitary life of a bachelor; you do not know the female sex; you will not know how to behave or what to do.'

'How to behave, what to do,' Tusmann interrupted. 'You must regard me as uncommonly thoughtless and imprudent, my good Herr Professor, if you believe me capable of acting blindly in such a matter, without first seeking counsel and reflecting upon it. I never take a step without weighing and considering it carefully; when I felt the dart of the dissolute god the ancients called Cupid, would I not exert all my faculties towards preparing myself suitably for this condition? Would anyone who hopes to pass a difficult examination not diligently study all the subjects he is to be asked questions on? Very well, most respected Herr Professor, my marriage is an examination for which I am preparing myself suitably and which I believe I shall pass. Behold, my dear man, this little book, which since I resolved on love and marriage I have carried everywhere with me and studied continually; behold it, and be assured that I am setting about this matter in a thorough and sensible fashion, and that when it comes to it, I shall not seem in the least inexperienced, notwithstanding the fact that I have, as I confess, to this moment been a stranger to the whole female sex.'

With these words the chancellery private secretary had drawn from his pocket a small, parchment-bound book and opened it at the title page, which read as follows: *A Short Treatise of the Politic Art of Correct Behaviour in Society of every Description: for the attainment of Judicious Comportment; translated, to meet the urgent needs of, and of the most exceptional utility to all who believe themselves sagacious, or who wish to become so, out of the Latin of Herr Thomasius. With an exhaustive index. Frankfurt and Leipzig. Johann Gross. 1710.*

'Notice', said Tusmann with a sweet smile, 'what the

worthy author expressly says in paragraph six of the seventh chapter, which deals purely with marriage and with how best to be the father of a family: *This is not a thing that should be hurried. He who marries when he has attained to the years of full manhood will be the more prudent in that he will be so much wiser. Marriages entered into too early in life make those who have entered into them shameless or deceitful, and exhaust the energies of both the body and the mind. The years of manhood are naturally not the beginning of youth, but the end of the latter should not arrive before that of the former.*

'And then, as regards the choice of the object one intends to love and to marry, the excellent Thomasius says in paragraph nine: *The middle course is the safest: do not select a woman too beautiful nor too ugly, one very rich nor one very poor, one more exalted nor one baser, but one who is of the same rank as yourself, and so in the case of most of the other qualities will the middle course also prove to be the best course.*

'This course I have taken and, following the advice given by Herr Thomasius in paragraph seventeen, have conducted conversation with the charming person of my choice not only once – since you can easily be deceived by the dissimulation of faults and the pretence of non-existent virtues – but frequently, since in the long run it is impossible to conceal completely what one is.'

'But,' said the goldsmith, 'my worthy Herr Tusmann, it is precisely this traffic or, as you like to call it, conversation with women that seems to me to require lengthy practice and experience if one is not to be basely deceived by them.'

'In this, too,' Tusmann replied, 'the great Thomasius stands by me, through his exhaustive instruction in how to contrive an intelligent and pleasant conversation and how, when conversing with women, one can best introduce a delightful humorous element. But, as my author says in his fifth chapter, one should employ humour as a cook employs salt; indeed even piquant remarks should be employed as a weapon not for harming others but for our own defence, as a hedgehog uses its spikes. And one should, as a prudent man, pay almost more attention to one's gestures than to one's words, in as much as what one conceals in what one says is often revealed by one's gestures, and words are commonly less capable of evoking friendship or enmity than are the other elements of one's appearance and behaviour.'

'I perceive already,' the goldsmith put in, 'that there is no confounding you: you are armed against everything. I will therefore wager that your comportment has gained for you completely the love of the lady of your choice.'

'I study,' said Tusmann, 'following the counsel of Thomasius, a deferential and amicable courteousness, for this is at once the most natural mark of love and the most natural means of engendering love in return, just as yawning will incite an entire company to yawn in imitation. Yet I do not take this deference too far, for I bear in mind that, as Thomasius teaches, women are not angels, good or bad, but merely humans and, indeed, in bodily and spiritual strength weaker creatures than we are, as the difference between the sexes sufficiently shows.'

'A year of bad luck to you,' cried the old man furiously, 'for going on with such rubbish and ruining what I intended to be an hour of relaxation after the completion of my great work!'

'Quiet, old man,' the goldsmith said, raising his voice. 'You should be glad we put up with you here at all: your uncouthness makes you an unwelcome guest who ought really to be thrown out. – Do not be put off by the old man, my worthy Herr Tusmann. You are well disposed towards the old days, you admire Thomasius; for my own part, I go much further back and admire only that age to which, as you see, my dress in part belongs. Yes, my dear sir, that age was surely more glorious than ours; moreover, it gave birth to that sorcery which you witnessed today in the Town Hall tower.'

'How so, most worthy Herr Professor?' asked the chancellery private secretary.

'Why,' the goldsmith continued, 'in those days there were many merry weddings at the Town Hall, and such weddings looked a little different from the weddings of today. Many a happy bride used to gaze down from that window, and so it is a pleasing piece of magic if an airy form now prophesies from what happened long ago what is yet to be. In general, I have to confess that in those days our Berlin used to be a much more colourful and cheerful place than it is now, when everything comes out of one mould and in order not to be bored people seek and find pleasure in boredom itself. There were festivals then, festivals such as cannot be imagined nowadays. Let me merely recall how in the spring of 1581 the Elector Augustus of Saxony and his lady and son Christian were taken across to Kölln in a glorious procession of some hundred horses. And the citizens of both towns, Berlin and Kölln, with those of Spandau, lined the road from the Köpenick Gate to the castle in full armour. The next day there was a magnificent joust and tournament, in which the Elector and Count Jost von Barby, with many more of the nobility, appeared clad in gold, with tall golden crests, golden lions'-heads at their shoulders, elbows and knees, and their arms and legs encased in flesh-coloured silk as though they were bare, like painted heathen warriors. Minstrels and musicians sat hidden in a golden Noah's Ark, and on top sat a little boy dressed in flesh-coloured silk, with wings, bow, quiver and blindfold like a picture of Cupid. Two more boys clad in white ostrich feathers, with gold-painted eyes and beaks like doves', guided the Ark, from which music sounded whenever the Elector won at the tilt. Thereupon certain doves were released from the Ark, and one of them settled on the pointed sable hat of our gracious Elector and beat its wings and sang a very lovely Italian aria, much finer than those our court singer Bernardo

Pasquino Gross of Mantua used to sing seventy years later, though not as charming as those sung by the prima donnas of the present day – who are, to be sure, when they demonstrate their art, more comfortably situated than that little dove. Then there was a tournament on foot, for which the Elector and the Count von Barby entered in a ship decorated in yellow and black and with a sail of gold taffeta. And the little boy who had been Cupid the day before sat behind the lords wearing a long, many-coloured coat and a pointed hat decorated in yellow and black and a long grey beard. Minstrels and musicians were clad in the same way. But around the ship there danced and leaped many nobles bedecked with the heads and tails of salmon, herrings and other fish, which made a very gay sight. At ten o'clock at night came a firework display using several thousand fireworks: there was a square fortress manned by soldiers all made of fireworks, and there was much fighting and fencing, and fiery horses and riders and strange birds and animals were shot off into the sky with a terrible banging and crackling. The display lasted for two hours.'

While the goldsmith was recounting all this the chancellery private secretary evidenced every sign of rapt attention and high delight. He punctuated the narration with little cries of 'Oh!' and 'Ah!', smirked, rubbed his hands together, fidgeted on his seat and gulped down one glass of wine after another as he did so.

'My excellent Herr Professor,' he cried at last in the falsetto that great pleasure always extorted from him, 'my dear, excellent Herr Professor, what marvellous things – and you describe them as vividly as if you had been there yourself.'

'Well,' the goldsmith replied, 'and is it not possible I was there myself?'

Failing to grasp the meaning of this strange remark, Tusmann was about to resume, when the old man said to the goldsmith morosely: 'Do not forget the fairest of the festivals enjoyed by the Berliners in that age you praise so highly, when the pyres blazed in the Neumarkt and there flowed the blood of the unfortunate sacrifices, who, martyred in the most fearful fashion, confessed to whatever the maddest lunacy and grossest superstition could dream up.'

'Ah,' the chancellery private secretary interposed, 'you allude to the iniquitous witch-trials that took place in the old days, my dear sir! Yes, yes, that was a bad thing, to be sure, but our Enlightenment has put an end to it.'

The goldsmith cast a strange glance at the old man and at Tusmann, and at length asked the latter with a mysterious smile: 'Do you know the story of the Jewish coiner Lippold, which happened in the year 1572?'

Before Tusmann could reply, the goldsmith went on: 'People accused the Jewish coiner Lippold of perpetrating gigantic frauds and of being in general an arrant knave, but he enjoyed the trust of the Elector and had control of the country's entire coinage and could moreover always lay his hands on any amount of money, so that, whether it was because he knew how to plead his cause or whether he had other means at his command to clear himself of guilt in the eyes of the Elector or whether some people with influence over his lord had, as they used to say, been squared – whatever the reason, he was on the point of being declared innocent of everything he was accused of, and only a few citizens were keeping watch on him in his little house in the Stralauerstrasse. One day, however, he had an angry scene with his wife, and she shouted at him in rage: "If the gracious Herr Elector only knew what a wicked rogue you are and what knavish tricks you can play with your magic book, you would be done for!" These words were retailed to the Elector, who had Lippold's house searched from top to bottom for the magic book, which was at length discovered and which, when those who understood it had read it, brought his knavery clearly to light. He had practised the black arts with a view to bringing the Elector wholly under his control and to ruling the entire country, and it was only through his Highness's godliness that the satanic magic had failed of its effect. Lippold was burned to death on the Neumarkt, but as the flames consumed his body and his magic book, a large mouse came out from under the scaffolding and ran into the fire. Many people regarded the mouse as Lippold's familiar.'

While the goldsmith was recounting this story, the old man had propped both his arms on the table, held his hands before his face and groaned and moaned like one riven by unendurable suffering. The chancellery private secretary, on the other hand, seemed not to pay very much attention to the goldsmith's words, but behaved in an immoderately amicable way and appeared at that moment to be preoccupied with something quite other than what the goldsmith was saying: for when the latter had finished, he began to smirk and asked in a sweet lisping voice: 'But just tell me, most worthy, most respected Herr Professor, was that really Demoiselle Albertine Vosswinkel who was looking down at us with her lovely eyes from the dilapidated window of the Town Hall tower?'

'What', the goldsmith rounded on him furiously, 'have you to do with Albertine Vosswinkel?'

'Well,' Tusmann replied meekly, 'good heavens, that is the charming lady I have undertaken to love and marry.'

'Sir,' the goldsmith cried, his face scarlet and his eyes ablaze with rage, 'I believe you must be possessed of the Devil or totally insane! You – you wretched decrepit old pedant, you who with all your book-learning and politic arts out of Thomasius cannot see three paces in front of your nose – *you* wish to marry the fair young Albertine Vosswinkel? Banish any such idea, or you could find yourself with your neck broken this equinoctial night.'

The chancellery private secretary was normally a gentle,

peaceable, indeed timid man who, even if he was assailed, could never speak sharply to anyone. The goldsmith's words were, however, too insolent for even him to bear, and there was also the consideration that Tusmann had drunk more strong wine than he was used to, so it happened, unprecedentedly, that he rose up in anger and screamed shrilly: 'I do not know, my unknown Herr Goldsmith, what gives you the right to address me in that fashion! I even think you have been trying to make a fool of me with all kinds of childish tricks and have the presumption to intend loving the Demoiselle Albertine yourself and have painted the lady's portrait on glass and by means of a *laterna magica* hidden under your cloak projected that lovely image on to the Town Hall tower! Oh, my dear sir, I too know all about such things, and if you think your tricks and coarse speeches can make me back down you are barking up quite the wrong tree!'

'Take care,' the goldsmith responded calmly with a curious smile, 'take care, Tusmann: you are dealing with strange people here.'

But at that moment the goldsmith's face vanished and in its stead a hideous fox's mask grinned across at the chancellery private secretary, who, seized with profound terror, collapsed back into his seat.

The old man evidenced no surprise whatever at the goldsmith's transformation: on the contrary, he all at once lost his former air of moroseness and cried with a laugh: 'An excellent jest! – but there's no profit in that kind of thing: I know better and can do things that have always been too hard for you, Leonhard.'

'Let us see,' said the goldsmith, who had now resumed his human face and was sitting quietly at the table, 'let us see what you can do.'

The old man drew a large black radish out of his pocket, cleaned and peeled it with a little knife which he had also brought forth, cut it into thin slices and laid them on the table. But when he smote one of the slices of radish with his clenched fist a beautifully stamped glittering gold piece appeared with a metallic clink. He took it up and threw it to the goldsmith, but when the goldsmith caught it the gold piece exploded into a thousand crackling sparks of fire. This seemed to annoy the old man: he began to stamp the slices of radish faster and faster and harder and harder, but they only exploded more and more noisily in the goldsmith's hand.

The chancellery private secretary was quite beside himself and bewildered with fear and terror, but at last he pulled himself out of the swoon which was threatening to engulf him and said in a trembling voice: 'I will now bid the most excellent gentlemen a very humble good evening,' and, seizing his hat and walking-stick, he rushed out of the door.

On the street outside he heard his two uncanny acquaintances burst into a piercing shriek of laughter behind him that froze the blood in his veins.

2

It was in a less devious fashion than the chancellery private secretary that the young painter Edmund Lehsen had made the acquaintanceship of the singular goldsmith Leonhard.

Edmund was sketching a group of trees from nature in a solitary spot in the Tiergarten when Leonhard came up to him and without ceremony looked over his shoulder at what he was doing. Edmund did not allow himself to be in the least distracted but diligently continued drawing, until the goldsmith cried: 'What an astonishing drawing, my dear young man: that won't end up as trees but as something quite different.'

'Do you see something there, sir?' said Edmund with a flashing glance.

'Well,' the goldsmith went on, 'out of those clusters of

leaves it seems to me there are all kinds of figures peering: now genii, now strange animals, now young girls, now flowers. And yet the whole should depict nothing but that group of trees standing before us with the rays of the evening sun sparkling through them, should it not?'

'Indeed, sir,' cried Edmund, 'either you possess a very profound insight, a penetrative eye, for such things, or I have succeeded in conveying my inner inspiration more happily than I usually do. When, amid nature, you abandon yourself wholly to your desires and longings, does it not seem to you too as if all kinds of wonderful forms were gazing at you with loving eyes through the trees and the undergrowth? That is what I wanted to give expression to in this drawing, and it appears I have done so.'

'I see,' said Leonhard in somewhat cold and dry tones. 'You wanted to abandon all real study, take a rest and exercise and enliven your imagination with a pleasant pastime.'

'Not at all, sir,' Edmund replied. 'It is precisely this manner of drawing from nature that I consider the best and most useful study. It is from such studies that I bestow poetry and imagination on the landscape. The landscape painter has to be just as much a poet as a portrait painter does, or he will never be anything but a bungler.'

'Heaven help us!' cried Leonhard. 'You too, my dear Edmund Lehsen!'

'You know me, sir?' Edmund interrupted him.

'Why should I not know you?' Leonhard replied. 'I first made your valued acquaintanceship at a time which you probably cannot recall very clearly, namely the moment of your birth. For the small amount of experience you could have possessed at that time you behaved extremely well, made uncommonly little trouble for your mama, let out a very pleasant-sounding cry of joy and vehemently desired to see the light of day – which, by my advice, was not denied you, since according to the most up-to-date physicians this does not merely do no harm to newborn children but is on the contrary beneficial to their minds and to their physical condition in general. Your papa was so delighted he hopped about the room on one leg and sang *Bei Männern, welche Liebe fühlen* from the *Magic Flute*. Afterwards he handed me your tiny person and asked me to draw up your horoscope, which I did. Thereafter I was a frequent visitor to your father's house, and you did not disdain to accept the bags of raisins and almonds which I brought with me. Later I travelled away – you would have been six or eight years old. Then I came here to Berlin, saw you and was pleased to learn that your father had sent you here from Müncheberg to study the noble art of painting – for Müncheberg possesses no great fund of pictures, marbles, bronzes, cameos or other art treasures needed for the pursuit of that study. In this respect your worthy home town cannot be compared with Rome, Florence or Dresden – although Berlin will be compared with them in the future perhaps, if brand-new antiques are fished out of the Tiber and transported here.'

'My God,' said Edmund, 'now I recall everything! Are you not Herr Leonhard?'

'I am,' the goldsmith replied, 'in any event called Leonhard, but I should be surprised if you could remember me from so early a period of your life.'

'Yet I do,' Edmund continued. 'I know I was very glad whenever you appeared at our house, because you always brought me all kinds of nice things and in general paid me a lot of attention, and at the same time I could not shake off a timid sense of awe, even a certain fear and oppression, which often persisted after you had left. But, even more, it is the tales my father told of you which have kept the memory of you lively within me. He was proud of your friendship, since you had with particular dexterity rescued him from all kinds of disagreeable events and involvements such as cannot fail to arise in the course of our life.

And he spoke with enthusiasm of how you had penetrated into the profound secret sciences, held sway over many hidden forces of nature, and sometimes – forgive me for saying so – he strongly hinted that, if the total truth were known, you were none other than Ahasuerus, the Wandering Jew!'

'Why not the Pied Piper of Hamelin or Old Everywhere-and-Nowhere or Peterkin or some other kobold?' the goldsmith interrupted. 'But I will not deny that there are indeed certain peculiar circumstances connected with me, of which I cannot speak without giving offence. I did indeed render your papa many a service through my secret arts: he was especially delighted with the horoscope which I drew up for you after your birth.'

'Well, now,' the young man said, his cheeks flushing red, 'the horoscope, you know, was not so delightful as all that. My father often repeated to me that your prophecy had been that something great would become of me, either as a great artist or a great fool. But at least I have this prophecy to thank that my father placed nothing in the way of my artistic inclination; do you not think your horoscope will prove true?'

'Oh, absolutely,' the goldsmith said composedly, 'there can be no doubt about it, for you are even now on the right road to becoming a great fool.'

'What, sir,' cried Edmund, taken aback, 'do you say that to my face? You –'

'It is', the goldsmith interrupted, 'entirely up to you whether you avoid the evil alternative of my horoscope and become a proficient artist. Your drawings, your sketches, betray a rich and lively imagination, an active power of expression, a bold dexterity in representation; on these foundations a gallant structure may be erected. Leave aside all modish extravagances and give yourself wholly to serious study. I applaud your aspiration to the dignity and simplicity of the old German artists, but here too you must avoid the reefs upon which so many come to grief. For it requires a profound heart, a strength of soul such as can withstand the enervation of modern art, to grasp the true spirit of the old German masters and to penetrate the meaning of their creations. Only then will the spark from your innermost being be ignited and only then will true inspiration fashion works which, without blind imitation, are worthy of a better age. Nowadays, however, young people think that, when they have put together some biblical picture or other, with figures thin as rakes, faces a yard long, stiff, angular clothing and false perspectives, they have been painting in the manner of the old exalted German masters. Such wretched, spiritually dead imitators are like the peasant boy who kept his eyes closed in church during the *Pater Noster* as though he had got the prayer by heart, explaining that if he didn't know the words he at any rate knew the tune.'

The goldsmith said much more that was true and beautiful about the noble art of painting and gave the artistically inclined Edmund some excellent instruction, so that Edmund, mightily impressed, asked at last how it was possible for Leonhard to have acquired so much knowledge without himself being a painter, and why he lived in such obscurity without seeking to impose his influence upon artistic endeavour of every kind.

'I have told you already', the goldsmith replied in a very gentle and serious tone, 'that it is long, indeed marvellously long experience that has sharpened my eye and my judgement. As for my obscurity, however, I am conscious that my presence would everywhere appear as something strange – a fact determined not only by the structure of my whole personality but also by the feeling I produce of possessing a certain inherent power – and that this could disrupt my entire peaceful existence here in Berlin. I recall a man who could in a certain sense be my ancestor and who has entered so into my flesh and blood that I am sometimes subject to the strange delusion I am him. I mean none other than Leonhard Turnhäuser zum Thurm from Switzerland, who in the year 1582 lived here in Berlin at the court of the Elector Johann Georg. At that time, as you will know, every chemist was called an alchemist and every astronomer an astrologer, and Turnhäuser performed some remarkable feats and was, moreover, an excellent physician. But he committed the error of wanting to assert his arts everywhere, of involving himself in everything, of being everywhere at hand with deeds and advice. This attracted hatred and envy to him, as a rich man who expends his wealth on luxuries attracts enemies, even if the wealth has been acquired honestly. Now it happened that the Elector became convinced that Turnhäuser was able to make gold, but, either because he was really unable to do so or for some other reason, Turnhäuser obstinately refused to set about making it. Then his enemies went to the Elector and said: "Do you not see what an impudent crafty fellow this is? He boasts of knowledge which he does not possess and carries on all kinds of sorcery and Jewish dealings, for which he ought to suffer a shameful death, like the Jew Lippold." It emerged that Turnhäuser had in reality been a goldsmith, and all the art and erudition he had amply demonstrated was then called into question. It was even alleged that all the ingenious writings, the momentous prognostications, he had published were not his own work but had been written for him by others in exchange for money. Enough: hatred, envy and slander brought it about that, to avoid the fate of the Jew Lippold, Turnhäuser had to leave Berlin and Brandenburg in the greatest secrecy. Then his enemies cried that he had gone over to the papist mob, which was, however, not the case. He went to Saxony and, without renouncing his arts and his erudition, pursued his goldsmith's trade.'

Edmund felt strangely drawn to the old goldsmith, and the latter rewarded the respectful confidence which

Edmund exhibited towards him, not only by remaining a stern but profoundly instructive critic of his work, but also by revealing to him certain secrets possessed by ancient painters in the preparation and mixing of colours which, when put into practice, proved wonderfully effective. Thus there arose between Edmund and Leonhard the relationship of beloved and promising pupil and fatherly teacher and friend.

Soon afterwards it happened that, on a lovely summer's evening at the Hofjäger in the Tiergarten, Counsellor Melchior Vosswinkel could not get a single one of the cigars he had brought with him to stay alight. None of them would draw. With mounting annoyance the counsellor threw one after the other to the ground and at length cried: 'God Almighty, have I, at great trouble and expense, procured cigars direct from Hamburg only to have the wretched things ruin my best hours of relaxation? How can I enjoy the pleasures of nature in a reasonable fashion or conduct a useful conversation? It's dreadful!'

He had to some extent directed these words to Edmund Lehsen, who was standing beside him and whose cigar was burning merrily. Edmund, though unacquainted with the counsellor, straight away drew out a full box of cigars and offered it amicably to the distracted man with the request that he would help himself, as he could vouch for the quality and combustibility of the cigars, even though he had not got them direct from Hamburg but had bought them from a shop in the Friedrichsstrasse.

With an 'I am much obliged to you,' the counsellor, now all joy and contentment, did indeed help himself, and as, barely touched by the burning spill, the pleasant weed began to emit fine light-grey clouds of smoke, he cried in delight: 'O my worthy sir, you really have rescued me from the most abominable straits! A thousand thanks – and I am almost impudent enough to ask you for another when this one is finished.'

Edmund answered that the box of cigars was at his command, and the two then parted. But as twilight was beginning to come on and Edmund, reflecting on an idea for a picture and absentmindedly paying no attention to the people around him, was making his way through the chairs and tables on his way out of the Hofjäger, the counsellor suddenly reappeared before him and asked very amicably whether he would not join him at his table. Desiring to escape into the woods, Edmund was on the point of refusing when he beheld a girl – the very image of youth, sweetness and charm – sitting at the table from which the counsellor had risen.

'My daughter Albertine,' the counsellor said to Edmund, who stood motionless gazing at the girl, almost forgetting to speak. At first glance he had recognized in Albertine the lovely and elegantly dressed woman he had encountered before one of his drawings at the previous year's exhibition. She had with acute perspicacity explained to the older woman and the two young girls who were with her the meaning of the fantastical picture, she had gone into the draughtsmanship and grouping, she had lauded the master who had created the work and remarked that he must be a very young and promising artist whom she would like to get to know. Edmund had stood close behind her and drunk in avidly the praise that flowed from those fairest of lips. But, for the sheer sweet fear he felt, and the anxious beating of his heart, he could not bring himself to step forward as the creator of the picture. Then Albertine had dropped the glove she had just removed from her hand; Edmund had quickly stooped to pick it up, Albertine had done likewise, and their heads had met with a loud bump! 'God in Heaven!' Albertine had cried, grasping her head in pain.

Edmund had started back in horror; had stepped on the old lady's little dog, which had squealed aloud; and had then trodden on the foot of a gouty professor, who had let out a fearsome roar and had called down upon the unfortunate Edmund all the torments of damnation. And people had come running from all the other rooms, and every lorgnette had been directed at Edmund, who, blushing scarlet and to the accompaniment of the whimpering of the injured little dog, the cursing of the professor, the scolding of the old lady and the laughter and tittering of the girls, had rushed out in despair, while several ladies had opened their smelling-bottles and Albertine had applied eau-de-Cologne to her bruised forehead.

Even then, at the critical moment of that ludicrous scene, Edmund had, without being clearly aware of it, fallen in love, and only the excruciating sense of the fool he had made of himself had kept him from seeking the girl out in every end and corner of the town. He could think of Albertine only as standing with a forehead swollen red and with the bitterest reproach, the most resolute rage, in her face and whole being.

But not the slightest trace of any of this was observable today. Albertine blushed again and again, to be sure, when she beheld the youth and seemed to be as confused and disconcerted as he was; but when the counsellor asked after his name and station, she interposed with a sweet smile that, unless she was very much mistaken, she beheld before her Herr Lehsen, the splendid artist whose drawings, whose pictures, had moved her so profoundly.

As you may imagine, these words went through Edmund like an electric shock. Delighted by what he had heard, he was about to break out into the choicest figures of speech when the counsellor forestalled him by thumping him violently in the chest and saying: 'My dear fellow! the cigar you promised me!' Then, as he ignited the cigar Edmund offered him with the glowing ashes of the one he had just finished smoking, he went on: 'So you are a painter, and, it seems, an excellent one, if my daughter Albertine, who has a very fine understanding of such things, says so. Well, I am very glad to hear it; I love painting or, in the words of my daughter Albertine, art in general, with a fervour quite uncommon – I absolutely dote on it! I am also a connoisseur – yes, truly, a genuine connoisseur of painting! I can no more be taken in than my daughter Albertine can; we have eyes – yes, eyes! Tell me, my dear painter, tell me honestly without any false modesty, you are, are you not, that splendid artist whose pictures I pass every day and have to stop and gaze at for minutes on end on account of the riveting beauty of their colours?'

Edmund could not quite understand how the counsellor could contrive to pass his paintings every day, since he could not remember ever having painted sign-boards. But a little interrogation revealed that what Melchior Voss-winkel was referring to was nothing other than the var-nished tea-trays, fire-screens and other things of that sort displayed in Stobwasser's on the Unter den Linden, which he did indeed contemplate with delight when he took four anchovies and a glass of Danzig brandy at the Sala Tarone at eleven o'clock each morning. He regarded these manu-factures as the highest thing ever achieved in art. Edmund was not a little rattled by this revelation and inwardly cursed the counsellor as his continuing insipid stream of words made any advance to Albertine impossible.

At length an acquaintance of the counsellor's appeared and drew him into conversation, and Edmund exploited this circumstance to sit down close beside Albertine, who seemed pleased to see him do so.

Everyone who knows Demoiselle Albertine Voss winkel knows that she is, as above mentioned, the very image of youth, charm and beauty; that, like all Berlin girls, she knows how to dress very tastefully in the finest fashion; that she sings in Zelter's academy, receives instruction in the fortepiano from Herr Lauska, can imitate the daintiest steps of the finest ballerina, has already furnished the exhibition with a beautifully embroidered tulip attended by sundry forget-me-nots and violets; and, although of a cheerful, exuberant temperament by nature, is yet able, especially when taking tea, to display sufficient refinement of sensibility. Everyone also knows, finally, that in a neat dainty hand she copies into a little morocco-covered book poems and aphorisms she has found especially pleasing in the writings of Goethe, Jean Paul and other gifted men and women and that she never confuses *mir* with *mich* or *Sie* with *Ihnen*. It was thus quite natural that, sitting beside the young painter who gave every sign of being consumed with the delight of an awakening love, Albertine should ascend into a sensibility even more rarefied than that usually displayed at tea-circles and readings and that she should begin in the most agreeable fashion to lisp melodiously of poetical temperament, childlike receptivity, seriousness of purpose and other things of that sort.

The evening breeze had sprung up and was wafting the sweet scent of flowers before it, and in the dim bushes two nightingales were singing in duet the tenderest amorous complaints. Then Albertine began to recite from a poem of Fouqué:

> '*A whispering and a rustling*
> *Goes through the springtime grove,*
> *Imprisoning mind and spirit*
> *As do the coils of love.*'

Grown bolder in the deeper twilight which had now sunk down, Edmund grasped Albertine's hand, pressed it to his breast and spoke on:

> '*If I too sang what softly*
> *These sounds around us say,*
> *The everlasting light of love*
> *Would shine from out my lay.*'

Albertine withdrew her hand, but only so as to remove the fine kid glove she was wearing and then to return the hand to the happy man, who was just about to kiss it passionately when the counsellor interposed: 'God alive, how cold it's got! – I wish I had a coat in my pocket . . . or brought one with me, I should have said. Put your shawl round you, Tinchen – it's Turkish, my dear painter, and cost fifty ducats cash. Put it on, Tinchen, I say, we are off home. Farewell, my dear sir.'

Inspired by an appropriate sense of tact, Edmund at this moment reached for his cigar-box and offered the counsellor a third cigar.

'Oh, may I!' cried Vosswinkel. 'What a very generous man you are, to be sure! The police will not permit smoking while walking about in the Tiergarten, so that the lovely grass doesn't get burned, but that only makes a pipe or cigar taste all the nicer.'

As the counsellor approached the lantern to ignite his cigar, Edmund asked Albertine softly and timidly if he might escort her home. She took his arm, they walked on ahead, and the counsellor seemed as he walked along to have taken it for granted that Edmund would accompany them.

Anyone who has been young and in love, or still is both (some never are), will be able to imagine how it seemed to Edmund that, at Albertine's side, he was not walking through the woods but floating with her high above the trees in a cloud of light.

According to Rosalind in Shakespeare's *As You Like It*, the marks of a lover are: a lean cheek, a blue eye and sunken, an inquestionable spirit, a beard neglected, hose ungartered, bonnet unbanded, sleeve unbuttoned, shoe untied and a careless desolation in everything about him. All this was, to be sure, as little applicable to Edmund as to the enamoured Orlando; but, as the latter abused the young plants with carving 'Rosalind' on their barks and hung odes upon hawthorns and elegies upon brambles, so Edmund abused a great quantity of paper, parchment,

paint and canvas with celebrating his beloved in sufficiently bad verses, and with drawing and painting her without
ever hitting her likeness, since his imagination soared far
beyond his artistic capabilities. When to these activities
there were added the strange somnambulistic stare of the
lovesick and a considerable amount of sighing at all times
of the day and night, the old goldsmith, of course, soon
divined the condition his youthful friend was in. When he
asked him about it, Edmund did not hesitate to reveal to
him his whole heart.

'Oh,' Leonhard cried when Edmund had concluded,
'you do not then consider it a bad thing to fall in love with
someone else's bride: Albertine Vosswinkel is as good as
married to Chancellery Private Secretary Tusmann.'

On receipt of this appalling information, Edmund was
instantly plunged into quite uncommonly intense despair.
Leonhard waited patiently until the first paroxysm was
over and then asked whether he really had it in mind to
marry Demoiselle Albertine Vosswinkel. Edmund assured
him that union with Albertine was the supreme desire
of his life and entreated the old man to stand by him with
all the power at his command, so that he might drive
the chancellery private secretary from the field and win the
fair maiden for himself.

The goldsmith's view was that, while a lusty young
artist might very well fall in love, there was really no profit
in his thinking straightaway of getting married. It was for
that very reason, he said, that even young Sternbald had
altogether declined to submit to marriage and, so far as he
knew, was still unmarried to that day. The point struck
home, for Tieck's *Sternbald* was Edmund's favourite book,
whose hero he would himself have very much liked to
have been. He pulled a very long face and almost burst into
tears.

'Well,' said the goldsmith, 'let happen what may, I will
rid you of the chancellery private secretary. How and by

what means you are to get into the counsellor's house and
become more and more intimate with Albertine is a matter
for you. In any event, my operations against the chancellery private secretary cannot begin before the night of the
equinox.'

Edmund was beside himself with joy at the goldsmith's
assurance, for he knew that the old man kept his word
when he promised something. In what manner the goldsmith began his operations against the chancellery private
secretary, the indulgent reader has already learned in our
first chapter.

3

And from all you have learned of Chancellery Private
Secretary Tusmann, my very dear reader, you will no
doubt have the man before your eyes at this moment in his
entirety. But I would nonetheless remind you that, so far
as concerns his outward parts, he was of small stature,
bald, a little crook-legged and somewhat grotesque in his
attire. With a coat of antiquated cut and with enormously
long skirts, he wore long, wide trousers and shoes which
rang on the pavement like courier's boots when he walked
– in which connection it should be remarked that when he
went down the street he would never do so with a steady,
measured pace, but rather in a series of giant, irregular
hops which took him along at an incredible speed, so that
the aforementioned skirts of his coat, taken by the breeze
he created, would spread themselves out like a pair of
wings. Although there was something indescribably comical about his face, the very good-natured smile which
played about his mouth charmed everyone, so that everyone liked him, even though they laughed heartily at his
pedantry and at his awkward behaviour. His chief passion
was – reading! He never went out without having both his
coat-pockets stuffed with books. He read wherever he

was, while going for a walk, in church, in the coffee-shop; he read indiscriminately whatever he came across, though only works of earlier times, since he hated modern authors. Thus today he would sit in the coffee-shop and study a book of algebra, tomorrow the cavalry regulations under Friedrich Wilhelm I, the next day that remarkable work from the year 1720, *Cicero Presented as a Great Windbag and Pettifogger in Ten Orations*. Tusmann was, moreover, gifted with a tremendous memory. He was accustomed to mark anything that struck him in a book he was reading and then read through again what he had marked, after which he never forgot it. Thus it came about that Tusmann developed into a polyhistor, a living encyclopaedia which was opened when any point of science or history was at issue. When it happened, as it occasionally did, that he was unable to furnish the required information on the instant, he hunted indefatigably through every library until he had discovered it and then joyously produced it. A remarkable thing about him was that in company he could be reading and to all appearance quite lost in his book and yet hear everything that was said. He would often interpolate an altogether apposite remark and if anything witty or humorous was said, he would indicate without looking up from his book his appreciation with a short laugh in the highest tenor.

Counsellor Vosswinkel had been to school with the chancellery private secretary at the Graue Kloster, and it was to this school friendship that the close association which existed between them was ascribed. Tusmann watched Albertine grow up and had on her twelfth birthday, after having presented her with a sweet-smelling bouquet of flowers tastefully arranged by the most celebrated gardener in Berlin, kissed her hand for the first time, and had even done so with a dignity, a gallantry, with which one would not have credited him. From that moment on, the notion began to arise in the counsellor's mind that his school friend might well marry Albertine. He felt that in this way his desire that Albertine should be married would be encompassed with the least amount of trouble and difficulty, and also that the frugal and easily satisfied Tusmann would be content to settle for a very modest dowry. For a long time he kept this plan to himself, but on Albertine's eighteenth birthday he revealed it to the chancellery private secretary. The latter was at first violently terrified: the daring idea of entering into marriage, and into marriage, moreover, with a young and beautiful girl, was more than he could support. Gradually, however, he grew used to it, and when, at the counsellor's instigation, Albertine one day presented him with a little purse which she had herself decorated in the liveliest colours and addressed him as 'dear Herr Chancellery Private Secretary' as she did so, his heart became wholly inflamed with love for the charming girl. He at once declared to the counsellor in confidence that he was resolved to marry Albertine and, as the counsellor embraced him as his son-in-law, regarded himself as already Albertine's bridegroom, although there still remained the little consideration that Albertine had to that moment heard not so much as a word about the whole transaction and could, indeed, hardly have a suspicion of it.

Very early on the morning after his strange adventure at the Town Hall tower and in the wine-shop on the Alexanderplatz, the chancellery private secretary, his face pale and distorted, rushed into the counsellor's room. The counsellor was considerably startled, for Tusmann had never before visited him at this hour and his whole appearance seemed to announce some terrible event.

'Secretary!' (as the counsellor was accustomed to call the chancellery private secretary for short), 'where have you come from? How strange you look! What has happened?'

Tusmann threw himself, exhausted, into the armchair,

and only after he had spent a couple of minutes recovering his breath did he begin in a thin whimpering voice: 'Counsellor, I have come from the Spandauerstrasse, where I have been running up and down since midnight! – I haven't set foot in my house, I haven't been to bed, I haven't closed my eyes!'

And then Tusmann told the counsellor of everything that had happened, from his first encounter with the fabulous goldsmith to the moment when, horrified at the mad behaviour of the uncanny sorcerer, he rushed out of the wine-shop.

'Secretary!' cried the counsellor, 'what has happened is that, contrary to your usual habits, you took strong drink late in the evening and afterwards fell into strange dreams.'

'What are you saying, Counsellor?' the chancellery private secretary replied. 'Slept, dreamed? Do you think me ill-informed about sleep and dreams? I can show you, from Nudow's *Theory of Sleep*, what sleep is, and that it is possible to sleep without dreaming, which is why Hamlet says: To sleep, *perchance* to dream. And as for dreams, you would know as much about them as I do if you had read the *Somnium Scipionis* and Artemidorus's celebrated work on dreams and the Frankfurt Dream Book. But you read nothing, and so you blunder vilely over everything.'

'Now, now, Secretary,' the counsellor interposed, 'do not get so agitated; I am willing to think that you let yourself be led into overstepping the mark a little yesterday and fell among a gang of malicious tricksters, who played mischief with you once the wine had gone to your head. But tell me, Secretary, why on earth, when you had happily escaped from them, you did not go straight home, why you wandered about the streets.'

'O Counsellor,' wailed the chancellery private secretary, 'O dear Counsellor, faithful school friend of the Graue Kloster! – do not insult me with vile doubts, but listen calmly when I tell you that it was only when I found myself in the street that the crazy devilment really began. For as I arrived at the Town Hall, a blinding candlelight burst through every window and merry dance music with Turkish drums pealed out. I don't know how it happened, but, although I do not enjoy any very great stature, I was able to raise myself on my toes high enough to see in through the window. What do I see? – O great Creator in Heaven! – whom do I behold? – None other than your daughter, Demoiselle Albertine Vosswinkel, wearing the neatest bridal gown and waltzing immoderately with a young man. I knock on the window, I call: "Dear Demoiselle Albertine Vosswinkel, what are you doing here in the middle of the night?" But then some low fellow comes down the Königsstrasse, pulls my legs away from under me as he goes past, and laughing loudly runs off as fast as he can go. I fall down flat in the vile muck of the roadway, I cry: "Nightwatchmen! Police! Patrol! Come quick – thief, thief! – he has stolen my legs!" But up in the Town Hall everything suddenly goes dark and still, and my voice fades away unregarded in the air. I am on the point of despair when the man returns and, running past as if frantic, throws my legs into my face. I then scramble up from the ground as fast as I can in my total confusion and run into the Spandauerstrasse. But when I reach the door of my house and have got the keys in my hand, I – yes, I myself – am already standing before it and gazing wildly at myself with the same big black eyes as are to be found in my own head. I recoil in terror and collide with a man who clasps me in his strong arms. From the staff he is carrying I recognize him as the nightwatchman. I am greatly relieved and say: "Dear nightwatchman, kind man, do be good enough to drive the *Doppelgänger* of Chancellery Private Secretary Tusmann away from that door, so that the real Chancellery Secretary Tusmann, who is I myself, can get into his house." "I think you are possessed, Tusmann!" the man snarls in a hollow voice, and I see that it is not the nightwatchman at all, but the dreadful goldsmith, who has me in his clasp. At that I am unmanned by fear, cold drops of sweat stand on my brow and I say: "My honoured Herr Professor, do not take it amiss that in the darkness I mistook you for the nightwatchman. O God! call me what you like – Monsieur Tusmann or whatever you wish – I don't mind what it is, only free me from that terrible spook, which stands wholly under your control." "Tusmann," the vile sorcerer begins in his odious hollow voice, "you shall henceforth be spared all interference if you swear here and now never again to think of marrying Albertine Vosswinkel." You can imagine, Counsellor, how I feel on hearing this detestable proposition. "Dear Herr Professor," I plead, "you are making my heart bleed. The waltz is an ugly, indecent dance, and just now Demoiselle Albertine Vosswinkel, dressed as my bride, was waltzing with a young man in a manner that deprived me of my senses; nonetheless, I cannot renounce that fairest of creatures, no, I cannot renounce her." Hardly have I pronounced these words, however, than the infamous goldsmith gives me a push, so that I at once begin to spin round. And, as if pursued by an irresistible force, I start waltzing up and down the Spandauerstrasse; instead of a lady I am holding in my arms a hideous broomstick which is scratching my face, while invisible hands beat me on the back and there is a teeming crowd of Chancellery Private Secretary Tusmanns waltzing with broomsticks all around me. At last, exhausted, I sink down unconscious. Morning dawns, I open my eyes and – feel the terror I felt, Counsellor, swoon with horror, old school friend! – find myself seated high up on the horse before the Great Elector with my head leaning against his cold, iron breast. Happily, the guard seemed to be asleep, so that I could clamber down, at the risk of my life, and make off unnoticed. I ran towards the Spandauerstrasse, but I was again seized by a senseless fear which finally drove me to you.'

'Secretary,' the counsellor said, 'do you suppose I am going to believe this crazy and tasteless story? Who ever heard of such a pantomime taking place in our enlightened Berlin?'

'See now, Counsellor,' the chancellery private secretary replied, 'the errors you fall into through your lack of reading. If, like me, you had read the *Microchronicon marchicum* of Hoftius, the rector of both schools in Berlin and Kölln on the Spree, you would know that more marvellous things even than that have happened. In fact, Counsellor, I almost believe that the goldsmith who has been playing tricks with me is accursed Satan himself.'

'I beg you,' the counsellor said, 'Secretary, stay away from me with this stupid superstition. Reflect! – isn't it true that you got drunk and climbed up to the Great Elector in the excitement of intoxication?'

Tears welled into the chancellery private secretary's eyes at Vosswinkel's suspicions, which he tried with all his might to refute.

The counsellor grew more and more serious. At last, when the chancellery private secretary continued to assert that everything had happened as he said, Vosswinkel began: 'Listen, Secretary: the more I reflect on your description of the goldsmith and the old Jew with whom, quite contrary to your usual propriety and frugal way of life, you were carousing late into the night, the more certain I am that the Jew is my old Manassa and that the sorcerer goldsmith is none other than the goldsmith Leonhard, who is to be seen now and then in Berlin. It is true I haven't read as many books as you, Secretary, but it doesn't require that to know that both of them, Manassa and Leonhard, are simple, honest people and anything but sorcerers. I am uncommonly surprised that you, Secretary, who ought to be experienced in the law, do not know that superstition is strictly prohibited and that a sorcerer would never get a licence to practise his art. Listen,

Secretary: I refuse to believe that the suspicion which I was forming in my mind is well founded! Yes, I refuse to believe that you have lost the desire to marry my beautiful daughter – that you are hiding your true intent behind a curtain of crazy stories, that you are saying: "Counsellor, we must part, for if I marry your daughter the Devil will steal away my legs and beat me on the back!" It would be sad, Secretary, if you were attempting lies and deception of that sort.'

The chancellery private secretary became quite beside himself at the counsellor's wicked suspicions. He asserted time after time that he loved Demoiselle Albertine beyond all measure, that, another Leander, another Troilus, he would face death for her sake and, as an innocent martyr, let Satan himself beat him black and blue before he would renounce his love.

During these asseverations of the chancellery private secretary there came a loud knocking on the door, and the aged Manassa of whom the counsellor had spoken walked in. The moment Tusmann saw the old man he cried: 'O Lord God in Heaven, that is the old Jew who yesterday stamped gold pieces out of a radish and threw them in the goldsmith's face! Now the accursed sorcerer himself is going to come in!'

He made to exit rapidly through the door, but the counsellor restrained him, saying: 'Now we shall hear what he has to say.'

Then the counsellor turned to Manassa and repeated what Tusmann had said of him and what was supposed to have taken place the previous night in the wine-shop on the Alexanderplatz. Manassa smiled mockingly at Tusmann and said: 'I do not know what the gentleman means. The gentleman came into the wine-house yesterday with the goldsmith Leonhard just as I was refreshing myself with a glass of wine after wearisome labour that lasted almost to midnight. The gentleman drank more than enough, could hardly stand on his feet and stumbled out into the street.'

'You see, Secretary,' cried the counsellor, 'it is just as I thought. This is what comes of your revolting boozing; you must give it up, completely, if you are to marry my daughter.'

Utterly annihilated by this undeserved reproach, the chancellery private secretary sank breathless into the armchair, closed his eyes and squeaked incomprehensibly.

'Here we have it,' the counsellor said. 'First the riotous night, then the hangover.'

Despite all his protestations Tusmann had to suffer the counsellor to tie a bandage around his head and pack him off to the Spandauerstrasse in a cab.

'What is new with you, Manassa?' the counsellor then asked the old man.

Manassa smirked in a friendly way and said that the counsellor could have no inkling of the good fortune he had come to tell him of. When the counsellor asked eagerly what it could be, Manassa revealed to him that his handsome young nephew, Benjamin Dümmerl, the possessor of almost a million who had been created a baron for his incredible services in Vienna and had just returned from Italy – that this nephew had suddenly fallen desperately in love with Demoiselle Albertine and desired her for his wife.

The young Baron Dümmerl was often to be seen in the theatre, where he boasted a private box, and even more often at every kind of concert, so that everyone knew that he was as long and thin as a beanstalk; that in his sallow face, shadowed by jet black curly hair and whiskers, he bore all the marks of the oriental; that he dressed himself in the latest and most bizarre mode of the English dandy; that he spoke various languages with the same accent; that he scraped at the violin and hammered at the piano; that he patched together execrable verse; that without possessing knowledge or taste he played at critic of the arts and would have liked to have been a literary Maecenas; that he affected wit and *esprit* though he possessed neither; that he was forward, importunate – in short, and in the blunt expression employed by those clever people among whom he would dearly have liked to include himself, an intolerable boor. And if you add to this that, his great wealth notwithstanding, a nasty pettiness and cupidity appeared in everything he did, it will not be surprising that even base souls who were otherwise devotees of Mammon soon deserted him.

As Manassa informed the counsellor of his charming nephew's intentions, the thought of the half-million which Benjie actually possessed passed very rapidly through Vosswinkel's mind, but at the same time there occurred to him an objection which in his view must make the whole thing perfectly impossible.

'Dear Manassa,' he began, 'you have forgotten that your good nephew is an adherent of the old faith and –'

'Oh,' Manassa interrupted, 'oh, Herr Counsellor, what of that? My nephew is in love with your daughter and desires to make her happy: a couple of drops of water will not matter to him; he will still be what he always was. Reflect on the matter, Herr Counsellor, and in a couple of days I shall return with my little baron and learn your answer.' And with that Manassa departed.

The counsellor at once began to reflect. Despite his boundless avarice and lack of character or conscience, he felt a strong repugnance at the idea of Albertine united with the repulsive Benjie and in a sudden attack of rectitude resolved to consult his old school friend.

4

Soon after she had become acquainted with Edmund Lehsen at the Hofjäger, Albertine discovered that the big oil painting of her father which hung in her room was altogether an ill likeness and an intolerably botched piece of work. She told the counsellor that, although several years had passed since he was painted, he looked at that moment much younger and handsomer than the painter had represented him, and she censured especially the dark, sullen expression of the face, the old-fashioned dress and the unnatural posy of roses which the counsellor was depicted as holding very daintily between two fingers, on which there sparkled majestic diamond rings.

Albertine was so eloquent and persistent about the picture that at length the counsellor himself came to regard it as atrocious and could not comprehend how the incompetent artist could have transformed his charming person into so hideous a caricature. The longer he looked at the portrait, the more agitated he became; finally he resolved to take it down and throw it into the lumber room.

Albertine then said that, though the wretched picture certainly deserved no better fate, she had grown so accustomed to having her father's likeness in her room that the sight of the empty wall would constantly disturb her. There was nothing for it: her father would have to have himself painted again by a skilled artist capable of producing an accurate portrait and this could be no other than young Edmund Lehsen, who had already the most beautiful speaking likenesses to his credit.

'Daughter,' the counsellor expostulated, 'what are you asking? Our young artists are absurdly inflated with pride and arrogance and demand unheard-of prices for their trifling works; and only Friedrichsdor will satisfy them, not ordinary talers!'

Albertine assured him that Lehsen, since he painted more for pleasure than as a means of livelihood, would certainly prove very cheap, and pressed the counsellor about it for so long that at last he agreed to go to Lehsen and speak to him.

It can be imagined with what joy Edmund declared himself ready to paint the counsellor; his joy increased to delirious delight when he learned it was Albertine who had given the counsellor the idea of being painted by him. He thought, rightly, that she wanted in this way to make it possible for them to meet one another. It was also quite natural that, when the counsellor rather anxiously raised the subject of the price of the portrait, he should assure him that he would take no payment at all but would count himself fortunate that his art had thus gained him admittance to the house of so excellent a man as the counsellor was.

'My God!' the counsellor exclaimed in the profoundest astonishment, 'what do I hear? My dear Herr Lehsen, no money whatever, not a Friedrichsdor for your labours? – not even the cost of paint and canvas in good current talers?'

Edmund said with a smile that these expenses were too insignificant even to be worth mentioning.

'But', the counsellor interposed meekly, 'perhaps you do not realize that this is a lifesize half-length portrait –' Lehsen replied that that made no difference.

At that, the counsellor clasped him violently to his breast and, moved to the point of tears, cried: 'O God in Heaven! do such exalted, unselfish souls still exist then in this wicked world? First the cigars, then this painting! You are an admirable man, or rather youth, my dear Herr Lehsen; in you there dwells that German virtue and probity which ought to be encouraged in our times. But believe me that, although I am a counsellor and dress in the French fashion, I feel the same way as you do and know how to value your high-mindedness, and you may count on my knowing how to show hospitality.'

Cunning Albertine had foreseen how Edmund would receive the counsellor's commission. Her objective was achieved. The counsellor overflowed with praise of the excellent youth and his freedom from avarice and concluded by saying that, since young people, especially painters, always had something fantastical about them and placed value on faded flowers and ribbons that had once belonged to a pretty girl and could become quite beside themselves over some knick-knack or other made by a pair of fair hands, Albertine might stitch together a little purse for Edmund and, if she wanted to, even enclose a lock of her lovely chestnut-brown hair and thus settle any obligation they might possibly have towards Lehsen. He said he expressly gave his permission for that and would answer for it to Chancellery Private Secretary Tusmann.

Albertine, still not informed of the counsellor's plans and intentions, failed to understand what Tusmann had to do with it and refrained from asking.

On the same evening Edmund had his painter's equipment brought to the counsellor's house, and the following morning he arrived for the first sitting. He asked the counsellor to imagine himself back at the happiest moment of his life: the moment when his late wife first assured him of her love, perhaps, or when Albertine was born, or when he had unexpectedly encountered a long-lost friend.

'Stop,' cried the counsellor, 'stop, Herr Lehsen: about three months ago I received notification from Hamburg that I had won a considerable sum in the lottery held there. I ran to my daughter with the letter open in my hand. I have never known a more joyful moment in my life; let us therefore choose that one, and so as to have it visibly before our eyes, let me get the letter and hold it open in my hand as I did then.'

Edmund was actually obliged to portray the counsellor in this posture and to reproduce clearly and legibly the contents of the open letter: *Sir, I have the honour to inform you*, etc. The opened envelope had to lie on a little table beside him, and the address *To Herr Counsellor, Administrator and Fire Committeeman Melchior Vosswinkel, Esquire,*

Berlin, had also to be clearly readable, together with a lifelike copy of the postmark: *Hamburg*. In addition to this, Edmund painted a portrait of a very handsome, amiable, elegantly clad man whose face did indeed bear some faint resemblance to the counsellor's, so that anyone who read the reproduction of the envelope could not possibly mistake whom the portrait was supposed to represent.

The counsellor was altogether delighted with the picture. He said that one could see from it how a skilful painter could capture the features of a handsome man, even though the subject was somewhat advanced in years, and that it was only now that he could see what the professor he had once heard address the Humanities Society had meant when he had asserted that a good portrait must also be a sound historical document: for when he now regarded his picture, he recalled each time the pleasing history of his win in the lottery and he could understand the nature of the amiable smile which, originating in his ego, was then reflected in his face.

Before Albertine could put the rest of her plan into effect, the counsellor anticipated her wishes and asked Edmund if he would now paint his daughter's portrait too. Edmund set to work at once. Albertine's portrait, however, proved much harder to get under way than the counsellor's had been. He drew, rubbed out, drew again, began to paint, threw the whole thing away, began again, changed the posture; now the room was too light, now too dark, etc., until the counsellor, who had attended the sittings, finally lost patience and stayed away.

Edmund now came morning and afternoon; if the portrait on the easel did not progress very much, the love affair between Edmund and Albertine did, as the couple grew closer and closer.

You will certainly have discovered, kind reader, that when one is in love, it is often necessary – if one's protestations, sweet love-sick speeches and fond desires are to obtain their due and proper force, so that they penetrate irresistibly into the depths of the heart – to seize the hand of the beloved and to press and kiss it and that then, in the course of these caresses and as if in obedience to a law of electricity, lip involuntarily touches lip and this law goes on to fulfil itself in a fiery stream of glowing kisses. Not only did Edmund often have to neglect his painting on this account; he was often constrained to leave the easel altogether.

So it happened that one morning Edmund was standing with Albertine at the white-curtained window and, so as to bestow more force on his protestations, had an arm around her waist and was pressing her hand ceaselessly to his mouth, when Chancellery Private Secretary Tusmann, his pockets stuffed with improving and entertaining books, passed by the counsellor's house. Although he was in a great hurry, for the clock was on the point of striking the hour at which he was accustomed to enter his office, he stopped for a moment and cast a satisfied glance up to the window of his supposed bride.

There he beheld, as if through a mist, Albertine standing with Edmund, and although he could see nothing clearly, his heart, he knew not why, began to beat more violently. A strange fear constrained him to do something unheard-of: to go up to the house at that uncommon hour and to make straight for Albertine's room.

As he entered, Albertine said very audibly: 'Yes, Edmund, forever, I will love you forever!' and thereupon pressed Edmund to her breast, and a whole firework display of electrical bolts, as described above, began to explode and crackle.

The chancellery private secretary involuntarily stepped forward and, as though struck by catalepsy, stood motionless and speechless in the middle of the room.

Lost in a transport of the highest rapture, the lovers had

failed to hear the ponderous tread of the chancellery private secretary's boots, the sound of the door being opened, his entry into the room, his advance to the middle of the floor. Now he suddenly squeaked in the highest falsetto: 'But Demoiselle Albertine Vosswinkel!'

The lovers sprang apart in alarm: Edmund made for the easel, Albertine for the chair in which she was supposed to be posing for her portrait.

'But,' the chancellery private secretary began after a short pause as he recovered his breath, 'Demoiselle Albertine Vosswinkel, what are you doing? First you go waltzing with this young gentleman, whom I do not have the honour of knowing, in the Town Hall in the depths of midnight, so that I, a bridegroom beaten black and blue, almost lose my senses, and now, in broad daylight at the window behind the curtains – O just God! is this fitting behaviour for a bride?'

'Who is a bride?' Albertine expostulated. 'Of whom are you speaking, Herr Chancellery Private Secretary?'

'O my Creator in Heaven!' wailed the chancellery private secretary, 'you ask, dear demoiselle, who is a bride, of whom I am speaking? Who else can it be but you? Are you not my revered, silently worshipped bride? Did your honoured Herr Papa not long ago promise me your dear, white hand, so worthy of kisses?'

'Herr Chancellery Private Secretary,' cried Albertine, quite beside herself, 'either you have been to the wine-shop already this morning – and my father says you go there nowadays far too often – or you are the victim of a strange madness. My father has not promised you my hand and cannot have thought of doing so.'

'Dearest Demoiselle Vosswinkel,' the chancellery private secretary interposed, 'think what you are saying! You have known me for many years: have I not always been a temperate, prudent man? Would I suddenly give myself over to odious wine-drinking and unseemly lunacies?

Dear Demoiselle Vosswinkel, come to a better opinion of my humble person.'

'Go!' said Albertine, in a half-choked voice, and fled, a handkerchief pressed to her eyes, into a corner of the room.

'No,' the chancellery private secretary replied, 'no, dear demoiselle, I must follow Thomasius's politic advice and stay. I shall not go until –' He made as if to follow Albertine.

While this was going on, Edmund, boiling with rage, had been dabbing at the dark-green background of the portrait. Now he could restrain himself no longer. 'Madman, pestiferous devil!' he cried, quite beside himself, leaped at Tusmann, wiped the paint-laden brush across his face three or four times, seized him and, after opening the door, gave him such a powerful push that he shot out of the room like an arrow. The counsellor, who was on the point of coming out of the door opposite, started back in horror as his green-painted school friend fell into his arms.

'Secretary,' he cried, 'for Heaven's sake, what a sight you are!'

Almost out of his senses at what had just taken place, the chancellery private secretary narrated in brief, broken sentences how Albertine had treated him and what he had suffered at Edmund's hands. The counsellor, seized with rage and annoyance, took him by the hand, went back with him to Albertine's room and exploded: 'What is this I hear? Is this the way to behave towards your bridegroom?'

'Bridegroom!' cried Albertine in panic.

'Yes indeed,' said the counsellor, 'bridegroom. I do not see why you should get so excited over something decided long ago. My dear secretary is your bridegroom, and in a few weeks we shall celebrate the happy wedding.'

'Never!' cried Albertine. 'Never will I marry the chancellery private secretary. How do you imagine I could love him, this old man . . . no . . .'

'What do you mean, love? What do you mean, old man?' the counsellor interposed. 'We are not speaking of love, we are speaking of marriage. My dear Secretary is, to be sure, no longer a frivolous youth but, as I am, of those years rightly called the best, and with it an honest, prudent, well-read, charming man and my school friend.'

'No!' cried Albertine in the most violent agitation and with tears welling from her eyes. 'No, I cannot endure him, I find him insupportable, I hate, I loathe him! Oh, my Edmund –'

And thereupon the girl, quite beside herself, fell almost fainting into the arms of Edmund, who pressed her impetuously to his bosom. The counsellor, frozen to the spot, opened wide his eyes as if he had seen a ghost and exclaimed: 'What is this, what do I behold –?'

'Yes,' the chancellery private secretary interposed in a wailing voice, 'Demoiselle Albertine seems not to want to know me at all, seems to harbour an uncommon inclination for that young gentleman, the painter, since she kisses him without blushing, but won't so much as give me her hand, even though I shortly intend to place the engagement ring upon her lovely finger.'

'Stand apart, I say!' the counsellor shouted and tore Albertine from Edmund's arms. The latter, however, cried that he would never let Albertine go, even if it should cost him his life.

'Ha!' the counsellor said mockingly, 'so that is it: a nice little love affair going on behind my back! Splendid behaviour, my young Herr Lehsen; this is what your unselfishness, your cigars and pictures, were all about. To insinuate yourself into my home, to seduce my daughter with dissolute arts. A fine thought, to abandon my daughter to a poverty-stricken, miserable, worthless canvas-dauber!'

Beside himself with rage at the counsellor's imprecations, Edmund seized the mahlstick and raised it into the air, but at that moment Leonhard rushed in through the door and cried in a thunderous voice: 'Stop, Edmund! Don't go too fast: Vosswinkel is an idiot and will change his mind.'

Amazed at Leonhard's unexpected appearance, the counsellor cried from the corner into which he had recoiled: 'Whatever are you doing here, Herr Leonhard?'

The chancellery private secretary, however, who had dived straight behind the sofa the moment he beheld the goldsmith and was crouching down as low as he could, wailed tearfully: 'O God in Heaven! Counsellor, take care! Be silent! Keep your mouth shut, dear school fellow! O God in Heaven, this is the professor – the dreadful magician of the Spandauerstrasse –'

'Come on out,' said the goldsmith, laughing. 'Come on out, Tusmann, don't be afraid, nothing else is going to happen to you; you have already been punished enough for your foolish desire to marry, since you are going to wear a green face for the rest of your life.'

'O God,' cried the chancellery private secretary, 'a green face! What will people, what will his excellency the Minister say? Will his excellency not think that I have coloured my face green out of sheer wordly vanity? I am done for, I shall lose my place, for the state cannot tolerate chancellery private secretaries with green faces! Oh what a poor wretch I am!'

'Now, now,' the goldsmith interrupted, 'now, now, Tusmann, don't go on so; there is hope for you, provided you see reason and abandon your mad idea of marrying Albertine.'

'I cannot do that. He shall not do that,' the counsellor and the chancellery private secretary cried together.

The goldsmith regarded them both with a penetrating glance, but as he was about to speak the door opened and the old man, Manassa, came in with his nephew, the Baron Benjamin Dümmerl of Vienna. Benjie went straight up to

Albertine, whom he now saw for the first time in his life, and, seizing her hand, said in a harsh voice: 'Ah, dear girl, here I am in person, to throw myself at your feet. But understand me! That is only a figure of speech; Baron Dümmerl does not throw himself at anyone's feet, not even at those of his Majesty the Emperor. What I mean is that you may give me a kiss.' With that, he stepped closer to Albertine and bent down, but at the same moment something happened which filled everyone except the goldsmith with profound astonishment.

Benjie's already conspicuous nose suddenly shot out to such a length that, passing close beside Albertine's face, it struck the wall opposite with a resounding crack. Benjie recoiled a few paces, and his nose at once shrank back again to its usual size. He approached Albertine and the same thing happened: his nose slid out and back like a trombone.

'Accursed sorcerer!' roared Manassa; then, drawing a coil of cord from his pocket and throwing it to the counsellor, he cried: 'Quick, throw this noose round the fellow's neck – I mean the goldsmith's – then we can pull him out of the room and everything will be all right again.' The counsellor seized the cord, but threw it round the old Jew's neck instead of the goldsmith's, and both at once began to bounce up and down from floor to ceiling, while Benjie continued with his nose concerto and Tusmann laughed and gabbled as if mad, until the counsellor sank down exhausted in the armchair.

'Now's the moment, now's the moment!' cried Manassa and opened his pocket; with one spring an enormous mouse leaped out and made straight for the goldsmith. But even as it was leaping, the goldsmith pierced it with a sharp golden needle, whereupon it vanished with a shrill cry, none knew where.

Then Manassa raised a clenched fist at the prostrate counsellor and, rage flashing from his fiery red eyes, cried: 'Ha, Melchior Vosswinkel, you are in league against me, with the damned sorcerer, whom you lured into your house; but you shall be accursed, accursed; you and your whole tribe shall be taken off like a sparrow's helpless brood. Grass shall grow at your door and all you undertake shall be like the actions of a starving man who in dreams imagines he is eating his fill; and the *dalles* shall make his home with you and consume your possessions; and you shall beg in rags at the doors of the despised Chosen People, who shall spurn you like a mangy dog. And you shall be thrown to the ground like a despised twig of wood, and instead of the sound of harps, moths shall be your companions! Accursed, accursed, accursed, Counsellor Melchior Vosswinkel!' And with that, the raging Manassa seized his nephew and stormed out of the room with him.

In fear and horror, Albertine had hidden her face in Edmund's bosom, while the latter held her in a close embrace and strove to retain his composure. The goldsmith then approached the couple and said gently with a smile: 'Do not be confused by all these fooleries. All will be well, I promise you. But now it is necessary for you to part, before Vosswinkel and Tusmann recover their senses.' Whereupon he left Vosswinkel's house in the company of Edmund.

5

The counsellor was shaken through and through, more by Manassa's curse than by the mad antics for which, as he well saw, the goldsmith had been responsible. And that curse was indeed sufficiently terrible, since it burdened the counsellor with the *dalles*. I do not know, indulgent reader, whether you understand what the *dalles* means. A Talmudist narrates how the wife of a poor Jew went one day up to the loft of her little house and found there a wasted, naked and exhausted man who begged her to give him food, drink and shelter. Greatly alarmed, the wife ran down to her husband and wailed: 'A naked and starving man has got into our house and is demanding food and shelter from us. But how can we give food to a stranger when we ourselves can hardly keep body and soul together?'

'I will go up to this stranger', the husband said, 'and see how to get him out of our house.'

'Why', he said to the stranger, 'have you sought refuge in my house, for I am poor and cannot give you food? Be off with you and enter a wealthy house, where the beasts for eating have long since been fattened and the guests long since invited for the feast.'

'How can you want to drive me from the shelter I have found?' the man replied. 'You can see that I am bare and naked: how can I go off into a wealthy house? But have a suit that fits me made and I will leave you.'

'It is better for me to sacrifice all I have to get the man out of my house quickly', thought the Jew, 'than that he should remain and consume everything I can gain through wearisome toil in the future.' He slaughtered the last calf he possessed, with which he and his wife had thought to feed themselves for many days, sold the meat and with the money acquired a smart suit for the stranger. But when he took the suit to the loft, the stranger, who had at first been small and wasted, had grown big and strong, so that the suit was altogether too small for him. The poor Jew was horrified at this, but the stranger said: 'Leave the folly of wanting to get me out of your house – I am the *dalles*.'

At that, the poor Jew wrung his hands and wailed and cried: 'God of my fathers, then I am chastised with the rod of wrath and miserable for ever: for if you are the *dalles*, you will not leave us but, consuming all we have, will grow ever bigger and stronger.' The *dalles* is poverty, which never departs from where it has once made its home but gets bigger and bigger.

But if the counsellor was dismayed at the curse of poverty which Manassa had in his rage loaded him with, he was also afraid of old Leonhard, who, apart from the strange magical arts he had at his command, also possessed something in his whole bearing which could not fail to awaken a timid awe. Against both of them he felt himself more or less helpless and he thus directed all his rage against Edmund Lehsen, to whom he attributed all the misfortunes that had befallen him. And if you add to all this Albertine's frank and firm declaration that she loved Edmund beyond bounds and would never agree to marry the pedantic old chancellery private secretary or the intolerable Baron Benjie, it cannot be surprising that the counsellor's wrath became immoderate and that he wished Edmund as far away as possible. But since he was unable to realize this desire in the way the late French government did – which in fact sent people it wanted to be rid of as far away as they could possibly go – he contented himself with writing Edmund a pleasant little letter into which he poured all the gall and poison which infected him and which ended with the demand that Edmund should never again set foot over his threshold.

You may imagine that this cruel separation from Albertine at once plunged Edmund into the state of despair in which Leonhard found him when, as he was accustomed to do, he visited the painter one evening.

'What good has your protection done me?' he exclaimed to the goldsmith. 'What good have been all your efforts to rid me of my hated rival? Your uncanny juggler's tricks have confused and terrified everyone, my dear girl included, and it is your activities alone which stand in my way as an insuperable obstacle. I shall flee, I shall flee, a dagger in my heart, to Rome!'

'Then', said the goldsmith, 'you would be doing what I most heartily desire. Recall that, when you first spoke of your love for Albertine, I then assured you that in my view a young artist might well fall in love but ought not to think straightaway of marriage, which would be altogether unprofitable to him. Half jokingly I presented to you the example of young Sternbald, but now I say to you quite seriously that, if you propose to become a real artist, you must abandon all thought of marriage. Go, joyful and free, to the homeland of art, study with all your enthusiasm its innermost nature; only then will the technical accomplishment which you can perhaps attain here too be of any use to you.'

'Ha!' cried Edmund, 'what a fool I was to confide in you about my love! Now I see that it is you, from whom I had a right to expect support by word and deed, that it is you, I say, who have been deliberately working against me and with mocking malice destroying my fairest hopes!'

'Ho, ho!' the goldsmith replied. 'Young man, moderate your language, be less vehement and reflect that you are much too inexperienced to see through my intentions. But I will set your mistaken anger down to your insane infatuation –'

'And,' Edmund went on, 'so far as art is concerned, I cannot see why, since as you know I do not lack the means to do so, I should not go to Rome and study art without in any way harming my inner union with Albertine. Indeed, my intention was, once I could be sure of possessing her, to travel to Italy and to stay there a whole year, and then, enriched with a true knowledge of art, to return to the arms of my bride.'

'What,' cried the goldsmith, 'Edmund, was that in fact your actual, serious intention?'

'Certainly,' the youth replied. 'Although I am on fire with love for dear Albertine, I am just as much drawn to the land which is the home of my art.'

'Can you give me your solemn word', the goldsmith resumed, 'that, if Albertine became yours, you would at once set out for Italy?'

'Why should I not,' the youth replied, 'since that has been my firm determination and would remain so even if Albertine were to become mine, which I must doubt will happen.'

'Well then,' cried the goldsmith gaily, 'in that case, Edmund, take heart: this firm intention has won you your beloved. I give you my word that in a few days Albertine shall be your bride. That I shall know how to bring it about you need not doubt.'

Edmund's eyes were alight with joy and delight. Hurrying away, the enigmatic goldsmith left the youth to all the sweet dreams and hopes he had aroused in his heart.

In a remote corner of the Tiergarten, Chancellery Private Secretary Tusmann lay, in the words of Celia in *As You Like It*, like a dropped acorn or like a wounded knight and bewailed his sorrows to the faithless autumn winds.

'O God of justice!' he lamented. 'Unhappy, pitiable chancellery private secretary, how have you deserved all this misfortune that has come upon you? Does Thomasius not say that marriage should in no way prejudice the attainment of wisdom? And yet, though you have done no more than taken the first step towards marriage, you have already almost lost your sweet reason. Why does the worthy Demoiselle Albertine Vosswinkel feel such an aversion to your humble but nonetheless sufficiently praiseworthy person? Are you a politician, who has no wife, or a jurist, who according to the teaching of Cleobulus ought to beat his wife a little when she is ill-behaved, that she should hesitate to marry you? O just God, what misery awaits you! Why, dear chancellery private secretary, do you have to come into open conflict with vile sorcerers and raving painters who regard your tender face as a canvas and throw on to it a confused Salvator Rosa? Yes, that is the worst! All my hopes reposed in my intimate friend Herr Streccius, who is an experienced chemist and knows how to help in every misfortune, but it is all in vain. The more I wash myself with the water he recommended, the greener I get, though the green changes through the most various shades and nuances, so that it has been spring, summer and autumn on my visage! Yes, it is this green which is driving me to my destruction, and if I cannot restore the white winter which is the most apposite season for my face, I shall fall into despair and throw myself into this vile frog-pond and die a green death!'

Tusmann had a right to such bitter complaints, for the greenness of his face was in truth a very sad matter: the colouring was no ordinary oil paint but seemed to be an artfully compounded tincture which, having penetrated into his skin, absolutely refused to go away. During the day-time the poor chancellery private secretary dared not go out except with a hat pulled down low over his eyes and a handkerchief held before his face; even when evening fell he only ventured to run at a moderate trot through distant streets. He was partly afraid of the mockery of the street urchins and partly dreaded encountering anyone from his office, where he had reported himself as being sick.

It may be that we feel the calamities which have befallen us more acutely in the silence of the night than we do during the bustling day; so it was that, as the clouds grew darker and darker, as the shadows of the wood spread blacker and blacker and as the rude autumn wind whistled in horrible mockery through trees and bushes, Tusmann, reflecting on the magnitude of his misery, fell into a state of utter despair. The dreadful thought of leaping into the green frog-pond and thus putting an end to his troubled existence came so vividly into the secretary's soul that he regarded it as a decisive sign of his destiny which he would have to obey.

'Yes,' he cried in a shrill voice as he sprang up from the ground where he had been lying, 'chancellery private secretary, it is all up with you! Despair, good Tusmann! No Thomasius can save you, away with you to a green death! Farewell, cruel Demoiselle Albertine Vosswinkel! You shall see your bridegroom, whom you have vilely rejected, never again! He is going to leap into the frog-pond!'

As if mad, he ran off to the nearby pool, which lay in the deep evening twilight like a broad overgrown path before him, and stopped close by the edge. The thought of the nearness of his death may have unhinged his mind, for he began to sing in a high, penetrating voice the English folksong whose refrain goes 'Green grow the rushes, o!', threw his *Political Economy*, *Handbook of Court and Country* and Hufeland's *Art of Long Life* into the water and was about to leap in after them with a mighty spring when he felt himself powerfully gripped from behind. At the same moment he heard the familiar voice of the sorcerer gold-smith: 'Tusmann, what are you doing? Do not be an ass, I beg of you, and cease these follies!'

The chancellery private secretary put forth all his strength to get free from the goldsmith's embrace, while at the same time, scarcely any longer capable of speech, he croaked: 'Herr Professor, I am desperate, and in that state all other considerations cease. Herr Professor, do not hold it against a desperate chancellery private secretary, who is well aware what custom and decency demand, but – I say it quite frankly – I wish the Devil would take you, together with your magic arts, together with your insolence, together with your accursed, your – your –'

The goldsmith released the chancellery private secretary and the latter straightaway tumbled into the high wet grass. Under the impression he was lying in the pool, he cried: 'O cold death, O green rushes, adieu! Your most humble servant, dear Demoiselle Albertine Vosswinkel. Farewell, honest counsellor. The unhappy bridegroom lies with the frogs, who in the summertime raise their voices in praise of the Lord!'

'Do you see, Tusmann,' said the goldsmith loudly, 'that

you are out of your senses and exhausted and wretched as well? You want to send me to the Devil; how if I myself were the Devil and were to twist your neck on this spot, here where you suppose yourself to be lying in the pond?'

Tusmann moaned, groaned and shuddered as if in the grip of a fever. 'But', the goldsmith went on, 'I mean well by you, Tusmann, and forgive your desperation everything. Get yourself up and come with me.'

The goldsmith helped the poor chancellery private secretary to his feet. Utterly annihilated, the latter whispered: 'I am in your power, honoured Herr Professor, do what you will with my poor mortal body, but I beg of you most humbly to spare my immortal soul.'

'Stop talking such insane rubbish and come along quickly,' the goldsmith cried, seizing the chancellery private secretary by the arm and walking away with him. But in the middle of the path that led across the Tiergarten to the tents he halted and said: 'Stop, Tusmann! You are completely wet and you look dreadful. Let me at least dry your face.'

With that, the goldsmith drew a blindingly white cloth from his pocket and did as he had said. When he now saw the bright lights of the tents gleaming through the bushes, Tusmann suddenly cried in alarm: 'For God's sake, honoured Herr Professor, wherever are you taking me? Not back to the town? Not to my house? Not back among people? Just God, I cannot let myself be seen! I would provoke a scandal!'

'I do not know, Tusmann,' the goldsmith replied, 'why you should be acting so timorously; don't be such a rabbit! In any event, you need something strong to drink – perhaps a glass of hot punch – or you will catch a fever from the cold. Just come along!'

The chancellery private secretary wept and wailed, spoke ceaselessly of his green face, of the vile Salvator Rosa on his visage, but the goldsmith paid not the slightest attention but drew him along with irresistible force. When they entered the brightly lit room, Tusmann covered his face with his handkerchief, as there were still a couple of people eating at the long table.

'Why, Tusmann,' the goldsmith said into the secretary's ear, 'are you thus concealing your honest visage?'

'Ah God,' the chancellery private secretary groaned, 'honoured Herr Professor, you must know why: my face, which the wrathful young painter daubed all over in green —'

'Nonsense!' cried the goldsmith; he grasped the chancellery private secretary with a firm hand, set him before the large mirror at the end of the room and illuminated him with a candle. Tusmann gazed at it involuntarily and could not prevent himself from uttering a loud 'Ah!' Not only had the hateful green completely vanished, but Tusmann's face had acquired a healthier coloration than it had had before, so that he looked in fact several years younger. In a transport of delight, the secretary sprang into the air with both feet and said in a saccharine voice: 'O just God, what do I see, what do I behold? Worthiest, uncommonly respected Herr Professor, it is certainly you alone to whom I owe this good fortune! Yes! now Demoiselle Albertine Vosswinkel, for whose sake I almost jumped into an abyss, will certainly not hesitate to choose me for her husband! Yes, worthiest Herr Professor, you have rescued me from the depths of wretchedness! I felt a certain pleasant sensation when you were pleased to pass your snow-white handkerchief over my humble face. Oh speak: were you really my benefactor?'

'I will not deny', the goldsmith replied, 'that it was I who washed away your green coloration, and you can assume from that that I am not so hostile towards you as you may perhaps think. It is only your absurd notion, which you acquired from the counsellor, that you could marry a beautiful young girl bubbling over with the joy of life – it is only this notion, I say, which I find unendurable in you; and since you now, having barely got over the tricks that have been played on you, again straightaway think about marriage, I would like to expunge this taste from you in the most emphatic way, which is altogether within my power. But I shall refrain and shall advise you instead to stay calm and do nothing until next Sunday at midday, when you will hear further. If you venture to see Albertine before then, I shall first make you dance before her eyes until your breath runs out, then transform you into the greenest possible frog and throw you into the pond here in the Tiergarten, if not into the Spree, where you can stay and croak until the end of your life! Fare you well! I have something more to do today which bids me hurry to the town. You will not be able to follow me. Fare you well!'

The goldsmith was right that no one could easily have followed him, for as if wearing Schlemihl's famous seven-league boots he vanished from the sight of the dismayed secretary with the single bound with which he departed through the door. It could thus happen that a minute later he suddenly appeared like a ghost in the counsellor's room and in a somewhat hoarse voice bade him good evening. The counsellor started violently but quickly pulled himself together and asked the goldsmith irascibly what he wanted so late at night; he then ordered him to be off and to leave him in peace with the absurd juggler's tricks which he no doubt had in mind to plague him with.

'Thus', the goldsmith replied very calmly, 'is the nature of man, and especially of counsellors. Precisely those who approach you with benevolent intent, and into whose arms you should confidently throw yourselves, precisely those do you thrust from you. You, dear Counsellor, are a poor, unhappy, pitiable man; I have come, I have sped through the darkness of the night, to take counsel with you as to how the mortal blow which is about to strike you may perhaps be deflected and –'

'Oh God,' cried the counsellor, quite beside himself, 'O God, there has been another bankruptcy in Hamburg, Bremen or London which threatens to ruin me! Oh, stricken counsellor that I am – and now that too!'

'No,' the goldsmith said, interrupting Vosswinkel's lamentations, 'I am referring to something else. Do you absolutely decline to give Albertine's hand to young Edmund Lehsen?'

'What absurd nonsense!' cried the counsellor. 'I? Give my daughter to that wretched dauber?'

'Well,' said the goldsmith, 'he painted you and Albertine very well.'

'Ho, ho!' the counsellor replied, 'that would be a fine bargain: my daughter for a couple of pretty pictures! I have sent the things back to him.'

'Edmund', the goldsmith went on, 'will be revenged on you if you refuse him Albertine.'

'I should like to know', the counsellor said, 'what revenge that wretch, that jackanapes, can take on Counsellor Melchior Vosswinkel.'

'That I shall tell you right away, my very excellent Herr Counsellor,' the goldsmith replied. 'Edmund is just now on the point of retouching your lovely picture in a way worthy of it. He is converting the cheerful, laughing face into a bitterly sullen one, with raised brows, dull eyes, a down-drawn mouth. Wrinkles on cheeks and forehead are being more deeply marked, the many grey hairs which powder is supposed to hide are being clearly indicated. Instead of the joyful tidings of your win at the lottery he is inscribing the highly distressing news in the letter you received the day before yesterday that the house of Campbell and Company of London is bankrupt; on the envelope there stand the words *To the failed Alderman*, etc., for he knows that six months ago you sought that dignity in vain. Out of the torn waistcoat pockets there fall ducats, talers and treasury notes, indicating the losses you have suffered. Altered thus, the picture will then be exhibited at the picture-dealer's at the bank building in the Jäger-strasse.'

'The Devil!' cried the counsellor. 'The rascal! No, he shan't do it! I call on the police, on justice –'

'As soon as fifty people have seen the picture inside the first quarter of an hour,' the goldsmith continued calmly, 'news of it will spread through the whole town, with a thousand additional details supplied by this or that wit. All the ridiculous and absurd things that have been said of you, and are still being said, will be refurbished in new and gleaming colours; everyone you meet will laugh at you to your face; and, what is the worst of all, there will be unceasing chatter about the loss you sustained through the collapse of Campbell, and your credit will be gone.'

'O God,' cried the counsellor. 'But he must hand me back the picture; yes, the villain, he must do so first thing tomorrow.'

'And', the goldsmith went on, 'if he did so – which I very much doubt – what good would it do you? He will etch your valued person as I have just described it on a copperplate, take many hundreds of impressions, illumin-ate them himself *con amore* and send them out all over the world, to Hamburg, Bremen, Lübeck, Stettin, even to London –'

'Stop,' the counsellor interrupted, 'stop! Go to the dreadful man, offer him fifty – offer him a hundred talers if he will leave my picture alone.'

'Ha, ha, ha!' the goldsmith laughed. 'You forget that money means nothing to Lehsen, that his parents are wealthy, that his great-aunt, Demoiselle Lehsen, who lives in the Breitstrasse, long ago bequeathed him her fortune, which amounts to not less than eighty thousand talers.'

'What?' cried the counsellor, growing pale with sudden astonishment, 'What do you say? Eighty? Listen, Herr Leonhard, I think that little Albertine is quite infatuated with young Lehsen; I am a good fellow, after all, a soft-hearted father; I cannot resist tears or pleadings – I like the young man, moreover. He is an excellent artist. You know that, so far as art is concerned, when I like a thing I become quite foolish over it. He possesses some nice qualities, dear good Lehsen. Eighty. You know what, Leonhard: out of sheer goodness of heart I shall give him my daughter, the dear young fellow!'

'Hm,' said the goldsmith. 'In that case there is something funny I must tell you. I have just come from the Tiergarten. Close by the big pond I found your friend and schoolfellow Chancellery Private Secretary Tusmann, who, in mad despair at Albertine's rejection of him, was about to throw himself into the water. It was only with difficulty that I succeeded in dissuading him from carrying out this dreadful resolve by representing to him that you, my excellent counsellor, would be sure to keep your faithfully given word and by fatherly admonition would induce Albertine no longer to refuse him her hand. If this does not happen, if you give Albertine's hand to young Lehsen, your friend will jump into the pond – that is as good as certain. Think what a commotion the terrible suicide of so respectable a man would cause! You – you alone – will be regarded as Tusmann's murderer. Everyone will ostracize you, you will no longer be invited out and if you go into any coffee-house to hear the latest gossip, you will be ejected. But that is not all. The chancellery private secretary is highly regarded by all his superiors; his reputation as a man of business is known throughout the town. Now, if you have brought him to the point of suicide through your vacillation and duplicity, it is out of the question that any official, of a legation or of a finance office, should ever enter your house again for the rest of your life – least of all those with influence. The authorities whose goodwill is needed for your business will henceforth ignore you completely. Simple commercial counsellors will mock at you, clerks will pursue you with murder weapons, and messengers, seeing you, will pull down their hats. Your title of counsellor will be taken from you, blow will follow blow, your credit will be gone, your fortune will disappear, things will get worse and worse, until at last, sunk into contempt, poverty and wretchedness –'

'Stop!' cried the counsellor. 'You are torturing me! Who could have thought that the secretary would be such an infatuated ass at his age? But you are right. Let happen what may, I must keep my word to him, or I am a ruined man. Yes, it is decided, the secretary shall have Albertine's hand.'

'You are forgetting the aspirations of Baron Dümmerl,' said the goldsmith. 'You are forgetting old Manassa's terrible curse! If Benjie is rejected, it is in him, Manassa, that you will possess your most terrible foe. He will oppose you in all your speculations. He will shun no means of curtailing your credit, he will employ every opportunity of harming you, he will not rest until he has reduced you to shame and disgrace, until the *dalles* which he has cursed you with has in reality entered your house. Enough: whichever of Albertine's three wooers you give her hand to, you will be undone, and that is why I called you a poor, pitiable man.'

The counsellor ran back and forth across the room as if he had taken leave of his senses and cried again and again: 'I am lost – a miserable, ruined man! If only I didn't have the girl on my hands! May the Devil take the lot of them –'

'Now, now,' the goldsmith began. 'I expect there exists a way of getting you out of all your difficulties.'

'What way?' said the counsellor, halting abruptly and staring fixedly at the goldsmith. 'I will try anything.'

'Have you', the goldsmith asked, 'ever seen *The Merchant of Venice*?'

'That is the play', the counsellor replied, 'in which Herr Devrient plays a murderous Jew named Shylock who lusts after the flesh of a wholesaler. Yes, I have seen the play, but what has it to do with me now?'

'If you know *The Merchant of Venice*,' the goldsmith went on, 'you will remember that there appears in it a certain wealthy Miss Portia, whose father has in his will made his daughter's hand the prize in a kind of lottery. Three caskets are set up, of which her wooers must choose and open one. The wooer who finds Portia's portrait in the casket he has chosen receives her hand. You, Counsellor, should as a living father do as Portia's dead father did. Tell the three wooers that, as you like them all equally, you intend to leave the decision to chance. Set up three closed caskets for the wooers to choose from, and he who finds Albertine's picture receives her hand.'

'What a curious suggestion!' cried the counsellor. 'And if I do proceed with it, do you believe, dear Herr Leonhard, that it will help me in the slightest? That even if chance has decided, I shall escape the rage and hatred of those who have not discovered the portrait and must therefore withdraw their suit?'

'Stop!' said the goldsmith. 'That precisely is the most important point! See here, Counsellor, I herewith promise you most solemnly to arrange the matter of the caskets in such a way that everything shall end happily and peaceably. The two who choose wrongly shall find in their caskets, not a disdainful dismissal, as the Princes of Morocco and Aragon did, but something which shall so greatly content them they will forget all about marrying Albertine and regard you, Counsellor, as the procurer of an altogether undreamed-of good fortune.'

'If only that were possible!' cried the counsellor.

'It is not only possible,' the goldsmith replied; 'it

shall, it must all happen as I have said. I give you my word.'

At this, the counsellor abandoned all resistance to the goldsmith's plan, and both agreed that the choosing of the bride should take place at midday the following Sunday. The goldsmith undertook to procure the three caskets.

6

It may be imagined that, when the counsellor told her of the unfortunate lottery in which her hand was to be the prize, and all her tears and pleadings failed to induce him to abandon his decision to hold it, Albertine fell into total despair. Lehsen, moreover, began to seem to her indifferent and inattentive in a way that no one who was really in love could be: he made not the slightest attempt to visit her in secret or even to send her a covert love-note. As twilight was falling on the Saturday before the fateful Sunday that was to decide her destiny, Albertine was sitting alone in her room. Wholly sunk in thought of the misfortune which threatened her, she wondered whether it might not be preferable to flee her father's house than to stay and await the fearful fate of being forced to marry the pedantic old chancellery private secretary or, which was worse, the revolting Baron Benjie. Then, however, she suddenly called to mind the enigmatic goldsmith and the strange magical means with which he had kept the importunate Benjie away from her. She was well aware that he was on the side of Lehsen, and the hope therefore dawned in her that if anyone was to help her at the moment of crisis it would have to be the goldsmith. She felt a lively desire to speak with him and was inwardly convinced she would not be in the least afraid if he should at that moment appear in a ghostly fashion before her.

And she was in fact not in the least afraid when she became aware that what she had taken for the stove was actually the goldsmith Leonhard, who approached her and in a soft, sonorous voice began as follows: 'Leave your sorrow, my dear child! Know that Edmund Lehsen, with whom you believe you are in love, is under my protection, that I exert all my powers on his behalf. Know further that it is I who gave your father the idea of the lottery, that it is I who have prepared the fateful caskets; now you may be well assured that no one but Edmund shall discover your picture.'

Albertine wanted to cry aloud for joy; the goldsmith went on: 'I could have procured your hand for Edmund in other ways, but I wanted wholly to placate his fellow suitors at the same time. That too will be done, and both of you, you and your father, will be safe from any vexations from the rejected wooers.'

Albertine overflowed with passionate gratitude. She would almost have fallen at the goldsmith's feet, she pressed his hand to her breast, she assured him that, notwithstanding the magic arts he practised, or even the ghostly fashion in which he had suddenly appeared in her room that evening, she felt nothing strange or sinister in his presence, and ended with the naive questions: what was his behaviour really all about and who really was he.

'My dear child,' the goldsmith began, smiling, 'I shall find it very hard to say who I really am. I am like many others, who know far better what people take them to be than what they really are! Learn, then, my dear child, that many take me to be none other than the goldsmith Leonhard Turnhäuser, who in the 1580s stood in such high repute at the court of the Elector Johann Georg and who, when malice and envy sought to destroy him, vanished, no one knew how or whither. Now, if such people as are usually called romantics or visionaries give me out to be that same Turnhäuser, and consequently a ghost, you can imagine what annoyance I have to endure from respectable, enlightened people, who as sound citizens and men of business could not give a rap for romanticism and poetry.

Even stalwart aestheticians, indeed, close in on me, persecute me like the scribes and doctors in the days of Johann Georg and try as much as they can to spoil and embitter for me the little bit of existence I claim for myself.

'Ah, my dear child, I can see already that, although I care for young Edmund Lehsen and for you with such solicitude and appear everywhere as a real *deus ex machina*, there will be many who share the view of those aestheticians and will in no way tolerate my presence in these events, since they are quite unable to believe that I really exist! As some measure of self-defence, I have never directly admitted that I am the Swiss goldsmith Leonhard Turnhäuser of the sixteenth century. These people are therefore free to assume that I am a clever trickster and to seek an explanation of any supernatural events that occur in Wiegleb's *Natural Magic* or elsewhere. At this moment, to be sure, I intend a piece of work which not even a Philodorus, a Philadelphia, a Cagliostro could equal, and which, being altogether inexplicable, will remain an everlasting offence to those people; I cannot refrain from it on that ground, however, since for the completion of the story of the wooing by three famous persons of the hand of the lovely Demoiselle Albertine Vosswinkel of Berlin it is absolutely indispensable. Now then, take courage, my dear child, rise early tomorrow, dress yourself in your most becoming clothes, wreathe your hair into the loveliest plaits and await whatever may then happen calmly and with modest patience.' Hereupon the goldsmith vanished as he had arrived.

On Sunday at the appointed hour, that is at precisely eleven o'clock, there appeared old Manassa with his hopeful nephew, Chancellery Private Secretary Tusmann and Edmund Lehsen with the goldsmith. The wooers, not excluding Baron Benjie, were almost startled when they beheld Albertine, for she had never before seemed to them so lovely. I can, however, assure any lady who sets store by tasteful costume and decorative ornament (and what lady here in Berlin does not do so?) that the cut of the dress Albertine was wearing was of exceptional elegance, that it was sufficiently short to reveal her dainty, white-shod feet, that the short sleeves and bodice were made of the costliest lace, that her white French kid gloves came only a little way above her elbows, permitting a view of the loveliest upper arm, that her coiffure consisted of nothing but a single, golden, gem-encrusted comb – in short, that all that was missing from the bridal attire was a myrtle crown among the dark tresses. But the real reason Albertine looked much more alluring than usual was no doubt the love and hope which gleamed in her eyes and blossomed on her cheeks.

In a fit of hospitality the counsellor had provided a buffet lunch. Manassa maliciously looked askance at the laden table, and when the counsellor invited him to help himself you could read in his face Shylock's answer: 'I will buy with you, sell with you, talk with you, walk with you, and so following; but I will not eat with you, drink with you, nor pray with you.'

Baron Benjie was less conscientious: he ate far more beef-steaks than was seemly and prattled childishly as he did so, as was his way.

At this fateful hour, the counsellor behaved altogether out of character: not only did he distribute Madeira and port quite relentlessly, and even betray that he had hundred-year-old Malaga in his cellar; he also, after lunch was over, addressed the suitors on the subject of how his daughter's hand was to be won in a well-worded speech such as you would not have thought him capable of. It had to be impressed upon them that only he who chose the casket containing Albertine's picture would win her for his bride.

As the clock struck twelve, the door of the room was

opened to reveal a table covered with an opulent carpet on which were standing three small caskets. The first, made of glittering gold, had upon its lid a wreath of sparkling ducats, in the middle of which stood the words: 'He who chooses me, let him be happy in the way he likes.' The second casket was finely worked in silver. On the lid there stood among many characters from foreign tongues the words: 'He who chooses me will get much more than he hoped for.' The third casket, carved plainly in ivory, bore the inscription: 'He who chooses me will possess the happiness he dreams of.'

Albertine took her place in an armchair behind the table; the counsellor placed himself at her side; Manassa and the goldsmith withdrew to the other side of the room. When they had drawn lots and the chancellery private secretary was elected to choose first, Benjie and Lehsen had to retreat into another room.

The chancellery private secretary stepped thoughtfully up to the table, regarded the caskets carefully and read the inscriptions again and again. Soon, however, he felt himself drawn irresistibly to the graceful intertwined characters on the silver casket.

'Just God,' he cried enthusiastically, 'what a lovely script! How pleasingly the Arabic here unites with the Latin hand! And "He who chooses me will get much more than he hoped for" – have I ever hoped that Demoiselle Albertine would ever make me happy with the gift of her dear hand? Have I not rather sunk into total despair? Did I not . . . in the pool . . . ? Well, then, here is comfort, here is my happiness! Counsellor, Demoiselle Albertine, I choose the silver casket!'

Albertine rose and handed the chancellery private secretary a little key, with which he at once opened the casket. But how he started back when he discovered, not Albertine's picture, but a little book bound in parchment which when he opened it proved to contain nothing but blank pages. He also found a small sheet of paper bearing the words:

> *Though thy toil be vain, yet hast thou won*
> *Great joy; this that thou findest*
> *Changeth thy ignorance to wisdom.*

'Just God,' the secretary stammered, 'a book . . . no, not a book – a packet of paper, instead of the picture! All hope is gone. O defeated chancellery private secretary! It is all up with you, it is all over! Away to the frog-pond!'

Tusmann made to depart, but the goldsmith stepped into his path and said: 'Tusmann, you are in error! No treasure could profit you more than that which you have found. The verses should have told you that already. Do me the favour of putting the book you took from the casket into your pocket.' Tusmann did so. 'Now', the goldsmith went on, 'think of a book you would at this moment like to be carrying with you.'

'O God,' said the secretary, 'in a thoughtless and un-christian way I threw Thomasius's *Short Introduction to Politic Policy* into the pond!'

'Reach into your pocket, take out the book,' cried the goldsmith. Tusmann did as he was bid, and behold! – the book was none other than Thomasius's.

'Ha! what is this?' cried the secretary, quite beside himself. 'My dear Thomasius rescued from the depreda-tions of vile frogs, who could never have learned anything from it!'

'Quiet,' the goldsmith interrupted, 'just put the book back into your pocket.' Tusmann did so. 'Think,' the goldsmith went on, 'think now of some rare work which you have perhaps long looked for in vain, which you could discover in no library.'

'O God!' said the secretary. 'As I like to cheer myself up by going to the opera now and then, I have wanted to inform myself about the noble *musica* and have tried in vain to get hold of a little book which sets out in an allegorical fashion the whole art of the composer and virtuoso. I mean nothing other than Johannes Beer's *Musical War, or Description of the Pitched Battle between the Two Heroines, Composition and Harmony, how They Took to the Field against One Another, Skirmished and after a Bloody Contest were at last Reconciled*.'

'Reach into your pocket,' cried the goldsmith, and the chancellery private secretary exclaimed aloud for joy when he opened the book, which had now become Johann Beer's *Musical War*. 'You now see', the goldsmith said, 'that through the book you found in the casket you have acquired the amplest, completest library anyone has ever possessed, and one, moreover, that you can carry about with you constantly. For if you have this remarkable book in your pocket, whenever you take it out it will become whatever work you desire to read.'

Without a glance at Albertine or the counsellor, the chancellery private secretary leaped quickly to a corner of the room, threw himself into an armchair, put the book into his pocket and took it out again; you could see from the joy that gleamed in his eyes that what the goldsmith had promised had gloriously come to pass.

Now it was Baron Benjie's turn to choose. He came in, made in his childishly clumsy way straight for the table, regarded the caskets through his lorgnette and murmured aloud the inscriptions. But soon a natural instinct fettered his attention to the golden casket with the glittering ducats on the lid. '"He who chooses me, let him be happy in the way he likes." Well now, ducats, I like them, and Albertine, I like her too; choosing here presents no problem!' Thus spoke Benjie, reached for the golden casket, received the key from Albertine, opened the casket and found – a little English file! He also found a sheet of paper bearing the words:

All that thy heart could painfully desire
Thou hast; all else an idle jest:
A business going onward, never back.

'Oh!' he cried in anger. 'What do I want with a file? Is it a portrait, is it Albertine's portrait? I shall take the casket and give it to Albertine as a wedding present. Come, my girl.'

With that he made to advance on Albertine, but the goldsmith held him back by the shoulders and said: 'Stop, dear sir, that is contrary to the agreement. You must be content with the file, and you undoubtedly will be as soon as you know the value, the inestimable value, of the precious treasure you have received, of which the verses already give you some idea. Have you a lovely milled ducat in your pocket?'

'Yes,' Benjie replied ill-humouredly. 'What of it?'

'Take one out of your pocket', the goldsmith went on, 'and file the edge away.'

Benjie did so with a dexterity that indicated long practice. And behold! the edge of the ducat appeared even brighter, and so with the second and third ducats: the more Benjie filed, the better milled they became. Up to that point, Manassa had quietly looked on at what had been taking place, but now he leaped at his nephew with his eyes glittering wildly and screamed in a dreadful hollow voice: 'God of my fathers – what is this . . . give me that file! Give me that file – it is the magical trick for which I sold my soul more than three hundred years ago. God of my fathers – give me that file!'

With that he made to wrench the file away from Benjie, but the latter pushed him back and cried: 'Get back, you old fool, it was I who found the file, not you!'

Whereupon Manassa in a towering rage cried: 'Viper – worm-eaten fruit of my tree, give me that file! May all the devils take you, accursed thief!'

Amid a stream of imprecations, Manassa then clutched at the baron and, foaming and gnashing his teeth, sought with all his might to wrench the file from him. Benjie, however, defended his treasure like a lioness her cubs, until at last Manassa weakened. Then the nephew seized his dear uncle roughly, threw him through the door so that his bones rattled, returned with the speed of an arrow, pushed a little table into the corner of the room opposite the chancellery private secretary, shook out a whole handful of ducats and began filing away zealously.

'Well,' said the goldsmith, 'now we are rid for ever of that dreadful fellow, old Manassa. They say he is a second Ahasuerus and has been haunting the world since the year 1572. At that time he was executed for devilish sorcery under the name of the Jewish coiner Lippold. But the Devil saved him from death at the price of his immortal soul. Many people who understand such things have observed him here in Berlin in various different guises, from which the tale has arisen that there exist at present not one but many, many Lippolds. Very well! Since I too have some experience in secret matters, I have now finished him off!'

You would certainly be extremely bored, dearly beloved reader, if I now went on to retail at length what, since it goes without saying, you already know: namely, that Edmund Lehsen chose the ivory casket with the inscription: 'He who chooses me will possess the happiness he dreams of' and found therein a speaking likeness of Albertine, with the verses:

> Thou hast chosen aright: read thy joy
> In thy beloved's eyes; what more
> Shall be her kiss shall teach thee.

and further, that Edmund, like Bassanio, followed the instructions of the final words and pressed his hotly blushing beloved to his heart and kissed her and that the counsellor was altogether contented and delighted at the happy outcome of the most involved marriage transaction there has ever been.

Baron Benjie had been filing as industriously as the chancellery private secretary had been reading on. Neither took any notice of what was taking place before the counsellor loudly announced that Edmund had chosen the casket in which Albertine's portrait was to be found and had consequently received her hand. The secretary seemed to be overjoyed at the news, for, in the way in which he usually expressed pleasure, he rubbed his hands together, jumped a short distance into the air two or three times and gave a refined laugh. Baron Benjie seemed to have lost all interest in the marriage; but he embraced the counsellor instead, called him a splendid gentleman who had, through the sterling gift of the file, rendered him totally happy and assured him that he could count on him in any business matter thereafter. Then he quickly went away.

The chancellery private secretary likewise thanked the counsellor, amid tears of profound emotion, for having through the gift of the rarest of books made him the happiest of men and – having exhausted himself in gallantries towards Albertine, Edmund and the old goldsmith – followed the baron as hastily as he could.

From then on, Benjie ceased to plague the literary world with aesthetic monstrosities, as he had done hitherto, but preferred to employ his time in filing ducats. Tusmann, on the other hand, ceased to be a burden to the librarians who had hitherto been obliged to spend all day fetching him old, long-forgotten books. In the counsellor's house, however, after a few weeks of joy and rapture, there was a sudden outbreak of terrible sorrow and affliction: the goldsmith had urgently admonished young Edmund to keep his promise and, for the sake of his art and of himself, to go to Italy. Painful though the separation from his beloved must be to him, Edmund was nonetheless conscious of a pressing desire to make a pilgrimage to the land of art, and Albertine too thought, in the midst of the bitterest tears, how interesting it would be at this or that afternoon tea to draw from her sewing-basket letters she had received from Rome.

Edmund has already been in Rome for over a year, and they say his letters to Albertine have grown steadily rarer and cooler. Who knows whether anything will ever come of the idea the two young people had of marrying one another? Albertine will in any event not remain single: she is much too pretty and much too rich for that. It has been noticed, moreover, that the junior barrister Gloxin, a handsome young man with a slim, tightly laced waist, two waistcoats and a neckerchief tied in the English fashion, frequently conducts Demoiselle Albertine Vosswinkel to the Tiergarten – having danced with her at balls all through the winter – and that the counsellor trips after the little couple with the air of a contented father. The junior barrister Gloxin has, in addition, taken his second examination at the Supreme Court and, according to the examiners who tortured him, passed it splendidly. This examination is supposed to prove that the junior barrister obviously has the idea of marriage in his head, since he has shown himself remarkably well versed in the subject of speculative ventures.

Perhaps Albertine will marry the nice junior barrister once he has attained to a decent position. We must wait and see what happens.